FYODOR M. DOSTOEVSKY

THE BROTHERS KARAMAZOV

I

*Translated from the Russian
by Constance Garnett*

Introduction by A. B. McMillin

Original Illustrations by Pietro Sarto

Distributed by
HERON BOOKS

Published by arrangement with
William Heinemann Ltd.

13 005

INTRODUCTION

'THE novel I am now writing *(The Brothers Karamazov)* is consuming all my time and strength... I am writing slowly and carefully, making corrections and polishing, for I wish to complete it satisfactorily: never have I regarded a work more seriously than I regard this one'. Thus wrote Dostoevsky in July 1879, and indeed work on this, his greatest novel, completely dominated the last three years of his life, being completed in November 1880, a mere three months before his death. In many ways it can be regarded as the culmination of his work: artistically it is the most satisfactory of the four great novels, with the various elements or planes best integrated into the structure as a whole. None of the great conversations in the novel exist simply for their own sake, but all are essential reflections of the moral questioning and intellectual striving of the characters, and this in turn is of supreme importance for the plot, for in Dostoevsky, as perhaps in no other writer, the characters are inseparable from their ideas, truly living them out and thus raising them from mere abstraction to a vital role in human existence. The novel is also a culmination in the sense that it brings to final expression many of the ideas that occupied the writer during his lifetime. Thus Alyosha may be seen as a stage of development is Dostoevsky's quest for a truly good christian man, a successor to Prince Myshkin in *The Idiot;* many of Ivan's ideas on moral responsibility are close to those of Raskolnikov in *Crime and Punishment;* Ivan's legend of the Grand Inquisitor expresses in an infinitely subtler form many of the ideas contained in Myshkin's attack on Catholicism.

INTRODUCTION

Stylistically, too, Dostoevsky was able to achieve greater harmony, along with symmetry of construction in this novel, without losing any of the characteristic breathless tension and dynamism that make it one of the most dramatic and purely exciting of all European classics.

Fyodor Mikhailovich Dostoevsky was born in Moscow on the 30th of October, 1821. His father was a doctor in one of the paupers' hospitals and a member of the petty nobility but of an irritable and unsociable disposition, subjecting his gentle wife and large family to a rigid and puritanical discipline amounting almost to despotism. In the oppressive atmosphere of their cramped little house filled with icons and religious pictures Fyodor and his brother Mikhail sought escape in the world of Pushkin, Scott, Hoffman and Schiller. After a private preparatory school he entered the Military Engineers' School in Petersburg where he suffered from both bullying and a lack of interest in his studies: in 1841 he received his commission but resigned it three years later, after the period of compulsory military service had expired, in order to devote himself entirely to literature. His father had been brutally murdered in 1839 during a serf uprising on the estate, and Fyodor inherited a small fortune which, however, was soon spent in a characteristically extravagant and impractical manner. After this he supported himself by translating the works of his youthful idol Balzac.

In the years 1844-45 he produced his first novel *Poor Folk* and was acclaimed by the poet Nekrasov with the words 'A new Gogol has arisen!'. The novel found similar favour with Belinsky, the leading radical critic, and with the reading public at large. Subsequent works like *The Double* (1846) were received much less rapturously, and Dostoevsky's short-lived friendship with the advanced circle of radical writers and critics soon foundered on the rocks of the writer's great personal vanity. In spite of this break Dostoevsky continued to take an active interest in the radical movement, and he joined a group of socialists that met regularly to discuss liberal ideas and read writers like Fourier; during the reaction which followed the 1848 revolution, however, the members of the group (known

INTRODUCTION

as the Petrashevtsy) were arrested and sentenced to death: this was commuted to eight years hard labour, but not before the prisoners had been stripped to the waist despite a severe frost and tied up with all ceremony to face the firing squad. Only then were the real sentences announced, a joke that resulted in one man losing his reason and another's hair turning white. Dostoevsky did not forget this nightmarish experience, and it is referred to in *The Idiot* and elsewhere.

From January 1850 to January 1854 the writer lived in the abject conditions of the penal settlement in Omsk. His experiences in these dismal surroundings, with no book to read except the Bible, are described in *Notes from the House of the Dead* (1861). His health was completely ruined in Siberia, with severe gastric disorders, rheumatism of the legs and a worsening of the nervous system that brought on frequent attacks of epilepsy. Returning to European Russia in his late thirties, after four years service as a private soldier, during which time he made an unsuccessful marriage, he is described as looking old, tired and haggard, with a nervous tic on his yellow, sunken cheeks. The greatest transformation, however, was not physical but spiritual : Dostoevsky returned from exile in 1859 a completely new man. Rejecting all his former liberal ideas, he was now a staunch advocate of autocracy, and a fervent convert to the simple, trusting religion of the Russian people. Of the radicalism and atheism of his youth not a trace remained.

Back in Petersburg he joined his brother in founding a successful journal *Time*, which by a stroke of bad luck was suppressed as the result of an error on the part of the censor: the writer was involved in great financial losses and, in typical fashion, embarked on a tour of the gambling halls of Europe in the company of one Apollinaria Suslova: a significant figure, since with her proud and cruel nature she revealed to Dostoevsky some of the dark and evil side of human nature. She is portrayed as Polina in *The Gambler*, and aspects of her equivocal and wilful character are reflected in many of his other heroines, including Katerina Ivanovna and Grushenka in *The Brothers Karamazov*. Returning to Russia he attempted to found another journal, *The Epoch*, but it failed to establish itself with the reading public. To add to his difficulties his wife and brother both died within a few months and he found himself with the latter's family to support at a time when his own financial position was extremely insecure.

To overcome these bleak circumstances Dostoevsky sold the copyright of his works for a ridiculously low sum, and undertook several further contracts for his publisher, involving him in frenzied, but highly fruitful writing, for this was the period of the great novels, *Crime and Punishment* (1866), *The Idiot* (1868) and *The Possessed* (1871-72). In order to be able to write more quickly he hired a secretary, Anna Snitkina, and before long married her (February 1867): she proved a devoted wife, and it was largely thanks to her stability and common sense that Dostoevsky overcame his financial difficulties: not, however, before they had lived four humiliating years abroad, beyond the reach of their many creditors. These years were marked by renewed fits of passion for gambling, bringing in their wake fresh squalor and misery for the couple, whose life was still further darkened by the loss of their first child. Thanks to his wife's forebearance and support Dostoevsky was finally able to return to Russia in 1871. By now all the great novels except *The Brothers Karamazov* had been written, and the latter was already being planned under the title *The Life of a Great Sinner.*

Henceforth Dostoevsky's life was more settled, emotionally and financially. His popularity grew steadily, reaching its peak with *A Writer's Diary* and *The Brothers Karamazov*, while his speech at the unveiling of a monument to Pushkin in 1880 won rapturous acclaim. In the winter of the same year, however, he fell seriously ill and died after a pulmonary haemorrhage on January 28th, 1881.

The novels of Dostoevsky's maturity strike one immediately by their great homogeneity as a group. All share the central themes of murder, lust and religious conflict, and all involve judicial proceedings to a greater or lesser extent. Even more striking are the links between the characters: Alyosha and Myshkin, Grushenka and Nastasya Filipovna, Katerina Ivanovna and Aglaya, Ivan and Raskolnikov; or one might compare the spiritual conflict in *The Possessed* between Stavrogin

INTRODUCTION

and Tikhon with that between Ivan and Father Zosima. Within the novels many of the characters have 'doubles': Svidrigailov *(Crime and Punishment)* is an evil reflection of Raskolnikov's dangerous ideas, and Smerdyakov—the brothers' other self—is a caricature of Ivan and his theory that 'all is permitted'. It was no coincidence that one of Dostoevsky's first works was called *The Double*. Many of the characters, too, are torn by an inner conflict or duality of nature, which the writer felt to be a Russian national trait: the sensualist Svidrigailov saw no difference between wanton bestiality and divine self-sacrifice: both were exhilarating experiences; Katerina Ivanovna and Grushenka alternate between satanic pride and self abasement, voluptuousness and spiritual sublimation; at the trial the prosecutor accuses Dmitri of wanting to 'leap across two precipices at once'.

In contrast to the homogeneity of material in Dostoevsky's *opus* as a whole is an astounding heterogeneity of style and content within each individual book. Never before had a writer combined the trapping of the sensational crime thriller with psychological analysis of such depth, or introduced metaphysics on the highest plane to a world of violence, greed and lust. Perhaps it is misleading to speak of psychological analysis in *The Brothers Karamazov*, for the characters are not formally or objectively analysed. Nor are they portrayed in a process of slow development—the breakneck pace of what is in many ways a cliff-hanging novel would not allow that. (Most of the novels were published in monthly journals.) We meet them at moments of crisis and maximum tension when their souls are most clearly revealed. Dostoevsky's method is to expose innermost motives and feelings, rather than to build up a broad, composite picture. There is none of the panoramic vision so typical of 19th century Russian literature and of Tolstoy in particular.

Despite the wide gulf separating, for example, Ivan's legend of the Grand Inquisitor and the mystery of the murder and Dmitri's sudden wealth, the actual plot in *The Brothers Karamazov* is much more tightly knit than in the earlier novels. Hitherto there had been only one central character, and now there were three, albeit three bound together by a bond even stronger than that of blood. Some critics have seen the brothers as representing three aspects of the author's own life, a belief reinforced by the fact that Fyodor Pavlovich has some of the features of Dostoevsky's own father: Dmitri is seen as representing the idealistic, Romantic stage, ending in tragedy; Ivan the atheist represents the socialist period and friendship with Belinsky, whilst Alyosha reflects the ideas and ideals of the writer after exile, with his 'discovery' of the simple Russian people and Russian God. This spiritual autobiography is developed on a universal plane, however, with the illegitimate son Smerdyakov representing the dark side of this complex joint personality, as well as showing in grotesque and evil distortion the harmfulness of Ivan's over-intellectual theories. The three brothers are linked by communal guilt for the murder of their father, for Smerdyakov is only the tool or agent: the responsibility lies with Dmitri who willed the deed, Ivan who prepared the ground, and Alyosha who for all his principles foresaw and was unable to prevent the crime. In *Crime and Punishment* only a sixth of the book led up to the murder, whilst the rest was given over to its solution. In *The Brothers Karamazov* half the book is devoted to events before the crime: by the time it actually happens it has the force of inevitability, for from the very start we are cast into an atmosphere where parricide is an ever-present possibility. In the early scene at the monastery Dmitri exclaims in disgust at his father, 'Why should a man like that live?', at which Fyodor Pavlovich cries out, 'Do you hear him, do you hear him, you monks, the parricide?' The conversation between Alyosha and Rakitin adds to the impression that it is only a matter of time before the murder takes place. The atmosphere becomes stiflingly oppressive, although no-one can feel sympathy for the old man, so revolting is he in his lecherousness, greed and buffoonery.

The tension of the book comes from the very close relationships within the family: all the brothers share the elemental Karamazov force, so sadly perverted in their father; none is able to relax and react passively to his surroundings, but all must engage in a constant search for truth and a meaning to

INTRODUCTION

life. Ivan's intellectual questioning leads him to reject not God, but the world He has created: his 'handing back the ticket' is the result not of facile atheism, but of his immense love for humanity, and Zosima says to him, 'Thank God that you have a mind lofty enough to be tormented in this way'. Dostoevsky sought to show the harmfulness of Ivan's powerful ideas by giving them a distorted reflection in the devil that appears to him and in the lackey Smerdyakov, whilst in Alyosha he expressed his own religious beliefs and aspirations, but it is perhaps a reflection of his deep-lying doubts that the youngest brother is unable to answer satisfactorily Ivan's searching questions. For the eldest brother Dmitri the driving force is erotic passion, which becomes for him an all-powerful, almost spiritual force. For still greater tension and dramatic cohesion the bonds of family unity, or rather conflict, are drawn tighter by their complex relations with the women; for example, Fyodor Pavlovitch and Dmitri both pursue Grushenka, whilst Katerina Ivanovna is torn between Dmitri and Ivan.

The Brothers Karamazov may be read on at least three different planes: as a gripping crime thriller, as a psychological document of unprecedented significance (this was Freud's reaction) and as a profound discussion of the world's greatest philosophical and religious issues. In combining these hitherto irreconcilable elements it has proved a major influence on many 20th century writers, like Joyce and Camus; in Russia, too, despite the considerable hostility aroused by his doctrine of humility and suffering, Dostoevsky's influence has been enormous. Some twenty five years after the writer's death Vyacheslav Ivanov, the Symbolist poet, described him as 'that maddening convict, whose chains still jangle in Russian literature, which has been stunned by his raving invasion'. Readers have been exhilerated, revolted, or simply overpowered by Dostoevsky, but, whatever one's reaction, his immense stature and influence can hardly be denied. And of all the novels it is The Brothers Karamazov that gives fullest expression to the many different aspects of his tormented genius.

A. B. McMillin

London, July 1967.

TRANSLATOR'S PREFACE

A FEW words about Dostoevsky himself may help the English reader to understand his work.

Dostoevsky was the son of a doctor. His parents were very hard-working and deeply religious people, but so poor that they lived with their five children in only two rooms. The father and mother spent their evenings in reading aloud to their children, generally from books of a serious character.

Though always sickly and delicate Dostoevsky came out third in the final examination of the Petersburg school of Engineering. There he had already begun his first work, "Poor Folk".

This story was published by the poet Nekrassov in his review and was received with acclamations. The shy, unknown youth found himself instantly something of a celebrity. A brilliant and successful career seemed to open before him, but those hopes were soon dashed. In 1849 he was arrested.

Though neither by temperament nor conviction a revolutionist, Dostoevsky was one of a little group of young men who met together to read Fourier and Proudhon. He was accused of "taking part in conversations against the censorship, of reading a letter from Byelinsky to Gogol, and of knowing of the intention to set up a printing press". Under Nicholas I. (that "stern and just man", as Maurice Baring calls him) this was enough, and he was condemned to death. After eight months' imprisonment he was with twenty-one others taken out to the Semyonovsky Square to be shot. Writing to his brother Mihail, Dostoevsky says: "They snapped swords over our heads, and they made us put on the white shirts worn by persons condemned to death. Thereupon we were bound in threes to stakes, to suffer execution. Being the third in the row, I concluded I had only a few minutes of life before me. I thought of you and your dear ones and I continued to kiss Plestcheiev and Dourov, who were next to me, and to bid them farewell. Suddenly the troops beat a tattoo, we were unbound, brought back upon the scaffold, and informed that his Majesty had spared us our lives." The sentence was commuted to hard labour.

One of the prisoners, Grigoryev, went mad as soon as he was untied and never regained his sanity.

The intense suffering of this experience left a lasting stamp on Dostoevsky's mind. Though his religious temper led him in the end to accept every suffering with resignation and to regard it as a blessing in his own case, he constantly recurs to the subject in his writings. He describes the awful agony of the condemned man and insists on the cruelty of inflicting such torture. Then followed four years of penal servitude, spent in the company of common criminals in Siberia, where he began the "Dead House", and some years of service in a disciplinary battalion.

He had shown signs of some obscure nervous disease before his arrest and this now developed into violent attacks of epilepsy, from which he suffered for the rest of his life. The fits occurred three or four times a year and were more frequent in periods of great strain. In 1859 he was allowed to return to Russia. He started a journal, "Vremya", which was forbidden by the censorship through a misunderstanding. In 1864 he lost his first wife and his brother Mihail. He was in terrible poverty, yet he took upon himself the payment of his brother's debts. He started another journal—"The Epoch", which within a few months was also prohibited. He was weighed down by debt, his brother's family was dependent on him, he was forced to write at heart-breaking speed, and is said never to have corrected his work. The later years of his life were much softened by the tenderness and devotion of his second wife.

In June 1880 he made his famous speech at the unveiling of the monument to Pushkin in Moscow and he was received with extraordinary demonstrations of love and honour.

A few months later Dostoevsky died. He was followed to the grave by a vast multitude of mourners, who "gave the hapless man the funeral of a king". He is still probably the most widely read writer in Russia.

In the words of a Russian critic, who seeks to explain the feeling inspired by Dostoevsky: "He was one of ourselves, a man of our blood and our bone, but one who has suffered and has seen so much more deeply than we that his insight impresses us as wisdom . . . that wisdom of the heart which we seek that we may learn from it how to live. All his other gifts came to him from nature, this he won for himself and through it he became great."

CONTENTS

PART I

PART II

PART I

BOOK I: THE HISTORY OF A FAMILY

CHAPTER I

FYODOR PAVLOVITCH KARAMAZOV

ALEXEY FYODOROVITCH KARAMAZOV was the third son of Fyodor Pavlovitch Karamazov, a landowner well known in our district in his own day, and still remembered among us owing to his gloomy and tragic death, which happened thirteen years ago, and which I shall describe in its proper place. For the present I will only say that this "landowner"— for so we used to call him, although he hardly spent a day of his life on his own estate—was a strange type, yet one pretty frequently to be met with, a type abject and vicious and at the some time senseless. But he was one of those senseless persons who are very well capable of looking after their worldly affairs, and, apparently, after nothing else. Fyodor Pavlovitch, for instance, began with next to nothing; his estate was of the smallest; he ran to dine at other men's tables, and fastened on them as a toady; yet at his death it appeared that he had a hundred thousand roubles in hard cash. At the same time, he was all his life one of the most senseless, fantastical fellows in the whole district. I repeat, it was not stupidity—the majority of these fantastical fellows are shrewd and intelligent enough—but just senselessness, and a peculiar national form of it.

He was married twice, and had three sons, the eldest, Dmitri, by his first wife, and two, Ivan and Alexey, by his second. Fyodor Pavlovitch's first wife, Adelaïda Ivanovna, belonged to a fairly rich and distinguished noble family, also landowners in our district, the Miüsovs. How it came to pass that an heiress, who was also a beauty, and moreover one of those vigorous, intelligent girls, so common in this generation, but sometimes also to be found in the last, could have married such a worthless puny weakling, as we all called him, I won't attempt to explain. I knew a young lady of the last "romantic" generation who after some years of an enigmatic passion for a gentleman, whom

1

she might quite easily have married at any moment, invented insuperable obstacles to their union, and ended by throwing herself one stormy night into a rather deep and rapid river from a high bank, almost a precipice, and so perished, entirely to satisfy her own caprice, and to be like Shakespeare's Ophelia. Indeed, if this precipice, a chosen and favourite spot of hers, had been less picturesque, if there had been a prosaic flat bank in its place, most likely the suicide would never have taken place. This is a fact, and probably there have been not a few similar instances in the last two or three generations. Adelaïda Ivanovna Miüsov's action was similarly, no doubt, an echo of other people's ideas, and was due to the irritation caused by lack of mental freedom. She wanted, perhaps, to show her feminine independence, to override class distinctions and the despotism of her family. And a pliable imagination persuaded her, we must suppose, for a brief moment, that Fyodor Pavlovitch, in spite of his parasitic position, was one of the bold and ironical spirits of that progressive epoch, though he was, in fact, an ill-natured buffoon and nothing more. What gave the marriage piquancy was that it was preceded by an elopement, and this greatly captivated Adelaïda Ivanovna's fancy. Fyodor Pavlovitch's position at the time made him specially eager for any such enterprise, for he was passionately anxious to make a career in one way or another. To attach himself to a good family and obtain a dowry was an alluring prospect. As for mutual love it did not exist, apparently, either in the bride or in him, in spite of Adelaïda Ivanovna's beauty. This was, perhaps, a unique case of the kind in the life of Fyodor Pavlovitch, who was always of a voluptuous temper, and ready to run after any petticoat on the slightest encouragement. She seems to have been the only woman who made no particular appeal to his senses.

Immediately after the elopement Adelaïda Ivanovna discerned in a flash that she had no feeling for her husband but contempt. The marriage accordingly showed itself in its true colours with extraordinary rapidity. Although the family accepted the event pretty quickly and apportioned the runaway bride her dowry, the husband and wife began to lead a most disorderly life, and there were everlasting scenes between them. It was said that the young wife showed incomparably more generosity and dignity than Fyodor Pavlovitch, who, as is now known, got hold of all her money up to twenty-five thousand roubles as soon as she received it, so that those thousands were lost to her for ever.

The little village and the rather fine town house which formed part of her dowry he did his utmost for a long time to transfer to his name, by means of some deeds of conveyance. He would probably have succeeded, merely from her moral fatigue and desire to get rid of him, and from the contempt and loathing he aroused by his persistent and shameless importunity. But, fortunately, Adelaïda Ivanovna's family intervened and circumvented his greediness. It is known for a fact that frequent fights took place between the husband and wife, but rumour had it that Fyodor Pavlovitch did not beat his wife but was beaten by her, for she was a hot-tempered, bold, dark-browed, impatient woman, possessed of remarkable physical strength. Finally, she left the house and ran away from Fyodor Pavlovitch with a destitute divinity student, leaving Mitya, a child three years old, in her husband's hands. Immediately Fyodor Pavlovitch introduced a regular harem into the house, and abandoned himself to orgies of drunkenness. In the intervals he used to drive all over the province, complaining tearfully to each and all of Adelaïda Ivanovna's having left him, going into details too disgraceful for a husband to mention in regard to his own married life. What seemed to gratify him and flatter his self-love most was to play the ridiculous part of the injured husband, and to parade his woes with embellishments.

"One would think that you'd got a promotion, Fyodor Pavlovitch, you seem so pleased in spite of your sorrow," scoffers said to him. Many even added that he was glad of a new comic part in which to play the buffoon, and that it was simply to make it funnier that he pretended to be unaware of his ludicrous position. But, who knows, it may have been simplicity. At last he succeeded in getting on the track of his runaway wife. The poor woman turned out to be in Petersburg, where she had gone with her divinity student, and where she had thrown herself into a life of complete emancipation. Fyodor Pavlovitch at once began hustling about, making preparations to go to Petersburg, with what object he could not himself have said. He would perhaps have really gone; but having determined to do so he felt at once entitled to fortify himself for the journey by another bout of reckless drinking. And just at that time his wife's family received the news of her death in Petersburg. She had died quite suddenly in a garret, according to one story, of typhus, or, as another version had it, of starvation. Fyodor Pavlovitch was drunk when he heard of his wife's death, and the story is that he ran out into the

3

street and began shouting with joy, raising his hands to Heaven: "Lord, now lettest Thou Thy servant depart in peace," but others say he wept without restraint like a little child, so much so that people were sorry for him, in spite of the repulsion he inspired. It is quite possible that both versions were true, that he rejoiced at his release and at the same time wept for her who released him. As a general rule, people, even the wicked, are much more naïve and simple-hearted than we suppose. And we ourselves are, too.

CHAPTER II

HE GETS RID OF HIS ELDEST SON

YOU can easily imagine what a father such a man could be and how he would bring up his children. His behaviour as a father was exactly what might be expected. He completely abandoned the child of his marriage with Adelaïda Ivanovna, not from malice, nor because of his matrimonial grievances, but simply because he forgot him. While he was wearying everyone with his tears and complaints, and turning his house into a sink of debauchery, a faithful servant of the family, Grigory, took the three-year-old Mitya into his care. If he hadn't looked after him there would have been no one even to change the baby's little shirt.

It happened moreover that the child's relations on his mother's side forgot him too at first. His grandfather was no longer living, his widow, Mitya's grandmother, had moved to Moscow, and was seriously ill, while his daughters were married, so that Mitya remained for almost a whole year in old Grigory's charge and lived with him in the servant's cottage. But if his father had remembered him (he could not, indeed, have been altogether unaware of his existence) he would have sent him back to the cottage, as the child would only have been in the way of his debaucheries. But a cousin of Mitya's mother, Pyotr Alexandrovitch Miüsov, happened to return from Paris. He lived for many years afterwards abroad, but was at that time quite a young man, and distinguished among the Miüsovs as a man of enlightened ideas and of European culture, who had been in the capitals and abroad. Towards the end of his life he became a Liberal of the type common in the forties and fifties. In the course of his career he had come into contact

4

with many of the most Liberal men of his epoch, both in Russia and abroad. He had known Proudhon and Bakunin personally, and in his declining years was very fond of describing the three days of the Paris Revolution of February 1848, hinting that he himself had almost taken part in the fighting on the barricades. This was one of the most grateful recollections of his youth. He had an independent property of about a thousand souls, to reckon in the old style. His splendid estate lay on the outskirts of our little town and bordered on the lands of our famous monastery, with which Pyotr Alexandrovitch began an endless lawsuit, almost as soon as he came into the estate, concerning the rights of fishing in the river or wood-cutting in the forest, I don't know exactly which. He regarded it as his duty as a citizen and a man of culture to open an attack upon the "clericals". Hearing all about Adelaïda Ivanovna, whom he, of course, remembered, and in whom he had at one time been interested, and learning of the existence of Mitya, he intervened, in spite of all his youthful indignation and contempt for Fyodor Pavlovitch. He made the latter's acquaintance for the first time, and told him directly that he wished to undertake the child's education. He used long afterwards to tell as a characteristic touch that when he began to speak of Mitya, Fyodor Pavlovitch looked for some time as though he did not understand what child he was talking about, and even as though he was surprised to hear that he had a little son in the house. The story may have been exaggerated, yet it must have been something like the truth.

Fyodor Pavlovitch was all his life fond of acting, of suddenly playing an unexpected part, sometimes without any motive for doing so, and even to his own direct disadvantage, as, for instance, in the present case. This habit, however, is characteristic of a very great number of people, some of them very clever ones, not like Fyodor Pavlovitch. Pyotr Alexandrovitch carried the business through vigorously, and was appointed, with Fyodor Pavlovitch, joint guardian of the child, who had a small property, a house and land, left him by his mother. Mitya did, in fact, pass into this cousin's keeping, but as the latter had no family of his own, and after securing the revenues of his estates was in haste to return at once to Paris, he left the boy in charge of one of his cousins, a lady living in Moscow. It came to pass that, settling permanently in Paris, he, too, forgot the child, especially when the revolution of February broke out, making an impression on his mind that he remembered all the rest of his life. The Moscow lady died, and Mitya passed into the care of one of her married daughters. I believe he changed his home a fourth time later on. I won't enlarge upon that now, as I shall have much to tell later of Fyodor Pavlovitch's first-born, and must confine myself now to the most essential facts about him, without which I could not begin my story.

In the first place, this Mitya, or rather Dmitri Fyodorovitch, was the only one of Fyodor Pavlovitch's three sons who grew up in the belief that he had property, and that he would be independent on coming of age. He spent an irregular boyhood and youth. He did not finish his studies at the gymnasium, he got into a military school, then went to the Caucasus, was promoted, fought a duel, and was degraded to the ranks, earned promotion again, led a wild life, and spent a good deal of money. He did not begin to receive any income from Fyodor Pavlovitch until he came of age, and until then got into debt. He saw and knew his father, Fyodor Pavlovitch, for the first time on coming of age, when he visited our neighbourhood on purpose to settle with him about his property. He seems not to have liked his father. He did not stay long with him, and made haste to get away, having only succeeded in obtaining a sum of money, and entering into an agreement for future payments from the estate, of the revenues and value of which he was unable (a fact worthy of note), upon this occasion, to get a statement from his father. Fyodor Pavlovitch remarked for the first time then (this, too, should be noted) that Mitya had a vague and exaggerated idea of his property. Fyodor Pavlovitch was very well satisfied with this, as it fell in with his own designs. He gathered only that the young man was frivolous, unruly, of violent passions, impatient, and dissipated, and that if he could only obtain ready money he would be satisfied, although only, of course, for a short time. So Fyodor Pavlovitch began to take advantage of this fact, sending him from time to time small doles, instalments. In the end, when, four years later, Mitya, losing patience, came a second time to our little town to settle up once for all with his father, it turned out to his amazement that he had nothing, that it was difficult to get an account even, that he had received the whole value of his property in sums of money from Fyodor Pavlovitch, and was perhaps even in debt to him, that by various agreements into which he had, of his own desire, entered at various previous dates, he had no right to expect anything more, and so on, and so on. The young man was overwhelmed, suspected deceit and cheating, and was almost beside

6

himself. And, indeed, this circumstance led to the catastrophe, the account of which forms the subject of my first introductory story, or rather the external side of it. But before I pass to that story I must say a little of Fyodor Pavlovitch's other two sons, and of their origin.

CHAPTER III

THE SECOND MARRIAGE AND THE SECOND FAMILY

VERY shortly after getting his four-year-old Mitya off his hands Fyodor Pavlovitch married a second time. His second marriage lasted eight years. He took this second wife, Sofya Ivanovna, also a very young girl, from another province, where he had gone upon some small piece of business in company with a Jew. Though Fyodor Pavlovitch was a drunkard and a vicious debauchee he never neglected investing his capital, and managed his business affairs very successfully, though, no doubt, not over-scrupulously. Sofya Ivanovna was the daughter of an obscure deacon, and was left from childhood an orphan without relations. She grew up in the house of a general's widow, a wealthy old lady of good position, who was at once her benefactress and tormentor. I do not know the details, but I have only heard that the orphan girl, a meek and gentle creature, was once cut down from a halter in which she was hanging from a nail in the loft, so terrible were her sufferings from the caprice and everlasting nagging of this old woman, who was apparently not bad-hearted but had become an insufferable tyrant through idleness.

Fyodor Pavlovitch made her an offer; inquiries were made about him and he was refused. But again, as in his first marriage, he proposed an elopement to the orphan girl. There is very little doubt that she would not on any account have married him if she had known a little more about him in time. But she lived in another province; besides, what could a little girl of sixteen know about it, except that she would be better at the bottom of the river than remaining with her benefactress? So the poor child exchanged a benefactress for a benefactor. Fyodor Pavlovitch did not get a penny this time, for the general's widow was furious. She gave them nothing and cursed them both. But he had not reckoned on a dowry; what allured him was the remarkable beauty of the innocent girl, above all her innocent appearance, which had a peculiar attraction for a vicious profligate, who had hitherto admired only the coarser types of feminine beauty.

"Those innocent eyes slit my soul up like a razor," he used to say afterwards, with his loathsome snigger. In a man so depraved this might, of course, mean no more than sensual attraction. As he had received no dowry with his wife, and had, so to speak, taken her "from the halter", he did not stand on ceremony with her. Making her feel that she had "wronged" him, he took advantage of her phenomenal meekness and submissiveness to trample on the elementary decencies of marriage. He gathered loose women into his house, and carried on orgies of debauchery in his wife's presence. To show what a pass things had come to, I may mention that Grigory, the gloomy, stupid, obstinate, argumentative servant, who had always hated his first mistress, Adelaïda Ivanovna, took the side of his new mistress. He championed her cause, abusing Fyodor Pavlovitch in a manner little befitting a servant, and on one occasion broke up the revels and drove all the disorderly women out of the house. In the end this unhappy young woman, kept in terror from her childhood, fell into that kind of nervous disease which is most frequently found in peasant women who are said to be "possessed by devils". At times after terrible fits of hysterics she even lost her reason. Yet she bore Fyodor Pavlovitch two sons, Ivan and Alexey, the eldest in the first year of marriage and the second three years later. When she died little Alexey was in his fourth year, and, strange as it seems, I know that he remembered his mother all his life, like a dream, of course. At her death almost exactly the same thing happened to the two little boys as to their elder brother, Mitya. They were completely forgotten and abandoned by their father. They were looked after by the same Grigory and lived in his cottage, where they were found by the tyrannical old lady who had brought up their mother. She was still alive, and had not, all those eight years, forgotten the insult done her. All that time she was obtaining exact information as to her Sofya's manner of life, and hearing of her illness and hideous surroundings she declared aloud two or three times to her retainers:

"It serves her right. God has punished her for her ingratitude."

Exactly three months after Sofya Ivanovna's death the general's widow suddenly appeared in our town, and went straight to Fyodor Pavlovitch's house. She spent only half an

hour in the town but she did a great deal. It was evening.
Fyodor Pavlovitch, whom she had not seen for those eight
years, came in to her drunk. The story is that instantly upon
seeing him, without any sort of explanation, she gave him two
good, resounding slaps on the face, seized him by a tuft of hair,
and shook him three times up and down. Then, without a word,
she went straight to the cottage to the two boys. Seeing, at the
first glance, that they were unwashed and in dirty linen, she
promptly gave Grigory, too, a box on the ear, and announcing
that she would carry off both the children she wrapped them
just as they were in a rug, put them in the carriage, and drove
off to her own town. Grigory accepted the blow like a devoted
slave, without a word, and when he escorted the old lady to her
carriage he made her a low bow and pronounced impressively
that "God would repay her for the orphans". "You are a
blockhead all the same," the old lady shouted to him as she
drove away.

Fyodor Pavlovitch, thinking it over, decided that it was a
good thing, and did not refuse the general's widow his formal
consent to any proposition in regard to his children's education.
As for the slaps she had given him, he drove all over the town
telling the story.

It happened that the old lady died soon after this, but she left
the boys in her will a thousand roubles each "for their instruc-
tion, and so that all be spent on them exclusively, with the condition that it be so portioned out as to last till they are twenty-
one, for it is more than adequate provision for such children.
If other people think fit to throw away their money, let them."
I have not read the will myself, but I heard there was something
queer of the sort, very whimsically expressed. The principal
heir, Yefim Petrovitch Polenov, the Marshal of Nobility of the
province, turned out, however, to be an honest man. Writing
to Fyodor Pavlovitch, and discerning at once that he could ex-
tract nothing from him for his children's education (though the
latter never directly refused but only procrastinated as he always
did in such cases, and was, indeed, at times effusively sentimental), Yefim Petrovitch took a personal interest in the
orphans. He became especially fond of the younger, Alexey,
who lived for a long while as one of his family. I beg the reader
to note this from the beginning. And to Yefim Petrovitch, a
man of a generosity and humanity rarely to be met with, the
young people were more indebted for their education and bringing up than to anyone. He kept the two thousand roubles left

to them by the general's widow intact, so that by the time they came of age their portions had been doubled by the accumulation of interest. He educated them both at his own expense, and certainly spent far more than a thousand roubles upon each of them. I won't enter into a detailed account of their boyhood and youth, but will only mention a few of the most important events. Of the elder, Ivan, I will only say that he grew into a somewhat morose and reserved, though far from timid boy. At ten years old he had realised that they were living not in their own home but on other people's charity, and that their father was a man of whom it was disgraceful to speak. This boy began very early, almost in his infancy (so they say at least), to show a brilliant and unusual aptitude for learning. I don't know precisely why, but he left the family of Yefim Petrovitch when he was hardly thirteen, entering a Moscow gymnasium, and boarding with an experienced and celebrated teacher, an old friend of Yefim Petrovitch. Ivan used to declare afterwards that this was all due to the "ardour for good works" of Yefim Petrovitch, who was captivated by the idea that the boy's genius should be trained by a teacher of genius. But neither Yefim Petrovitch nor this teacher was living when the young man finished at the gymnasium and entered the university. As Yefim Petrovitch had made no provision for the payment of the tyrannical old lady's legacy, which had grown from one thousand to two, it was delayed, owing to formalities inevitable in Russia, and the young man was in great straits for the first two years at the university, as he was forced to keep himself all the time he was studying. It must be noted that he did not even attempt to communicate with his father, perhaps from pride, from contempt for him, or perhaps from his cool common sense, which told him that from such a father he would get no real assistance. However that may have been, the young man was by no means despondent and succeeded in getting work, at first giving sixpenny lessons and afterwards getting paragraphs on street incidents into the newspapers under the signature of "Eye-Witness". These paragraphs, it was said, were so interesting and piquant that they were soon taken. This alone showed the young man's practical and intellectual superiority over the masses of needy and unfortunate students of both sexes who hang about the offices of the newspapers and journals, unable to think of anything better than everlasting entreaties for copying and translations from the French. Having once got into touch with the editors Ivan Fyodorovitch always kept up his connection with them, and in his latter years at the university he published brilliant reviews of books upon various special subjects, so that he became well known in literary circles. But only in his last year he suddenly succeeded in attracting the attention of a far wider circle of readers, so that a great many people noticed and remembered him. It was rather a curious incident. When he had just left the university and was preparing to go abroad upon his two thousand roubles Ivan Fyodorovitch published in one of the more important journals a strange article, which attracted general notice, on a subject of which he might have been supposed to know nothing, as he was a student of natural science. The article dealt with a subject which was being debated everywhere at the time—the position of the ecclesiastical courts. After discussing several opinions on the subject he went on to explain his own view. What was most striking about the article was its tone, and its unexpected conclusion. Many of the Church party regarded him unquestioningly as on their side. And yet not only the secularists but even atheists joined them in their applause. Finally some sagacious persons opined that the article was nothing but an impudent satirical burlesque. I mention this incident particularly because this article penetrated into the famous monastery in our neighbourhood, where the inmates, being particularly interested in the question of the ecclesiastical courts, were completely bewildered by it. Learning the author's name, they were interested in his being a native of the town and the son of "that Fyodor Pavlovitch". And just then it was that the author himself made his appearance among us.

Why Ivan Fyodorovitch had come among us I remember asking myself at the time with a certain uneasiness. This fateful visit, which was the first step leading to so many consequences, I never fully explained to myself. It seemed strange on the face of it that a young man so learned, so proud, and apparently so cautious should suddenly visit such an infamous house and a father who had ignored him all his life, hardly knew him, never thought of him, and would not under any circumstances have given him money, though he was always afraid that his sons Ivan and Alexey would also come to ask him for it. And here the young man was staying in the house of such a father, had been living with him for two months, and they were on the best possible terms. This last fact was a special cause of wonder to many others as well as to me. Pyotr Alexandrovitch Miüsov, of whom we have spoken already, the cousin of Fyodor Pavlovitch's first wife, happened to be in the neighbourhood again on a visit to his estate. He had come from Paris, which was his permanent home. I remember that he was more surprised than anyone when he made the acquaintance of the young man, who interested him extremely, and with whom he sometimes argued and, not without an inner pang, compared himself in acquirements.

"He is proud," he used to say, "he will never be in want of pence; he has got money enough to go abroad now. What does he want here? Everyone can see that he hasn't come for money, for his father would never give him any. He has no taste for drink and dissipation, and yet his father can't do without him. They get on so well together!"

That was the truth; the young man had an unmistakable influence over his father, who positively appeared to be behaving more decently and even seemed at times ready to obey his son, though often extremely and even spitefully perverse.

It was only later that we learned that Ivan had come partly at the request of, and in the interests of, his elder brother, Dmitri, whom he saw for the first time on this very visit, though he had before leaving Moscow been in correspondence with him about an important matter of more concern to Dmitri than himself. What that business was the reader will learn fully in due time. Yet even when I did know of this special circumstance I still felt Ivan Fyodorovitch to be an enigmatic figure, and thought his visit rather mysterious.

I may add that Ivan appeared at the time in the light of a mediator between his father and his elder brother Dmitri, who was in open quarrel with his father and even planning to bring an action against him.

The family, I repeat, was now united for the first time, and some of its members met for the first time in their lives. The younger brother, Alexey, had been a year already among us, having been the first of the three to arrive. It is of that brother Alexey I find it most difficult to speak in this introduction. Yet I must give some preliminary account of him, if only to explain one queer fact, which is that I have to introduce my hero to the reader wearing the cassock of a novice. Yes, he had been for the last year in our monastery, and seemed willing to be cloistered there for the rest of his life.

CHAPTER IV

THE THIRD SON, ALYOSHA

HE was only twenty, his brother Ivan was in his twenty-fourth year at the time, while their elder brother Dmitri was twenty-seven. First of all, I must explain that this young man, Alyosha, was not a fanatic, and, in my opinion at least, was not even a mystic. I may as well give my full opinion from the beginning. He was simply an early lover of humanity, and that he adopted the monastic life was simply because at that time it struck him, so to say, as the ideal escape for his soul struggling from the darkness of worldly wickedness to the light of love. And the reason this life struck him in this way was that he found in it at that time, as he thought, an extraordinary being, our celebrated elder, Zossima, to whom he became attached with all the warm first love of his ardent heart. But I do not dispute that he was very strange even at that time, and had been so indeed from his cradle. I have mentioned already, by the way, that though he lost his mother in his fourth year he remembered her all his life—her face, her caresses, "as though she stood living before me". Such memories may persist, as everyone knows, from an even earlier age, even from two years old, but scarcely standing out through a whole lifetime like spots of light out of darkness, like a corner torn out of a huge picture, which has all faded and disappeared except that fragment. That is how it was with him. He remembered one still summer evening, an open window, the slanting rays of the setting sun (that he recalled most vividly of all); in a corner of the room the holy image, before it a lighted lamp, and on her knees before the image his mother, sobbing hysterically with cries and moans, snatching him up in both arms, squeezing him close till it hurt, and praying for him to the Mother of God, holding him out in both arms to the image as though to put him under the Mother's protection . . . and suddenly a nurse runs in and snatches him from her in terror. That was the picture! And Alyosha remembered his mother's face at that minute. He used to say that it was frenzied but beautiful as he remembered. But he rarely cared to speak of this memory to anyone. In his childhood and youth he was by no means expansive, and talked little indeed, but not from shyness or a sullen unsociability; quite the contrary, from something different, from a sort of inner preoccupation entirely personal and unconcerned with other

13

people, but so important to him that he seemed, as it were, to forget others on account of it. But he was fond of people: he seemed throughout his life to put implicit trust in people: yet no one ever looked on him as a simpleton or naïve person. There was something about him which made one feel at once (and it was so all his life afterwards) that he did not care to be a judge of others—that he would never take it upon himself to criticise and would never condemn anyone for anything. He seemed, indeed, to accept everything without the least condemnation though often grieving bitterly: and this was so much so that no one could surprise or frighten him even in his earliest youth. Coming at twenty to his father's house, which was a very sink of filthy debauchery, he, chaste and pure as he was, simply withdrew in silence when to look on was unbearable, but without the slightest sign of contempt or condemnation. His father, who had once been in a dependent position, and so was sensitive and ready to take offence, met him at first with distrust and sullenness. "He does not say much," he used to say, "and thinks the more." But soon, within a fortnight indeed, he took to embracing him and kissing him terribly often, with drunken tears, with sottish sentimentality, yet he evidently felt a real and deep affection for him, such as he had never been capable of feeling for anyone before.

Everyone, indeed, loved this young man wherever he went, and it was so from his earliest childhood. When he entered the household of his patron and benefactor, Yefim Petrovitch Polenov, he gained the hearts of all the family, so that they looked on him quite as their own child. Yet he entered the house at such a tender age that he could not have acted from design nor artfulness in winning affection. So that the gift of making himself loved directly and unconsciously was inherent in him, in his very nature, so to speak. It was the same at school, though he seemed to be just one of those children who are distrusted, sometimes ridiculed, and even disliked by their schoolfellows. He was dreamy, for instance, and rather solitary. From his earliest childhood he was fond of creeping into a corner to read, and yet he was a general favourite all the while he was at school. He was rarely playful or merry, but anyone could see at the first glance that this was not from any sullenness. On the contrary he was bright and good-tempered. He never tried to show off among his schoolfellows. Perhaps because of this he was never afraid of anyone, yet the boys immediately understood that he was not proud of his fearlessness and seemed to be

14

unaware that he was bold and courageous. He never resented an insult. It would happen that an hour after the offence he would address the offender or answer some question with as trustful and candid an expression as though nothing had happened between them. And it was not that he seemed to have forgotten or intentionally forgiven the affront, but simply that he did not regard it as an affront, and this completely conquered and captivated the boys. He had one characteristic which made all his schoolfellows from the bottom class to the top want to mock at him, not from malice but because it amused them. This characteristic was a wild fanatical modesty and chastity. He could not bear to hear certain words and certain conversations about women. There are "certain" words and conversations unhappily impossible to eradicate in schools. Boys pure in mind and heart, almost children, are fond of talking in school among themselves, and even aloud, of things, pictures, and images of which even soldiers would sometimes hesitate to speak. More than that, much that soldiers have no knowledge or conception of is familiar to quite young children of our intellectual and higher classes. There is no moral depravity, no real corrupt inner cynicism in it, but there is the appearance of it, and it is often looked upon among them as something refined, subtle, daring, and worthy of imitation. Seeing that Alyosha Karamazov put his fingers in his ears when they talked of "that", they used sometimes to crowd round him, pull his hands away, and shout nastiness into both ears, while he struggled, slipped to the floor, tried to hide himself without uttering one word of abuse, enduring their insults in silence. But at last they left him alone and gave up taunting him with being a "regular girl", and, what's more, they looked upon it with compassion as a weakness. He was always one of the best in the class but was never first.

At the time of Yefim Petrovitch's death Alyosha had two more years to complete at the provincial gymnasium. The inconsolable widow went almost immediately after his death for a long visit to Italy with her whole family, which consisted only of women and girls. Alyosha went to live in the house of two distant relations of Yefim Petrovitch, ladies whom he had never seen before. On what terms he lived with them he did not know himself. It was very characteristic of him, indeed, that he never cared at whose expense he was living. In that respect he was a striking contrast to his elder brother Ivan, who struggled with poverty for his first two years in the university, maintained himself by his own efforts, and had from childhood been bitterly conscious of living at the expense of his benefactor. But this strange trait in Alyosha's character must not, I think, be criticised too severely, for at the slightest acquaintance with him anyone would have perceived that Alyosha was one of those youths, almost of the type of religious enthusiast, who, if they were suddenly to come into possession of a large fortune, would not hesitate to give it away for the asking, either for good works or perhaps to a clever rogue. In general he seemed scarcely to know the value of money, not, of course, in a literal sense. When he was given pocket-money, which he never asked for, he was either terribly careless of it so that it was gone in a moment, or he kept it for weeks together, not knowing what to do with it.

In later years Pyotr Alexandrovitch Miüsov, a man very sensitive on the score of money and bourgeois honesty, pronounced the following judgment, after getting to know Alyosha:

"Here is perhaps the one man in the world whom you might leave alone without a penny, in the centre of an unknown town of a million inhabitants, and he would not come to harm, he would not die of cold and hunger, for he would be fed and sheltered at once; and if he were not, he would find a shelter for himself, and it would cost him no effort or humiliation. And to shelter him would be no burden, but, on the contrary, would probably be looked on as a pleasure."

He did not finish his studies at the gymnasium. A year before the end of the course he suddenly announced to the ladies that he was going to see his father about a plan which had occurred to him. They were sorry and unwilling to let him go. The journey was not an expensive one, and the ladies would not let him pawn his watch, a parting present from his benefactor's family. They provided him liberally with money and even fitted him out with new clothes and linen. But he returned half the money they gave him, saying that he intended to go third class. On his arrival in the town he made no answer to his father's first inquiry why he had come before completing his studies, and seemed, so they say, unusually thoughtful. It soon became apparent that he was looking for his mother's tomb. He practically acknowledged at the time that that was the only object of his visit. But it can hardly have been the whole reason for it. It is more probable that he himself did not understand and could not explain what had suddenly arisen in his soul, and drawn him irresistibly into a new, unknown, but inevitable path.

Fyodor Pavlovitch could not show him where his second wife was buried, for he had never visited her grave since he had thrown earth upon her coffin, and in the course of years had entirely forgotten where she was buried.

Fyodor Pavlovitch, by the way, had for some time previously not been living in our town. Three or four years after his wife's death he had gone to the south of Russia and finally turned up in Odessa, where he spent several years. He made the acquaintance at first, in his own words, "of a lot of low Jews, Jewesses, and Jewkins", and ended by being received by "Jews high and low alike". It may be presumed that at this period he developed a peculiar faculty for making and hoarding money. He finally returned to our town only three years before Alyosha's arrival. His former acquaintances found him looking terribly aged, although he was by no means an old man. He behaved not exactly with more dignity but with more effrontery. The former buffoon showed an insolent propensity for making buffoons of others. His depravity with women was not simply what it used to be, but even more revolting. In a short time he opened a great number of new taverns in the district. It was evident that he had perhaps a hundred thousand roubles or not much less. Many of the inhabitants of the town and district were soon in his debt, and, of course, had given good security. Of late, too, he looked somehow bloated and seemed more irresponsible, more uneven, had sunk into a sort of incoherence, used to begin one thing and go on with another, as though he were letting himself go altogether. He was more and more frequently drunk. And, if it had not been for the same servant Grigory, who by that time had aged considerably too, and used to look after him sometimes almost like a tutor, Fyodor Pavlovitch might have got into terrible scrapes. Alyosha's arrival seemed to affect even his moral side, as though something had awakened in this prematurely old man which had long been dead in his soul.

"Do you know," he used often to say, looking at Alyosha, "that you are like her, 'the crazy woman' "—that was what he used to call his dead wife, Alyosha's mother. Grigory it was who pointed out the "crazy woman's" grave to Alyosha. He took him to our town cemetery and showed him in a remote corner a cast-iron tombstone, cheap but decently kept, on which were inscribed the name and age of the deceased and the date of her death, and below a four-lined verse, such as are commonly used on old-fashioned middle-class tombs. To

Alyosha's amazement this tomb turned out to be Grigory's doing. He had put it up on the poor "crazy woman's" grave at his own expense, after Fyodor Pavlovítch, whom he had often pestered about the grave, had gone to Odessa, abandoning the grave and all his memories. Alyosha showed no particular emotion at the sight of his mother's grave. He only listened to Grigory's minute and solemn account of the erection of the tomb; he stood with bowed head and walked away without uttering a word. It was perhaps a year before he visited the cemetery again. But this little episode was not without an influence upon Fyodor Pavlovitch—and a very original one. He suddenly took a thousand roubles to our monastery to pay for requiems for the soul of his wife; but not for the second, Alyosha's mother, the "crazy woman", but for the first, Adelaïda Ivanovna, who used to thrash him. In the evening of the same day he got drunk and abused the monks to Alyosha. He himself was far from being religious; he had probably never put a penny candle before the image of a saint. Strange impulses of sudden feeling and sudden thought are common in such types.

I have mentioned already that he looked bloated. His countenance at this time bore traces of something that testified unmistakably to the life he had led. Besides the long fleshy bags under his little, always insolent, suspicious, and ironical eyes; besides the multitude of deep wrinkles in his little fat face, the Adam's apple hung below his sharp chin like a great, fleshy goitre, which gave him a peculiar, repulsive, sensual appearance; add to that a long rapacious mouth with full lips, between which could be seen little stumps of black decayed teeth. He slobbered every time he began to speak. He was fond indeed of making fun of his own face, though, I believe, he was well satisfied with it. He used particularly to point to his nose, which was not very large, but very delicate and conspicuously aquiline. "A regular Roman nose," he used to say. "With my goitre I've quite the countenance of an ancient Roman patrician of the decadent period." He seemed proud of it.

Not long after visiting his mother's grave Alyosha suddenly announced that he wanted to enter the monastery, and that the monks were willing to receive him as a novice. He explained that this was his strong desire, and that he was solemnly asking his consent as his father. The old man knew that the elder Zossima, who was living in the monastery hermitage, had made a special impression upon his "gentle boy".

"That is the most honest monk among them, of course," he observed, after listening in thoughtful silence to Alyosha, and seeming scarcely surprised at his request. "H'm! . . . So that's where you want to be, my gentle boy?"

He was half drunk, and suddenly he grinned his slow half-drunken grin, which was not without a certain cunning and tipsy slyness. "H'm! . . . I had a presentiment that you would end in something like this. Would you believe it? You were making straight for it. Well, to be sure you have your own two thousand. That's a dowry for you. And I'll never desert you, my angel. And I'll pay what's wanted for you there, if they ask for it. But, of course, if they don't ask, why should we worry them? What do you say? You know, you spend money like a canary, two grains a week. H'm! . . . Do you know that near one monastery there's a place outside the town where every baby knows there are none but 'the monks' wives' living, as they are called. Thirty women, I believe. I have been there myself. You know, it's interesting in its own way, of course, as a variety. The worst of it is it's awfully Russian. There are no French women there. Of course they could get them fast enough, they have plenty of money. If they get to hear of it they'll come along. Well, there's nothing of that sort here, no 'monks' wives', and two hundred monks. They're honest. They keep the fasts. I admit it. . . . H'm. . . . So you want to be a monk? And do you know I'm sorry to lose you, Alyosha; would you believe it, I've really grown fond of you? Well, it's a good opportunity. You'll pray for us sinners; we have sinned too much here. I've always been thinking who would pray for me, and whether there's anyone in the world to do it. My dear boy, I'm awfully stupid about that. You wouldn't believe it. Awfully. You see, however stupid I am about it, I keep thinking, I keep thinking—from time to time, of course, not all the while. It's impossible, I think, for the devils to forget to drag me down to hell with their hooks when I die. Then I wonder—hooks? Where would they get them? What of? Iron hooks? Where do they forge them? Have they a foundry there of some sort? The monks in the monastery probably believe that there's a ceiling in hell, for instance. Now I'm ready to believe in hell, but without a ceiling. It makes it more refined, more enlightened, more Lutheran, that it. And, after all, what does it matter whether it has a ceiling or hasn't? But, do you know, there's a damnable question involved in it? If there's no ceiling there can be no hooks, and if there are no hooks it all breaks down, which is unlikely again, for then there would be none to drag me down to hell, and if they don't drag me down what justice is there in the world? *Il faudrait les inventer*, those hooks, on purpose for me alone, for, if you only knew, Alyosha, what a blackguard I am.''

"But there are no hooks there," said Alyosha, looking gently and seriously at his father.

"Yes, yes, only the shadows of hooks. I know, I know. That's how a Frenchman described hell: *'J'ai vu l'ombre d'un cocher qui avec l'ombre d'une brosse frottait l'ombre d'une carrosse.'* How do you know there are no hooks, darling? When you've lived with the monks you'll sing a different tune. But go and get at the truth there, and then come and tell me. Anyway, it's easier going to the other world if one knows what there is there. Besides, it will be more seemly for you with the monks than here with me, with a drunken old man and young harlots . . . though you're like an angel, nothing touches you. And I dare say nothing will touch you there. That's why I let you go, because I hope for that. You've got all your wits about you. You will burn and you will burn out; you will be healed and come back again. And I will wait for you. I feel that you're the only creature in the world who has not condemned me. My dear boy, I feel it, you know. I can't help feeling it."

And he even began blubbering. He was sentimental. He was wicked and sentimental.

CHAPTER V

ELDERS

SOME of my readers may imagine that my young man was a sickly, ecstatic, poorly developed creature, a pale, consumptive dreamer. On the contrary, Alyosha was at this time a well-grown, red-cheeked, clear-eyed lad of nineteen, radiant with health. He was very handsome, too, graceful, moderately tall, with hair of a dark brown, with a regular, rather long, oval-shaped face, and wide-set dark grey, shining eyes; he was very thoughtful, and apparently very serene. I shall be told, perhaps, that red cheeks are not incompatible with fanaticism and mysticism; but I fancy that Alyosha was more of a realist than anyone. Oh! no doubt in the monastery he fully believed in miracles, but, to my thinking, miracles are never a stumbling-block to the realist. It is not miracles that dispose realists to belief. The genuine realist, if he is an unbeliever, will always find strength and ability to disbelieve in the miraculous, and if he is confronted with a miracle as an irrefutable fact he would rather disbelieve his own senses than admit the fact. Even if he admits it, he admits it as a fact of nature till then unrecognised by him. Faith does not, in the realist, spring from the miracle but the miracle from faith. If the realist once believes, then he is bound by his very realism to admit the miraculous also. The Apostle Thomas said that he would not believe till he saw, but when he did see he said: "My Lord and my God!" Was it the miracle forced him to believe? Most likely not, but he believed solely because he desired to believe and possibly he fully believed in his secret heart even when he said: "I do not believe till I see."

I shall be told, perhaps, that Alyosha was stupid, undeveloped, had not finished his studies, and so on. That he did not finish his studies is true, but to say that he was stupid or dull would be a great injustice. I'll simply repeat what I have said above. He entered upon this path only because, at that time, it alone struck his imagination and presented itself to him as offering an ideal means of escape for his soul from darkness to light. Add to that that he was to some extent a youth of our last epoch—that is, honest in nature, desiring the truth, seeking for it and believing in it, and seeking to serve it at once with all the strength of his soul, seeking for immediate action, and ready to sacrifice anything, life itself, for it. Though these young men unhappily fail to understand that the sacrifice of life is, in many cases, the easiest of all sacrifices, and that to sacrifice, for instance, five or six years of their seething youth to hard and tedious study, if only to multiply tenfold their powers of serving the truth and the cause they have set before them as their goal— such a sacrifice is utterly beyond the strength of many of them. The path Alyosha chose was a path going in the opposite direction, but he chose it with the same thirst for swift achievement. As soon as he reflected seriously he was convinced of the existence of God and immortality, and at once he instinctively said to himself: "I want to live for immortality, and I will accept no compromise." In the same way, if he had decided that God and immortality did not exist, he would at once have become an atheist and a socialist. For socialism is not merely the labour question, it is before all things the atheistic question, the question of the form taken by atheism to-day, the question of the tower of Babel built without God, not to mount to Heaven from earth but to set up Heaven on earth. Alyosha would have found it strange and impossible to go on living as before. It is written: "Give all that thou hast to the poor and follow Me, if thou wouldst be perfect."

Alyosha said to himself: "I can't give two roubles instead of 'all', and only go to mass instead of 'following Him'." Perhaps his memories of childhood brought back our monastery, to which his mother may have taken him to mass. Perhaps the slanting sunlight and the holy image to which his poor "crazy" mother had held him up still acted upon his imagination. Brooding on these things he may have come to us perhaps only to see whether here he could sacrifice all or only "two roubles", and in the monastery he met this elder. I must digress to explain what an "elder" is in Russian monasteries, and I am sorry that I do not feel very competent to do so. I will try, however, to give a superficial account of it in a few words. Authorities on the subject assert that the institution of "elders" is of recent date, not more than a hundred years old in our monasteries, though in the orthodox East, especially in Sinai and Athos, it has existed over a thousand years. It is maintained that it existed in ancient times in Russia also, but through the calamities which overtook Russia—the Tartars, civil war, the interruption of relations with the East after the destruction of Constantinople—this institution fell into oblivion. It was revived among us towards the end of last century by one of the great "ascetics", as they called him, Païssy Velitchkovsky, and his disciples. But to this day it exists in few monasteries only, and has sometimes been almost persecuted as an innovation in Russia. It flourished especially in the celebrated Kozelski Optin Monastery. When and how it was introduced into our monastery I cannot say. There had already been three such elders and Zossima was the last of them. But he was almost dying of weakness and disease, and they had no one to take his place. The question for our monastery was an important one, for it had not been distinguished by anything in particular till then: they had neither relics of saints, nor wonder-working ikons, nor glorious traditions, nor historical exploits. It had flourished and been glorious all over Russia through its elders, to see and hear whom pilgrims had flocked for thousands of miles from all parts.

What was such an elder? An elder was one who took your soul, your will, into his soul and his will. When you choose an elder, you renounce your own will and yield it to him in complete submission, complete self-abnegation. This novitiate, this terrible school of abnegation, is undertaken voluntarily, in the hope of self-conquest, of self-mastery, in order, after a life of obedience, to attain perfect freedom, that is, from self; to escape the lot of those who have lived their whole life without finding their true selves in themselves. This institution of elders is not founded on theory, but was established in the East from the practice of a thousand years. The obligations due to an elder are not the ordinary "obedience" which has always existed in our Russian monasteries. The obligation involves confession to the elder by all who have submitted themselves to him, and to the indissoluble bond between him and them.

The story is told, for instance, that in the early days of Christianity one such novice, failing to fulfil some command laid upon him by his elder, left his monastery in Syria and went to Egypt. There, after great exploits, he was found worthy at last to suffer torture and a martyr's death for the faith. When the Church, regarding him as a saint, was burying him, suddenly, at the deacon's exhortation "Depart all ye unbaptized", the coffin containing the martyr's body left its place and was cast forth from the church, and this took place three times. And only at last they learnt that this holy man had broken his vow of obedience and left his elder, and, therefore, could not be forgiven without the elder's absolution in spite of his great deeds. Only after this could the funeral take place. This, of course, is only an old legend. But here is a recent instance.

A monk was suddenly commanded by his elder to quit Athos, which he loved as a sacred place and a haven of refuge, and to go, first to Jerusalem to do homage to the Holy Places and then to go to the north to Siberia: "There is the place for thee and not here." The monk, overwhelmed with sorrow, went to the Œcumenical Patriarch at Constantinople and besought him to release him from his obedience. But the Patriarch replied that not only was he unable to release him but there was not and could not be on earth a power which could release him except the elder who had himself laid that duty upon him. In this way the elders were endowed in certain cases with unbounded and inexplicable authority. That is why in many of our monasteries the institution was at first resisted almost to persecution. Meantime the elders immediately began to be highly esteemed among the people. Masses of the ignorant people as well as men of distinction flocked, for instance, to the elders of our monastery to confess their doubts, their sins, and their sufferings, and ask for counsel and admonition. Seeing this, the opponents of the elders declared that the sacrament of confession was being arbitrarily and frivolously degraded, though the continual opening of the heart to the elder by the monk or the layman had nothing of the character of the sacrament. In the end, however, the institution of elders has been retained and is becoming established in Russian monasteries. It is true, perhaps, that this instrument, which had stood the test of a thousand years for the moral regeneration of a man from slavery to freedom and to moral perfectibility, may be a two-edged weapon and it may lead some not to humility and complete self-control but to the most Satanic pride, that is, to bondage and not to freedom.

The elder Zossima was sixty-five. He came of a family of landowners, had been in the army in early youth, and served in the Caucasus as an officer. He had, no doubt, impressed Alyosha by some peculiar quality of his soul. Alyosha lived in the cell of the elder, who was very fond of him and let him wait upon him. It must be noted that Alyosha was bound by no obligation and could go where he pleased and be absent for whole days. Though he wore the monastic dress it was voluntarily, not to be different from others. No doubt he liked to do so. Possibly his youthful imagination was deeply stirred by the power and fame of his elder. It was said that so many people had for years past come to confess their sins to Father Zossima and to entreat him for words of advice and healing, that he had acquired the keenest intuition and could tell from an unknown face what a new-comer wanted, and what was the suffering on his conscience. He sometimes astounded and almost alarmed his visitors by his knowledge of their secrets before they had spoken a word.

Alyosha noticed that many, almost all, went in to the elder for the first time with apprehension and uneasiness, but came out with bright and happy faces. Alyosha was particularly struck by the fact that Father Zossima was not at all stern. On the contrary, he was always almost gay. The monks used to say that he was more drawn to those who were more sinful, and the greater the sinner the more he loved him. There were, no doubt, up to the end of his life, among the monks some who hated and envied him, but they were few in number and they were silent, though among them were some of great dignity in the monastery, one, for instance, of the older monks distinguished for his strict keeping of fasts and vows of silence. But the majority were on Father Zossima's side and very many of them loved him with

all their hearts, warmly and sincerely. Some were almost fanatically devoted to him, and declared, though not quite aloud, that he was a saint, that there could be no doubt of it, and, seeing that his end was near, they anticipated miracles and great glory to the monastery in the immediate future from his relics. Alyosha had unquestioning faith in the miraculous power of the elder, just as he had unquestioning faith in the story of the coffin that flew out of the church. He saw many who came with sick children or relatives and besought the elder to lay hands on them and to pray over them, return shortly after— some the next day—and, falling in tears at the elder's feet, thank him for healing their sick.

Whether they had really been healed or were simply better in the natural course of the disease was a question which did not exist for Alyosha, for he fully believed in the spiritual power of his teacher and rejoiced in his fame, in his glory, as though it were his own triumph. His heart throbbed, and he beamed, as it were, all over when the elder came out to the gates of the hermitage into the waiting crowd of pilgrims of the humbler class who had flocked from all parts of Russia on purpose to see the elder and obtain his blessing. They fell down before him, wept, kissed his feet, kissed the earth on which he stood, and wailed, while the women held up their children to him and brought him the sick "possessed with devils". The elder spoke to them, read a brief prayer over them, blessed them, and dismissed them. Of late he had become so weak through attacks of illness that he was sometimes unable to leave his cell, and the pilgrims waited for him to come out for several days. Alyosha did not wonder why they loved him so, why they fell down before him and wept with emotion merely at seeing his face. Oh! he understood that for the humble soul of the Russian peasant, worn out by grief and toil, and still more by the everlasting injustice and everlasting sin, his own and the world's, it was the greatest need and comfort to find someone or something holy to fall down before and worship.

"Among us there is sin, injustice, and temptation, but yet, somewhere on earth there is someone holy and exhalted. He has the truth; he knows the truth; so it is not dead upon the earth; so it will come one day to us, too, and rule over all the earth according to the promise."

Alyosha knew that this was just how the people felt and even reasoned. He understood it, but that the elder Zossima was this saint and custodian of God's truth—of that he had no more doubt than the weeping peasants and the sick women who held out their children to the elder. The conviction that after his death the elder would bring extraordinary glory to the monastery was even stronger in Alyosha than in anyone there, and, of late, a kind of deep flame of inner ecstasy burnt more and more strongly in his heart. He was not at all troubled at this elder's standing as a solitary example before him.

"No matter. He is holy. He carries in his heart the secret of renewal for all: that power which will, at last, establish truth on the earth, and all men will be holy and love one another, and there will be no more rich nor poor, no exalted nor humbled, but all will be as the children of God, and the true Kingdom of Christ will come." That was the dream in Alyosha's heart.

The arrival of his two brothers, whom he had not known till then, seemed to make a great impression on Alyosha. He more quickly made friends with his half-brother Dmitri (though he arrived later) than with his own brother Ivan. He was extremely interested in his brother Ivan, but when the latter had been two months in the town, though they had met fairly often, they were still not intimate. Alyosha was naturally silent, and he seemed to be expecting something, ashamed about something, while his brother Ivan, though Alyosha noticed at first that he looked long and curiously at him, seemed soon to have left off thinking of him. Alyosha noticed it with some embarrassment. He ascribed his brother's indifference at first to the disparity of their age and education. But he also wondered whether the absence of curiosity and sympathy in Ivan might be due to some other cause entirely unknown to him. He kept fancying that Ivan was absorbed in something—something inward and important— that he was striving towards some goal, perhaps very hard to attain, and that that was why he had no thought for him. Alyosha wondered, too, whether there was not some contempt on the part of the learned atheist for him—a foolish novice. He knew for certain that his brother was an atheist. He could not take offence at this contempt, if it existed; yet, with an uneasy embarrassment which he did not himself understand, he waited for his brother to come nearer to him. Dmitri used to speak of Ivan with the deepest respect and with a peculiar earnestness. From him Alyosha learnt all the details of the important affair which had of late formed such a close and remarkable bond between the two elder brothers. Dmitri's enthusiastic references to Ivan were the more striking in Alyosha's eyes since Dmitri was, compared with Ivan, almost uneducated, and the two brothers were such a contrast in personality and character that it would be difficult to find two men more unlike.

It was at this time that the meeting, or rather, gathering of the members of this inharmonious family took place in the cell of the elder who had such an extraordinary influence on Alyosha. The pretext for this gathering was a false one. It was at this time that the discord between Dmitri and his father seemed at its acutest stage and their relations had become insufferably strained. Fyodor Pavlovitch seems to have been the first to suggest, apparently in joke, that they should all meet in Father Zossima's cell, and that, without appealing to his direct intervention, they might more decently come to an understanding under the conciliating influence of the elder's presence. Dmitri, who had never seen the elder, naturally supposed that his father was trying to intimidate him, but, as he secretly blamed himself for his outbursts of temper with his father on several recent occasions, he accepted the challenge. It must be noted that he was not, like Ivan, staying with his father, but living apart at the other end of the town. It happened that Pyotr Alexandrovitch Miüsov, who was staying in the district at the time, caught eagerly at the idea. A Liberal of the forties and fifties, a freethinker and atheist, he may have been led on by boredom or the hope of frivolous diversion. He was suddenly seized with the desire to see the monastery and the holy man. As his lawsuit with the monastery still dragged on, he made it the pretext for seeing the Superior, in order to attempt to settle it amicably. A visitor coming with such laudable intentions might be received with more attention and consideration than if he came from simple curiosity. Influences from within the monastery were brought to bear on the elder, who of late had scarcely left his cell, and had been forced by illness to deny even his ordinary visitors. In the end he consented to see them, and the day was fixed.

"Who has made me a judge over them?" was all he said, smilingly, to Alyosha.

Alyosha was much perturbed when he heard of the proposed visit. Of all the wrangling, quarrelsome party, Dmitri was the only one who could regard the interview seriously. All the others would come from frivolous motives, perhaps insulting to the elder. Alyosha was well aware of that. Ivan and Miüsov would come from curiosity, perhaps of the coarsest kind, while his father might be contemplating some piece of buffoonery. Though he sad nothing, Alyosha thoroughly understood his father. The boy, I repeat, was far from being so simple as everyone thought him. He awaited the day with a heavy heart. No doubt he was always pondering in his mind how the family discord could be ended. But his chief anxiety concerned the elder. He trembled for him, for his glory, and dreaded any affront to him, especially the refined, courteous irony of Miüsov and the supercilious half-utterances of the highly educated Ivan. He even wanted to venture on warning the elder, telling him something about them, but, on second thoughts, said nothing. He only sent word the day before, through a friend, to his brother Dmitri, that he loved him and expected him to keep his promise. Dmitri wondered, for he could not remember what he had promised, but he answered by letter that he would do his utmost not to let himself be provoked "by vileness", but that, although he had a deep respect for the elder and for his brother Ivan, he was convinced that the meeting was either a trap for him or an unworthy farce.

"Nevertheless I would rather bite out my tongue than be lacking in respect to the sainted man whom you reverence so highly," he wrote in conclusion. Alyosha was not greatly cheered by the letter.

BOOK II: AN UNFORTUNATE GATHERING

CHAPTER I

THEY ARRIVE AT THE MONASTERY

IT was a warm, bright day at the end of August. The interview with the elder had been fixed at half-past eleven, immediately after late mass. Our visitors did not take part in the service, but arrived just as it was over. First an elegant open carriage, drawn by two valuable horses, drove up with Miüsov and a distant relative of his, a young man of twenty, called Pyotr Fomitch Kalganov. This young man was preparing to enter the university. Miüsov, with whom he was staying for the time, was trying to persuade him to go abroad to the university of Zürich or Jena. The young man was still undecided. He was thoughtful and absent-minded. He was nice-looking, strongly built, and rather tall. There was a strange fixity in his gaze at times. Like all very absent-minded people he would sometimes stare at a person without seeing him. He was silent and rather awkward, but sometimes, when he was alone with anyone, he became talkative and effusive, and would laugh at anything or nothing. But his animation vanished as quickly as it appeared. He was always well and even elaborately dressed; he had already some independent fortune and expectations of much more. He was a friend of Alyosha's.

In an ancient, jolting, but roomy, hired carriage, with a pair of old pinkish-grey horses, a long way behind Miüsov's carriage, came Fyodor Pavlovitch, with his son Ivan. Dmitri was late, though he had been informed of the time the evening before. The visitors left their carriage at the hotel, outside the precincts, and went to the gates of the monastery on foot. Except Fyodor Pavlovitch, none of the party had ever seen the monastery, and Miüsov had probably not even been to church for thirty years. He looked about him with curiosity, together with assumed ease. But, except the church and the domestic buildings, though these too were ordinary enough, he found nothing of interest in the interior of the monastery. The last of the worshippers were coming out of the church, bareheaded and crossing themselves. Among the humbler people were a few of higher rank—two or three ladies and a very old general. They were all staying at the hotel. Our visitors were at once surrounded by beggars, but none of them gave them anything, except young Kalganov, who took a ten-copeck piece out of his purse, and, nervous and embarrassed—God knows why!—hurriedly gave it to an old woman, saying: "Divide it equally." None of his companions made any remark upon it, so that he had no reason to be embarrassed; but, perceiving this, he was even more overcome.

It was strange that their arrival did not seem expected, and that they were not received with special honour, though one of them had recently made a donation of a thousand roubles, while another was a very wealthy and highly cultured landowner, upon whom all in the monastery were in a sense dependent, as a decision of the lawsuit might at any moment put their fishing rights in his hands. Yet no official personage met them.

Miüsov looked absent-mindedly at the tombstones round the church, and was on the point of saying that the dead buried here must have paid a pretty penny for the right of lying in this "holy place", but refrained. His liberal irony was rapidly changing almost into anger.

"Who the devil is there to ask in this imbecile place? We must find out, for time is passing," he observed suddenly, as though speaking to himself.

All at once there came a bald-headed, elderly man with ingratiating little eyes, wearing a full, summer overcoat. Lifting his hat, he introduced himself with a honeyed lisp as Maximov, a landowner of Tula. He at once entered into our visitors' difficulty.

"Father Zossima lives in the hermitage, apart, four hundred paces from the monastery, the other side of the copse."

"I know it's the other side of the copse," observed Fyodor Pavlovitch, "but we don't remember the way. It is a long time since we've been here."

"This way, by this gate, and straight across the copse . . . the copse. Come with me, won't you? I'll show you. I have to go. . . . I am going myself. This way, this way."

They came out of the gate and turned toward the copse. Maximov, a man of sixty, ran rather than walked, turning sideways to stare at them all, with an incredible degree of nervous curiosity. His eyes looked starting out of his head.

"You see, we have come to the elder upon business of our own," observed Miüsov severely. "That personage has granted us an audience, so to speak, and so, though we thank you for showing us the way, we cannot ask you to accompany us."

"I've been there. I've been already; *un chevalier parfait*," and Maximov snapped his fingers in the air.

"Who is a *chevalier?*" asked Miüsov.

"The elder, the splendid elder, the elder! The honour and glory of the monastery, Zossima. Such an elder!"

But his incoherent talk was cut short by a very pale, wan-looking monk of medium height, wearing a monk's cap, who overtook them. Fyodor Pavlovitch and Miüsov stopped.

The monk, with an extremely courteous, profound bow, announced:

"The Father Superior invites all of you gentlemen to dine with him after your visit to the hermitage. At one o'clock, not later. And you also," he added, addressing Maximov.

"That I certainly will, without fail," cried Fyodor Pavlovitch, hugely delighted at the invitation. "And, believe me, we've all given our word to behave properly here. . . . And you, Pyotr Alexandrovitch, will you go, too?"

"Yes, of course. What have I come for but to study all the customs here? The only obstacle to me is your company. . . ."

"Yes, Dmitri Fyodorovitch is non-existent as yet."

"It would be a capital thing if he didn't turn up. Do you suppose I like all this business, and in your company, too? So we will come to dinner. Thank the Father Superior," he said to the monk.

"No, it is my duty now to conduct you to the elder," answered the monk.

"If so I'll go straight to the Father Superior—to the Father Superior," babbled Maximov.

"The Father Superior is engaged just now. But as you please——" the monk hesitated.

"Impertinent old man!" Miüsov observed aloud, while Maximov ran back to the monastery.

"He's like Von Sohn," Fyodor Pavlovitch said suddenly.

"Is that all you can think of? . . . In what way is he like Von Sohn? Have you ever seen Von Sohn?"

"I've seen his portrait. It's not the features, but something indefinable. He's a second Von Sohn. I can always tell from the physiognomy."

"Ah, I dare say you are a connoisseur in that. But, look here, Fyodor Pavlovitch, you said just now that we had given our word to behave properly. Remember it. I advise you to control yourself. But, if you begin to play the fool I don't intend to be associated with you here. . . . You see what a man he is"—he turned to the monk—"I'm afraid to go among decent people with him." A fine smile, not without a certain slyness, came on to the pale, bloodless lips of the monk, but he made no reply, and was evidently silent from a sense of his own dignity. Miüsov frowned more than ever.

"Oh, devil take them all! An outer show elaborated through centuries, and nothing but charlatanism and nonsense underneath," flashed through Miüsov's mind.

"Here's the hermitage. We've arrived," cried Fyodor Pavlovitch. "The gates are shut."

And he repeatedly made the sign of the cross to the saints painted above and on the sides of the gates.

"When you go to Rome you must do as the Romans do. Here in this hermitage there are twenty-five saints being saved. They look at one another, and eat cabbages. And not one woman goes in at this gate. That's what is remarkable. And that really is so. But I did hear that the elder receives ladies," he remarked suddenly to the monk.

"Women of the people are here too now, lying in the portico there waiting. But for ladies of higher rank two rooms have been built adjoining the portico, but outside the precincts—you can see the windows—and the elder goes out to them by an inner passage when he is well enough. They are always outside the precincts. There is a Harkov lady, Madame Hohlakov, waiting there now with her sick daughter. Probably he has promised to come out to her, though of late he has been so weak that he has hardly shown himself even to the people."

"So then there are loopholes, after all, to creep out of the hermitage to the ladies. Don't suppose, Holy Father, that I mean any harm. But do you know that at Athos not only the visits of women are not allowed, but no creature of the female sex—no hens, nor turkey-hens, nor cows."

"Fyodor Pavlovitch, I warn you I shall go back and leave you here. They'll turn you out when I'm gone."

"But I'm not interfering with you, Pyotr Alexandrovitch. Look," he cried suddenly, stepping within the precincts, "what a vale of roses they live in!"

Though there were no roses now, there were numbers of rare and beautiful autumn flowers growing wherever there was space for them, and evidently tended by a skilful hand; there were flower-beds round the church, and between the tombs; and the one-storeyed wooden house where the elder lived was also surrounded with flowers.

"And was it like this in the time of the last elder, Varsonofy? He didn't care for such elegance. They say he used to jump up and thrash even ladies with a stick," observed Fyodor Pavlovitch, as he went up the steps.

"The elder Varsonofy did sometimes seem rather strange, but a great deal that's told is foolishness. He never thrashed anyone," answered the monk. "Now, gentlemen, if you will wait a minute I will announce you."

"Fyodor Pavlovitch, for the last time, your compact, do you hear? Behave properly or I will pay you out!" Miüsov had time to mutter again.

"I can't think why you are so agitated," Fyodor Pavlovitch observed sarcastically. "Are you uneasy about your sins? They say he can tell by one's eyes what one has come about. And what a lot you think of their opinion! you, a Parisian, and so advanced. I'm surprised at you."

32

But Miüsov had no time to reply to this sarcasm. They were asked to come in. He walked in, somewhat irritated.

"Now, I know myself, I am annoyed, I shall lose my temper and begin to quarrel—and lower myself and my ideas," he reflected.

CHAPTER II

THE OLD BUFFOON

THEY entered the room almost at the same moment that the elder came in from his bedroom. There were already in the cell, awaiting the elder, two monks of the hermitage, one the Father Librarian and the other Father Païssy, a very learned man, so they said, in delicate health, though not old. There was also a tall young man, who looked about two-and-twenty, standing in the corner throughout the interview. He had a broad, fresh face, and clever, observant, narrow brown eyes, and was wearing ordinary dress. He was a divinity student, living under the protection of the monastery. His expression was one of unquestioning, but self-respecting, reverence. Being in a subordinate and dependent position, and so not on an equality with the guests, he did not greet them with a bow.

Father Zossima was accompanied by a novice, and by Alyosha. The two monks rose and greeted him with a very deep bow, touching the ground with their fingers; then kissed his hand. Blessing them, the elder replied with as deep a reverence to them and asked their blessing. The whole ceremony was performed very seriously and with an appearance of feeling, not like an everyday rite. But Miüsov fancied that it was all done with intentional impressiveness. He stood in front of the other visitors. He ought—he had reflected upon it the evening before —from simple politeness, since it was the custom here, to have gone up to receive the elder's blessing, even if he did not kiss his hand. But when he saw all this bowing and kissing on the part of the monks he instantly changed his mind. With dignified gravity he made a rather deep, conventional bow and moved away to a chair. Fyodor Pavlovitch did the same, mimicking Miüsov like an ape. Ivan bowed with great dignity and courtesy, but he too kept his hands at his sides, while Kalganov was so confused that he did not bow at all. The elder let fall the hand raised to bless them and, bowing to them again, asked

33

them all to sit down. The blood rushed to Alyosha's cheeks. He was ashamed. His forebodings were coming true.

Father Zossima sat down on a very old-fashioned mahogany sofa, covered with leather, and made his visitors sit down in a row along the opposite wall on four mahogany chairs, covered with shabby black leather. The monks sat, one at the door and the other at the window. The divinity student, the novice, and Alyosha remained standing. The cell was not very large and had a faded look. It contained nothing but the most necessary furniture, of coarse and poor quality. There were two pots of flowers in the window, and a number of holy pictures in the corner. Before one huge ancient ikon of the Virgin a lamp was burning. Near it were two other holy pictures in shining settings, and, next them, carved cherubims, china eggs, a Catholic cross of ivory, with a Mater Dolorosa embracing it, and several foreign engravings from the great Italian artists of past centuries. Next to these costly and artistic engravings were several of the roughest Russian prints of saints and martyrs, such as are sold for a few farthings at all the fairs. On the other walls were portraits of Russian bishops, past and present.

Miüsov took a cursory glance at all these "conventional" surroundings and bent an intent look upon the elder. He had a high opinion of his own insight, a weakness excusable in him as he was fifty, an age in which a clever man of the world of established position can hardly help taking himself rather seriously. At the first moment he did not like Zossima. There was, indeed, something in the elder face which many people besides Miüsov might not have liked. He was a short, bent, little man, with very weak legs, and though he was only sixty-five, he looked at least ten years older. His face was very thin and covered with a network of fine wrinkles, particularly numerous about his eyes, which were small, light-coloured, quick, and shining like two bright points. He had a sprinkling of grey hair about his temples. His pointed beard was small and scanty, and his lips, which smiled frequently, were as thin as two threads. His nose was not long, but sharp, like a bird's beak.

"To all appearances a malicious soul, full of petty pride," thought Miüsov. He felt altogether dissatisfied with his position.

A cheap little clock on the wall struck twelve hurriedly, and served to begin the conversation.

"Precisely to our time," cried Fyodor Pavlovitch, "but no sign of my son Dmitri. I apologise for him, sacred elder!" (Alyosha shuddered all over at "sacred elder".) "I am always punctual myself, minute for minute, remembering that punctuality is the courtesy of kings . . ."

"But you are not a king, anyway," Miüsov muttered, losing his self-restraint at once.

"Yes; that's true. I'm not a king, and, would you believe it, Pyotr Alexandrovitch, I was aware of that myself. But, there! I always say the wrong thing. Your reverence," he cried, with sudden pathos, "you behold before you a buffoon in earnest! I introduce myself as such. It's an old habit, alas! And if I sometimes talk nonsense out of place it's with an object, with the object of amusing people and making myself agreeable. One must be agreeable, mustn't one? I was, seven years ago, in a little town where I had business, and I made friends with some merchants there. We went to the captain of police because we had to see him about something, and to ask him to dine with us. He was a tall, fat, fair, sulky man, the most dangerous type in such cases. It's their liver. I went straight up to him, and with the ease of a man of the world, you know, 'Mr. Ispravnik,' said I, 'be our Napravnik'. 'What do you mean by Napravnik?' said he. I saw, at the first half-second, that it had missed fire. He stood there so glum. 'I wanted to make a joke,' said I, 'for the general diversion, as Mr. Napravnik is our well-known Russian orchestra conductor and what we need for the harmony of our undertaking is someone of that sort.' And I explained my comparison very reasonably, didn't I? 'Excuse me,' said he, 'I am an Ispravnik, and I do not allow puns to be made on my calling.' He turned and walked away. I followed him, shouting, 'Yes, yes, you are an Ispravnik, not a Napravnik.' 'No,' he said, 'since you called me a Napravnik I am one.' And would you believe it, it ruined our business! And I'm always like that, always like that. Always injuring myself with my politeness. Once, many years ago, I said to an influential person: 'Your wife is a ticklish lady,' in an honourable sense, of the moral qualities, so to speak. But he asked me, 'Why, have you tickled her?' I thought I'd be polite, so I couldn't help saying 'Yes', and he gave me a fine tickling on the spot. Only that happened long ago, so I'm not ashamed to tell the story. I'm always injuring myself like that."

"You're doing it now," muttered Miüsov, with disgust.

Father Zossima scrutinised them both in silence.

"Am I? Would you believe it, I was aware of that, too, Pyotr Alexandrovitch, and let me tell you, indeed, I foresaw I should as soon as I began to speak. And do you know I foresaw, too, that you'd be the first to remark on it. The minute I see my joke isn't coming off, your reverence, both my cheeks feel as though they were drawn down to the lower jaw and there is almost a spasm in them. That's been so since I was young, when I had to make jokes for my living in noblemen's families. I am an inveterate buffoon, and have been from my birth up, your reverence, it's as though it were a craze in me. I dare say it's a devil within me. But only a little one. A more serious one would have chosen another lodging. But not your soul, Pyotr Alexandrovitch; you're not a lodging worth having either. But I do believe—I believe in God, though I have had doubts of late. But now I sit and await words of wisdom. I'm like the philosopher Diderot, your reverence. Did you ever hear, most Holy Father, how Diderot went to see the Metropolitan Platon, in the time of the Empress Catherine? He went in and said straight out, 'There is no God'. To which the great Bishop lifted up his finger and answered, 'The fool has said in his heart there is no God'. And he fell down at his feet on the spot. 'I believe,' he cried, 'and will be christened.' And so he was. Princess Dashkov was his godmother, and Potyomkin his godfather."

"Fyodor Pavlovitch, this is unbearable! You know you're telling lies and that that stupid anecdote isn't true. Why are you playing the fool?" cried Miüsov in a shaking voice.

"I suspected all my life that it wasn't true," Fyodor Pavlovitch cried with conviction. "But I'll tell you the whole truth, gentlemen. Great elder! Forgive me, the last thing about Diderot's christening I made up just now. I never thought of it before. I made it up to add piquancy. I play the fool, Pyotr Alexandrovitch, to make myself agreeable. Though I really don't know myself, sometimes, what I do it for. And as for Diderot, I heard as far as 'the fool hath said in his heart' twenty times from the gentry about here when I was young. I heard your aunt, Pyotr Alexandrovitch, tell the story. They all believe to this day that the infidel Diderot came to dispute about God with the Metropolitan Platon. . . ."

Miüsov got up, forgetting himself in his impatience. He was furious, and conscious of being ridiculous.

What was taking place in the cell was really incredible. For forty or fifty years past, from the times of former elders, no visitors had entered that cell without feelings of the profoundest veneration. Almost everyone admitted to the cell felt that a great favour was being shown him. Many remained kneeling during the whole visit. Of these visitors, many had been men of high rank and learning, some even freethinkers, attracted by curiosity, but all without exception had shown the profoundest reverence and delicacy, for here there was no question of money, but only, on the one side love and kindness, and on the other penitence and eager desire to decide some spiritual problem or crisis. So that such buffoonery amazed and bewildered the spectators, or at least some of them. The monks, with unchanged countenances, waited, with earnest attention, to hear what the elder would say, but seemed on the point of standing up, like Miüsov. Alyosha stood, with hanging head, on the verge of tears. What seemed to him strangest of all was that his brother Ivan, on whom alone he had rested his hopes, and who alone had such influence on his father that he could have stopped him, sat now quite unmoved, with downcast eyes, apparently waiting with interest to see how it would end, as though he had nothing to do with it. Alyosha did not dare to look at Rakitin, the divinity student, whom he knew almost intimately. He alone in the monastery knew Rakitin's thoughts.

"Forgive me," began Miüsov, addressing Father Zossima, "for perhaps I seem to be taking part in this shameful foolery. I made a mistake in believing that even a man like Fyodor Pavlovitch would understand what was due on a visit to so honoured a personage. I did not suppose I should have to apologise simply for having come with him. . . ."

Pyotr Alexandrovitch could say no more, and was about to leave the room, overwhelmed with confusion.

"Don't distress yourself, I beg." The elder got on to his feeble legs, and taking Pyotr Alexandrovitch by both hands, made him sit down again. "I beg you not to disturb yourself. I particularly beg you to be my guest." And with a bow he went back and sat down again on his little sofa.

"Great elder, speak! Do I annoy you by my vivacity?" Fyodor Pavlovitch cried suddenly, clutching the arms of his chair in both hands, as though ready to leap up from it if the answer were unfavourable.

"I earnestly beg you, too, not to disturb yourself, and not to be uneasy," the elder said impressively. "Do not trouble. Make yourself quite at home. And, above all, do not be so ashamed of yourself, for that is at the root of it all."

"Quite at home? To be my natural self? Oh, that is much too much, but I accept it with grateful joy. Do you know, blessed Father, you'd better not invite me to be my natural self. Don't risk it. . . . I will not go so far as that myself. I warn you for your own sake. Well, the rest is still plunged in the mists of uncertainty, though there are people who'd be pleased to describe me for you. I mean that for you, Pyotr Alexandrovitch. But as for you, holy being, let me tell you, I am brimming over with ecstasy."

He got up, and throwing up his hands, declaimed: "Blessed be the womb that bare thee, and the paps that gave thee suck— the paps especially. When you said just now, 'Don't be so ashamed of yourself, for that is at the root of it all', you pierced right through me by that remark, and read me to the core. Indeed, I always feel when I meet people that I am lower than all, and that they all take me for a buffoon. So I say, 'Let me really play the buffoon. I am not afraid of your opinion, for you are, every one of you, worse than I am'. That is why I am a buffoon. It is from shame, great elder, from shame; it's simply over-sensitiveness that makes me rowdy. If I had only been sure that everyone would accept me as the kindest and wisest of men, oh, Lord, what a good man I should have been then! Teacher!" he fell suddenly on his knees, "what must I do to gain eternal life?"

It was difficult even now to decide whether he was joking or really moved.

Father Zossima, lifting his eyes, looked at him, and said with a smile:

"You have known for a long time what you must do. You have sense enough: don't give way to drunkenness and incontinence of speech; don't give way to sensual lust; and, above all, to the love of money. And close your taverns. If you can't close all, at least two or three. And, above all—don't lie."

"You mean about Diderot?"

"No, not about Diderot. Above all, don't lie to yourself. The man who lies to himself and listens to his own lie comes to such a pass that he cannot distinguish the truth within him, or around him, and so loses all respect for himself and for others. And having no respect he ceases to love, and in order to occupy and distract himself without love he gives way to passions and coarse pleasures, and sinks to bestiality in his vices, all from continual lying to other men and to himself. The man who lies to himself can be more easily offended than anyone. You know it is sometimes very pleasant to take offence, isn't it? A man may know that nobody has insulted him, but that he has invented the insult for himself, has lied and exaggerated to make it picturesque, has caught at a word and made a mountain out of a molehill—he knows that himself, yet he will be the first to take offence, and will revel in his resentment till he feels great pleasure in it, and so pass to genuine vindictiveness. But get up, sit down, I beg you. All this, too, is deceitful posturing . . ."

"Blessed man! Give me your hand to kiss."

Fyodor Pavlovitch skipped up, and imprinted a rapid kiss on the elder's thin hand. "It is, it is pleasant to take offence. You said that so well, as I never heard it before. Yes, I have been all my life taking offence, to please myself, taking offence on æsthetic grounds, for it is not so much pleasant as distinguished sometimes to be insulted—that you had forgotten, great elder, it is distinguished! I shall make a note of that. But I have been lying, lying positively my whole life long, every day and hour of it. Of a truth, I am a lie, and the father of lies. Though I believe I am not the father of lies. I am getting mixed in my texts. Say, the son of lies, and that will be enough. Only . . . my angel . . . I may sometimes talk about Diderot! Diderot will do no harm, though sometimes a word will do harm. Great elder, by the way, I was forgetting, though I had been meaning for the last two years to come here on purpose to ask and to find out something. Only do tell Pyotr Alexandrovitch not to interrupt me. Here is my question: Is it true, great Father, that the story is told somewhere in the 'Lives of the Saints' of a holy saint martyred for his faith who, when his head was cut off at last, stood up, picked up his head, and, 'courteously kissing it', walked a long way, carrying it in his hands? Is that true or not, honoured Father?"

"No, it is untrue," said the elder.

"There is nothing of the kind in all the lives of the saints. What saint do you say the story is told of?" asked the Father Librarian.

"I do not know what saint. I do not know, and can't tell, I was deceived. I was told the story. I had heard it, and do you know who told it? Pyotr Alexandrovitch Miüsov here, who was so angry just now about Diderot. He it was who told the story."

"I have never told it you, I never speak to you at all."

"It is true you did not tell me, but you told it when I was present. It was three years ago. I mentioned it because by that ridiculous story you shook my faith, Pyotr Alexandrovitch. You knew nothing of it, but I went home with my faith shaken, and I have been getting more and more shaken ever since. Yes,

Pyotr Alexandrovitch, you were the cause of a great fall. That was not a Diderot!"

Fyodor Pavlovitch got excited and pathetic, though it was perfectly clear to everyone by now that he was playing a part again. Yet Miüsov was stung by his words.

"What nonsense, and it is all nonsense," he muttered. "I may really have told it, some time or other . . . but not to you. I was told it myself. I heard it in Paris from a Frenchman. He told me it was read at our mass from the 'Lives of the Saints' . . . he was a very learned man who had made a special study of Russian statistics and had lived a long time in Russia. . . . I have not read the 'Lives of the Saints' myself, and I am not going to read them . . . all sorts of things are said at dinner —we were dining then."

"Yes, you were dining then, and so I lost my faith!" said Fyodor Pavlovitch, mimicking him.

"What do I care for your faith?" Miüsov was on the point of shouting, but he suddenly checked himself, and said with contempt: "You defile everything you touch."

The elder suddenly rose from his seat. "Excuse me, gentlemen, for leaving you a few minutes," he said, addressing all his guests. "I have visitors awaiting me who arrived before you. But don't tell lies, all the same," he added, turning to Fyodor Pavlovitch with a good-humoured face. He went out of the cell. Alyosha and the novice flew to escort him down the steps. Alyosha was breathless: he was glad to get away, but he was glad, too, that the elder was good-humoured and not offended. Father Zossima was going towards the portico to bless the people waiting for him there. But Fyodor Pavlovitch persisted in stopping him at the door of the cell.

"Blessed man!" he cried, with feeling. "Allow me to kiss your hand once more. Yes, with you I could still talk, I could still get on. Do you think I always lie and play the fool like this? Believe me, I have been acting like this all the time on purpose to try you. I have been testing you all the time to see whether I could get on with you. Is there room for my humility beside your pride? I am ready to give you a testimonial that one can get on with you! But now, I'll be quiet; I will keep quiet all the time. I'll sit in a chair and hold my tongue. Now it is for you to speak, Pyotr Alexandrovitch. You are the principal person left now—for ten minutes."

CHAPTER III

PEASANT WOMEN WHO HAVE FAITH

NEAR the wooden portico below, built on to the outer wall of the precinct, there was a crowd of about twenty peasant women. They had been told that the elder was at last coming out, and they had gathered together in anticipation. Two ladies, Madame Hohlakov and her daughter, had also come out into the portico to wait for the elder, but in a separate part of it set aside for women of rank.

Madame Hohlakov was a wealthy lady, still young and attractive, and always dressed with taste. She was rather pale, and had lively black eyes. She was not more than thirty-three, and had been five years a widow. Her daughter, a girl of fourteen, was partially paralysed. The poor child had not been able to walk for the last six months, and was wheeled about in a long reclining chair. She had a charming little face, rather thin from illness, but full of gaiety. There was a gleam of mischief in her big dark eyes with their long lashes. Her mother had been intending to take her abroad ever since the spring, but they had been detained all the summer by business connected with their estate. They had been staying a week in our town, where they had come more for purposes of business than devotion, but had visited Father Zossima once already, three days before. Though they knew that the elder scarcely saw anyone, they had now suddenly turned up again, and urgently entreated "the happiness of looking once again on the great healer".

The mother was sitting on a chair by the side of her daughter's invalid carriage, and two paces from her stood an old monk, not one of our monastery but a visitor from an obscure religious house in the far north. He too sought the elder's blessing.

But Father Zossima, on entering the portico, went first straight to the peasants who were crowded at the foot of the three steps that led up into the portico. Father Zossima stood on the top step, put on his stole, and began blessing the women who thronged about him. One crazy woman was led up to him. As soon as she caught sight of the elder she began shrieking and writhing as though in the pains of childbirth. Laying the stole on her forehead, he read a short prayer over her, and she was at once soothed and quieted.

I do not know how it may be now, but in my childhood I

41

often happened to see and hear these "possessed" women in the villages and monasteries. They used to be brought to mass; they would squeal and bark like a dog so that they were heard all over the church. But when the sacrament was carried in and they were led up to it, at once the "possession" ceased, and the sick women were always soothed for a time. I was greatly impressed and amazed at this as a child; but then I heard from country neighbours and from my town teachers that the whole illness was simulated to avoid work, and that it could always be cured by suitable severity; various anecdotes were told to confirm this. But later on I learnt with astonishment from medical specialists that there is no pretence about it, that it is a terrible illness to which women are subject, specially prevalent among us in Russia, and that it is due to the hard lot of the peasant woman. It is a disease, I was told, arising from exhausting toil too soon after hard, abnormal and unassisted labour in childbirth, and from the hopeless misery, from beatings, and so on, which some women were not able to endure like others. The strange and instant healing of the frantic and struggling woman as soon as she was led up to the holy sacrament, which had been explained to me as due to malingering and the trickery of the "clericals", arose probably in the most natural manner. Both the women who supported her and the invalid herself fully believed as a truth beyond question that the evil spirit in possession of her could not hold out if the sick woman were brought to the sacrament and made to bow down before it. And so, with a nervous and psychically deranged woman, a sort of convulsion of the whole organism always took place, and was bound to take place, at the moment of bowing down to the sacrament, aroused by the expectation of the miracle of healing and the implicit belief that it would come to pass; and it did come to pass, though only for a moment. It was exactly the same now as soon as the elder touched the sick woman with the stole.

Many of the women in the crowd were moved to tears of ecstasy by the effect of the moment: some strove to kiss the hem of his garment, others cried out in sing-song voices.

He blessed them all and talked with some of them. The "possessed" woman he knew already. She came from a village only six versts from the monastery, and had been brought to him before.

"But here is one from afar." He pointed to a woman by no means old but very thin and wasted, with a face not merely

42

sunburnt but almost blackened by exposure. She was kneeling and gazing with a fixed stare at the elder; there was something almost frenzied in her eyes.

"From afar off, Father, from afar off! From two hundred miles from here. From afar off, Father, from afar off!" the woman began in a sing-song voice as though she were chanting a dirge, swaying her head from side to side with her cheeks resting in her hand.

There is silent and long-suffering sorrow to be met with among the peasantry. It withdraws into itself and is still. But there is a grief that breaks out, and from that minute it bursts into tears and finds vent in wailing. This is particularly common with women. But it is no lighter a grief than the silent. Lamentations comfort only by lacerating the heart still more. Such grief does not desire consolation. It feeds on the sense of its hopelessness. Lamentations spring only from the constant craving to re-open the wound.

"You are of the tradesman class?" said Father Zossima, looking curiously at her.

"Townfolk we are, Father, townfolk. Yet we are peasants though we live in the town. I have come to see you, oh Father! We heard of you, Father, we heard of you. I have buried my little son, and I have come on a pilgrimage. I have been in three monasteries, but they told me, 'Go, Nastasya, go to them' —that is to you. I have come; I was yesterday at the service, and to-day I have come to you."

"What are you weeping for?"

'It's my little son I'm grieving for, Father. He was three years old—three years all but three months. For my little boy, Father, I'm in anguish, for my little boy. He was the last one left. We had four, my Nikita and I, and now we've no children, our dear ones have all gone. I buried the first three without grieving overmuch, and now I have buried the last I can't forget him. He seems always standing before me. He never leaves me. He has withered my heart. I look at his little clothes, his little shirt, his little boots, and I wail. I lay out all that is left of him, all his little things. I look at them and wail. I say to Nikita, my husband, let me go on a pilgrimage, master. He is a driver. We're not poor people, Father, not poor; he drives our own horse. It's all our own, the horse and the carriage. And what good is it all to us now? My Nikita has begun drinking while I am away. He's sure to. It used to be so before. As soon as I turn my back he gives way to it. But now I don't think about him. It's three months since I left home. I've forgotten him. I've forgotten everything. I don't want to remember. And what would our life be now together? I've done with him, I've done. I've done with them all. I don't care to look upon my house and my goods. I don't care to see anything at all!"

"Listen, mother," said the elder. "Once in olden times a holy saint saw in the Temple a mother like you weeping for her little one, her only one, whom God had taken. 'Knowest thou not,' said the saint to her, 'how bold these little ones are before the throne of God? Verily there are none bolder than they in the Kingdom of Heaven. "Thou didst give us life, oh Lord," they say, "and scarcely had we looked upon it when Thou didst take it back again." And so boldly they ask and ask again that God gives them at once the rank of angels. Therefore,' said the saint, 'thou too, oh mother, rejoice and weep not, for thy little one is with the Lord in the fellowship of the angels'. That's what the saint said to the weeping mother of old. He was a great saint and he could not have spoken falsely. Therefore you too, mother, know that your little one is surely before the throne of God, is rejoicing and happy, and praying to God for you, and therefore weep, but rejoice."

The woman listened to him, looking down with her cheek in her hand. She sighed deeply.

"My Nikita tried to comfort me with the same words as you. 'Foolish one,' he said, 'why weep? Our son is no doubt singing with the angels before God.' He says that to me, but he weeps himself. I see that he cries like me. 'I know, Nikita,' said I. 'Where could he be if not with the Lord God? Only, here with us now he is not as he used to sit beside us before.' And if only I could look upon him one little time, if only I could peep at him one little time, without going up to him, without speaking, if I could be hidden in a corner and only see him for one little minute, hear him playing in the yard, calling in his little voice, 'Mammy, where are you?' If only I could hear him pattering with his little feet about the room just once, only once; for so often, so often I remember how he used to run to me and shout and laugh, if only I could hear his little feet I should know him! But he's gone, Father, he's gone, and I shall never hear him again. Here's his little sash, but him I shall never see or hear now."

She drew out of her bosom her boy's little embroidered sash, and as soon as she looked at it she began shaking with sobs,

hiding her eyes with her fingers through which the tears flowed in a sudden stream.

"It is Rachel of old," said the elder, "weeping for her children, and will not be comforted because they are not. Such is the lot set on earth for you mothers. Be not comforted. Consolation is not what you need. Weep and be not consoled, but weep. Only every time that you weep be sure to remember that your little son is one of the angels of God, that he looks down from there at you and sees you, and rejoices at your tears, and points at them to the Lord God; and a long while yet will you keep that great mother's grief. But it will turn in the end into quiet joy, and your bitter tears will be only tears of tender sorrow that purifies the heart and delivers it from sin. And I shall pray for the peace of your child's soul. What was his name?"

"Alexey, Father."

"A sweet name. After Alexey, the man of God?"

"Yes, Father."

"What a saint he was! I will remember him, mother, and your grief in my prayers, and I will pray for your husband's health. It is a sin for you to leave him. Your little one will see from heaven that you have forsaken his father, and will weep over you. Why do you trouble his happiness? He is living, for the soul lives for ever, and though he is not in the house he is near you, unseen. How can he go into the house when you say that the house is hateful to you? To whom is he to go if he find you not together, his father and mother? He comes to you in dreams now, and you grieve. But then he will send you gentle dreams. Go to your husband, mother; go this very day."

"I will go, Father, at your word. I will go. You've gone straight to my heart. My Nikita, my Nikita, you are waiting for me," the woman began in a sing-song voice; but the elder had already turned away to a very old woman, dressed like a dweller in the town, not like a pilgrim. Her eyes showed that she had come with an object, and in order to say something. She said she was the widow of a non-commissioned officer, and lived close by in the town. Her son Vasenka was in the commissariat service, and had gone to Irkutsk in Siberia. He had written twice from there, but now a year had passed since he had written. She did inquire about him, but she did not know the proper place to inquire.

"Only the other day Stepanida Ilyinishna—she's a rich

merchant's wife—said to me, 'You go, Prohorovna, and put your son's name down for prayer in the church, and pray for the peace of his soul as though he were dead. His soul will be troubled,' she said, 'and he will write you a letter.' And Stepanida Ilyinishna told me it was a certain thing which had been many times tried. Only I am in doubt. . . . Oh, you light of ours! is it true or false, and would it be right?"

"Don't think of it. It's shameful to ask the question. How is it possible to pray for the peace of a living soul? And his own mother too! It's a great sin, akin to sorcery. Only for your ignorance it is forgiven you. Better pray to the Queen of Heaven, our swift defence and help, for his good health, and that she may forgive you for your error. And another thing I will tell you, Prohorovna. Either he will soon come back to you, your son, or he will be sure to send a letter. Go, and henceforward be in peace. Your son is alive, I tell you."

"Dear Father, God reward you, our benefactor, who prays for all of us and for our sins!"

But the elder had already noticed in the crowd two glowing eyes fixed upon him. An exhausted, consumptive-looking, though young peasant woman was gazing at him in silence. Her eyes besought him, but she seemed afraid to approach.

"What is it, my child?"

"Absolve my soul, Father," she articulated softly and slowly, sank on her knees and bowed down at his feet. "I have sinned, Father. I am afraid of my sin."

The elder sat down on the lower step. The woman crept closer to him, still on her knees.

"I am a widow these three years," she began in a half-whisper, with a sort of shudder. "I had a hard life with my husband. He was an old man. He used to beat me cruelly. He lay ill; I thought, looking at him, if he were to get well, if he were to get up again, what then? And then the thought came to me——"

"Stay!" said the elder, and he put his ear close to her lips.

The woman went on in a low whisper, so that it was almost impossible to catch anything. She had soon done.

"Three years ago?" asked the elder.

"Three years. At first I didn't think about it, but now I've begun to be ill, and the thought never leaves me."

"Have you come from far?"

"Over three hundred miles away."

"Have you told it in confession?"

"I have confessed it. Twice I have confessed it."

"Have you been admitted to Communion?"

"Yes. I am afraid. I am afraid to die."

"Fear nothing and never be afraid; and don't fret. If only your penitence fail not, God will forgive all. There is no sin, and there can be no sin on all the earth, which the Lord will not forgive to the truly repentant! Man cannot commit a sin so great as to exhaust the infinite love of God. Can there be a sin which could exceed the love of God? Think only of repentance, continual repentance, but dismiss fear altogether. Believe that God loves you as you cannot conceive; that He loves you with your sin, in your sin. It has been said of old that over one repentant sinner there is more joy in heaven than over ten righteous men. Go, and fear not. Be not bitter against men. Be not angry if you are wronged. Forgive the dead man in your heart what wrong he did you. Be reconciled with him in truth. If you are penitent, you love. And if you love you are of God. All things are atoned for, all things are saved by love. If I, a sinner, even as you are, am tender with you and have pity on you, how much more will God. Love is such a priceless treasure that you can redeem the whole world by it, and expiate not only your own sins but the sins of others."

He signed her three times with the cross, took from his own neck a little ikon and put it upon her. She bowed down to the earth without speaking.

He got up and looked cheerfully at a healthy peasant woman with a tiny baby in her arms.

"From Vyshegorye, dear Father."

"Five miles you have dragged yourself with the baby. What do you want?"

"I've come to look at you. I have been to you before—or have you forgotten? You've no great memory if you've forgotten me. They told us you were ill. Thinks I, I'll go and see him for myself. Now I see you, and you're not ill! You'll live another twenty years. God bless you! There are plenty to pray for you; how should you be ill?"

"I thank you for all, daughter."

"By the way, I have a thing to ask, not a great one. Here are sixty copecks. Give them, dear Father, to someone poorer than me. I thought as I came along, better give through him. He'll know whom to give to."

"Thanks, my dear, thanks! You are a good woman. I love you. I will do so certainly. Is that your little girl?"

"My little girl, Father, Lizaveta."

"May the Lord bless you both, you and your babe Lizaveta! You have gladdened my heart, mother. Farewell, dear children farewell, dear ones."

He blessed them all and bowed low to them.

CHAPTER IV

A LADY OF LITTLE FAITH

A VISITOR looking on the scene of his conversation with the peasants and his blessing them shed silent tears and wiped them away with her handkerchief. She was a sentimental society lady of genuinely good disposition in many respects. When the elder went up to her at last she met him enthusiastically.

"Ah, what I have been feeling, looking on at this touching scene! . . ." She could not go on for emotion. "Oh, I understand the people's love for you. I love the people myself. I want to love them. And who could help loving them, our splendid Russian people, so simple in their greatness!"

"How is your daughter's health? You wanted to talk to me again?"

"Oh, I have been urgently begging for it, I have prayed for it! I was ready to fall on my knees and kneel for three days at your windows until you let me in. We have come, great healer, to express our ardent gratitude. You have healed my Lise, healed her completely, merely by praying over her last Thursday and laying your hands upon her. We have hastened here to kiss those hands, to pour out our feelings and our homage."

"What do you mean by healed? But she is still lying down in her chair."

"But her night fevers have entirely ceased ever since Thursday," said the lady with nervous haste. "And that's not all. Her legs are stronger. This morning she got up well; she had slept all night. Look at her rosy cheeks, her bright eyes! She used to be always crying, but now she laughs and is gay and happy. This morning she insisted on my letting her stand up, and she stood up for a whole minute without any support. She wagers that in a fortnight she'll be dancing a quadrille. I've called in Doctor Herzenstube. He shrugged his shoulders and said: 'I am amazed; I can make nothing of it.' And would you

48

have us not come here to disturb you, not fly here to thank you?
Lise, thank him—thank him!"

Lise's pretty little laughing face became suddenly serious. She
rose in her chair as far as she could and, looking at the elder,
clasped her hands before him, but could not restrain herself and
broke into laughter.

"It's at him," she said, pointing to Alyosha, with childish
vexation at herself for not being able to repress her mirth.

If anyone had looked at Alyosha standing a step behind the
elder he would have caught a quick flush crimsoning his cheeks
in an instant. His eyes shone and he looked down.

"She has a message for you, Alexey Fyodorovitch. How are
you?" the mother went on, holding out her exquisitely gloved
hand to Alyosha.

The elder turned round and all at once looked attentively at
Alyosha. The latter went nearer to Lise and, smiling in a
strangely awkward way, held out his hand to her too. Lise
assumed an important air.

"Katerina Ivanovna has sent you this through me." She
handed him a little note. "She particularly begs you to go and
see her as soon as possible; that you will not fail her, but will
be sure to come."

"She asks me to go and see her? Me? What for?" Alyosha
muttered in great astonishment. His face at once looked
anxious.

"Oh, it's all to do with Dmitri Fyodorovitch and—what has
happened lately," the mother explained hurriedly. "Katerina
Ivanovna has made up her mind, but she must see you about
it. . . . Why, of course, I can't say. But she wants to see
you at once. And you will go to her, of course. It is a Christian
duty."

"I have only seen her once," Alyosha protested with the
same perplexity.

"Oh, she is such a lofty, incomparable creature! If only for
her suffering. . . . Think what she has gone through, what
she is enduring now! Think what awaits her! It's all terrible,
terrible!"

"Very well, I will come," Alyosha decided, after rapidly
scanning the brief, enigmatic note, which consisted of an urgent
entreaty that he would come, without any sort of explanation.

"Oh, how sweet and generous that would be of you!" cried
Lise with sudden animation. "I told mamma you'd be sure not
to go. I said you were saving your soul. How splendid you

are! I've always thought you were splendid. How glad I am to tell you so!"

"Lise!" said her mother impressively, though she smiled after she had said it.

"You have quite forgotten us, Alexey Fyodorovitch," she said; "you never come to see us. Yet Lise has told me twice that she is never happy except with you."

Alyosha raised his downcast eyes and again flushed, and again smiled without knowing why. But the elder was no longer watching him. He had begun talking to a monk who, as mentioned before, had been awaiting his entrance by Lise's chair. He was evidently a monk of the humblest, that is of the peasant, class, of a narrow outlook, but a true believer, and, in his own way, a stubborn one. He announced that he had come from the far north from Obdorsk, from Saint Sylvester, and was a member of a poor monastery, consisting of only ten monks. The elder gave him his blessing and invited him to come to his cell whenever he liked.

"How can you presume to do such deeds?" the monk asked suddenly, pointing solemnly and significantly at Lise. He was referring to her "healing".

"It's too early, of course, to speak of that. Relief is not complete cure, and may proceed from different causes. But if there has been any healing, it is by no power but God's will. It's all from God. Visit me, Father," he added to the monk. "It's not often I can see visitors. I am ill, and I know that my days are numbered."

"Oh, no, no! God will not take you from us. You will live a long, long time yet," cried the lady. "And in what way are you ill? You look so well, so gay and happy."

"I am extraordinarily better to-day. But I know that it's only for a moment. I understand my disease now thoroughly. If I seem so happy to you, you could never say anything that would please me so much. For men are made for happiness, and anyone who is completely happy has a right to say to himself: 'I am doing God's will on earth.' All the righteous, all the saints, all the holy martyrs were happy."

"Oh, how you speak! What bold and lofty words!" cried the lady. "You seem to pierce with your words. And yet—happiness, happiness—where is it? Who can say of himself that he is happy? Oh, since you have been so glad as to let us see you once more to-day, let me tell you what I could not utter last time, what I dared not say, all I am suffering and have been for so long! I am suffering! Forgive me! I am suffering!"

And in a rush of fervent feeling she clasped her hands before him.

"From what specially?"

"I suffer . . . from lack of faith."

"Lack of faith in God?"

"Oh, no, no! I dare not even think of that. But the future life—it is such an enigma! And no one, no one can solve it. Listen! You are a healer, you are deeply versed in the human soul, and of course I dare not expect you to believe me entirely, but I assure you on my word of honour that I am not speaking lightly now. The thought of the life beyond the grave distracts me to anguish, to terror. And I don't know to whom to appeal, and have not dared to all my life. And now I am so bad as to ask you. Oh, God! What will you think of me now?"

She clasped her hands.

"Don't distress yourself about my opinion of you," said the elder. "I quite believe in the sincerity of your suffering."

"Oh, how thankful I am to you! You see, I shut my eyes and ask myself, 'If everyone has faith, where did it come from?' And then they do say that it all comes from terror at the menacing phenomena of nature, and that none of it's real. And I say to myself, 'What if I've been believing all my life, and when I come to die there's nothing but the burdocks growing on my grave?' as I read in some author. It's awful! How—how can I get back my faith? But I only believed when I was a little child, mechanically, without thinking of anything. How, how is one to prove it? I have come now to lay my soul before you and to ask you about it. If I let this chance slip, no one all my life will answer me. How can I prove it? How can I convince myself? Oh, how unhappy I am! I stand and look about me and see that scarcely anyone else cares; no one troubles his head about it, and I'm the only one who can't stand it. It's deadly—deadly!"

"No doubt. But there's no proving it, though you can be convinced of it."

"How?"

"By the experience of active love. Strive to love your neighbour actively and indefatigably. In as far as you advance in love you will grow surer of the reality of God and of the immortality of your soul. If you attain to perfect self-forgetfulness in the love of your neighbour, then you will believe without

51

doubt, and no doubt can possibly enter your soul. This has been tried. This is certain.''

"In active love? There's another question—and such a question! You see, I so love humanity that—would you believe it? —I often dream of forsaking all that I have, leaving Lise, and becoming a sister of mercy. I close my eyes and think and dream, and at that moment I feel full of strength to overcome all obstacles. No wounds, no festering sores could at that moment frighten me. I would bind them up and wash them with my own hands. I would nurse the afflicted. I would be ready to kiss such wounds.''

"It is much, and well that your mind is full of such dreams and not others. Some time, unawares, you may do a good deed in reality.''

"Yes. But could I endure such a life for long?'' the lady went on fervently, almost frantically. "That's the chief question —that's my most agonising question. I shut my eyes and ask myself: 'Would you persevere long on that path?' And if the patient whose wounds you are washing did not meet you with gratitude, but worried you with his whims, without valuing or remarking your charitable services, began abusing you and rudely commanding you, and complaining to the superior authorities of you (which often happens when people are in great suffering)—what then? Would you persevere in your love, or not?' And do you know, I came with horror to the conclusion that, if anything could dissipate my love to humanity, it would be ingratitude. In short, I am a hired servant, I expect my payment at once—that is, praise, and the repayment of love with love. Otherwise I am incapable of loving anyone.''

She was in a very paroxysm of self-castigation, and, concluding, she looked with defiant resolution at the elder.

"It's just the same story as a doctor once told me,'' observed the elder. "He was a man getting on in years, and undoubtedly clever. He spoke as frankly as you, though in jest, in bitter jest. 'I love humanity,' he said, 'but I wonder at myself. The more I love humanity in general, the less I love man in particular. In my dreams,' he said, 'I have often come to making enthusiastic schemes for the service of humanity, and perhaps I might actually have faced crucifixion if it had been suddenly necessary; and yet I am incapable of living in the same room with anyone for two days together, as I know by experience. As soon as anyone is near me, his personality disturbs my self-complacency and restricts my freedom. In twenty-four hours I begin to hate the best of men: one because he's too long over his dinner; another because he has a cold and keeps on blowing his nose. I become hostile to people the moment they come close to me. But it has always happened that the more I detest men individually the more ardent becomes my love for humanity."

"But what's to be done? What can one do in such a case? Must one despair?"

"No. It is enough that you are distressed at it. Do what you can, and it will be reckoned unto you. Much is done already in you since you can so deeply and sincerely know yourself. If you have been talking to me so sincerely, simply to gain approbation for your frankness, as you did from me just now, then of course you will not attain to anything in the achievement of real love; it will all get no further than dreams, and your whole life will slip away like a phantom. In that case you will naturally cease to think of the future life too, and will of yourself grow calmer after a fashion in the end."

"You have crushed me! Only now, as you speak, I understand that I was really only seeking your approbation for my sincerity when I told you I could not endure ingratitude. You have revealed me to myself. You have seen through me and explained me to myself!"

"Are you speaking the truth? Well, now, after such a confession, I believe that you are sincere and good at heart. If you do not attain happiness, always remember that you are on the right road, and try not to leave it. Above all, avoid falsehood, every kind of falsehood, especially falseness to yourself. Watch over your own deceitfulness and look into it every hour, every minute. Avoid being scornful, both to others and to yourself. What seems to you bad within you will grow purer from the very fact of your observing it in yourself. Avoid fear, too, though fear is only the consequence of every sort of falsehood. Never be frightened at your own faint-heartedness in attaining love. Don't be frightened overmuch even at your evil actions. I am sorry I can say nothing more consoling to you, for love in action is a harsh and dreadful thing compared with love in dreams. Love in dreams is greedy for immediate action, rapidly performed and in the sight of all. Men will even give their lives if only the ordeal does not last long but is soon over, with all looking on and applauding as though on the stage. But active love is labour and fortitude, and for some people too, perhaps, a complete science. But I predict that just when you see with horror that in spite of all your efforts you are getting further from your goal instead of nearer to it—at that very moment I predict that you will reach it and behold clearly the miraculous power of the Lord who has been all the time loving and mysteriously guiding you. Forgive me for not being able to stay longer with you. They are waiting for me. Good-bye."

The lady was weeping.

"Lise, Lise! Bless her—bless her!" she cried, starting up suddenly.

"She does not deserve to be loved. I have seen her naughtiness all along," the elder said jestingly. "Why have you been laughing at Alexey?"

Lise had in fact been occupied in mocking at him all the time. She had noticed before that Alyosha was shy and tried not to look at her, and she found this extremely amusing. She waited intently to catch his eye. Alyosha, unable to endure her persistent stare, was irresistibly and suddenly drawn to glance at her, and at once she smiled triumphantly in his face. Alyosha was even more disconcerted and vexed. At last he turned away from her altogether and hid behind the elder's back. After a few minutes, drawn by the same irresistible force, he turned again to see whether he was being looked at or not, and found Lise almost hanging out of her chair to peep sideways at him, eagerly waiting for him to look. Catching his eye, she laughed so that the elder could not help saying: "Why do you make fun of him like that, naughty girl?"

Lise suddenly and quite unexpectedly blushed. Her eyes flashed and her face became quite serious. She began speaking quickly and nervously in a warm and resentful voice:

"Why has he forgotten everything, then? He used to carry me about when I was little. We used to play together. He used to come to teach me to read, do you know. Two years ago, when he went away, he said that he would never forget me, that we were friends for ever, for ever, for ever! And now he's afraid of me all at once. Am I going to eat him? Why doesn't he want to come near me? Why doesn't he talk? Why won't he come and see us? It's not that you won't let him. We know that he goes everywhere. It's not good manners for me to invite him. He ought to have thought of it first, if he hasn't forgotten me. No, now he's saving his soul! Why have you put that long gown on him? If he runs he'll fall."

And suddenly she hid her face in her hand and went off into

54

irresistible, prolonged, nervous, inaudible laughter. The elder listened to her with a smile, and blessed her tenderly. As she kissed his hand she suddenly pressed it to her eyes and began crying.

"Don't be angry with me. I'm silly and good for nothing . . . and perhaps Alyosha's right, quite right, in not wanting to come and see such a ridiculous girl."

"I will certainly send him," said the elder.

CHAPTER V

SO BE IT! SO BE IT!

THE elder's absence from his cell had lasted for about twenty-five minutes. It was more than half-past twelve, but Dmitri, on whose account they had all met there, had still not appeared. But he seemed almost to be forgotten, and when the elder entered the cell again, he found his guests engaged in eager conversation. Ivan and the two monks took the leading share in it. Miüsov, too, was trying to take a part, and apparently very eagerly, in the conversation. But he was unsuccessful in this also. He was evidently in the background, and his remarks were treated with neglect, which increased his irritability. He had had intellectual encounters with Ivan before and he could not endure a certain carelessness Ivan showed him.

"Hitherto at least I have stood in the front ranks of all that is progressive in Europe, and here the new generation positively ignores us," he thought.

Fyodor Pavlovitch, who had given his word to sit still and be quiet, had actually been quiet for some time, but he watched his neighbour Miüsov with an ironical little smile, obviously enjoying his discomfiture. He had been waiting for some time to pay off old scores, and now he could not let the opportunity slip. Bending over his shoulder he began teasing him again in a whisper.

"Why didn't you go away just now, after the 'courteously kissing'? Why did you consent to remain in such unseemly company? It was because you felt insulted and aggrieved, and you remained to vindicate yourself by showing off your intelligence. Now you won't go till you've displayed your intellect to them."

"You again? . . . On the contrary, I'm just going."

"You'll be the last, the last of all to go!" Fyodor Pavlovitch delivered him another thrust, almost at the moment of Father Zossima's return.

The discussion died down for a moment, but the elder, seating himself in his former place, looked at them all as though cordially inviting them to go on. Alyosha, who knew every expression of his face, saw that he was fearfully exhausted and making a great effort. Of late he had been liable to fainting fits from exhaustion. His face had the pallor that was common before such attacks, and his lips were white. But he evidently did not want to break up the party. He seemed to have some special object of his own in keeping them. What object? Alyosha watched him intently.

"We are discussing this gentleman's most interesting article," said Father Iosif, the librarian, addressing the elder, and indicating Ivan. "He brings forward much that is new, but I think the argument cuts both ways. It is an article written in answer to a book by an ecclesiastical authority on the question of the ecclesiastical court, and the scope of its jurisdiction."

"I'm sorry I have not read your article, but I've heard of it," said the elder, looking keenly and intently at Ivan.

"He takes up a most interesting position," continued the Father Librarian. "As far as Church jurisdiction is concerned he is apparently quite opposed to the separation of Church from State."

"That's interesting. But in what sense?" Father Zossima asked Ivan.

The latter, at last, answered him, not condescendingly, as Alyosha had feared, but with modesty and reserve, with evident good will and apparently without the slightest *arrière-pensée*.

"I start from the position that this confusion of elements, that is, of the essential principles of Church and State, will, of course, go on for ever, in spite of the fact that it is impossible for them to mingle, and that the confusion of these elements cannot lead to any consistent or even normal results, for there is falsity at the very foundation of it. Compromise between the Church and State in such questions as, for instance, jurisdiction is, to my thinking, impossible in any real sense. My clerical opponent maintains that the Church holds a precise and defined position in the State. I maintain, on the contrary, that the Church ought to include the whole State, and not simply to occupy a corner in it, and, if this is, for some reason, impossible at present, then it ought, in reality, to be set up as the direct and chief aim of the future development of Christian society!"

"Perfectly true," Father Païssy, the silent and learned monk, assented with fervour and decision.

"The purest Ultramontanism!" cried Miüsov impatiently, crossing and recrossing his legs.

"Oh, well, we have no mountains," cried Father Iosif, and turning to the elder he continued: "Observe the answer he makes to the following 'fundamental and essential' propositions of his opponent, who is, you must note, an ecclesiastic. First, that 'no social organisation can or ought to arrogate to itself power to dispose of the civic and political rights of its members'. Secondly, that 'criminal and civil jurisdiction ought not to belong to the Church, and is inconsistent with its nature, both as a divine institution and as an organisation of men for religious objects', and, finally, in the third place, 'the Church is a kingdom not of this world'."

"A most unworthy play upon words for an ecclesiastic!" Father Païssy could not refrain from breaking in again. "I have read the book which you have answered," he added, addressing Ivan, "and was astounded at the words 'the Church is a kingdom not of this world'. If it is not of this world, then it cannot exist on earth at all. In the Gospel, the words 'not of this world are not used in that sense. To play with such words is indefensible. Our Lord Jesus Christ came to set up the Church upon earth. The Kingdom of Heaven, of course, is not of this world but in Heaven; but it is only entered through the Church which has been founded and established upon earth. And so a frivolous play upon words in such a connection is unpardonable and improper. The Church is, in truth, a kingdom and ordained to rule, and in the end must undoubtedly become the kingdom ruling over all the earth. For that we have the divine promise."

He ceased speaking suddenly, as though checking himself. After listening attentively and respectfully Ivan went on, addressing the elder with perfect composure and as before with ready cordiality:

"The whole point of my article lies in the fact that during the first three centuries Christianity only existed on earth in the Church and was nothing but the Church. When the pagan Roman Empire desired to become Christian, it inevitably happened that, by becoming Christian, it included the Church but remained a pagan State in very many of its departments. In reality this was bound to happen. But Rome as a State retained too much of the pagan civilisation and culture, as, for example, in the very objects and fundamental principles of the State. The Christian Church entering into the State could, of course, surrender no part of its fundamental principles—the rock on which it stands—and could pursue no other aims than those which have been ordained and revealed by God Himself, and among them that of drawing the whole world, and therefore the ancient pagan State itself, into the Church. In that way (that is, with a view to the future) it is not the Church that should seek a definite position in the State, like 'every social organisation', or as 'an organisation of men for religious purposes' (as my opponent calls the Church, but, on the contrary, every earthly State should be, in the end, completely transformed into the Church and should become nothing else but a Church, rejecting every purpose incongruous with the aims of the Church. All this will not degrade it in any way or take from its honour and glory as a great State, nor from the glory of its rulers, but only turns it from a false, still pagan, and mistaken path to the true and rightful path, which alone leads to the eternal goal. This is why the author of the book 'On the Foundations of Church Jurisdiction' would have judged correctly if, in seeking and laying down those foundations, he had looked upon them as only a temporary compromise inevitable in our sinful and imperfect days. But as soon as the author ventures to declare that the foundations which he predicates now, part of which Father Iosif just enumerated, are the permanent, essential, and eternal foundations, he is going directly against the Church and its sacred and eternal vocation. That is the gist of my article.''

"That is, in brief,'' Father Païssy began again, laying stress on each word, ''according to certain theories only too clearly formulated in the nineteenth century, the Church ought to be transformed into the State, as though this would be an advance from a lower to a higher form, so as to disappear into it, making way for science, for the spirit of the age, and civilisation. And if the Church resists and is unwilling, some corner will be set apart for her in the State, and even that under control—and this will be so everywhere in all modern European countries. But Russian hopes and conceptions demand not that the Church should pass as from a lower into a higher type into the State, but, on the contrary, that the State should end by being worthy to become only the Church and nothing else. So be it! So be it!''

"Well, I confess you've reassured me somewhat," Miüsov said smiling, again crossing his legs. "So far as I understand, then, the realisation of such an ideal is infinitely remote, at the second coming of Christ. That's as you please. It's a beautiful Utopian dream of the abolition of war, diplomacy, banks, and so on—something after the fashion of socialism, indeed. But I imagined that it was all meant seriously, and that the Church might be *now* going to try criminals and sentence them to beating, prison, and even death."

"But if there were none but the ecclesiastical court, the Church would not even now sentence a criminal to prison or to death. Crime and the way of regarding it would inevitably change, not all at once of course, but fairly soon," Ivan replied calmly, without flinching.

"Are you serious?" Miüsov glanced keenly at him.

"If everything became the Church, the Church would exclude all the criminal and disobedient, and would not cut off their heads," Ivan went on. "I ask you, what would become of the excluded? He would be cut off then not only from men, as now, but from Christ. By his crime he would have transgressed not only against men but against the Church of Christ. This is so even now, of course, strictly speaking, but it is not clearly enunciated, and very, very often the criminal of to-day compromises with his conscience: 'I steal,' he says, 'but I don't go against Church. I'm not an enemy of Christ.' That's what the criminal of to-day is continually saying to himself, but when the Church takes the place of the State it will be difficult for him, in opposition to the Church all over the world, to say: 'All men are mistaken, all in error, all mankind are the false Church. I, a thief and murderer, am the only true Christian Church.' It will be very difficult to say this to himself; it requires a rare combination of unusual circumstances. Now, on the other side, take the Church's own view of crime: is it not bound to renounce the present almost pagan attitude, and to change from a mechanical cutting off of its tainted member for the preservation of Society, as at present, into completely and honestly adopting the idea of the regeneration of the man, of his reformation and salvation?"

"What do you mean? I fail to understand again," Miüsov interrupted. "Some sort of dream again. Something shapeless and even incomprehensible. What is excommunication? What sort of exclusion? I suspect you are simply amusing yourself, Ivan Fyodorovitch."

"Yes, but you know, in reality it is so now," said the elder suddenly, and all turned to him at once. "If it were not for the Church of Christ there would be nothing to restrain the criminal from evil doing, no real chastisement for it afterwards; none, that is, but the mechanical punishment spoken of just now, which in the majority of cases only embitters the heart; and not the real punishment, the only effectual one, the only deterrent and softening one, which lies in the recognition of sin by conscience."

"How is that, may one inquire?" asked Miüsov, with lively curiosity.

"Why," began the elder, "all these sentences to exile with hard labour, and formerly with flogging also, reform no one, and what's more, deter hardly a single criminal, and the number of crimes does not diminish but is continually on the increase. You must admit that. Consequently the security of society is not preserved, for although the obnoxious member is mechanically cut off and sent far away out of sight, another criminal always comes to take his place at once, and often two of them. If anything does preserve society, even in our time, and does regenerate and transform the criminal, it is only the law of Christ speaking in his conscience. It is only by recognising his wrongdoing as a son of a Christian society—that is, of the Church—that he recognises his sin against society—that is, against the Church. So that it is only against the Church, and not against the State, that the criminal of to-day can recognise that he has sinned. If society, as a Church, had jurisdiction then it would know whom to bring back from exclusion and to re-unite to itself. Now the Church having no real jurisdiction, but only the power of moral condemnation, withdraws of her own accord from punishing the criminal actively. She does not excommunicate him but simply persists in fatherly exhortation of him. What is more, the Church even tries to preserve all Christian communion with the criminal. She admits him to Church services, to the holy sacrament, gives him alms, and treats him more as a captive than as a convict. And what would become of the criminal, O Lord, if even the Christian society—that is, the Church—were to reject him even as the civil law rejects him and cuts him off? What would become of him if the Church punished him with her excommunication as the direct consequence of the secular law? There could be no more terrible despair, at least for a Russian criminal, for Russian criminals still have faith. Though, who knows, perhaps than a fearful thing would happen, perhaps the despairing heart of the criminal would lose its faith, and then what would become of him? But the Church, like a tender, loving mother, holds aloof from active punishment herself, as the sinner is too severely punished already by the civil law, and there must be at least someone to have pity on him. The Church holds aloof, above all, because its judgment is the only one that contains the truth, and therefore cannot practically and morally be united to any other judgment even as a temporary compromise. She can enter into no compact about that. The foreign criminal, they say, rarely repents, for the very doctrines of to-day confirm him in the idea that his crime is not a crime but only a reaction against an unjustly oppressive force. Society cuts him off completely by a force that triumphs over him mechanically and (so at least they say of themselves in Europe) accompanies this exclusion with hatred, forgetfulness, and the most profound indifference as to the ultimate fate of the erring brother. In this way it all takes place without the compassionate intervention of the Church, for in many cases there are no churches there at all, for though ecclesiastics and splendid church buildings remain, the churches themselves have long ago striven to pass from Church into State and to disappear in it completely. So it seems at least in Lutheran countries. As for Rome, it was proclaimed a State instead of a Church a thousand years ago. And so the criminal is no longer conscious of being a member of the Church and sinks into despair. If he returns to society, often it is with such hatred that society itself instinctively cuts him off. You can judge for yourself how it must end. In many cases it would seem to be the same with us, but the difference is that besides the established law courts we have the Church too, which always keeps up relations with the criminal as a dear and still precious son. And besides that, there is still preserved, though only in thought, the judgment of the Church, which though no longer existing in practice is still living as a dream for the future, and is, no doubt, instinctively recognised by the criminal in his soul. What was said here just now is true too, that is, that if the jurisdiction of the Church were introduced in practice in its full force, that is, if the whole of the society were changed into the Church, not only the judgment of the Church would have influence on the reformation of the criminal such as it never has now, but possibly also the crimes themselves would be incredibly diminished. And there can be no doubt that the Church would look upon the criminal and the crime of the future in many cases quite differently and would succeed in restoring the excluded, in restraining those who plan evil, and in regenerating the fallen. It is true," said Father Zossima, with a smile, "the Christian society now is not ready and is only resting on some seven righteous men, but as they are never lacking, it will continue still unshaken in expectation of its complete transformation from a society almost heathen in character into a single universal and all-powerful Church. So be it, so be it! Even though at the end of the ages, for it is ordained to come to pass! And there is no need to be troubled about times and seasons, for the secret of the times and seasons is in the wisdom of God, in His foresight and His love. And what in human reckoning seems still afar off may by the Divine ordinance be close at hand, on the eve of its appearance. And so be it, so be it!"

"So be it, so be it!" Father Païssy repeated austerely and reverently.

"Strange, extremely strange!" Miüsov pronounced, not so much with heat as with latent indignation.

"What strikes you as so strange?" Father Iosif inquired cautiously.

"Why, it's beyond anything!" cried Miüsov, suddenly breaking out. "The State is eliminated and the Church is raised to the position of the State. It's not simply Ultramontanism, it's arch-ultramontanism! It's beyond the dreams of Pope Gregory the Seventh!"

"You are completely misunderstanding it," said Father Païssy sternly. "Understand the Church is not to be transformed into the State. That is Rome and its dream. That is the third temptation of the devil. On the contrary, the State is transformed into the Church, will ascend and become a Church over the whole world—which is the complete opposite of Ultramontanism and Rome, and your interpretation, and is only the glorious destiny ordained for the Orthodox Church. This star will arise in the east!"

Miüsov was significantly silent. His whole figure expressed extraordinary personal dignity. A supercilious and condescending smile played on his lips. Alyosha watched it all with a throbbing heart. The whole conversation stirred him profoundly. He glanced casually at Rakitin, who was standing immovable in his place by the door listening and watching intently though with downcast eyes. But from the colour in his cheeks Alyosha guessed that Rakitin was probably no less excited, and he knew what caused his excitement.

"Allow me to tell you one little anecdote, gentlemen," Miüsov said impressively, with a peculiarly majestic air. "Some years ago, soon after the *coup d'état* of December, I happened to be calling in Paris on an extremely influential personage in the Government, and I met a very interesting man in his house. This individual was not precisely a detective but was a sort of superintendent of a whole regiment of political detectives—a rather powerful position in its own way. I was prompted by curiosity to seize the opportunity of conversation with him. And as he had not come as a visitor but as a subordinate official bringing a special report, and as he saw the reception given me by his chief he deigned to speak with some openness, to a certain extent only, of course. He was rather courteous than open, as Frenchmen know how to be courteous, especially to a foreigner. But I thoroughly understood him. The subject was the socialist revolutionaries who were at that time persecuted. I will quote only one most curious remark dropped by this person. 'We are not particularly afraid,' said he, 'of all these socialists, anarchists, infidels, and revolutionists; we keep watch on them and know all their goings on. But there are a few peculiar men among them who believe in God and are Christians, but at the same time are socialists. Those are the people we are most afraid of. They are dreadful people! The socialist who is a Christian is more to be dreaded than a socialist who is an atheist.' The words struck me at the time, and now they have suddenly come back to me here, gentlemen."

"You apply them to us, and look upon us as socialists?" Father Païssy asked directly, without beating about the bush.

But before Pyotr Alexandrovitch could think what to answer, the door opened, and the guest so long expected, Dmitri Fyodorovitch, came in. They had, in fact, given up expecting him, and his sudden appearance caused some surprise for a moment.

CHAPTER VI

WHY IS SUCH A MAN ALIVE?

DMITRI FYODOROVITCH, a young man of eight-and-twenty, of medium height and agreeable countenance, looked older than his years. He was muscular, and showed signs of considerable physical strength. Yet there was something not healthy in his face. It was rather thin, his cheeks were hollow, and there was an unhealthy sallowness in their colour. His rather large, prominent, dark eyes had an expression of firm determination, and yet there was a vague look in them, too. Even when he was excited and talking irritably, his eyes somehow did not follow his mood, but betrayed something else, sometimes quite incongruous with what was passing. "It's hard to tell what he's thinking," those who talked to him sometimes declared. People who saw something pensive and sullen in his eyes were startled by his sudden laugh, which bore witness to mirthful and light-hearted thoughts at the very time when his eyes were so gloomy. A certain strained look in his face was easy to understand at this moment. Everyone knew or had heard of the extremely restless and dissipated life which he had been leading of late, as well as of the violent anger to which he had been roused in his quarrels with his father. There were several stories current in the town about it. It is true that he was irascible by nature, "of an unstable and unbalanced mind", as our justice of the peace, Katchalnikov, happily described him.

He was stylishly and irreproachably dressed in a carefully buttoned frock-coat. He wore black gloves and carried a top hat. Having only lately left the army, he still had moustaches and no beard. His dark brown hair was cropped short, and combed forward on his temples. He had the long determined stride of a military man. He stood still for a moment on the threshold, and glancing at the whole party went straight up to the elder, guessing him to be their host. He made him a low bow, and asked his blessing. Father Zossima, rising in his chair, blessed him. Dmitri kissed his hand respectfully, and with intense feeling, almost anger, he said:

"Be so generous as to forgive me for having kept you waiting so long, but Smerdyakov, the valet sent me by my father, in reply to my inquiries, told me twice over that the appointment was for one. Now I suddenly learn——"

"Don't disturb yourself," interposed the elder. "No matter. You are a little late. It's of no consequence. . . ."

"I'm extremely obliged to you, and expected no less from your goodness."

Saying this, Dmitri bowed once more. Then, turning suddenly towards his father, made him, too, a similarly low and respectful bow. He had evidently considered it beforehand, and made this bow in all seriousness, thinking it his duty to show his respect and good intentions.

64

Although Fyodor Pavlovitch was taken unawares, he was equal to the occasion. In response to Dmitri's bow he jumped up from his chair and made his son a bow as low in return. His face was suddenly solemn and impressive, which gave him a positively malignant look. Dmitri bowed generally to all present, and without a word walked to the window with his long, resolute stride, sat down on the only empty chair, near Father Païssy, and, bending forward, prepared to listen to the conversation he had interrupted.

Dmitri's entrance had taken no more than two minutes, and the conversation was resumed. But this time Miüsov thought it unnecessary to reply to Father Païssy's persistent and almost irritable question.

"Allow me to withdraw from this discussion," he observed with a certain well-bred nonchalance. "It's a subtle question, too. Here Ivan Fyodorovitch is smiling at us. He must have something interesting to say about that also. Ask him."

"Nothing special, except one little remark," Ivan replied at once. "European Liberals in general, and even our liberal dilettanti, often mix up the final results of socialism with those of Christianity. This wild notion is, of course, a characteristic feature. But it's not only Liberals and dilettanti who mix up socialism and Christianity, but, in many cases, it appears, the police—the foreign police, of course—do the same. Your Paris anecdote is rather to the point, Pyotr Alexandrovitch."

"I ask your permission to drop this subject altogether," Miüsov repeated. "I will tell you instead, gentlemen, another interesting and rather characteristic anecdote of Ivan Fyodorovitch himself. Only five days ago, in a gathering here, principally of ladies, he solemnly declared in argument that there was nothing in the whole world to make men love their neighbours. That there was no law of nature that man should love mankind, and that, if there had been any love on earth hitherto, it was not owing to a natural law but simply because men have believed in immortality. Ivan Fyodorovitch added in parenthesis that the whole natural law lies in that faith, and that if you were to destroy in mankind the belief in immortality, not only love but every living force maintaining the life of the world would at once be dried up. Moreover, nothing then would be immoral, everything would be lawful, even cannibalism. That's not all. He ended by asserting that for every individual, like ourselves, who does not believe in God or immortality, the moral law of nature must immediately be changed into the exact contrary of the former religious law, and that egoism, even to crime, must become, not only lawful but even recognised as the inevitable, the most rational, even honourable outcome of his position. From this paradox, gentlemen, you can judge of the rest of our eccentric and paradoxical friend Ivan Fyodorovitch's theories."

"Excuse me," Dmitri cried suddenly. "If I've heard aright, crime must not only be permitted but even recognised as the inevitable and the most rational outcome of his position for every infidel! Is that so or not?"

"Quite so," said Father Païssy.

"I'll remember it."

Having uttered these words Dmitri ceased speaking as suddenly as he had begun. Everyone looked at him with curiosity.

"Is that really your conviction as to the consequences of the disappearance of the faith in immortality?" the elder asked Ivan suddenly.

"Yes. That was my contention. There is no virtue if there is no immortality."

"You are blessed in believing that, or else most unhappy."

"Why unhappy?" Ivan asked, smiling.

"Because, in all probability you don't believe yourself in the immortality of your soul, nor in what you have written yourself in your article on Church jurisdiction."

"Perhaps you are right! . . . But I wasn't altogether joking," Ivan suddenly and strangely confessed, flushing quickly.

"You were not altogether joking. That's true. The question is still fretting your heart, and not answered. But the martyr likes sometimes to divert himself with his despair, as it were driven to it by despair itself. Meanwhile, in your despair, you, too, divert yourself with magazine articles, and discussions in society, though you don't believe your own arguments, and with an aching heart mock at them inwardly. . . . That question you have not answered, and it is your great grief, for it clamours for an answer."

"But can it be answered by me? Answered in the affirmative?" Ivan went on asking strangely, still looking at the elder with the same inexplicable smile.

"If it can't be decided in the affirmative, it will never be decided in the negative. You know that that is the peculiarity of your heart, and all its suffering is due to it. But thank the Creator who has given you a lofty heart capable of such suffering; of thinking and seeking higher things, for our dwelling is in the heavens. God grant that your heart will attain the answer on earth, and may God bless your path."

The elder raised his hand and would have made the sign of the cross over Ivan from where he stood. But the latter rose from his seat, went up to him, received his blessing, and kissing his hand went back to his place in silence. His face looked firm and earnest. This action and all the preceding conversation, which was so surprising from Ivan, impressed everyone by its strangeness and a certain solemnity, so that all were silent for a moment, and there was a look almost of apprehension in Alyosha's face. But Miüsov suddenly shrugged his shoulders. And at the same moment Fyodor Pavlovitch jumped up from his seat.

"Most pious and holy elder," he cried, pointing to Ivan, "that is my son, flesh of my flesh, the dearest of my flesh! He is my most dutiful Karl Moor, so to speak, while this son who has just come in, Dmitri, against whom I am seeking justice from you, is the undutiful Franz Moor—they are both out of Schiller's *Robbers,* and so I am the reigning Count von Moor! Judge and save us! We need not only your prayers but your prophecies!"

"Speak without buffoonery, and don't begin by insulting the members of your family," answered the elder, in a faint, exhausted voice. He was obviously getting more and more fatigued, and his strength was failing.

"An unseemly farce which I foresaw when I came here!" cried Dmitri indignantly. He too leapt up. "Forgive it, reverend Father," he added, addressing the elder. "I am not a cultivated man, and I don't even know how to address you properly, but you have been deceived and you have been too good-natured in letting us meet here. All my father wants is a scandal. Why he wants it only he can tell. He always has some motive. But I believe I know why——"

"They all blame me, all of them!" cried Fyodor Pavlovitch in his turn. "Pyotr Alexandrovitch here blames me too. You have been blaming me, Pyotr Alexandrovitch, you have!" he turned suddenly to Miüsov, although the latter was not dreaming of interrupting him. "They all accuse me of having hidden the children's money in my boots, and cheated them, but isn't there a court of law? There they will reckon out for you, Dmitri Fyodorovitch, from your notes, your letters, and your agreements, how much money you had, how much you have spent, and how much you have left. Why does Pyotr Alexandrovitch refuse to pass judgment? Dmitri is not a stranger to him. Because they are all against me, while Dmitri Fyodorovitch is in debt to me, and not a little, but some thousands of which I have documentary proof. The whole town is echoing with his debaucheries. And where he was stationed before, he several times spent a thousand or two for the seduction of some respectable girl; we know all about that, Dmitri Fyodorovitch, in its most secret details. I'll prove it. . . . Would you believe it, holy Father, he has captivated the heart of the most honourable of young ladies of good family and fortune, daughter of a gallant colonel, formerly his superior officer, who had received many honours and had the Anna Order on his breast. He compromised the girl by his promise of marriage, now she is an orphan and here; she is betrothed to him, yet before her very eyes he is dancing attendance on a certain enchantress. And although this enchantress has lived in, so to speak, civil marriage with a respectable man, yet she is of an independent character, an unapproachable fortress for everybody, just like a legal wife—for she is virtuous, yes, holy Fathers, she is virtuous. Dmitri Fyodorovitch wants to open this fortress with a golden key, and that's why he is insolent to me now, trying to get money from me, though he has wasted thousands on this enchantress already. He's continually borrowing money for the purpose. From whom do you think? Shall I say, Mitya?"

"Be silent!" cried Dmitri, "wait till I'm gone. Don't dare in my presence to asperse the good name of an honourable girl! That you should utter a word about her is an outrage, and I won't permit it!"

He was breathless.

"Mitya! Mitya!" cried Fyodor Pavlovitch hysterically, squeezing out a tear. "And is your father's blessing nothing to you? If I curse you, what then?"

"Shameless hypocrite!" exclaimed Dmitri furiously.

"He says that to his father! his father! What would he be with others? Gentlemen, only fancy; there's a poor but honourable man living here, burdened with a numerous family, a captain who got into trouble and was discharged from the army, but not publicly, not by court-martial, with no slur on his honour. And three weeks ago Dmitri seized him by the beard in a tavern, dragged him out into the street and beat him publicly, and all because he is an agent in a little business of mine."

"It's all a lie! Outwardly it's the truth, but inwardly a lie!"

Dmitri was trembling with rage. "Father, I don't justify my action. Yes, I confess it publicly, I behaved like a brute to that captain, and I regret it now, and I'm disgusted with myself for my brutal rage. But this captain, this agent of yours, went to that lady whom you call an enchantress, and suggested to her from you that she should take I O Us of mine which were in your possession, and should sue me for the money so as to get me into prison, by means of them, if I persisted in claiming an account from you of my property. Now you reproach me for having a weakness for that lady when you yourself incited her to captivate me! She told me so to my face. . . . She told me the story and laughed at you. . . . You wanted to put me in prison because you are jealous of me with her, because you'd begun to force your attentions upon her; and I know all about that, too; she laughed at you for that as well—you hear—she laughed at you as she described it. So here you have this man, this father who reproaches his profligate son! Gentlemen, forgive my anger, but I foresaw that this crafty old man had only brought you together to create a scandal. I had come to forgive him if he held out his hand; to forgive him and ask forgiveness! But as he has just this minute insulted not only me but an honourable young lady for whom I feel such reverence that I dare not take her name in vain, I have made up my mind to show up his game, though he is my father. . . ."

He could not go on. His eyes were glittering and he breathed with difficulty. But everyone in the cell was stirred. All except Father Zossima got up from their seats uneasily. The monks looked austere but waited for guidance from the elder. He sat still, pale, not from excitement but from the weakness of disease. An imploring smile lighted up his face; from time to time he raised his hand, as though to check the storm, and, of course, a gesture from him would have been enough to end the scene; but he seemed to be waiting for something and watched them intently as though trying to make out something which was not perfectly clear to him. At last Miüsov felt completely humiliated and disgraced.

"We are all to blame for this scandalous scene," he said hotly. "But I did not foresee it when I came, though I knew with whom I had to deal. This must be stopped at once! Believe me, your reverence, I had no precise knowledge of the details that have just come to light. I was unwilling to believe them, and I learn for the first time. . . . A father is jealous of his son's relations with a woman of loose behaviour and intrigues with the creature to get his son into prison! This is the company in which I have been forced to be present! I was deceived. I declare to you all that I was as much deceived as anyone."

"Dmitri Fyodorovitch," yelled Fyodor Pavlovitch suddenly, in an unnatural voice, "if you were not my son I would challenge you this instant to a duel . . . with pistols, at three paces . . . across a handkerchief," he added, stamping with both feet.

With old liars who have been acting all their lives there are moments when they enter so completely into their part that they tremble or shed tears of emotion in earnest, although at that very moment, or a second later, they are able to whisper to themselves: "You know you are lying, you shameless old sinner! You're acting now, in spite of your 'holy' wrath."

Dmitri frowned painfully, and looked with unutterable contempt at his father.

"I thought . . . I thought," he said, in a soft and, as it were, controlled voice, "that I was coming to my native place with the angel of my heart, my betrothed, to cherish his old age, and I find nothing but a depraved profligate, a despicable clown!"

"A duel!" yelled the old wretch again, breathless and spluttering at each syllable. "And you, Pyotr Alexandrovitch Miüsov, let me tell you that there has never been in all your family a loftier, and more honest—you hear—more honest woman than this 'creature', as you have dared to call her! And you, Dmitri Fyodorovitch, have abandoned your betrothed for that 'creature', so you must yourself have thought that your betrothed couldn't hold a candle to her. That's the woman called a 'creature'!"

"Shameful!" broke from Father Iosif.

"Shameful and disgraceful!" Kalganov, flushing crimson, cried in a boyish voice, trembling with emotion. He had been silent till that moment.

"Why is such a man alive?" Dmitri, beside himself with rage, growled in a hollow voice, hunching up his shoulders till he looked almost deformed. "Tell me, can he be allowed to go on defiling the earth?" He looked round at everyone and pointed at the old man. He spoke evenly and deliberately.

"Listen, listen, monks, to the parricide!" cried Fyodor Pavlovitch, rushing up to Father Iosif. "That's the answer to your 'shameful'! What is shameful? That 'creature', that 'woman of loose behaviour' is perhaps holier than you are yourselves, you monks who are seeking salvation! She fell perhaps in her youth, ruined by her environment. But she loved much, and Christ Himself forgave the woman 'who loved much'."

"It was not for such love Christ forgave her," broke impatiently from the gentle Father Iosif.

"Yes, it was for such, monks, it was! You save your souls here, eating cabbage, and think you are the righteous. You eat a gudgeon a day, and you think you bribe God with gudgeon."

"This is unendurable!" was heard on all sides in the cell.

But this unseemly scene was cut short in a most unexpected way. Father Zossima rose suddenly from his seat. Almost distracted with anxiety for the elder and everyone else, Alyosha succeeded, however, in supporting him by the arm. Father Zossima moved towards Dmitri and reaching him sank on his knees before him. Alyosha thought that he had fallen from weakness, but this was not so. The elder distinctly and deliberately bowed down at Dmitri's feet till his forehead touched the floor. Alyosha was so astounded that he failed to assist him when he got up again. There was a faint smile on his lips.

"Good-bye! Forgive me, all of you!" he said, bowing on all sides to his guests.

Dmitri stood for a few moments in amazement. Bowing down to him—what did it mean? Suddenly he cried aloud: "Oh God!" hid his face in his hands, and rushed out of the room. All the guests flocked out after him, in their confusion not saying good-bye, or bowing to their host. Only the monks went up to him again for a blessing.

"What did it mean, falling at his feet like that? Was it symbolic or what?" said Fyodor Pavlovitch, suddenly quieted and trying to reopen conversation without venturing to address anybody in particular. They were all passing out of the precincts of the hermitage at the moment.

"I can't answer for a madhouse and for madmen," Miüsov answered at once ill-humouredly, "but I will spare myself your company, Fyodor Pavlovitch, and, trust me, for ever. Where's that monk?"

"That monk," that is, the monk who had invited them to dine with the Superior, did not keep them waiting. He met them as soon as they came down the steps from the elder's cell, as though he had been waiting for them all the time.

"Reverend Father, kindly do me a favour. Convey my

71

deepest respect to the Father Superior, apologise for me, personally, Miüsov, to his reverence, telling him that I deeply regret that owing to unforeseen circumstances I am unable to have the honour of being present at his table, greatly as I should desire to do so," Miüsov said irritably to the monk.

"And that unforeseen circumstance, of course, is myself," Fyodor Pavlovitch cut in immediately. "Do you hear, Father; this gentleman doesn't want to remain in my company or else he'd come at once. And you shall go, Pyotr Alexandrovitch, pray go to the Father Superior and good appetite to you. I will decline, and not you. Home, home, I'll eat at home, I don't feel equal to it here, Pyotr Alexandrovitch, my amiable relative."

"I am not your relative and never have been, you contemptible man!"

"I said it on purpose to madden you, because you always disclaim the relationship, though you really are a relation in spite of your shuffling. I'll prove it by the church calendar. As for you, Ivan, stay if you like. I'll send the horses for you later. Propriety requires you to go to the Father Superior, Pyotr Alexandrovitch, to apologise for the disturbance we've been making. . . ."

"Is it true that you are going home? Aren't you lying?"

"Pyotr Alexandrovitch! How could I dare after what's happened! Forgive me, gentlemen, I was carried away! And upset besides! And, indeed, I am ashamed. Gentlemen, one man has the heart of Alexander of Macedon and another the heart of the little dog Fido. Mine is that of the little dog Fido. I am abashed! After such an escapade how can I go to dinner, to gobble up the monastery's sauces? I am ashamed, I can't. You must excuse me!"

"The devil only knows, what if he deceives us," thought Miüsov, still hesitating, and watching the retreating buffoon with distrustful eyes. The latter turned round, and noticing that Miüsov was watching him, waved him a kiss.

"Well, are you coming to the Superior?" Miüsov asked Ivan abruptly.

"Why not? I was especially invited yesterday."

"Unfortunately I feel myself compelled to go to this confounded dinner," said Miüsov with the same irritability, regardless of the fact that the monk was listening. "We ought, at least, to apologise for the disturbance, and explain that it was not our doing. What do you think?"

"Yes, we must explain that it wasn't our doing. Besides, father won't be there," observed Ivan.

"Well, I should hope not! Confound this dinner!"

They all walked on, however. The monk listened in silence. On the road through the copse he made one observation, however—that the Father Superior had been waiting a long time, and that they were more than half an hour late. He received no answer. Miüsov looked with hatred at Ivan.

"Here he is, going to the dinner as though nothing had happened," he thought. "A brazen face, and the conscience of a Karamazov!"

CHAPTER VII

A YOUNG MAN BENT ON A CAREER

ALYOSHA helped Father Zossima to his bedroom and seated him on his bed. It was a little room furnished with the bare necessities. There was a narrow iron bedstead, with a strip of felt for a mattress. In the corner, under the ikons, was a reading-desk with a cross and the Gospel lying on it. The elder sank exhausted on the bed. His eyes glittered and he breathed hard. He looked intently at Alyosha, as though considering something.

"Go, my dear boy, go. Porfiry is enough for me. Make haste, you are needed there, go and wait at the Father Superior's table."

"Let me stay here," Alyosha entreated.

"You are more needed there. There is no peace there. You will wait, and be of service. If evil spirits rise up, repeat a prayer. And remember, my son (the elder liked to call him that), this is not the place for you in the future. When it is God's will to call me, leave the monastery. Go away for good."

Alyosha started.

"What is it? This is not your place for the time. I bless you for great service in the world. Yours will be a long pilgrimage. And you will have to take a wife, too. You will have to bear *all* before you come back. There will be much to do. But I don't doubt of you, and so I send you forth. Christ is with you. Do not abandon Him and He will not abandon you. You will see great sorrow, and in that sorrow you will be happy. This is my last message to you: in sorrow seek happi-

73

ness. Work, work unceasingly. Remember my words, for although I shall talk with you again, not only my days but my hours are numbered."

Alyosha's face again betrayed strong emotion. The corners of his mouth quivered.

"What is it again?" Father Zossima asked, smiling gently. "The worldly may follow the dead with tears, but here we rejoice over the father who is departing. We rejoice and pray for him. Leave me, I must pray. Go, and make haste. Be near your brothers. And not near one only but near both."

Father Zossima raised his hand to bless him. Alyosha could make no protest, though he had a great longing to remain. He longed, moreover, to ask the significance of his bowing to Dmitri, the question was on the tip of his tongue, but he dared not ask it. He knew that the elder would have explained it unasked if he had thought fit. But evidently it was not his will. That action had made a terrible impression on Alyosha; he believed blindly in its mysterious significance. Mysterious, and perhaps awful.

As he hastened out of the hermitage precincts to reach the monastery in time to serve at the Father Superior's dinner, he felt a sudden pang at his heart, and stopped short. He seemed to hear again Father Zossima's words, foretelling his approaching end. What he had foretold so exactly must infallibly come to pass. Alyosha believed that implicitly. But how could he be left without him? How could he live without seeing and hearing him? Where should he go? He had told him not to weep, and to leave the monastery. Good God! It was long since Alyosha had known such anguish. He hurried through the copse that divided the monastery from the hermitage, and unable to bear the burden of his thoughts, he gazed at the ancient pines beside the path. He had not far to go—about five hundred paces. He expected to meet no one at that hour, but at the first turn of the path he noticed Rakitin. He was waiting for someone.

"Are you waiting for me?" asked Alyosha, overtaking him.

"Yes," grinned Rakitin. "You are hurrying to the Father Superior, I know; he has a banquet. There's not been such a banquet since the Superior entertained the Bishop and General Pahatov, do you remember? I shan't be there, but you go and hand the sauces. Tell me one thing, Alexey, what does that vision mean? That's what I want to ask you."

"What vision?"

"That bowing to your brother, Dmitri. And didn't he tap the ground with his forehead, too!"

"You speak of Father Zossima?"

"Yes, of Father Zossima."

"Tapped the ground?"

"Ah, an irreverent expression! Well, what of it? Anyway, what does that vision mean?"

"I don't know what it means, Misha."

"I knew he wouldn't explain it to you! There's nothing wonderful about it, of course, only the usual holy mummery. But there was an object in the performance. All the pious people in the town will talk about it and spread the story through the province, wondering what it meant. To my thinking the old man really has a keen nose; he sniffed a crime. Your house stinks of it."

"What crime?"

Rakitin evidently had something he was eager to speak of.

"It'll be in your family, this crime. Between your brothers and your rich old father. So Father Zossima flopped down to be ready for what may turn up. If something happens later on, it'll be: 'Ah, the holy man foresaw it, prophesied it!' though it's a poor sort of prophecy, flopping like that. 'Ah, but it was symbolic,' they'll say, 'an allegory', and the devil knows what all! It'll be remembered to his glory: 'He predicted the crime and marked the criminal!' That's always the way with these crazy fanatics; they cross themselves at the tavern and throw stones at the temple. Like your elder, he takes a stick to a just man and falls at the feet of a murderer."

"What crime? What murderer? What do you mean?"

Alyosha stopped dead. Rakitin stopped, too.

"What murderer? As though you didn't know! I'll bet you've thought of it before. That's interesting, too, by the way. Listen, Alyosha, you always speak the truth, though you're always between two stools. Have you thought of it or not? Answer."

"I have," answered Alyosha in a low voice. Even Rakitin was taken aback.

"What? Have you really?" he cried.

"I . . . I've not exactly thought it," muttered Alyosha, "but directly you began speaking so strangely, I fancied I had thought of it myself."

"You see? (And how well you expressed it!) Looking at

your father and your brother Mitya to-day you thought of a crime. Then I'm not mistaken?"

"But wait, wait a minute," Alyosha broke in uneasily. "What has led you to see all this? Why does it interest you? That's the first question."

"Two questions, disconnected, but natural. I'll deal with them separately. What led me to see it? I shouldn't have seen it if I hadn't suddenly understood your brother Dmitri, seen right into the very heart of him all at once. I caught the whole man from one trait. These very honest but passionate people have a line which mustn't be crossed. If it were, he'd run at your father with a knife. But your father's a drunken and abandoned old sinner, who can never draw the line—if they both let themselves go, they'll both come to grief."

"No, Misha, no. If that's all, you've reassured me! It won't come to that."

"But why are you trembling? Let me tell you; he may be honest—your Mitya (he is stupid, but honest), but he's—a sensualist. That's the very definition and inner essence of him. It's your father has handed him on his low sensuality. Do you know, I simply wonder at you, Alyosha, how you can have kept your purity. You're a Karamazov too, you know! In your family sensuality is carried to a disease. But now, these three sensualists are watching one another, with their knives in their belts. The three of them are knocking their heads together, and you may be the fourth."

"You are mistaken about that woman. Dmitri—despises her," said Alyosha, with a sort of shudder.

"Grushenka? No, brother, he doesn't despise her. Since he has openly abandoned his betrothed for her, he doesn't despise her. There's something here, my dear boy, that you don't understand yet. A man will fall in love with some beauty, with a woman's body, or even with a part of a woman's body (a sensualist can understand that) and he'll abandon his own children for her, sell his father and mother, and his country, Russia, too. If he's honest, he'll steal; if he's humane, he'll murder; if he's faithful, he'll deceive. Pushkin, the poet of women's feet, sung of their feet in his verse. Others don't sing their praises, but they can't look at their feet without a thrill—and it's not only their feet. Contempt's no help here, brother, even if he did despise Grushenka. He does, but he can't tear himself away."

"I understand that," Alyosha jerked out suddenly.

"Really? Well, I dare say you do understand, since you blurt it out at the first word," said Rakitin, malignantly. "That escaped you unawares, and the confession's the more precious. So it's a familiar subject; you've thought about it already, about sensuality, I mean! Oh, you virgin soul! You're a quiet one, Alyosha, you're a saint, I know, but the devil only knows what you've thought about, and what you know already! You are pure, but you've been down into the depths. . . . I've been watching you a long time. You're a Karamazov yourself; you're a thorough Karamazov—no doubt birth and selection have something to answer for. You're a sensualist from your father, a crazy saint from your mother. Why do you tremble? Is it true, then? Do you know, Grushenka has been begging me to bring you along, 'I'll pull off his cassock', she says. You can't think how she keeps begging me to bring you. I wondered why she took such an interest in you. Do you know, she's an extraordinary woman, too!"

"Thank her and say I'm not coming," said Alyosha, with a strained smile. "Finish what you were saying, Misha. I'll tell you my idea after."

"There's nothing to finish. It's all clear. It's the same old tune, brother. If even you are a sensualist at heart what of your brother Ivan? He's a Karamazov, too. What is at the root of all you Karamazovs is that you're all sensual, grasping and crazy! Your brother Ivan writes theological articles in joke, for some idiotic, unknown motive of his own, though he's an atheist, and he admits it's a fraud himself—that's your brother Ivan. He's trying to get Mitya's betrothed for himself, and I fancy he'll succeed, too. And, what's more, it's with Mitya's consent. For Mitya will surrender his betrothed to him to be rid of her, and escape to Grushenka. And he's ready to do that in spite of all his nobility and disinterestedness. Observe that. Those are the most fatal people! Who the devil can make you out? He recognises his vileness and goes on with it! Let me tell you, too, the old man, your father, is standing in Mitya's way now. He has suddenly gone crazy over Grushenka. His mouth waters at the sight of her. It's simply on her account he made that scene in the cell just now, simply because Miüsov called her an 'abandoned creature'. He's worse than a tom cat in love. At first she was only employed by him in connection with his taverns and in some other shady business, but now he has suddenly realised all she is and has gone wild about her. He keeps pestering her with his offers, not honourable ones, of course. And they'll come into collision, the precious father and son, on that path! But Grushenka favours neither of them, she's still playing with them, and teasing them both, considering which she can get most out of. For though she could filch a lot of money from the papa he wouldn't marry her, and maybe he'll turn stingy in the end, and keep his purse shut. That's where Mitya's value comes in, he has no money but he's ready to marry her. Yes, ready to marry her! to abandon his betrothed, a rare beauty, Katerina Ivanovna, who's rich, and the daughter of a colonel, and to marry Grushenka, who has been the mistress of a dissolute old merchant, Samsonov, a coarse, uneducated, provincial mayor. Some murderous conflict may well come to pass from all this, and that's what your brother Ivan is waiting for. It would suit him down to the ground. He'll carry off Katerina Ivanovna, for whom he is languishing, and pocket her dowry of sixty thousand. That's very alluring to start with, for a man of no consequence and a beggar. And, take note, he won't be wronging Mitya, but doing him the greatest service. For I know as a fact that Mitya only last week, when he was with some gipsy girls drunk in a tavern, cried out aloud that he was unworthy of his betrothed Katya, but that his brother Ivan, he was the man who deserved her. And Katerina Ivanovna will not in the end refuse such a fascinating man as Ivan. She's hesitating between the two of them already. And how has that Ivan won you all, so that you all worship him? He is laughing at you, and enjoying himself at your expense."

"How do you know? How can you speak so confidently?" Alyosha asked sharply, frowning.

"Why do you ask, and are frightened at my answer? It shows that you know I'm speaking the truth."

"You don't like Ivan. Ivan wouldn't be tempted by money."

"Really? And the beauty of Katerina Ivanovna? It's not only the money, though a fortune of sixty thousand is an attraction."

"Ivan is above that. He wouldn't make up to anyone for thousands. It is not money, it's not comfort Ivan is seeking. Perhaps it's suffering he is seeking?"

"What wild dream now? Oh, you—aristocrats!"

"Ah, Misha, he has a stormy spirit. His mind is in bondage. He is haunted by a great, unsolved doubt. He is one of those who don't want millions but an answer to their questions."

"That's plagiarism, Alyosha. You're quoting your elder's

phrases. Ah, Ivan has set you a problem!" cried Rakitin, with undisguised malice. His face changed, and his lips twitched. "And the problem's a stupid one. It is no good guessing it. Rack your brains—you'll understand it. His article is absurd and ridiculous. And did you hear his stupid theory just now: if there's no immortality of the soul, then there's no virtue, and everything is lawful. (And, by the way, do you remember how your brother Mitya cried out: 'I will remember!'?) An attractive theory for scoundrels!—(I'm being abusive, that's stupid.) Not for scoundrels, but for pedantic poseurs, 'haunted by profound, unsolved doubts'. He's showing off, and what it all comes to is, 'on the one hand we cannot but admit' and 'on the other it must be confessed!' His whole theory is a fraud! Humanity will find in itself the power to live for virtue even without believing in immortality. It will find it in love for freedom, for equality, for fraternity."

Ratikin could hardly restrain himself in his heat, but, suddenly, as though remembering something, he stopped short.

"Well, that's enough," he said, with a still more crooked smile. "Why are you laughing? Do you think I'm a vulgar fool?"

"No, I never dreamed of thinking you a vulgar fool. You are clever but . . . never mind, I was silly to smile. I understand your getting hot about it, Misha. I guess from your warmth that you are not indifferent to Katerina Ivanovna yourself; I've suspected that for a long time, brother, that's why you don't like my brother Ivan. Are you jealous of him?"

"And jealous of her money, too? Won't you add that?"

"I'll say nothing about money. I am not going to insult you."

"I believe it, since you say so, but confound you, and your brother Ivan with you. Don't you understand that one might very well dislike him, apart from Katerina Ivanovna. And why the devil should I like him? He condescends to abuse me, you know. Why haven't I a right to abuse him?"

"I never heard of his saying anything about you, good or bad. He doesn't speak of you at all."

"But I heard that the day before yesterday at Katerina Ivanovna's he was abusing me for all he was worth—you see what an interest he takes in your humble servant. And which is the jealous one after that, brother, I can't say. He was so good as to express the opinion that, if I don't go in for tne career of an archimandrite in the immediate future and don't become a monk, I shall be sure to go to Petersburg and get on to some solid magazine as a reviewer, that I shall write for the next ten years, and in the end become the owner of the magazine, and bring it out on the liberal and atheistic side, with a socialistic tinge, with a tiny gloss of socialism, but keeping a sharp look-out all the time, that is, keeping in with both sides and hood-winking the fools. According to your brother's account, the tinge of socialism won't hinder me from laying by the proceeds and investing them under the guidance of some Jew, till at the end of my career I build a great house in Petersburg and move my publishing offices to it, and let out the upper storeys to lodgers. He has even chosen the place for it, near the new stone bridge across the Neva, which they say is to be built in Petersburg."

"Ah, Misha, that's just what will really happen, every word of it," cried Alyosha, unable to restrain a good-humoured smile.

"You are pleased to be sarcastic, too, Alexey Fyodorovitch."

"No, no, I'm joking, forgive me. I've something quite different in my mind. But, excuse me, who can have told you all this? You can't have been at Katerina Ivanovna's yourself when he was talking about you?"

"I wasn't there, but Dmitri Fyodorovitch was; and I heard him tell it with my own ears; if you want to know, he didn't tell me, but I overheard him, unintentionally, of course, for I was sitting in Grushenka's bedroom and I couldn't go away because Dmitri Fyodorovitch was in the next room."

"Oh yes, I'd forgotten she was a relation of yours."

"A relation! That Grushenka a relation of mine!" cried Rakitin, turning crimson. "Are you mad? You're out of your mind!"

"Why, isn't she a relation of yours? I heard so."

"Where can you have heard it? You Karamazovs brag of being an ancient, noble family, though your father used to run about playing the buffoon at other men's tables, and was only admitted to the kitchen as a favour. I may be only a priest's son, and dirt in the eyes of noblemen like you, but don't insult me so lightly and wantonly. I have a sense of honour, too, Alexey Fyodorovitch, I couldn't be a relation of Grushenka, a common harlot. I beg you to understand that!"

Rakitin was intensely irritated.

"Forgive me, for goodness' sake, I had no idea . . . besides . . . how can you call her a harlot? Is she . . . that sort of woman?" Alyosha flushed suddenly. "I tell you again, I heard that she was a relation of yours. You often go to see her, and you told me yourself you're not her lover. I never dreamed that you of all people had such contempt for her! Does she really deserve it?"

"I may have reasons of my own for visiting her. That's not your business. But as for relationship, your brother, or even your father is more likely to make her yours, than mine. Well, here we are. You'd better go to the kitchen. Hullo! what's wrong, what is it? Are we late? They can't have finished dinner so soon! Have the Karamazovs been making trouble again? No doubt they have. Here's your father and your brother Ivan after him. They've broken out from the Father Superior's. And look, Father Isidor's shouting out something after them from the steps. And your father's shouting and waving his arms. I expect he's swearing. Bah! and there goes Miüsov driving away in his carriage. You see, he's going. And there's old Maximov running!—there must have been a row. There can't have been any dinner. Surely they've not been beating the Father Superior! Or have they, perhaps, been beaten? It would serve them right!"

There was reason for Rakitin's exclamations. There had been a scandalous, an unprecedented scene. It had all come from the impulse of a moment.

CHAPTER VIII

THE SCANDALOUS SCENE

M IÜSOV, as a man of breeding and delicacy, could not but feel some inward qualms when he reached the Father Superior's with Ivan: he felt ashamed of having lost his temper. He felt that he ought to have disdained that despicable wretch, Fyodor Pavlovitch, too much to have been upset by him in Father Zossima's cell, and so to have forgotten himself. "The monks were not to blame, in any case," he reflected, on the steps. "And if they're decent people here (and the Father Superior, I understand, is a nobleman) why not be friendly and courteous with them? I won't argue, I'll fall in with everything, I'll win them by politeness, and . . . and . . . show them that I've nothing to do with that Æsop, that buffoon, that Pierrot, and have merely been taken in over this affair, just as they have."

He determined to drop his litigation with the monastery and relinquish his claims to the wood-cutting and fishery rights at once. He was the more ready to do this because the rights had become much less valuable, and he had indeed the vaguest idea where the wood and river in question were.

These excellent intentions were strengthened when he entered the Father Superior's dining-room, though, strictly speaking, it was not a dining-room, for the Father Superior had only two rooms altogether; they were, however, much larger and more comfortable than Father Zossima's. But there was no great luxury about the furnishing of these rooms either. The furniture was of mahogany, covered with leather, in the old-fashioned style of 1820; the floor was not even stained, but everything was shining with cleanliness, and there were many choice flowers in the windows; the most sumptuous thing in the room at the moment was, of course, the beautifully decorated table. The cloth was clean, the service shone; there were three kinds of well-baked bread, two bottles of wine, two of excellent mead, and a large glass jug of kvas—both the latter made in the monastery, and famous in the neighbourhood. There was no vodka. Rakitin related afterwards that there were five dishes: fish-soup made of sterlets, served with little fish patties; then boiled fish served in a special way; then salmon cutlets, ice pudding and compote, and, finally, blancmange. Rakitin found out about all these good things, for he could not resist peeping into the kitchen, where he already had a footing. He had a footing everywhere, and got information about everything. He was of an uneasy and envious temper. He was well aware of his own considerable abilities, and nervously exaggerated them in his self-conceit. He knew he would play a prominent part of some sort, but Alyosha, who was attached to him, was distressed to see that his friend Rakitin was dishonourable, and quite unconscious of being so himself, considering, on the contrary, that because he would not steal money left on the table he was a man of the highest integrity. Neither Alyosha nor anyone else could have influenced him in that.

Rakitin, of course, was a person of too little consequence to be invited to the dinner, to which Father Iosif, Father Païssy, and one other monk were the only inmates of the monastery invited. They were already waiting when Miüsov, Kalganov, and Ivan arrived. The other guest, Maximov, stood a little aside, waiting also. The Father Superior stepped into the middle of the room to receive his guests. He was a tall, thin, but still vigorous old man, with black hair streaked with grey, and a long, grave, ascetic face. He bowed to his guests in silence. But this time they approached to receive his blessing. Miüsov even tried to kiss his hand, but the Father Superior drew it back in time to avoid the salute. But Ivan and Kalganov went through the ceremony in the most simple-hearted and complete manner, kissing his hand as peasants do.

"We must apologise most humbly, your reverence," began Miüsov, simpering affably, and speaking in a dignified and respectful tone. "Pardon us for having come along without the gentleman you invited, Fyodor Pavlovitch. He felt obliged to decline the honour of your hospitality, and not without reason. In the reverend Father Zossima's cell he was carried away by the unhappy dissension with his son, and let fall words which were quite out of keeping . . . in fact, quite unseemly . . . as (he glanced at the monks) your reverence is, no doubt, already aware. And therefore, recognising that he had been to blame, he felt sincere regret and shame, and begged me, and his son Ivan Fyodorovitch, to convey to you his apologies and regrets. In brief, he hopes and desires to make amends later. He asks your blessing, and begs you to forget what has taken place."

As he uttered the last word of his tirade, Miüsov completely recovered his self-complacency, and all traces of his former irritation disappeared. He fully and sincerely loved humanity again.

The Father Superior listened to him with dignity, and, with a slight bend of the head, replied:

"I sincerely deplore his absence. Perhaps at our table he might have learnt to like us, and we him. Pray be seated, gentlemen."

He stood before the holy image, and began to say grace, aloud. All bent their heads reverently, and Maximov clasped his hands before him, with peculiar fervour.

It was at this moment that Fyodor Pavlovitch played his last prank. It must be noted that he really had meant to go home, and really had felt the impossibility of going to dine with the Father Superior as though nothing had happened, after his disgraceful behaviour in the elder's cell. Not that he was so very much ashamed of himself—quite the contrary perhaps. But still he felt it would be unseemly to go to dinner. Yet his creaking carriage had hardly been brought to the steps of the hotel, and he had hardly got into it, when he suddenly stopped short. He remembered his own words at the elder's: "I always feel when I meet people that I am lower than all, and that they all take me for a buffoon; so I say let me play the buffoon, for you are, every one of you, stupider and lower than I." He longed to avenge himself on everyone for his own unseemliness. He suddenly recalled how he had once in the past been asked: "Why do you hate so and so, so much?" And he had answered them, with his shameless impudence: "I'll tell you. He has done me no harm. But I played him a dirty trick, and ever since I have hated him."

Remembering that now, he smiled quietly and malignantly, hesitating for a moment. His eyes gleamed, and his lips positively quivered. "Well, since I have begun, I may as well go on," he decided. His predominant sensation at that moment might be expressed in the following words: "Well, there is no rehabilitating myself now. So let me shame them for all I am worth. I will show them I don't care what they think—that's all!"

He told the coachman to wait, while with rapid steps he returned to the monastery and straight to the Father Superior's. He had no clear idea what he would do, but he knew that he could not control himself, and that a touch might drive him to the utmost limits of obscenity, but only to obscenity, to nothing criminal, nothing for which he could be legally punished. In the last resort, he could always restrain himself, and had marvelled indeed at himself, on that score, sometimes. He appeared in the Father Superior's dining-room at the moment when the prayer was over and all were moving to the table. Standing in the doorway, he scanned the company, and laughing his prolonged, impudent, malicious chuckle, looked them all boldly in the face. "They thought I had gone, and here I am again," he cried to the whole room.

For one moment everyone stared at him without a word; and at once everyone felt that something revolting, grotesque, positively scandalous, was about to happen. Miüsov passed immediately from the most benevolent frame of mind to the most savage. All the feelings that had subsided and died down in his heart revived instantly.

"No! this I cannot endure!" he cried. "I absolutely cannot! and . . . I certainly cannot!"

The blood rushed to his head. He positively stammered; but he was beyond thinking of style, and he seized his hat.

"What is it he cannot?" cried Fyodor Pavlovitch, "that he

absolutely cannot and certainly cannot? Your reverence, am I to come in or not? Will you receive me as your guest?''

"You are welcome with all my heart,'' answered the Superior. "Gentlemen!'' he added, "I venture to beg you most earnestly to lay aside your dissensions, and to be united in love and family harmony—with prayer to the Lord at our humble table.''

"No, no, it is impossible!'' cried Miüsov, beside himself.

"Well, if it is impossible for Pyotr Alexandrovitch, it is impossible for me, and I won't stop. That is why I came. I will keep with Pyotr Alexandrovitch everywhere now. If you will go away, Pyotr Alexandrovitch, I will go away too; if you remain, I will remain. You stung him by what you said about family harmony, Father Superior, he does not admit he is my relation. That's right, isn't it, Von Sohn? Here's Von Sohn. How are you, Von Sohn?''

"Do you mean me?'' muttered Maximov, puzzled.

"Of course I mean you,'' cried Fyodor Pavlovitch. "Who else? The Father Superior could not be Von Sohn.''

"But I am not Von Sohn either. I am Maximov.''

"No, you are Von Sohn. Your reverence, do you know who Von Sohn was? It was a famous murder case. He was killed in a house of harlotry. I believe that is what such places are called among you—he was killed and robbed, and in spite of his venerable age, he was nailed up in a box and sent from Petersburg to Moscow in the luggage van, and while they were nailing him up, the harlots sang songs and played the harp, that is to say, the piano. So this is that very Von Sohn. He has risen from the dead, hasn't he, Von Sohn?''

"What is happening? What's this?'' voices were heard in the group of monks.

"Let us go,'' cried Miüsov, addressing Kalganov.

"No, excuse me,'' Fyodor Pavlovitch broke in shrilly, taking another step into the room. "Allow me to finish. There in the cell you blamed me for behaving disrespectfully just because I spoke of eating gudgeon, Pyotr Alexandrovitch. Miüsov, my relation, prefers to have *plus de noblesse que de sincérité* in his words, but I prefer to have *plus de sincérité que de noblesse,* and —damn the *noblesse!* That's right, isn't it, Von Sohn? Allow me, Father Superior, though I am a buffoon and play the buffoon, yet I am the soul of honour, and I want to speak my mind. Yes, I am the soul of honour, while in Pyotr Alexandrovitch there is wounded vanity and nothing else. I came here perhaps to have a look and speak my mind. My son Alexey

85

is here, being saved. I am his father; I care for his welfare, and it is my duty to care. While I've been playing the fool, I have been listening and having a look on the sly; and now I want to give you the last act of the performance. You know how things are with us? As a thing falls, so it lies. As a thing once has fallen, so it must lie for ever. Not a bit of it! I want to get up again. Holy Father, I am indignant with you. Confession is a great sacrament, before which I am ready to bow down reverently; but there in the cell they all kneel down and confess aloud. Can it be right to confess aloud? It was ordained by the holy fathers to confess in secret: then only your confession will be a mystery, and so it was of old. But how can I explain to him before everyone that I did this and that? . . . well, you understand what—sometimes it would not be proper to talk about it—so it is really a scandal! No, fathers, one might be carried along with you to the Flagellants, I dare say . . . at the first opportunity I shall write to the Synod, and I shall take my son Alexey home."

We must note here that Fyodor Pavlovitch knew where to look for the weak spots. There had been at one time malicious rumours which had even reached the Archbishop (not only regarding our monastery but in others where the institution of elders existed) that too much respect was paid to the elders, even to the detriment of the authority of the Superior, that the elders abused the sacrament of confession and so on and so on—absurd charges which had died away of themselves everywhere. But the spirit of folly, which had caught up Fyodor Pavlovitch, and was bearing him on the current of his own nerves into lower and lower depths of ignominy, prompted him with this old slander. Fyodor Pavlovitch did not understand a word of it, and he could not even put it sensibly, for on this occasion no one had been kneeling and confessing aloud in the elder's cell, so that he could not have seen anything of the kind. He was only speaking from confused memory of old slanders. But as soon as he had uttered his foolish tirade he felt he had been talking absurd nonsense, and at once longed to prove to his audience, and above all to himself, that he had not been talking nonsense. And though he knew perfectly well that with each word he would be adding more and more absurdity, he could not restrain himself, and plunged forward blindly.

"How disgraceful!" cried Pyotr Alexandrovitch.

"Pardon me!" said the Father Superior. "It was said of old, 'Many have begun to speak against me and have uttered evil sayings about me. And hearing it I have said to myself: it is the correction of the Lord and He has sent it to heal my vain soul'. And so we humbly thank you, honoured guest!" and he made Fyodor Pavlovitch a low bow.

"Tut—tut—tut! sanctimoniousness and stock phrases! Old phrases and old gestures. The old lies and formal prostrations. We know all about them. A kiss on the lips and a dagger in the heart, as in Schiller's *Robbers*. I don't like falsehood, fathers, I want the truth. But the truth is not to be found in eating gudgeon and that I proclaim aloud! Father monks, why do you fast? Why do you expect reward in heaven for that? Why, for reward like that I will come and fast too! No, saintly monk, you try being virtuous in the world, do good to society, without shutting yourself up in a monastery at other people's expense, and without expecting a reward up aloft for it—you'll find that a bit harder. I can talk sense, too, Father Superior. What have they got here?" He went up to the table. "Old port wine, mead brewed by the Eliseyev Brothers. Fie, fie, fathers! That is something beyond gudgeon. Look at the bottles the fathers have brought out, he! he! he! And who has provided it all? The Russian peasant, the labourer, brings here the farthing earned by his horny hand, wringing it from his family and the tax-gatherer! You bleed the people, you know, holy fathers."

"This is too disgraceful!" said Father Iosif.

Father Païssy kept obstinately silent. Miüsov rushed from the room, and Kalganov after him.

"Well, Father, I will follow Pyotr Alexandrovitch! I am not coming to see you again. You may beg me on your knees, I shan't come. I sent you a thousand roubles, so you have begun to keep your eye on me. He, he, he! No, I'll say no more. I am taking my revenge for my youth, for all the humiliation I endured." He thumped the table with his fist in a paroxysm of simulated feeling. "This monastery has played a great part in my life! It has cost me many bitter tears. You used to set my wife, the crazy one, against me. You cursed me with bell and book, you spread stories about me all over the place. Enough, fathers! This is the age of Liberalism, the age of steamers and railways. Neither a thousand, nor a hundred roubles, no, nor a hundred farthings will you get out of me!"

It must be noted again that our monastery never had played any great part in his life, and he never had shed a bitter tear owing to it. But he was so carried away by his simulated emotion that he was for one moment almost believing it himself. He was so touched he was almost weeping. But at that very instant he felt that it was time to draw back.

The Father Superior bowed his head at his malicious lie, and again spoke impressively:

"It is written again, 'Bear circumspectly and gladly dishonour that cometh upon thee by no act of thine own, be not confounded and hate not him who hath dishonoured thee'. And so will we."

"Tut, tut, tut! Bethinking thyself and the rest of the rigmarole. Bethink yourselves, fathers, I will go. But I will take my son Alexey away from here for ever, on my parental authority. Ivan Fyodorovitch, my most dutiful son, permit me to order you to follow me. Von Sohn, what have you to stay for? Come and see me now in the town. It is fun there. It is only one short verst. Instead of lenten oil I will give you sucking-pig and kasha. We will have dinner with some brandy and liqueur to it. . . . I've cloudberry wine Hey, Von Sohn, don't lose your chance." He went out, shouting and gesticulating.

It was at that moment Rakitin saw him and pointed him out to Alyosha.

"Alexey!" his father shouted, from far off, catching sight of him. "You come home to me to-day, for good, and bring your pillow and mattress, and leave no trace behind."

Alyosha stood rooted to the spot, watching the scene in silence. Meanwhile, Fyodor Pavlovitch had got into the carriage, and Ivan was about to follow him in grim silence without even turning to say good-bye to Alyosha. But at this point another almost incredible scene of grotesque buffoonery gave the finishing touch to the episode. Maximov suddenly appeared by the side of the carriage. He ran up, panting, afraid of being too late. Rakitin and Alyosha saw him running. He was in such a hurry that in his impatience he put his foot on the step on which Ivan's left foot was still resting, and clutching the carriage he kept trying to jump in. "I am going with you!" he kept shouting, laughing a thin mirthful laugh with a look of reckless glee in his face. "Take me, too."

"There!" cried Fyodor Pavlovitch, delighted. "Did I not say he was Von Sohn. It is Von Sohn himself, risen from the dead. Why, how did you tear yourself away? What did you *vonsohn* there? And how could you get away from the dinner? You must be a brazen-faced fellow! I am that myself, but I am surprised at you, brother! Jump in, jump in! Let him pass, Ivan. It will be fun. He can lie somewhere at our feet. Will you lie at our feet, Von Sohn? Or perch on the box with the coachman? Skip on to the box, Von Sohn!"

But Ivan, who had by now taken his seat, without a word gave Maximov a violent punch in the breast and sent him flying. It was quite by chance he did not fall.

"Drive on!" Ivan shouted angrily to the coachman.

"Why, what are you doing, what are you about? Why did you do that?" Fyodor Pavlovitch protested.

But the carriage had already driven away. Ivan made no reply.

"Well, you are a fellow," Fyodor Pavlovitch said again.

After a pause of two minutes, looking askance at his son, "Why, it was you got up all this monastery business. You urged it, you approved of it. Why are you angry now?"

"You've talked rot enough. You might rest a bit now," Ivan snapped sullenly.

Fyodor Pavlovitch was silent again for two minutes.

"A drop of brandy would be nice now," he observed sententiously, but Ivan made no response.

"You shall have some, too, when we get home."

Ivan was still silent.

Fyodor Pavlovitch waited another two minutes.

"But I shall take Alyosha away from the monastery, though you will dislike it so much, most honoured Karl von Moor."

Ivan shrugged his shoulders contemptuously, and turning away stared at the road. And they did not speak again all the way home.

BOOK III: THE SENSUALISTS

CHAPTER I

IN THE SERVANTS' QUARTERS

THE Karamazovs' house was far from being in the centre of the town, but it was not quite outside it. It was a pleasant-looking old house of two storeys, painted grey, with a red iron roof. It was roomy and snug, and might still last many years. There were all sorts of unexpected little cupboards and closets and staircases. There were rats in it, but Fyodor Pavlovitch did not altogether dislike them. "One doesn't feel so solitary when one's left alone in the evening," he used to say. It was his habit to send the servants away to the lodge for the night and to lock himself up alone. The lodge was a roomy and solid building in the yard. Fyodor Pavlovitch used to have the cooking done there, although there was a kitchen in the house; he did not like the smell of cooking, and, winter and summer alike, the dishes were carried in across the courtyard. The house was built for a large family; there was room for five times as many, with their servants. But at the time of our story there was no one living in the house but Fyodor Pavlovitch and his son Ivan. And in the lodge there were only three servants: old Grigory, and his old wife Marfa, and a young man called Smerdyakov. Of these three we must say a few words. Of old Grigory we have said something already. He was firm and determined and went blindly and obstinately for his object, if once he had been brought by any reasons (and they were often very illogical ones) to believe that it was immutably right. He was honest and incorruptible. His wife, Marfa Ignatyevna, had obeyed her husband's will implicitly all her life, yet she had pestered him terribly after the emancipation of the serfs. She was set on leaving Fyodor Pavlovitch and opening a little shop in Moscow with their small savings. But Grigory decided then, once for all, that "the woman's talking nonsense, for every woman is dishonest", and that they ought not to leave their old master, whatever he might be, for "that was now their duty".

"Do you understand what duty is?" he asked Marfa Ignatyevna.

"I understand what duty means, Grigory Vassilyevitch, but why it's our duty to stay here I never shall understand," Marfa answered firmly.

"Well, don't understand then. But so it shall be. And you hold your tongue."

And so it was. They did not go away, and Fyodor Pavlovitch promised them a small sum for wages, and paid it regularly. Grigory knew, too, that he had an indisputable influence over his master. It was true, and he was aware of it. Fyodor Pavlovitch was an obstinate and cunning buffoon, yet, though his will was strong enough "in some of the affairs of life", as he expressed it, he found himself, to his surprise, extremely feeble in facing certain other emergencies. He knew his weaknesses and was afraid of them. There are positions in which one has to keep a sharp look-out. And that's not easy without a trustworthy man, and Grigory was a most trustworthy man. Many times in the course of his life Fyodor Pavlovitch had only just escaped a sound thrashing through Grigory's intervention, and on each occasion the old servant gave him a good lecture. But it wasn't only thrashings that Fyodor Pavlovitch was afraid of. There were graver occasions, and very subtle and complicated ones, when Fyodor Pavlovitch could not have explained the extraordinary craving for someone faithful and devoted, which sometimes unaccountably came upon him all in a moment. It was almost a morbid condition. Corrupt and often cruel in his lust, like some noxious insect, Fyodor Pavlovitch was sometimes, in moments of drunkenness, overcome by superstitious terror and a moral convulsion which took an almost physical form. "My soul's simply quaking in my throat at those times," he used to say. At such moments he liked to feel that there was near at hand, in the lodge if not in the room, a strong, faithful man, virtuous and unlike himself, who had seen all his debauchery and knew all his secrets, but was ready in his devotion to overlook all that, not to oppose him, above all, not to reproach him or threaten him with anything, either in this world or in the next, and, in case of need, to defend him—from whom? From somebody unknown, but terrible and dangerous. What he needed was to feel that there was *another* man, an old and tried friend, that he might call him in his sick moments merely to look at his face, or, perhaps, exchange some quite irrelevant words with him. And if the old servant were not angry, he felt comforted, and if he were angry, he was more dejected. It happened even (very rarely, however) that Fyodor Pavlovitch went at night to the lodge to wake Grigory and fetch him for a moment. When the old man came, Fyodor Pavlovitch would begin talking about the most trivial matters, and would soon let him go again, sometimes even with a jest. And after he had gone, Fyodor Pavlovitch would get into bed with a curse and sleep the sleep of the just. Something of the same sort had happened to Fyodor Pavlovitch on Alyosha's arrival. Alyosha "pierced his heart" by "living with him, seeing everything and blaming nothing". Moreover, Alyosha brought with him something his father had never known before: a complete absence of contempt for him and an invariable kindness, a perfectly natural unaffected devotion to the old man who deserved it so little. All this was a complete surprise to the old profligate, who had dropped all family ties. It was a new and surprising experience for him, who had till then loved nothing but "evil". When Alyosha had left him, he confessed to himself that he had learnt something he had not till then been willing to learn.

I have mentioned already that Grigory had detested Adelaïda Ivanovna, the first wife of Fyodor Pavlovitch and the mother of Dmitri, and that he had, on the contrary, protected Sofya Ivanovna, the poor "crazy woman", against his master and anyone who chanced to speak ill or lightly of her. His sympathy for the unhappy wife had become something sacred to him, so that even now, twenty years after, he could not bear a slighting allusion to her from anyone, and would at once check the offender. Externally, Grigory was cold, dignified and taciturn, and spoke, weighing his words, without frivolity. It was impossible to tell at first sight whether he loved his meek, obedient wife; but he really did love her, and she knew it.

Marfa Ignatyevna was by no means foolish; she was probably, indeed, cleverer than her husband, or, at least, more prudent than he in worldly affairs, and yet she had given in to him in everything without question or complaint ever since her marriage, and respected him for his spiritual superiority. It was remarkable how little they spoke to one another in the course of their lives, and only of the most necessary daily affairs. The grave and dignified Grigory thought over all his cares and duties alone, so that Marfa Ignatyevna had long grown used to knowing that he did not need her advice. She felt that her husband respected her silence, and took it as a sign of her good sense. He had never beaten her but once, and then only slightly. Once during the year after Fyodor Pavlovitch's marriage with Adelaïda Ivanovna, the village girls and women—at that time serfs—were called together before the house to sing and dance. They were beginning "in the Green Meadows" when Marfa, at that time a young woman, skipped forward and danced "the Russian Dance", not in the village fashion but as she had danced it when she was a servant in the service of the rich Miüsov family, in their private theatre, where the actors were taught to dance by a dancing master from Moscow. Grigory saw how his wife danced, and, an hour later, at home in their cottage, he gave her a lesson, pulling her hair a little. But there it ended: the beating was never repeated, and Marfa Ignatyevna gave up dancing.

God had not blessed them with children. One child was born but it died. Grigory was fond of children, and was not ashamed of showing it. When Adelaïda Ivanovna had run away, Grigory took Dmitri, then a child of three years old, combed his hair and washed him in a tub with his own hands, and looked after him for almost a year. Afterwards he had looked after Ivan and Alyosha, for which the general's widow had rewarded him with a slap in the face; but I have already related all that. The only happiness his own child had brought him had been in the anticipation of its birth. When it was born he was overwhelmed with grief and horror. The baby had six fingers. Grigory was so crushed by this that he was not only silent till the day of the christening but kept away in the garden. It was spring, and he spent three days digging the kitchen garden. The third day was fixed for christening the baby: meantime Grigory had reached a conclusion. Going into the cottage where the clergy were assembled and the visitors had arrived, including Fyodor Pavlovitch, who was to stand godfather, he suddenly announced that the baby "ought not to be christened at all". He announced this quietly, briefly, forcing out his words, and gazing with dull intentness at the priest.

"Why not?" asked the priest with good-humoured surprise.

"Because it's a dragon," muttered Grigory.

"A dragon? What dragon?"

Grigory did not speak for some time. "It's a confusion of nature," he muttered vaguely but firmly, and obviously unwilling to say more.

They laughed, and of course christened the poor baby. Grigory prayed earnestly at the font, but his opinion of the new-born child remained unchanged. Yet he did not interfere in any way. As long as the sickly infant lived he scarcely looked at it, tried indeed not to notice it, and for the most part kept out of the cottage. But when, at the end of a fortnight, the baby died of thrush, he himself laid the child in its little coffin, looked at it in profound grief, and when they were filling up the shallow little grave he fell on his knees and bowed down to the earth. He did not for years afterwards mention his child, nor did Marfa speak of the baby before him, and, even if Grigory were not present, she never spoke of it above a whisper. Marfa observed that, from the day of the burial, he devoted himself to "religion", and took to reading the "Lives of the Saints", for the most part sitting alone and in silence, and always putting on his big, round, silver-rimmed spectacles. He rarely read aloud, only perhaps in Lent. He was fond of the Book of Job, and had somehow got hold of a copy of the sayings and sermons of "the God-fearing Father Isaac the Syrian", which he read persistently for years together, understanding very little of it, but perhaps prizing and loving it the more for that. Of late he had begun to listen to the doctrines of the sect of Flagellants settled in the neighbourhood. He was evidently shaken by them, but judged it unfitting to go over to the new faith. His habit of theological reading gave him an expression of still greater gravity.

He was perhaps predisposed to mysticism. And the birth of his deformed child, and its death, had, as though by special design, been accompanied by another strange and marvellous event, which, as he said later, had left a "stamp" upon his soul. It happened that, on the very night after the burial of his child, Marfa was awakened by the wail of a new-born baby. She was frightened and waked her husband. He listened and said he thought it was more like someone groaning, "it might be a woman". He got up and dressed. It was a rather warm night in May. As he went down the steps, he distinctly heard groans coming from the garden. But the gate from the yard into the garden was locked at night, and there was no other way of entering it, for it was enclosed all round by a strong, high fence. Going back to the house, Grigory lighted a lantern, took the garden key, and taking no notice of the hysterical fears of his wife, who was still persuaded that she heard a child crying, and that it was her own baby crying and calling for her, went into the garden in silence. There he heard at once that the groans came from the bath-house that stood near the garden gate, and that they were the groans of a woman. Opening the door of the bath-house, he saw a sight which petrified him. An idiot girl, who wandered about the streets and was known to the whole town by the nickname of Lizaveta Smerdyastchaya (Stinking Lizaveta), had got into the bath-house and had just given birth to a child. She lay dying with the baby beside her. She said nothing, for she had never been able to speak. But her story needs a chapter to itself.

CHAPTER II

LIZAVETA

THERE was one circumstance which struck Grigory particularly, and confirmed a very unpleasant and revolting suspicion. This Lizaveta was a dwarfish creature, "not five foot within a wee bit", as many of the pious old women said pathetically about her, after her death. Her broad, healthy, red face had a look of blank idiocy and the fixed stare in her eyes was unpleasant, in spite of their meek expression. She wandered about, summer and winter alike, barefooted, wearing nothing but a hempen smock. Her coarse, almost black hair curled like lamb's wool, and formed a sort of huge cap on her head. It was always crusted with mud, and had leaves, bits of stick, and shavings clinging to it, as she always slept on the ground and in the dirt. Her father, a homeless, sickly drunkard, called Ilya, had lost everything and lived many years as a workman with some well-to-do tradespeople. Her mother had long been dead. Spiteful and diseased, Ilya used to beat Lizaveta inhumanly whenever she returned to him. But she rarely did so, for everyone in the town was ready to look after her as being an idiot, and so specially dear to God. Ilya's employers, and many others in the town, especially of the tradespeople, tried to clothe her better, and always rigged her out with high boots and a sheepskin coat for the winter. But although she allowed them to dress her up without resisting, she usually went away, preferably to the cathedral porch, and taking off all that had been given her—kerchief, sheepskin, skirt or boots—she left them there and walked away barefoot in her smock as before. It happened on one occasion that a new governor of the province, making a tour of inspection in our town, saw Lizaveta, and was wounded in his tenderest susceptibilities. And though he was told she was an idiot, he pronounced that for a young woman of twenty to wander about in nothing but a smock was a breach of the proprieties, and must not occur again. But the governor went his way, and Lizaveta was left as she was. At last her father died, which made her even more acceptable in the eyes of the religious persons of the town, as an orphan. In fact, everyone seemed to like her; even the boys did not tease her, and the boys of our town, especially the schoolboys, are a mischievous set. She would walk into strange houses, and no one drove her away Everyone was kind to her and gave her something. If she were given a copper, she would take it, and at once drop it in the alms-jug of the church or prison. If she were given a roll or bun in the market, she would hand it to the first child she met. Sometimes she would stop one of the richest ladies in the town and give it to her, and the lady would be pleased to take it. She herself never tasted anything but black bread and water. If she went into an expensive shop, where there were costly goods or money lying about, no one kept watch on her, for they knew that if she saw thousands of roubles overlooked by them, she would not have touched a farthing. She scarcely ever went to church. She slept either in the church porch or climbed over a hurdle (there are many hurdles instead of fences to this day in our town) into a kitchen garden. She used at least once a week to turn up "at home", that is at the house of her father's former employers, and in the winter went there every night, and slept either in the passage or the cowhouse. People were amazed that she could stand such a life, but she was accustomed to it, and although she was so tiny, she was of a robust constitution. Some of the townspeople declared that she did all this only from pride, but that is hardly credible. She could hardly speak, and only from time to time uttered an inarticulate grunt. How could she have been proud?

It happened, one clear, warm, moonlight night in September (many years ago), five or six drunken revellers were returning from the club at a very late hour, according to our provincial notions. They passed through the "back-way", which led between the back gardens of the houses, with hurdles on either side. This way leads out on to the bridge over the long, stinking pool which we were accustomed to call a river. Among the nettles and burdocks under the hurdle our revellers saw Lizaveta asleep. They stopped to look at her, laughing, and began jesting with unbridled licentiousness. It occurred to one young gentleman to make the whimsical inquiry whether anyone could possibly look upon such an animal as a woman, and so'forth. . . . They all pronounced with lofty repugnance that it was impossible. But Fyodor Pavlovitch, who was among them, sprang forward and declared that it was by no means impossible, and that, indeed, there was a certain piquancy about it, and so on. . . . . It is true that at that time he was overdoing his part as a buffoon. He liked to put himself forward and entertain the company, ostensibly on equal terms, of course, though in reality he was on a servile footing with them. It was

just at the time when he had received the news of his first wife's death in Petersburg, and, with crape upon his hat, was drinking and behaving so shamelessly that even the most reckless among us were shocked at the sight of him. The revellers, of course, laughed at this unexpected opinion; and one of them even began challenging him to act upon it. The others repelled the idea even more emphatically, although still with the utmost hilarity, and at last they went on their way. Later on, Fyodor Pavlovitch swore that he had gone with them, and perhaps it was so, no one knows for certain, and no one ever knew. But five or six months later, all the town was talking, with intense and sincere indignation, of Lizaveta's condition, and trying to find out who was the miscreant who had wronged her. Then suddenly a terrible rumour was all over the town that this miscreant was no other than Fyodor Pavlovitch. Who set the rumour going? Of that drunken band five had left the town and the only one still among us was an elderly and much-respected civil counsellor, the father of grown-up daughters, who could hardly have spread the tale, even if there had been any foundation for it. But rumour pointed straight at Fyodor Pavlovitch, and persisted in pointing at him. Of course this was no great grievance to him: he would not have troubled to contradict a set of tradespeople. In those days he was proud, and did not condescend to talk except in his own circle of the officials and nobles, whom he entertained so well.

At the time Grigory stood up for his master vigorously. He provoked quarrels and altercations in defence of him and succeeded in bringing some people round to his side. "It's the wench's own fault," he asserted, and the culprit was Karp, a dangerous convict who had escaped from prison and whose name was well known to us, as he had hidden in our town. This conjecture sounded plausible, for it was remembered that Karp had been in the neighbourhood just at that time in the autumn, and had robbed three people. But this affair and all the talk about it did not estrange popular sympathy from the poor idiot. She was better looked after than ever. A well-to-do merchant's widow named Kondratyev arranged to take her into her house at the end of April, meaning not to let her go out until after the confinement. They kept a constant watch over her, but in spite of their vigilance she escaped on the very last day, and made her way into Fyodor Pavlovitch's garden. How, in her condition, she managed to climb over the high, strong fence remained a mystery. Some maintained that she must have been lifted over by somebody; others hinted at something more uncanny. The most likely explanation is that it happened naturally—that Lizaveta, accustomed to clambering over hurdles to sleep in gardens, had somehow managed to climb this fence, in spite of her condition, and had leapt down, injuring herself.

Grigory rushed to Marfa and sent her to Lizaveta, while he ran to fetch an old midwife who lived close by. They saved the baby, but Lizaveta died at dawn. Grigory took the baby, brought it home, and making his wife sit down, put it on her lap. "A child of God—an orphan is akin to all," he said, "and to us above others. Our little lost one has sent us this, who has come from the devil's son and a holy innocent. Nurse him and weep no more."

So Marfa brought up the child. He was christened Pavel, to which people were not slow in adding "Fyodorovitch" (son of Fyodor). Fyodor Pavlovitch did not object to any of this, and thought it amusing, though he persisted vigorously in denying his responsibility. The townspeople were pleased at his adopting the foundling. Later on, Fyodor Pavlovitch invented a surname for the child, calling him Smerdyakov, after his mother's nickname.

So this Smerdyakov became Fyodor Pavlovitch's second servant, and was living in the lodge with Grigory and Marfa at the time our story begins. He was employed as cook. I ought to say something of this Smerdyakov, but I am ashamed of keeping my readers' attention so long occupied with these common menials, and I will go back to my story, hoping to say more of Smerdyakov in the course of it.

CHAPTER III

THE CONFESSION OF A PASSIONATE HEART IN VERSE

ALYOSHA remained for some time irresolute after hearing the command his father shouted to him from the carriage. But in spite of his uneasiness he did not stand still. That was not his way. He went at once to the kitchen to find out what his father had been doing above. Then he set off, trusting that on the way he would find some answer to the doubt tormenting him. I hasten to add that his father's shouts, commanding him to return home "with his mattress and pillow", did not frighten him in the least. He understood perfectly that those peremptory shouts were merely "a flourish" to produce an effect. In the same way a tradesman in our town who was celebrating his name-day with a party of friends, getting angry at being refused more vodka, smashed up his own crockery and furniture and tore his own and his wife's clothes, and finally broke his windows, all for the sake of effect. Next day, of course, when he was sober, he regretted the broken cups and saucers. Alyosha knew that his father would let him go back to the monastery next day, possibly even that evening. Moreover, he was fully persuaded that his father might hurt anyone else but would not hurt him. Alyosha was certain that no one in the whole world ever would want to hurt him, and, what is more, he knew that no one could hurt him. This was for him an axiom, assumed once for all without question, and he went his way without hesitation, relying on it.

But at that moment an anxiety of a different sort disturbed him, and worried him the more because he could not formulate it. It was the fear of a woman, of Katerina Ivanovna, who had so urgently entreated him in the note handed to him by Madame Hohlakov to come and see her about something. This request and the necessity of going had at once aroused an uneasy feeling in his heart, and this feeling had grown more and more painful all the morning in spite of the scenes at the hermitage and at the Father Superior's. He was not uneasy because he did not know what she would speak of and what he must answer. And he was not afraid of her simply as a woman. Though he knew little of women, he had spent his life, from early childhood till he entered the monastery, entirely with women. He was afraid of that woman, Katerina Ivanovna. He had been afraid of her from the first time he saw her. He had only seen her two or three times, and had only chanced to say a few words to her. He thought of her as a beautiful, proud, imperious girl. It was not her beauty which troubled him, but something else. And the vagueness of his apprehension increased the apprehension itself. The girl's aims were of the noblest, he knew that. She was trying to save his brother Dmitri simply through generosity, though he had already behaved badly to her. Yet, although Alyosha recognised and did justice to all these fine and generous sentiments, a shiver began to run down his back as soon as he drew near her house.

He reflected that he would not find Ivan, who was so intimate a friend, with her, for Ivan was certainly now with his father.

Dmitri he was even more certain not to find there, and he had a foreboding of the reason. And so his conversation would be with her alone. He had a great longing to run and see his brother Dmitri before that fateful interview. Without showing him the letter, he could talk to him about it. But Dmitri lived a long way off, and he was sure to be away from home too. Standing still for a minute, he reached a final decision. Crossing himself with a rapid and accustomed gesture, and at once smiling, he turned resolutely in the direction of his terrible lady.

He knew her house. If he went by the High Street and then across the market-place, it was a long way round. Though our town is small, it is scattered, and the houses are far apart. And meanwhile his father was expecting him, and perhaps had not yet forgotten his command. He might be unreasonable, and so he had to make haste to get there and back. So he decided to take a short cut by the back-way, for he knew every inch of the ground. This meant skirting fences, climbing over hurdles, and crossing other people's back-yards, where everyone he met knew him and greeted him. In this way he could reach the High Street in half the time.

He had to pass the garden adjoining his father's, and belonging to a little tumbledown house with four windows. The owner of this house, as Alyosha knew, was a bedridden old woman, living with her daughter, who had been a genteel maidservant in generals' families in Petersburg. Now she had been at home a year, looking after her sick mother. She always dressed up in fine clothes, though her old mother and she had sunk into such poverty that they went every day to Fyodor Pavlovitch's kitchen for soup and bread, which Marfa gave readily. Yet, though the young woman came up for soup, she had never sold any of her dresses, and one of these even had a long train—a fact which Alyosha had learned from Rakitin, who always knew everything that was going on in the town. He had forgotten it as soon as he heard it, but now, on reaching the garden, he remembered the dress with the train, raised his head, which had been bowed in thought, and came upon something quite unexpected.

Over the hurdle in the garden, Dmitri, mounted on something, was leaning forward, gesticulating violently, beckoning to him, obviously afraid to utter a word for fear of being overheard. Alyosha ran up to the hurdle.

"It's a good thing you looked up. I was nearly shouting to you," Mitya said in a joyful, hurried whisper. "Climb in here quickly! How splendid that you've come! I was just thinking of you!"

Alyosha was delighted too, but he did not know how to get over the hurdle. Mitya put his powerful hand under his elbow to help him jump. Tucking up his cassock, Alyosha leapt over the hurdle with the agility of a bare-legged street urchin.

"Well done! Now come along," said Mitya in an enthusiastic whisper.

"Where?" whispered Alyosha, looking about him and finding himself in a deserted garden with no one near but themselves. The garden was small, but the house was at least fifty paces away.

"There's no one here. Why do you whisper?" asked Alyosha.

"Why do I whisper? Deuce take it!" cried Dmitri at the top of his voice. "You see what silly tricks nature plays one. I am here in secret, and on the watch. I'll explain later on, but, knowing it's a secret, I began whispering like a fool, when there's no need. Let us go. Over there. Till then be quiet. I want to kiss you.

> *Glory to God in the world,*
> *Glory to God in me . . .*

I was just repeating that, sitting here, before you came."

The garden was about three acres in extent, and planted with trees only along the fence at the four sides. There were apple-trees, maples, limes and birch-trees. The middle of the garden was an empty grass space, from which several hundredweight of hay was carried in the summer. The garden was let out for a few roubles for the summer. There were also plantations of raspberries and currants and gooseberries laid out along the sides; a kitchen garden had been planted lately near the house.

Dmitri led his brother to the most secluded corner of the garden. There, in a thicket of lime-trees and old bushes of black currant, elder, snowball-tree, and lilac, there stood a tumble-down green summer-house, blackened with age. Its walls were of lattice-work, but there was still a roof which could give shelter. God knows when this summer-house was built. There was a tradition that it had been put up some fifty years before by a retired colonel called Von Schmidt, who owned the house at that time. It was all in decay, the floor was rotting, the planks were loose, the woodwork smelled musty. In the summer-

101

house there was a green wooden table fixed in the ground, and round it were some green benches upon which it was still possible to sit. Alyosha had at once observed his brother's exhilarated condition, and on entering the arbour he saw half a bottle of brandy and a wineglass on the table.

"That's brandy," Mitya laughed. "I see your look: 'He's drinking again!' Distrust the apparition.

> *Distrust the worthless, lying crowd,*
> *And lay aside thy doubts.*

I'm not drinking, I'm only 'indulging', as that pig, your Rakitin, says. He'll be a civil councillor one day, but he'll always talk about 'indulging'. Sit down. I could take you in my arms, Alyosha, and press you to my bosom till I crush you, for in the whole world—in reality—in re-al-i-ty—(can you take it in?) I love no one but you!"

He uttered the last words in a sort of exaltation.

"No one but you and one 'jade' I have fallen in love with, to my ruin. But being in love doesn't mean loving. You may be in love with a woman and yet hate her. Remember that! I can talk about it gaily still. Sit down here by the table and I'll sit beside you and look at you, and go on talking. You shall keep quiet and I'll go on talking, for the time has come. But on reflection, you know, I'd better speak quietly, for here—here—you can never tell what ears are listening. I will explain everything, as they say, 'the story will be continued'. Why have I been longing for you? Why have I been thirsting for you all these days, and just now? (It's five days since I've cast anchor here.) Because it's only to you I can tell everything; because I must, because I need you, because to-morrow I shall fly from the clouds, because to-morrow life is ending and beginning. Have you ever felt, have you ever dreamt of falling down a precipice into a pit? That's just how I'm falling, but not in a dream. And I'm not afraid, and don't you be afraid. At least, I am afraid, but I enjoy it. It's not enjoyment though, but ecstasy. Damn it all, whatever it is! A strong spirit, a weak spirit, a womanish spirit—whatever it is! Let us praise nature: you see what sunshine, how clear the sky is, the leaves are all green, it's still summer; four o'clock in the afternoon and the stillness! Where were you going?"

"I was going to father's, but I meant to go to Katerina Ivanovna's first."

"To her, and to father! Oo! what a coincidence! Why was I waiting for you? Hungering and thirsting for you in every cranny of my soul and even in my ribs? Why, to send you to father and to her, Katerina Ivanovna, so as to have done with her and with father. To send an angel. I might have sent anyone, but I wanted to send an angel. And here you are on your way to see father and her."

"Did you really mean to send me?" cried Alyosha with a distressed expression.

"Stay! You knew it! And I see you understand it all at once. But be quiet, be quiet for a time. Don't be sorry, and don't cry."

Dmitri stood up, thought a moment, and put his finger to his forehead.

"She's asked you, written to you a letter or something, that's why you're going to her? You wouldn't be going except for that?"

"Here is her note." Alyosha took it out of his pocket. Mitya looked through it quickly.

"And you were going the back-way! Oh, gods, I thank you for sending him by the back-way, and he came to me like the golden fish to the silly old fishermen in the fable! Listen, Alyosha, listen, brother! Now I mean to tell you everything, for I must tell someone. An angel in heaven I've told already; but I want to tell an angel on earth. You are an angel on earth. You will hear and judge and forgive. And that's what I need, that someone above me should forgive. Listen! If two people break away from everything on earth and fly off into the unknown, or at least one of them, and before flying off or going to ruin he comes to someone else and says, 'Do this for me'— some favour never asked before that could only be asked on one's deathbed—would that other refuse, if he were a friend or a brother?"

"I will do it, but tell me what it is, and make haste," said Alyosha.

"Make haste! H'm! . . . Don't be in a hurry, Alyosha, you hurry and worry yourself. There's no need to hurry now. Now the world has taken a new turning. Ah, Alyosha, what a pity you can't understand ecstasy. But what am I saying to him? As though you didn't understand it. What an ass I am, what am I saying: 'Be noble, oh, man!' Who says that?"

Alyosha made up his mind to wait. He felt that, perhaps, indeed, his work lay here. Mitya sank into thought for a moment, with his elbow on the table and his head in his hand. Both were silent.

"Alyosha," said Mitya, "you're the only one who won't laugh. I should like to begin—my confession—with Schiller's 'Hymn to Joy', *An die Freude!* I don't know German, I only know it's called that. Don't think I'm talking nonsense because I'm drunk. I'm not a bit drunk. Brandy's all very well, but I need two bottles to make me drunk:

> *Silenus with his rosy phiz*
> *Upon his stumbling ass.*

But I've not drunk a quarter of a bottle, and I'm not Silenus. I'm not Silenus, though I am strong,* for I've made a decision once for all. Forgive me the pun; you'll have to forgive me a lot more than puns to-day. Don't be uneasy. I'm not spinning it out. I'm talking sense, and I'll come to the point in a minute. I won't keep you in suspense. Stay, how does it go?"

He raised his head, thought a minute, and began with enthusiasm:

> *"Wild and fearful in his cavern*
> *Hid the naked troglodyte,*
> *And the homeless nomad wandered*
> *Laying waste the fertile plain.*
> *Menacing with spear and arrow*
> *In the woods the hunter strayed. . . .*
> *Woe to all poor wretches stranded*
> *On those cruel and hostile shores!*

> *"From the peak of high Olympus*
> *Came the mother Ceres down,*
> *Seeking in those savage regions*
> *Her lost daughter Proserpine.*
> *But the Goddess found no refuge,*
> *Found no kindly welcome there,*
> *And no temple bearing witness*
> *To the worship of the gods.*

> *"From the fields and from the vineyards*
> *Came no fruits to deck the feasts,*

* In Russian, "silen".

104

Only flesh of blood-stained victims
Smouldered on the altar-fires,
And where'er the grieving goddess
Turns her melancholy gaze,
Sunk in vilest degradation
Man his loathsomeness displays."

Mitya broke into sobs and seized Alyosha's hand.

"My dear, my dear, in degradation, in degradation now, too. There's a terrible amount of suffering for man on earth, a terrible lot of trouble. Don't think I'm only a brute in an officer's uniform, wallowing in dirt and drink. I hardly think of anything but of that degraded man—if only I'm not lying. I pray God I'm not lying and showing off. I think about that man because I am that man myself.

Would he purge his soul from vileness
And attain to light and worth,
He must turn and cling for ever
To his ancient Mother Earth.

But the difficulty is how am I to cling for ever to Mother Earth. I don't kiss her. I don't cleave her bosom. Am I to become a peasant or a shepherd? I go on and I don't know whether I'm going to shame or to light and joy. That's the trouble, for everything in the world is a riddle! And whenever I've happened to sink into the vilest degradation (and it's always been happening) I always read that poem about Ceres and man. Has it reformed me? Never! For I'm a Karamazov. For when I do leap into the pit, I go headlong with my heels up, and am pleased to be falling in that degrading attitude, and pride myself upon it. And in the very depths of that degradation I begin a hymn of praise. Let me be accursed. Let me be vile and base, only let me kiss the hem of the veil in which my God is shrouded. Though I may be following the devil, I am Thy son, O Lord, and I love Thee, and I feel the joy without which the world cannot stand.

Joy everlasting fostereth
The soul of all creation,
It is her secret ferment fires
The cup of life with flame.
'Tis at her beck the grass hath turned
Each blade towards the light

And solar systems have evolved
From chaos and dark night,
Filling the realms of boundless space
Beyond the sage's sight.
At bounteous nature's kindly breast,
All things that breathe drink Joy,
And birds and beasts and creeping things
All follow where She leads.
Her gifts to man are friends in need,
The wreath, the foaming must,
To angels—vision of God's throne,
To insects—sensual lust.

But enough poetry! I am in tears; let me cry. It may be foolishness that everyone would laugh at. But you won't laugh. Your eyes are shining, too. Enough poetry. I want to tell you now about the insects to whom God gave 'sensual lust'.

To insects—sensual lust.

I am that insect, brother, and it is said of me specially. All we Karamazovs are such insects, and, angel as you are, that insect lives in you, too, and will stir up a tempest in your blood. Tempests, because sensual lust is a tempest—worse than a tempest! Beauty is a terrible and awful thing! It is terrible because it has not been fathomed and never can be fathomed, for God sets us nothing but riddles. Here the boundaries meet and all contradictions exist side by side. I am not a cultivated man, brother, but I've thought a lot about this. It's terrible what mysteries there are! Too many riddles weigh men down on earth. We must solve them as we can, and try to keep a dry skin in the water. Beauty! I can't endure the thought that a man of lofty mind and heart begins with the ideal of the Madonna and ends with the ideal of Sodom. What's still more awful is that a man with the ideal of Sodom in his soul does not renounce the ideal of the Madonna, and his heart may be on fire with that ideal, genuinely on fire, just as in his days of youth and innocence. Yes, man is broad, too broad, indeed. I'd have him narrower. The devil only knows what to make of it! What to the mind is shameful is beauty and nothing else to the heart. Is there beauty in Sodom? Believe me, that for the immense mass of mankind beauty is found in Sodom. Did you know that secret? The awful thing is that beauty is mysterious as well

106

as terrible. God and the devil are fighting there and the battle-field is the heart of man. But a man always talks of his own ache. Listen, now to come to facts.''

CHAPTER IV

THE CONFESSION OF A PASSIONATE HEART—IN ANECDOTE

"I WAS leading a wild life then. Father said just now that I spent several thousand roubles in seducing young girls. That's a swinish invention, and there was nothing of the sort. And if there was, I didn't need money simply for *that*. With me money is an accessory, the overflow of my heart, the frame-work. To-day she would be my lady, to-morrow a wench out of the streets in her place. I entertained them both. I threw away money by the handful on music, rioting, and gipsies. Sometimes I gave it to the ladies, too, for they'll take it greedily, that must be admitted, and be pleased and thankful for it. Ladies used to be fond of me; not all of them, but it happened, it happened. But I always liked side-paths, little dark back-alleys behind the main road—there one finds adventures and surprises, and precious metal in the dirt. I am speaking figuratively, brother. In the town I was in, there were no such back-alleys in the literal sense, but morally there were. If you were like me, you'd know what that means. I loved vice, I loved the ignominy of vice. I loved cruelty; am I not a bug, am I not a noxious insect? In fact, Karamazov! Once we went, a whole lot of us, for a picnic, in seven sledges. It was dark, it was winter, and I began squeezing a girl's hand, and forced her to kiss me. She was the daughter of an official, a sweet, gentle, submissive creature. She allowed me, she allowed me much in the dark. She thought, poor thing, that I should come next day to make her an offer. (I was looked upon as a good match, too.) But I didn't say a word to her for five months. I used to see her in a corner at dances (we were always having dances), her eyes watching me. I saw how they glowed with fire—a fire of gentle indignation. This game only tickled that insect lust I cherished in my soul. Five months later she married an official and left the town, still angry, and still, perhaps, in love with me. Now they live happily. Observe that I told no one. I didn't boast of it. Though I'm full of low desires, and love what's low, I'm not dishonourable. You're blushing; your eyes flashed. Enough

107

of this filth with you. And all this was nothing much—wayside blossoms *à la* Paul de Kock—though the cruel insect had already grown strong in my soul. I've a perfect album of reminiscences, brother. God bless them, the darlings. I tried to break it off without quarrelling. And I never gave them away. I never bragged of one of them. But that's enough. You can't suppose I brought you here simply to talk of such nonsense. No, I'm going to tell you something more curious; and don't be surprised that I'm glad to tell you, instead of being ashamed.''

"You say that because I blushed," Alyosha said suddenly. "I wasn't blushing at what you were saying or at what you've done. I blushed because I am the same as you are."

"You? Come, that's going a little too far!"

"No, it's not too far," said Alyosha warmly (obviously the idea was not a new one). "The ladder's the same. I'm at the bottom step, and you're above, somewhere about the thirteenth. That's how I see it. But it's all the same. Absolutely the same in kind. Anyone on the bottom step is bound to go up to the top one."

"Then one ought not to step on at all."

"Anyone who can help it had better not."

"But can you?"

"I think not."

"Hush, Alyosha, hush, darling! I could kiss your hand, you touch me so. That rogue Grushenka has an eye for men. She told me once that she'd devour you one day. There, there, I won't! From this field of corruption fouled by flies, let's pass to my tragedy, also befouled by flies, that is by every sort of vileness. Although the old man told lies about my seducing innocence, there really was something of the sort in my tragedy, though it was only once, and then it did not come off. The old man who has reproached me with what never happened does not even know of this fact; I never told anyone about it. You're the first, except Ivan, of course—Ivan knows everything. He knew about it long before you. But Ivan's a tomb."

"Ivan's a tomb?"

"Yes."

Alyosha listened with great attention.

"I was lieutenant in a line regiment, but still I was under supervision, like a kind of convict. Yet I was awfully well received in the little town. I spent money right and left. I was thought to be rich; I thought so myself. But I must have pleased them in other ways as well. Although they shook their heads over me, they liked me. My colonel, who was an old man, took a sudden dislike to me. He was always down upon me, but I had powerful friends, and, moreover, all the town was on my side, so he couldn't do me much harm. I was in fault myself for refusing to treat him with proper respect. I was proud. This obstinate old fellow, who was really a very good sort, kind-hearted and hospitable, had had two wives, both dead. His first wife, who was of a humble family, left a daughter as unpretentious as herself. She was a young woman of four-and-twenty when I was there, and was living with her father and an aunt, her mother's sister. The aunt was simple and illiterate; the niece was simple but lively. I like to say nice things about people. I never knew a woman of more charming character than Agafya—fancy, her name was Agafya Ivanovna! And she wasn't bad-looking either, in the Russian style: tall, stout, with a full figure, and beautiful eyes, though a rather coarse face. She had not married, although she had had two suitors. She refused them, but was as cheerful as ever. I was intimate with her, not in 'that' way, it was pure friendship. I have often been friendly with women quite innocently. I used to talk to her with shocking frankness, and she only laughed. Many women like such freedom, and she was a girl too, which made it very amusing. Another thing, one could never think of her as a young lady. She and her aunt lived in her father's house with a sort of voluntary humility, not putting themselves on an equality with other people. She was a general favourite, and of use to everyone, for she was a clever dressmaker. She had a talent for it. She gave her services freely without asking for payment, but if anyone offered her payment she didn't refuse. The colonel, of course, was a very different matter. He was one of the chief personages in the district. He kept open house, entertained the whole town, gave suppers and dances. At the time I arrived and joined the battalion all the town was talking of the expected return of the colonel's second daughter, a great beauty, who had just left a fashionable school in the capital. This second daughter is Katerina Ivanovna, and she was the child of the second wife, who belonged to a distinguished general's family; although, as I learnt on good authority, she too brought the colonel no money. She had connections, and that was all. There may have been expectations, but they had come to nothing.

"Yet, when the young lady came from boarding-school on a visit, the whole town revived. Our most distinguished ladies—

two 'Excellencies' and a colonel's wife—and all the rest following their lead, at once took her up and gave entertainments in her honour. She was the belle of the balls and picnics, and they got up *tableaux vivants* in aid of distressed governesses I took no notice, I went on as wildly as before, and one of my exploits at the time set all the town talking. I saw her eyes taking my measure one evening at the battery commander's, but I didn't go up to her, as though I disdained her acquaintance. I did go up and speak to her at an evening party not long after. She scarcely looked at me, and compressed her lips scornfully. 'Wait a bit. I'll have my revenge,' thought I. I behaved like an awful fool on many occasions at that time, and I was conscious of it myself. What made it worse was that I felt that 'Katenka' was not an innocent boarding-house miss but a person of character, proud and really high-principled; above all, she had education and intellect, and I had neither. You think I meant to make her an offer? No, I simply wanted to avenge myself, because I was such a hero and she didn't seem to feel it.

"Meanwhile, I spent my time in drink and riot, till the lieutenant-colonel put me under arrest for three days. Just at that time father sent me six thousand roubles in return for my sending him a deed giving up all claims upon him—settling our accounts, so to speak, and saying that I wouldn't expect anything more. I didn't understand a word of it at the time. Until I came here, Alyosha, till the last few days, indeed, perhaps even now, I haven't been able to make head or tail of my money affairs with father. But never mind that, we'll talk of it later.

"Just as I received the money, I got a letter from a friend telling me something that interested me immensely. The authorities, I learnt, were dissatisfied with our lieutenant-colonel. He was suspected of irregularities; in fact, his enemies were preparing a surprise for him. And then the commander of the division arrived, and kicked up the devil of a shindy. Shortly afterwards he was ordered to retire. I won't tell you how it all happened. He had enemies, certainly. Suddenly there was a marked coolness in the town towards him and all his family. His friends all turned their backs on him. Then I took my first step. I met Agafya Ivanovna, with whom I'd always kept up a friendship, and said: 'Do you know there's a deficit of 4500 roubles of government money in your father's accounts?'

" 'What do you mean? What makes you say so? The general was here not long ago, and everything was all right.'

" 'Then it was, but now it isn't.'

"She was terribly scared.

" 'Don't frighten me!' she said. 'Who told you so?'

" 'Don't be uneasy,' I said, 'I won't tell anyone. You know I'm as silent as the tomb. I only wanted, in view of "possibilities", to add that when they demand that 4500 roubles from your father, and he can't produce it, he'll be tried, and made to serve as a common soldier in his old age, unless you like to send me your young lady secretly. I've just had money paid me. I'll give her four thousand, if you like, and keep the secret religiously.'

" 'Ah, you scoundrel!' That's what she said. 'You wicked scoundrel! How dare you!'

"She went away furiously indignant, while I shouted after her once more that the secret should be kept sacred. Those two simple creatures, Agafya and her aunt, I may as well say at once, behaved like perfect angels all through this business. They genuinely adored their 'Katya', thought her far above them, and waited on her hand and foot. But Agafya told her of our conversation. I found that out afterwards. She didn't keep it back, and of course that was all I wanted.

"Suddenly the new major arrived to take command of the battalion. The old lieutenant-colonel was taken ill at once, couldn't leave his room for two days, and didn't hand over the government money. Dr. Kravchenko declared that he really was ill. But I knew for a fact, and had known for a long time, that for the last four years the money had never been in his hands except when the Commander made his visits of inspection. He used to lend it to a trustworthy person, a merchant of our town called Trifonov, an old widower, with a big beard and gold-rimmed spectacles. He used to go to the fair, do a profitable business with the money, and return the whole sum to the colonel, bringing with it a present from the fair, as well as interest on the loan. But this time (I heard all about it quite by chance from Trifonov's son and heir, a drivelling youth and one of the most vicious in the world)—this time, I say, Trifonov brought nothing back from the fair. The lieutenant-colonel flew to him. 'I've never received any money from you, and couldn't possibly have received any.' That was all the answer he got. So now our lieutenant-colonel is confined to the house, with a towel round his head, while they're all three busy putting ice on it. All at once an orderly arrives on the scene with the book and the order to 'hand over the battalion money immediately, within two hours'. He signed the book (I saw the signature in

111

the book afterwards), stood up, saying he would put on his uniform, ran to his bedroom, loaded his double-barrelled gun with a service bullet, took the boot off his right foot, fixed the gun against his chest, and began feeling for the trigger with his foot. But Agafya, remembering what I had told her, had her suspicions. She stole up and peeped into the room just in time. She rushed in, flung herself upon him from behind, threw her arms round him, and the gun went off, hit the ceiling, but hurt no one. The others ran in, took away the gun, and held him by the arms. I heard all about this afterwards. I was at home, it was getting dusk, and I was just preparing to go out. I had dressed, brushed my hair, scented my handkerchief, and taken up my cap, when suddenly the door opened, and facing me in the room stood Katerina Ivanovna.

"It's strange how things happen sometimes. No one had seen her in the street, so that no one knew of it in the town. I lodged with two decrepit old ladies, who looked after me. They were most obliging old things, ready to do anything for me, and at my request were as silent afterwards as two cast-iron posts. Of course I grasped the position at once. She walked in and looked straight at me, her dark eyes determined, even defiant, but on her lips and round her mouth I saw uncertainty.

" 'My sister told me,' she began, 'that you would give me 4500 roubles if I came to you for it—myself. I have come . . . give me the money!'

"She couldn't keep it up. She was breathless, frightened, her voice failed her, and the corners of her mouth and the lines round it quivered. Alyosha, are you listening, or are you asleep?"

"Mitya, I know you will tell the whole truth," said Alyosha in agitation.

"I am telling it. If I tell the whole truth just as it happened I shan't spare myself. My first idea was a—Karamazov one. Once I was bitten by a centipede, brother, and laid up a fortnight with fever from it. Well, I felt a centipede biting at my heart then—a noxious insect, you understand? I looked her up and down. You've seen her? She's a beauty. But she was beautiful in another way then. At that moment she was beautiful because she was noble, and I was a scoundrel; she in all the grandeur of her generosity and sacrifice for her father, and I— a bug! And, scoundrel as I was, she was altogether at my mercy, body and soul. She was hemmed in. I tell you frankly, that thought, that venomous thought, so possessed my heart

that it almost swooned with suspense. It seemed as if there could be no resisting it; as though I should act like a bug, like a venomous spider, without a spark of pity. I could scarcely breathe. Understand, I should have gone next day to ask for her hand, so that it might end honourably, so to speak, and that nobody would or could know. For though I'm a man of base desires, I'm honest. And at that very second some voice seemed to whisper in my ear: 'But when you come to-morrow to make your proposal, that girl won't even see you; she'll order her coachman to kick you out of the yard. "Publish it through all the town," she would say, "I'm not afraid of you." ' I looked at the young lady, my voice had not deceived me. That is how it would be, not a doubt of it. I could see from her face now that I should be turned out of the house. My spite was roused. I longed to play her the nastiest swinish cad's trick: to look at her with a sneer, and on the spot where she stood before me to stun her with a tone of voice that only a shopman could use.

" 'Four thousand! What do you mean? I was joking. You've been counting your chickens too easily, madam. Two hundred, if you like, with all my heart. But four thousand is not a sum to throw away on such frivolity. You've put yourself out to no purpose.'

"I should have lost the game, of course. She'd have run away. But it would have been an infernal revenge. It would have been worth it all. I'd have howled with regret all the rest of my life, only to have played that trick. Would you believe it, it has never happened to me with any other woman, not one, to look at her at such a moment with hatred. But, on my oath, I looked at her for three seconds, or five perhaps, with fearful hatred—that hate which is only a hair's-breadth from love, from the maddest love!

"I went to the window, put my forehead against the frozen pane, and I remember the ice burnt my forehead like fire. I did not keep her long, don't be afraid. I turned round, went up to the table, opened the drawer and took out a banknote for five thousand roubles (it was lying in a French dictionary). Then I showed it her in silence, folded it, handed it to her, opened the door into the passage, and, stepping back, made her a deep bow, a most respectful, a most impressive bow, believe me! She shuddered all over, gazed at me for a second, turned horribly pale—white as a sheet, in fact—and all at once, not impetuously but softly, gently, bowed down to my feet—not a

113

boarding-school curtsey but a Russian bow, with her forehead to the floor. She jumped up and ran away. I was wearing my sword. I drew it and nearly stabbed myself with it on the spot; why, I don't know. It would have been frightfully stupid, of course. I suppose it was from delight. Can you understand that one might kill oneself from delight? But I didn't stab myself. I only kissed my sword and put it back in the scabbard—which there was no need to have told you, by the way. And I fancy that in telling you about my inner conflict I have laid it on rather thick to glorify myself. But let it pass, and to hell with all who pry into the human heart! Well, so much for that 'adventure' with Katerina Ivanovna. So now Ivan knows of it, and you—no one else."

Dmitri got up, took a step or two in his excitement, pulled out his handkerchief and mopped his forehead, then sat down again, not in the same place as before, but on the opposite side, so that Alyosha had to turn quite round to face him.

CHAPTER V

THE CONFESSION OF A PASSIONATE HEART—"HEELS UP"

"NOW," said Alyosha, "I understand the first half."

"You understand the first half. That half is a drama, and it was played out there. The second half is a tragedy, and it is being acted here."

"And I understand nothing of that second half so far," said Alyosha.

"And I? Do you suppose I understand it?"

"Stop, Dmitri. There's one important question. Tell me, you were betrothed, you are betrothed still?"

"We weren't betrothed at once, not for three months after that adventure. The next day I told myself that the incident was closed, concluded, that there would be no sequel. It seemed to me caddish to make her an offer. On her side she gave no sign of life for the six weeks that she remained in the town; except, indeed, for one action. The day after her visit the maid-servant slipped round with an envelope addressed to me. I tore it open; it contained the change out of the banknote. Only 4500 was needed, but there was a discount of about 200 on changing it. She only sent me about 260 roubles, I don't remember exactly, but not a note, not a word of explanation. I searched the packet for a pencil mark—n-nothing! Well, I spent the rest of the money on such an orgy that the new major was obliged to reprimand me.

"Well, the lieutenant-colonel produced the battalion money, to the astonishment of everyone, for nobody believed that he had the money untouched. He'd no sooner paid it than he fell ill, took to his bed, and, three weeks later, softening of the brain set in, and he died five days afterwards. He was buried with military honours, for he had not had time to receive his discharge. Ten days after his funeral, Katerina Ivanovna, with her aunt and sister, went to Moscow. And, behold, on the very day they went away (I hadn't seen them, didn't see them off or take leave) I received a tiny note, a sheet of thin blue paper, and on it only one line in pencil: 'I will write to you. Wait. K.' And that was all.

"I'll explain the rest now, in two words. In Moscow their fortunes changed with the swiftness of lightning and the unexpectedness of an Arabian fairy tale. That general's widow, their nearest relation, suddenly lost the two nieces who were her heiresses and next-of-kin—both died in the same week of smallpox. The old lady, prostrated with grief, welcomed Katya as a daughter, as her one hope, clutched at her, altered her will in Katya's favour. But that concerned the future. Meanwhile she gave her, for present use, eighty thousand roubles, as a marriage portion, to do what she liked with. She was an hysterical woman. I saw something of her in Moscow, later.

"Well, suddenly I received by post four thousand five hundred roubles. I was speechless with surprise, as you may suppose. Three days later came the promised letter. I have it with me now. I always keep it, and shall keep it till I die. Shall I show you? You must read it. She offers to be my wife, offers herself to me. 'I love you madly,' she says, 'even if you don't love me, never mind. Be my husband. Don't be afraid. I won't hamper you in any way. I will be your chattel. I will be the carpet under your feet. I want to love you for ever. I want to save you from yourself.' Alyosha, I am not worthy to repeat those lines in my vulgar words and in my vulgar tone, my everlastingly vulgar tone, that I can never cure myself of. That letter stabs me even now. Do you think I don't mind—that I don't mind still? I wrote her an answer at once, as it was impossible for me to go to Moscow. I wrote to her with tears. One thing I shall be ashamed of for ever. I referred to her being rich and having a dowry while I was only a stuck-up beggar! I mentioned money! I ought to have borne it in silence, but it slipped from my pen. Then I wrote at once to Ivan, and told him all I could about it in a letter of six pages, and sent him to her. Why do you look like that? Why are you staring at me? Yes, Ivan fell in love with her; he's in love with her still. I know that. I did a stupid thing, in the world's opinion; but perhaps that one stupid thing may be the saving of us all now. Oo! Don't you see what a lot she thinks of Ivan, how she respects him? When she compares us, do you suppose she can love a man like me, especially after all that has happened here?''

"But I'm convinced that she does love a man like you, and not a man like him."

"She loves her own *virtue*, not me." The words broke involuntarily, and almost malignantly, from Dmitri. He laughed, but a minute later his eyes gleamed, he flushed crimson and struck the table violently with his fist.

"I swear, Alyosha," he cried, with intense and genuine anger at himself; "you may not believe me, but as God is holy, and as Christ is God, I swear that though I smiled at her lofty sentiments just now, I know that I am a million times baser in soul than she, and that these lofty sentiments of hers are as sincere as a heavenly angel's. That's the tragedy of it—that I know that for certain. What if anyone does show off a bit? Don't I do it myself? And yet I'm sincere, I'm sincere. As for Ivan, I can understand how he must be cursing nature now—with his intellect, too! To see the preference given—to whom, to what? To a monster who, though he is betrothed and all eyes are fixed on him, can't restrain his debaucheries—and before the very eyes of his betrothed! And a man like me is preferred, while he is rejected. And why? Because a girl wants to sacrifice her life and destiny out of gratitude. It's ridiculous! I've never said a word of this to Ivan, and Ivan of course has never dropped a hint of the sort to me. But destiny will be accomplished, and the best man will hold his ground while the undeserving one will vanish into his back-alley for ever—his filthy back-alley, his beloved back-alley, where he is at home and where he will sink in filth and stench at his own free will and with enjoyment. I've been talking foolishly. I've no words left. I use them at random, but it will be as I have said. I shall drown in the back-alley, and she will marry Ivan.''

"Stop, Dmitri," Alyosha interrupted again with great anxiety. "There's one thing you haven't made clear yet: you are still betrothed all the same, aren't you? How can you break off the engagement if she, your betrothed, doesn't want to?"

"Yes, formally and solemnly betrothed. It was all done on my arrival in Moscow, with great ceremony, with ikons, all in fine style. The general's wife blessed us, and—would you believe it?—congratulated Katya. 'You've made a good choice,' she said, 'I see right through him.' And—would you believe it?—she didn't like Ivan and hardly greeted him. I had a lot of talk with Katya in Moscow. I told her about myself—sincerely, honourably. She listened to everything.

> *There was sweet confusion,*
> *There were tender words.*

Though there were proud words, too. She wrung out of me a mighty promise to reform. I gave my promise, and here——"

"What?"

"Why, I called to you and brought you out here to-day, this very day—remember it—to send you—this very day again—to Katerina Ivanovna, and——"

"What?"

"To tell her that I shall never come to see her again. Say 'He sends you his compliments'."

"But is that possible?"

"That's just the reason I'm sending you, in my place, because it's impossible. And, how could I tell her myself?"

"And where are you going?"

"To the back-alley."

"To Grushenka then!" Alyosha exclaimed mournfully, clasping his hands. "Can Rakitin really have told the truth? I thought that you had just visited her, and that was all."

"Can a betrothed man pay such visits? Is such a thing possible and with such a betrothed, and before the eyes of all the world? Confound it, I have some honour! As soon as I began visiting Grushenka, I ceased to be betrothed, and to be an honest man. I understand that. Why do you look at me? You see, I went in the first place to beat her. I had heard, and I know for a fact now, that that captain, father's agent, had given Grushenka an I O U of mine for her to sue me for payment, so as to put an end to me. They wanted to scare me. I went to beat her. I had had a glimpse of her before. She doesn't strike one at first sight. I knew about her old merchant, who's lying ill now, paralysed; but he's leaving her a decent little sum. I knew, too, that she was fond of money, that she hoarded it, and lent it at a wicked rate of interest, that she's a merciless cheat and swindler. I went to beat her, and I stayed. The storm broke—it struck me down like the plague. I'm plague-stricken still, and I know that everything is over, that there will never be anything more for me. The cycle of the ages is accomplished. That's my position. And though I'm a beggar, as fate would have it, I had three thousand just then in my pocket. I drove with Grushenka to Mokroe, a place twenty-five versts from here. I got gypsies there and champagne and made all the peasants there drunk on it, and all the women and girls. I sent the thousands flying. In three days' time I was stripped bare, but a hero. Do you suppose the hero had gained his end? Not a sign of it from her. I tell you that rogue, Grushenka, has a supple curve all over her body. You can see it in her little foot, even in her little toe. I saw it, and kissed it, but that was all, I swear! 'I'll marry you if you like,' she said, 'you're a beggar, you know. Say that you won't beat me, and will let me do anything I choose, and perhaps I will marry you.' She laughed, and she's laughing still!"

Dmitri leapt up with a sort of fury. He seemed all at once as though he were drunk. His eyes became suddenly bloodshot.

"And do you really mean to marry her?"

"At once, if she will. And if she won't, I shall stay all the same. I'll be the porter at her gate. Alyosha!" he cried. He stopped short before him, and taking him by the shoulders began shaking him violently. "Do you know, you innocent boy, that this is all delirium, senseless delirium, for there's a tragedy here. Let me tell you, Alexey, that I may be a low man, with low and degraded passions, but a thief and a pickpocket Dmitri Karamazov never can be. Well, then; let me tell you that I am a thief and a pickpocket. That very morning, just before I went to beat Grushenka, Katerina Ivanovna sent for me, and in strict secrecy (why I don't know, I suppose she had some reason) asked me to go to the chief town of the province and to post three thousand roubles to Agafya Ivanovna in Moscow, so that nothing should be known of it in the town here. So I had that three thousand roubles in my pocket when I went to see Grushenka, and it was that money we spent at Mokroe. Afterwards I pretended I had been to the town, but did not show her the post-office receipt. I said I had sent the money and would bring the receipt, and so far I haven't brought it. I've forgotten it. Now what do you think you're going to her to-day to say, 'He sends his compliments,' and she'll ask you, 'What about the money?' You might still have said to her, 'He's a degraded sensualist, and a low creature, with uncontrolled passions. He didn't send your money then, but wasted it, because, like a low brute, he couldn't control himself.' But still you might have added, 'He isn't a thief though. Here is your three thousand; he sends it back. Send it yourself to Agafya Ivanovna. But he told me to say, "He sends his compliments".' But, as it is, she will ask, 'But where is the money?'"

"Mitya, you are unhappy, yes! But not as unhappy as you think. Don't worry yourself to death with despair."

"What, do you suppose I'd shoot myself because I can't get three thousand to pay back? That's just it. I shan't shoot myself. I haven't the strength now. Afterwards, perhaps. But now I'm going to Grushenka. I don't care what happens."

"And what then?"

"I'll be her husband if she deigns to have me, and when lovers come, I'll go into the next room. I'll clean her friends' goloshes, blow up their samovar, run their errands."

"Katerina Ivanovna will understand it all," Alyosha said solemnly. "She'll understand how great this trouble is and will forgive. She has a lofty mind, and no one could be more unhappy than you. She'll see that for herself."

"She won't forgive everything," said Dmitri, with a grin. "There's something in it, brother, that no woman could forgive. Do you know what would be the best thing to do?"

"What?"

"Pay back the three thousand."

"Where can we get it from? I say, I have two thousand. Ivan will give you another thousand—that makes three. Take it and pay it back."

"And when would you get it, your three thousand? You're not of age, besides, and you must—you absolutely must—take my farewell to her to-day, with the money or without it, for I can't drag on any longer, things have come to such a pass. To-morrow is too late. I shall send you to father."

"To father?"

"Yes, to father first. Ask him for three thousand."

"But, Mitya, he won't give it."

"As though he would! I know he won't. Do you know the meaning of despair, Alexey?"

119

"Yes."

"Listen. Legally he owes me nothing. I've had it all from him, I know that. But morally he owes me something, doesn't he? You know he started with twenty-eight thousand of my mother's money and made a hundred thousand with it. Let him give me back only three out of the twenty-eight thousand, and he'll draw my soul out of hell, and it will atone for many of his sins. For that three thousand—I give you my solemn word —I'll make an end of everything, and he shall hear nothing more of me. For the last time I give him the chance to be a father. Tell him God Himself sends him this chance."

"Mitya, he won't give it for anything."

"I know he won't. I know it perfectly well. Now, especially. That's not all. I know something more. Now, only a few days ago, perhaps only yesterday he found out for the first time *in earnest* (underline *in earnest*) that Grushenka is really perhaps not joking, and really means to marry me. He knows her nature; he knows the cat. And do you suppose he's going to give me money to help to bring that about when he's crazy about her himself? And that's not all, either. I can tell you more than that. I know that for the last five days he has had three thousand drawn out of the bank, changed into notes of a hundred roubles, packed into a large envelope, sealed with five seals, and tied across with red tape. You see how well I know all about it! On the envelope is written: 'To my angel, Grushenka, when she will come to me.' He scrawled it himself in silence and in secret, and no one knows that the money's there except the valet, Smerdyakov, whom he trusts like himself. So now he has been expecting Grushenka for the last three or four days; he hopes she'll come for the money. He has sent her word of it, and she has sent him word that perhaps she'll come. And if she does go to the old man, can I marry her after that? You understand now why I'm here in secret and what I'm on the watch for."

"For her?"

"Yes, for her. Foma has a room in the house of these sluts here. Foma comes from our parts; he was a soldier in our regiment. He does jobs for them. He's watchman at night and goes grouse shooting in the day-time; and that's how he lives. I've established myself in his room. Neither he nor the women of the house know the secret—that is, that I am on the watch here."

"No one but Smerdyakov knows, then?"

"No one else. He will let me know if she goes to man."

"It was he told you about the money, then?"

"Yes. It's a dead secret. Even Ivan doesn't know about the money, or anything. The old man is sending Ivan to Tchermashnya on a two or three days' journey. A purchaser has turned up for the copse: he'll give eight thousand for the timber. So the old man keeps asking Ivan to help him by going to arrange it. It will take him two or three days. That's what the old man wants, so that Grushenka can come while he's away."

"Then he's expecting Grushenka to-day?"

"No, she won't come to-day; there are signs. She's certain not to come," cried Mitya suddenly. "Smerdyakov thinks so, too. Father's drinking now. He's sitting at table with Ivan. Go to him, Alyosha, and ask for the three thousand."

"Mitya, dear, what's the matter with you?" cried Alyosha, jumping up from his place, and looking keenly at his brother's frenzied face. For one moment the thought struck him that Dmitri was mad.

"What is it? I'm not insane," said Dmitri, looking intently and earnestly at him. "No fear. I am sending you to father, and I know what I'm saying. I believe in miracles."

"In miracles?"

"In a miracle of Divine Providence. God knows my heart. He sees my despair. He sees the whole picture. Surely He won't let something awful happen. Alyosha, I believe in miracles. Go!"

"I am going. Tell me, will you wait for me here?"

"Yes. I know it will take some time. You can't go at him point-blank. He's drunk now. I'll wait three hours—four, five, six, seven. Only remember you must go to Katerina Ivanovna to-day, if it has to be at midnight, *with the money or without the money*, and say, 'He sends his compliments to you'. I want you to say that verse to her: 'He sends his compliments to you.'"

"Mitya! And what if Grushenka comes to-day—if not to-day, to-morrow, or the next day?"

"Grushenka? I shall see her. I shall rush out and prevent it."

"And if——?"

"If there's an 'if' it will be murder. I couldn't endure it."

"Who will be murdered?"

"The old man. I shan't kill her."

"Brother, what are you saying?"

"Oh, I don't know. . . . I don't know. Perhaps I shan't kill him, and perhaps I shall. I'm afraid that he will suddenly become so loathsome to me with his face at that moment. I hate his ugly throat, his nose, his eyes, his shameless snigger. I feel a physical repulsion. That's what I'm afraid of. That's what may be too much for me."

"I'll go, Mitya. I believe that God will order things for the best, that nothing awful may happen."

"And I will sit and wait for the miracle. And if it doesn't come to pass——"

Alyosha went thoughtfully towards his father's house.

CHAPTER VI

SMERDYAKOV

HE did in fact find his father still at table. Though there was a dining-room in the house, the table was laid as usual in the drawing-room, which was the largest room, and furnished with old-fashioned ostentation. The furniture was white and very old, upholstered in old, red, silky material. In the spaces between the windows there were mirrors in elaborate white and gilt frames, of old-fashioned carving. On the walls, covered with white paper, which was torn in many places, there hung two large portraits—one of some prince who had been governor of the district thirty years before, and the other of some bishop, also long since dead. In the corner opposite the door there were several ikons, before which a lamp was lighted at nightfall . . . not so much for devotional purposes as to light the room. Fyodor Pavlovitch used to go to bed very late, at three or four o'clock in the morning, and would wander about the room at night or sit in an armchair, thinking. This had become a habit with him. He often slept quite alone in the house, sending his servants to the lodge; but usually Smerdyakov remained, sleeping on a bench in the hall.

When Alyosha came in, dinner was over, but coffee and preserves had been served. Fyodor Pavlovitch liked sweet things with brandy after dinner. Ivan was also at table, sipping coffee. The servants, Grigory and Smerdyakov, were standing by. Both the gentlemen and the servants seemed in singularly good spirits. Fyodor Pavlovitch was roaring with laughter. Before he entered the room, Alyosha heard the shrill laugh he knew so well, and could tell from the sound of it that his father had only reached the good-humoured stage, and was far from being completely drunk.

"Here he is! Here he is!" yelled Fyodor Pavlovitch, highly delighted at seeing Alyosha. "Join us. Sit down. Coffee is a lenten dish, but it's hot and good. I don't offer you brandy, you're keeping the fast. But would you like some? No; I'd better give you some of our famous liqueur. Smerdyakov, go to the cupboard, the second shelf on the right. Here are the keys. Look sharp!"

Alyosha began refusing the liqueur.

"Never mind. If you won't have it, we will," said Fyodor Pavlovitch, beaming. "But stay—have you dined?"

"Yes," answered Alyosha, who had in truth only eaten a piece of bread and drunk a glass of kvass in the Father Superior's kitchen. "Though I should be pleased to have some hot coffee."

"Bravo, my darling! He'll have some coffee. Does it want warming? No, it's boiling. It's capital coffee: Smerdyakov's making. My Smerdyakov's an artist at coffee and at fish patties, and at fish soup, too. You must come one day and have some fish soup. Let me know beforehand. . . . But, stay, didn't I tell you this morning to come home with your mattress and pillow and all? Have you brought your mattress? He, he, he!"

"No, I haven't," said Alyosha, smiling, too.

"Ah, but you were frightened, you were frightened this morning, weren't you? There, my darling, I couldn't do anything to vex you. Do you know, Ivan, I can't resist the way he looks one straight in the face and laughs? It makes me laugh all over. I'm so fond of him. Alyosha, let me give you my blessing—a father's blessing."

Alyosha rose, but Fyodor Pavlovitch had already changed his mind.

"No, no," he said, "I'll just make the sign of the cross over you, for now. Sit still. Now we've a treat for you, in your own line, too. It'll make you laugh. Balaam's ass has begun talking to us here—and how he talks! How he talks!"

Balaam's ass, it appeared, was the valet, Smerdyakov. He was a young man of about four-and-twenty, remarkably unsociable and taciturn. Not that he was shy or bashful. On the contrary, he was conceited and seemed to despise everybody. But we must pause to say a few words about him now. He was brought up by Grigory and Marfa, but the boy grew up "with no sense of gratitude", as Grigory expressed it; he was an unfriendly boy, and seemed to look at the world mistrustfully. In his childhood he was very fond of hanging cats, and burying them with great ceremony. He used to dress up in a sheet as though it were a surplice, and sang, and waved some object over the dead cat as though it were a censer. All this he did on the sly, with the greatest secrecy. Grigory caught him once at this diversion and gave him a sound beating. He shrank into a corner and sulked there for a week. "He doesn't care for you or me, the monster," Grigory used to say to Marfa, "and he doesn't care for anyone. Are you a human being?" he said, addressing the boy directly. "You're not a human being. You grew from the mildew in the bath-house.* That's what you are." Smerdyakov, it appeared afterwards, could never forgive him those words. Grigory taught him to read and write, and when he was twelve years old began teaching him the Scriptures. But this teaching came to nothing. At the second or third lesson the boy suddenly grinned.

"What's that for?" asked Grigory, looking at him threateningly from under his spectacles.

"Oh, nothing. God created light on the first day, and the sun, moon, and stars on the fourth day. Where did the light come from on the first day?"

Grigory was thunderstruck. The boy looked sarcastically at his teacher. There was something positively condescending in his expression. Grigory could not restrain himself. "I'll show you where!" he cried, and gave the boy a violent slap on the cheek. The boy took the slap without a word, but withdrew into his corner again for some days. A week later he had his first attack of the disease to which he was subject all the rest of his life—epilepsy. When Fyodor Pavlovitch heard of it, his attitude to the boy seemed changed at once. Till then he had taken no notice of him, though he never scolded him, and always gave him a copeck when he met him. Sometimes, when he was in good humour, he would send the boy something sweet from his table. But as soon as he heard of his illness, he showed an active interest in him, sent for a doctor, and tried remedies, but the disease turned out to be incurable. The fits occurred, on an average, once a month, but at various intervals. The fits varied, too, in violence: some were light and some were very severe. Fyodor Pavlovitch strictly forbade Grigory to use corporal

* A proverbial expression in Russia.

punishment on the boy and began allowing him to come up-stairs to him. He forbade him to be taught anything whatever for a time, too. One day, when the boy was about fifteen, Fyodor Pavlovitch noticed him lingering by the bookcase, and reading the titles through the glass. Fyodor Pavlovitch had a fair number of books—over a hundred—but no one ever saw him reading. He at once gave Smerdyakov the key of the book-case. "Come, read. You shall be my librarian. You'll be better sitting reading than hanging about the courtyard. Come, read this," and Fyodor Pavlovitch gave him "Evenings in a Cottage near Dikanka".

He read a little, but didn't like it. He did not once smile, and ended by frowning.

"Why? Isn't it funny?" asked Fyodor Pavlovitch.

Smerdyakov did not speak.

"Answer, stupid!"

"It's all untrue," mumbled the boy, with a grin.

"Then go to the devil! You have the soul of a lackey. Stay, here's Smaragdov's 'Universal History'. That's all true. Read that."

But Smerdyakov did not get through ten pages of Smaragdov. He thought it dull. So the bookcase was closed again.

Shortly afterwards Marfa and Grigory reported to Fyodor Pavlovitch that Smerdyakov was gradually beginning to show an extraordinary fastidiousness. He would sit before his soup, take up his spoon and look into the soup, bend over it, examine it, take a spoonful and hold it to the light.

"What is it? A beetle?" Grigory would ask.

"A fly, perhaps," observed Marfa.

The squeamish youth never answered, but he did the same with his bread, his meat, and everything he ate. He would hold a piece on his fork to the light, scrutinise it microscopically, and only after long deliberation decide to put it in his mouth.

"Ach! What fine gentlemen's airs!" Grigory muttered, looking at him.

When Fyodor Pavlovitch heard of this development in Smerdyakov he determined to make him his cook, and sent him to Moscow to be trained. He spent some years there and came back remarkably changed in appearance. He looked extra-ordinarily old for his age. His face had grown wrinkled, yellow, and strangely emasculate. In character he seemed almost exactly the same as before he went away. He was just as unsociable, and showed not the slightest inclination for any companionship. In Moscow, too, as we heard afterwards, he had always been silent. Moscow itself had little interest for him; he saw very little there, and took scarcely any notice of anything. He went once to the theatre, but returned silent and displeased with it. On the other hand, he came back to us from Moscow well dressed, in a clean coat and clean linen. He brushed his clothes most scrupulously twice a day invariably, and was very fond of cleaning his smart calf boots with a special English polish, so that they shone like mirrors. He turned out a first-rate cook. Fyodor Pavlovitch paid him a salary, almost the whole of which Smerdyakov spent on clothes, pomade, perfumes, and such things. But he seemed to have as much contempt for the female sex as for men; he was discreet, almost unapproachable, with them. Fyodor Pavlovitch began to regard him rather differently. His fits were becoming more frequent, and on the days he was ill Marfa cooked, which did not suit Fyodor Pavlovitch at all.

"Why are your fits getting worse?" asked Fyodor Pavlovitch, looking askance at his new cook. "Would you like to get married? Shall I find you a wife?"

But Smerdyakov turned pale with anger, and made no reply. Fyodor Pavlovitch left him with an impatient gesture. The great thing was that he had absolute confidence in his honesty. It happened once, when Fyodor Pavlovitch was drunk, that he dropped in the muddy court-yard three hundred-rouble notes which he had only just received. He only missed them next day, and was just hastening to search his pockets when he saw the notes lying on the table. Where had they come from? Smerdyakov had picked them up and brought them in the day before.

"Well, my lad, I've never met anyone like you," Fyodor Pavlovitch said shortly, and gave him ten roubles. We may add that he not only believed in his honesty but had, for some reason, a liking for him, although the young man looked as morosely at him as at everyone and was always silent. He rarely spoke. If it had occurred to anyone to wonder at the time what the young man was interested in, and what was in his mind, it would have been impossible to tell by looking at him. Yet he used sometimes to stop suddenly in the house, or even in the yard or street, and would stand still for ten minutes, lost in thought. A physiognomist studying his face would have said that there was no thought in it, no reflection, but only a sort of contemplation. There is a remarkable picture by the painter Kramskoy, called "Contemplation". There is a forest in winter, and on a roadway through the forest, in absolute solitude, stands a peasant in a torn kaftan and bark shoes. He stands, as it were, lost in thought. Yet he is not thinking; he is "contemplating". If anyone touched him he would start and look at one as though awakening and bewildered. It's true he would come to himself immediately; but if he were asked what he had been thinking about, he would remember nothing. Yet probably he has hidden within himself the impression which had dominated him during the period of contemplation. Those impressions are dear to him and no doubt he hoards them imperceptibly, and even unconsciously. How and why, of course, he does not know either. He may suddenly, after hoarding impressions for many years, abandon everything and go off to Jerusalem on a pilgrimage for his soul's salvation, or perhaps he will suddenly set fire to his native village, and perhaps do both. There are a good many "contemplatives" among the peasantry. Well, Smerdyakov was probably one of them, and he probably was greedily hoarding up his impressions, hardly knowing why.

CHAPTER VII

THE CONTROVERSY

BUT Balaam's ass had suddenly spoken. The subject was a strange one. Grigory had gone in the morning to make purchases, and had heard from the shopkeeper Lukyanov the story of a Russian soldier which had appeared in the newspaper of that day. This soldier had been taken prisoner in some remote part of Asia, and was threatened with an immediate agonising death if he did not renounce Christianity and follow Islam. He refused to deny his faith, and was tortured, flayed alive, and died, praising and glorifying Christ. Grigory had related the story at table. Fyodor Pavlovitch always liked, over the dessert after dinner, to laugh and talk, if only with Grigory. This afternoon he was in a particularly good-humoured and expansive mood. Sipping his brandy and listening to the story, he observed that they ought to make a saint of a soldier like that, and to take his skin to some monastery. "That would make the people flock, and bring the money in."

Grigory frowned, seeing that Fyodor Pavlovitch was by no

means touched, but, as usual, was beginning to scoff. At that moment Smerdyakov, who was standing by the door, smiled. Smerdyakov often waited at table towards the end of dinner, and since Ivan's arrival in our town he had done so every day.

"What are you grinning at?" asked Fyodor Pavlovitch, catching the smile instantly, and knowing that it referred to Grigory.

"Well, my opinion is," Smerdyakov began suddenly and unexpectedly in a loud voice, "that if that laudable soldier's exploit was so very great there would have been, to my thinking, no sin in it if he had on such an emergency renounced, so to speak, the name of Christ and his own christening, to save by that same his life, for good deeds, by which, in the course of years, to expiate his cowardice."

"How could it not be a sin? You're talking nonsense. For that you'll go straight to hell and be roasted there like mutton,'' put in Fyodor Pavlovitch.

It was at this point that Alyosha came in, and Fyodor Pavlovitch, as we have seen, was highly delighted at his appearance.

"We're on your subject, your subject," he chuckled gleefully, making Alyosha sit down to listen.

"As for mutton, that's not so, and there'll be nothing there for this, and there shouldn't be either, if it's according to justice," Smerdyakov maintained stoutly.

"How do you mean 'according to justice'?" Fyodor Pavlovitch cried still more gaily, nudging Alyosha with his knee.

"He's a rascal, that's what he is!" burst from Grigory. He looked Smerdyakov wrathfully in the face.

"As for being a rascal, wait a little, Grigory Vassilyevitch," answered Smerdyakov with perfect composure. "You'd better consider yourself that, once I am taken prisoner by the enemies of the Christian race, and they demand from me to curse the name of God and to renounce my holy christening, I am fully entitled to act by my own reason, since there would be no sin in it."

"But you've said that before. Don't waste words. Prove it," cried Fyodor Pavlovitch.

"Soup-maker!" muttered Grigory contemptuously.

"As for being a soup-maker, wait a bit, too, and consider for yourself, Grigory Vassilyevitch, without abusing me. For as soon as I say to those enemies, 'No, I'm not a Christian, and I curse my true God', then at once, by God's high judgment, I become immediately and specially anathema accursed, and am cut off from the Holy Church, exactly as though I were a heathen, so that at that very instant, not only when I say it aloud but when I think of saying it, before a quarter of a second has passed, I am cut off. Is that so or not, Grigory Vassilyevitch?''

He addressed Grigory with obvious satisfaction, though he was really answering Fyodor Pavlovitch's questions, and was well aware of it, and intentionally pretending that Grigory had asked the questions.

"Ivan,'' cried Fyodor Pavlovitch suddenly, "stoop down for me to whisper. He's got this all up for your benefit. He wants you to praise him. Praise him.''

Ivan listended with perfect seriousness to his father's excited whisper.

"Stay, Smerdyakov, be quiet a minute,'' cried Fyodor Pavlovitch once more. "Ivan, your ear again.''

Ivan bent down again with a perfectly grave face.,

"I love you as I do Alyosha. Don't think I don't love you. Some brandy?''

"Yes.'' "But you're rather drunk yourself,'' thought Ivan, looking steadily at his father.

He was watching Smerdyakov with great curiosity.

"You're anathema accursed, as it is,'' Grigory suddenly burst out, "and how dare you argue, you rascal, after that, if . . .''

"Don't scold him, Grigory, don't scold him,'' Fyodor Pavlovitch cut him short.

"You should wait, Grigory Vassilyevitch, if only a short time, and listen, for I haven't finished all I had to say. For at the very moment I become accursed, at that same highest moment I become exactly like a heathen, and my christening is taken off me and becomes of no avail. Isn't that so?''

"Make haste and finish, my boy,'' Fyodor Pavlovitch urged him, sipping from his wineglass with relish.

"And if I've ceased to be a Christian, then I told no lie to the enemy when they asked whether I was a Christian or not a Christian, seeing I had already been relieved by God Himself of my Christianity by reason of the thought alone, before I had time to utter a word to the enemy. And if I have already been discharged, in what manner and with what sort of justice can I be held responsible as a Christian in the other world for having denied Christ, when, through the very thought alone, before denying Him I had been relieved from my christening? If I'm no longer a Christian, then I can't renounce Christ, for I've nothing then to renounce. Who will hold an unclean Tatar responsible, Grigory Vassilyevitch, even in heaven, for not having been born a Christian? And who would punish him for that, considering that you can't take two skins off one ox? For God Almighty Himself, even if He did make the Tatar responsible, when he dies would give him the smallest possible punishment, I imagine (since he must be punished), judging that he is not to blame if he has come into the world an unclean heathen, from heathen parents. The Lord God can't surely take a Tatar and say he was a Christian? That would mean that the Almighty would tell a real untruth. And can the Lord of Heaven and earth tell a lie, even in one word?"

Grigory was thunderstruck and looked at the orator, his eyes nearly starting out of his head. Though he did not clearly understand what was said, he had caught something in this rigmarole, and stood, looking like a man who has just hit his head against a wall. Fyodor Pavlovitch emptied his glass and went off into his shrill laugh.

"Alyosha! Alyosha! What do you say to that? Ah, you casuist! He must have been with the Jesuits somewhere, Ivan. Oh, you stinking Jesuits, who taught you? But you're talking nonsense, you casuist, nonsense, nonsense, nonsense. Don't cry, Grigory, we'll reduce him to smoke and ashes in a moment. Tell me this, oh, ass; you may be right before your enemies, but you have renounced your faith all the same in your own heart, and you say yourself that in that very hour you became anathema accursed. And if once you're anathema they won't pat you on the head for it in hell. What do you say to that, my fine Jesuit?"

"There is no doubt that I have renounced it in my own heart, but there was no special sin in that. Or if there was sin, it was the most ordinary."

"How's that the most ordinary?"

"You lie, accursed one!" hissed Grigory.

"Consider yourself, Grigory Vassilyevitch," Smerdyakov went on, staid and unruffled, conscious of his triumph, but, as it were, generous to the vanquished foe. "Consider yourself, Grigory Vassilyevitch; it is said in the Scripture that if you have faith, even as a mustard seed, and bid a mountain move into the sea, it will move without the least delay at your bidding. Well, Grigory Vassilyevitch, if I'm without faith and you have so great a faith that you are continually swearing at me, you

try yourself telling this mountain, not to move into the sea, for that's a long way off, but even to our stinking little river which runs at the bottom of the garden. You'll see for yourself that it won't budge, but will remain just where it is however much you shout at it, and that shows, Grigory Vassilyevitch, that you haven't faith in the proper manner, and only abuse others about it. Again, taking into consideration that no one in our day, not only you but actually no one, from the highest person to the lowest peasant, can shove mountains into the sea—except perhaps some one man in the world, or, at most, two, and they most likely are saving their souls in secret somewhere in the Egyptian desert, so you wouldn't find them—if so it be, if all the rest have no faith, will God curse all the rest? that is, the population of the whole earth, except about two hermits in the desert, and in His well-known mercy will He not forgive one of them? And so I'm persuaded that though I may once have doubted I shall be forgiven if I shed tears of repentance."

"Stay!" cried Fyodor Pavlovitch, in a transport of delight. "So you do suppose there are two who can move mountains? Ivan, make a note of it, write it down. There you have the Russian all over!"

"You're quite right in saying it's characteristic of the people's faith," Ivan assented, with an approving smile.

"You agree. Then it must be so, if you agree. It's true, isn't it, Alyosha? That's the Russian faith all over, isn't it?"

"No, Smerdyakov has not the Russian faith at all," said Alyosha firmly and gravely.

"I'm not talking about his faith. I mean those two in the desert, only that idea. Surely that's Russian, isn't it?"

"Yes, that's purely Russian," said Alyosha smiling.

"Your words are worth a gold piece, oh, ass, and I'll give it to you to-day. But as to the rest you talk nonsense, nonsense, nonsense. Let me tell you, stupid, that we here are all of little faith, only from carelessness, because we haven't time; things are too much for us, and, in the second place, the Lord God has given us so little time, only twenty-four hours in the day, so that one hasn't even time to get sleep enough, much less to repent of one's sins. While you have denied your faith to your enemies when you'd nothing else to think about but how to show your faith! So I consider, brother, that it constitutes a sin."

"Constitute a sin it may, but consider yourself, Grigory Vassilyevitch, that it only extenuates it, if it does constitute. If I had believed then in very truth, as I ought to have believed,

131

then it really would have been sinful if I had not faced tortures for my faith, and have gone over to the pagan Mohammedan faith. But, of course, it wouldn't have come to torture then, because I should only have had to say at that instant to the mountain 'Move and crush the tormentor', and it would have moved and at the very instant have crushed him like a black-beetle, and I should have walked away as though nothing had happened, praising and glorifying God. But, suppose at that very moment I had tried all that, and cried to that mountain, 'Crush these tormentors,' and it hadn't crushed them, how could I have helped doubting, pray, at such a time, and at such a dread hour of mortal terror? And apart from that, I should know already that I could not attain to the fullness of the Kingdom of Heaven (for since the mountain had not moved at my word, they could not think very much of my faith up aloft, and there could be no very great reward awaiting me in the world to come). So why should I let them flay the skin off me as well, and to no good purpose? For even though they had flayed my skin half off my back, even then the mountain would not have moved at my word or at my cry. And at such a moment not only doubt might come over one but one might lose one's reason from fear, so that one would not be able to think at all. And, therefore, how should I be particularly to blame if, not seeing my advantage or reward there or here, I should, at least, save my skin. And so trusting fully in the grace of the Lord I should cherish the hope that I might be altogether forgiven.''

CHAPTER VIII

OVER THE BRANDY

THE controversy was over. But strange to say Fyodor Pavlo-vitch, who had been so gay, suddenly began frowning. He frowned and gulped brandy, and it was already a glass too much.

"Get along with you, Jesuits!" he cried to the servants. "Go away, Smerdyakov. I'll send you the gold piece I promised you to-day, but be off! Don't cry, Grigory. Go to Marfa. She'll comfort you and put you to bed. The rascals won't let us sit in peace after dinner," he snapped peevishly, as the servants promptly withdrew at his word.

"Smerdyakov always pokes himself in now, after dinner. It's

you he's so interested in. What have you done to fascinate him?'' he added to Ivan.

"Nothing whatever,'' answered Ivan. "He's pleased to have a high opinion of me; he's a lackey and a mean soul. Raw material for revolution, however, when the time comes.''

"For revolution?''

"There will be others and better ones. But there will be some iike him as well. His kind will come first, and better ones after.''

"And when will the time come?''

"The rocket will go off and fizzle out, perhaps. The peasants are not very fond of listening to these soup-makers, so far.''

"Ah, brother, but a Balaam's ass like that thinks and thinks, and the devil knows where he gets to.''

"He's storing up ideas,'' said Ivan, smiling.

"You see, I know he can't hear me, nor anyone else, even you, though you fancy that he has a high opinion of me. Worse still with Alyosha, he despises Alyosha. But he doesn't steal, that's one thing, and he's not a gossip; he holds his tongue, and doesn't wash our dirty linen in public. He makes capital fish pasties too. But, damn him, is he worth talking about so much?''

"Of course he isn't.''

"And as for the ideas he may be hatching, the Russian peasant, generally speaking, needs thrashing. That I've always maintained. Our peasants are swindlers, and don't deserve to be pitied, and it's a good thing they're still flogged sometimes. Russia is rich in birches. If they destroyed the forests, it would be the ruin of Russia. I stand up for the clever people. We've left off thrashing the peasants, we've grown so clever, but they go on thrashing themselves. And a good thing too. 'For with what measure ye mete it shall be measured to you again,' or how does it go? Anyhow, it will be measured. But Russia's all swinishness. My dear, if you only knew how I hate Russia. . . . That is, not Russia, but all this vice! But maybe I mean Russia. *Tout cela c'est de la cochonnerie.* . . . Do you know what I like? I like wit.''

"'You've had another glass. That's enough.''

"Wait a bit. I'll have one more, and then another, and then I'll stop. No, stay, you interrupted me. At Mokroe I was talking to an old man, and he told me: 'There's nothing we like so much as sentencing girls to be thrashed, and we always give the lads the job of thrashing them. And the girl he has thrashed to-day, the young man will ask in marriage to-morrow. So it quite suits the girls, too,' he said. There's a set of de Sades for you! But it's clever, anyway. Shall we go over and have a look at it, eh? Alyosha, are you blushing? Don't be bashful, child. I'm sorry I didn't stay to dinner at the Superior's and tell the monks about the girls at Mokroe. Alyosha, don't be angry that I offended your Superior this morning. I lost my temper. If there is a God, if He exists, then, of course, I'm to blame, and I shall have to answer for it. But if there isn't a God at all, what do they deserve, your fathers? It's not enough to cut their heads off, for they keep back progress. Would you believe it, Ivan, that that lacerates my sentiments? No, you don't believe it, as I see from your eyes. You believe what people say, that I'm nothing but a buffoon. Alyosha, do you believe that I'm nothing but a buffoon?"

"No, I don't believe it."

"And I believe you don't, and that you speak the truth. You look sincere and you speak sincerely. But not Ivan. Ivan's supercilious. . . . I'd make an end of your monks, though, all the same. I'd take all the mystic stuff and suppress it, once for all, all over Russia, so as to bring all the fools to reason. And the gold and the silver that would flow into the mint!"

"But why suppress it?" asked Ivan.

"That Truth may prevail. That's why."

"Well, if Truth were to prevail, you know, you'd be the first to be robbed and suppressed."

"Ah! I dare say you're right. Ah, I'm an ass!!" burst out Fyodor Pavlovitch, striking himself lightly on the forehead.

"Well, your monastery may stand then, Alyosha, if that's how it is. And we clever people will sit snug and enjoy our brandy. You know, Ivan, it must have been so ordained by the Almighty Himself. Ivan, speak, is there a God or not? Stay, speak the truth, speak seriously. Why are you laughing again?"

"I'm laughing that you should have made a clever remark just now about Smerdyakov's belief in the existence of two saints who could move mountains."

"Why, am I like him now, then?"

"Very much."

"Well, that shows I'm a Russian, too, and I have a Russian characteristic. And you may be caught in the same way, though you are a philosopher. Shall I catch you? What do you bet that I'll catch you to-morrow? Speak, all the same, is there a God, or not? Only, be serious. I want you to be serious now."

"No, there is no God."

"Alyosha, is there a God?"

"There is."

"Ivan, and is there immortality of some sort, just a little, just a tiny bit?"

"There is no immortality either."

"None at all?"

"None at all."

"There's absolute nothingness then. Perhaps there is just something? Anything is better than nothing!"

"Absolute nothingness."

"Alyosha, is there immortality?"

"There is."

"God and immortality?"

"God and immortality. In God is immortality."

"H'm! It's more likely Ivan's right. Good Lord! To think what faith, what force of all kinds, man has lavished for nothing, on that dream and for how many thousand years. Who is it laughing at man? Ivan! For the last time, once for all, is there a God or not? I ask for the last time!"

"And for the last time there is not."

"Who is laughing at mankind, Ivan?"

"It must be the devil," said Ivan, smiling.

"And the devil? Does he exist?"

"No, there's no devil either."

"It's a pity. Damn it all, what wouldn't I do to the man who first invented God! Hanging on a bitter aspen tree would be too good for him."

"There would have been no civilisation if they hadn't invented God."

"Wouldn't there have been? Without God?"

"No. And there would have been no brandy either. But I must take your brandy away from you, anyway."

"Stop, stop, stop, dear boy, one more little glass. I've hurt Alyosha's feelings. You're not angry with me, Alyosha? My dear little Alexey!"

"No, I am not angry. I know your thoughts. Your heart is better than your head."

"My heart better than my head, is it? Oh Lord! And that from you. Ivan, do you love Alyosha?"

"Yes."

"You must love him." (Fyodor Pavlovitch was by this time very drunk.) "Listen, Alyosha, I was rude to your elder this morning. But I was excited. But there's wit in that elder, don't you think, Ivan?"

"Very likely."

"There is, there is. *Il y a du Piron là-dedans.* He's a Jesuit, a Russian one, that is. As he's an honourable person there's a hidden indignation boiling within him at having to pretend and affect holiness."

"But, of course, he believes in God."

"Not a bit of it. Didn't you know? Why, he tells everyone so, himself. That is, not everyone but all the clever people who come to him. He said straight out to Governor Schultz not long ago: 'Credo, but I don't know in what.' "

"Really?"

"He really did. But I respect him. There's something of Mephistopheles about him, or rather of 'The hero of our time'. . . . Arbenin, or what's his name? . . . You see, he's a sensualist. He's such a sensualist that I should be afraid for my daughter or my wife if she went to confess to him. You know, when he begins telling stories. . . . The year before last he invited us to tea, tea with liqueur (the ladies send him liqueur) and began telling us about old times till we nearly split our sides. . . . Especially how he once cured a paralysed woman. 'If my legs were not bad I know a dance I could dance you,' he said. What do you say to that? 'I've plenty of tricks in my time,' said he. He did Demidov, the merchant, out of sixty-thousand."

"What! he stole it?"

"He brought him the money as a man he could trust, saying: 'Take care of it for me, friend, there'll be a police search at my place to-morrow.' And he kept it. 'You have given it to the Church,' he declared. I said to him: 'You're a scoundrel,' I said. 'No,' said he, 'I'm not a scoundrel, but I'm broad-minded.' But that wasn't he, that was someone else. I've muddled him with someone else . . . without noticing it. Come, another glass and that's enough. Take away the bottle, Ivan. I've been telling lies. Why didn't you stop me, Ivan, and tell me I was lying?"

"I knew you'd stop of yourself."

"That's a lie. You did it from spite, from simple spite against me. You despise me. You have come to me and despised me in my own house."

"Well, I'm going away. You've had too much brandy."

"I've begged you, for Christ's sake, to go to Tchermashnya for a day or two, and you don't go."

"I'll go to-morrow if you're so set upon it."

"You won't go. You wan't to keep an eye on me. That's what you want, spiteful fellow. That's why you won't go."

The old man persisted. He had reached that state of drunkenness when the drunkard who has till then been inoffensive tries to pick a quarrel and to assert himself.

"Why are you looking at me? Why do you look like that? Your eyes look at me and say: 'You ugly drunkard!' Your eyes are mistrustful. They're contemptuous. . . . You've come here with some design. Alyosha, here, looks at me and his eyes shine. Alyosha doesn't despise me. Alexey, you mustn't love Ivan."

"Don't be ill-tempered with my brother. Leave off attacking him," Alyosha said emphatically.

"Oh, all right. Ugh! my head aches. Take away the brandy, Ivan. It's the third time I've told you."

He mused, and suddenly a slow, cunning grin spread over his face.

"Don't be angry with a feeble old man, Ivan. I know you don't love me, but don't be angry all the same. You've nothing to love me for. You go to Tchermashnya. I'll come to you myself and bring you a present. I'll show you a little wench there. I've had my eye on her a long time. She's still running about barefoot. Don't be afraid of barefooted wenches—don't despise them—they're pearls!"

And he kissed his hand with a smack.

"To my thinking," he revived at once, seeming to grow sober the instant he touched on his favourite topic. "To my thinking . . . Ah, you boys! You children, little suckling-pigs, to my thinking . . . I never thought a woman ugly in my life—that's been my rule! Can you understand that? How could you understand it? You've milk in your veins, not blood. You're not out of your shells yet. My rule has been that you can always find something devilishly interesting in every woman that you wouldn't find in any other. Only, one must know how to find it, that's the point! That's a talent! To my mind there are no ugly women. The very fact that she is a woman is half the battle . . . but how could you understand that? Even in *vieilles filles*, even in them you may discover something that makes you simply wonder that men have been such fools as to let them

137

grow old without noticing them. Bare-footed girls or un-attractive ones, you must take by surprise. Didn't you know that? You must astound them till they're fascinated, upset, ashamed that such a gentleman should fall in love with such a little slut. It's a jolly good thing that there always are and will be masters and slaves in the world, so there always will be a little maid-of-all-work and her master, and you know that's all that's needed for happiness. Stay . . . listen, Alyosha, I always used to surprise your mother, but in a different way. I paid no attention to her at all, but all at once, when the minute came, I'd be all devotion to her, crawl on my knees, kiss her feet, and I always, always—I remember it as though it were to-day—re-duced her to that tinkling, quiet, nervous, queer little laugh. It was peculiar to her. I knew her attacks always used to begin like that, the next day she would begin shrieking hysterically, and that this little laugh was not a sign of delight, but it made a very good counterfeit. That's the great thing, to know how to take everyone. Once Belavsky—he was a handsome fellow, and rich—used to like to come here and hang about her—sud-denly gave me a slap in the face in her presence. And she—such a mild sheep—why, I thought she would have knocked me down for that blow. How she set on me! 'You're beaten, beaten now,' she said. 'You've taken a blow from him. You have been trying to sell me to him,' she said. . . . 'And how dared he strike you in my presence! Don't dare come near me again, never, never! Run at once, challenge him to a duel!' . . . I took her to the monastery them to bring her to her senses. The holy Fathers prayed her back to reason. But I swear, by God, Alyosha, I never insulted the poor crazy girl! Only once, perhaps, in the first year; then she was very fond of praying. She used to keep the feasts of Our Lady particularly and used to turn me out of her room then. 'I'll knock that mysticism out of her,' thought I 'Here,' said I, 'you see your holy image. Here it is. Here I take it down. You believe it's miraculous, but here, I'll spit on it directly and nothing will happen to me for it!' . . . When she saw it, good Lord! I thought she would kill me. But she only jumped up, wrung her hands, then suddenly hid her face in them, began trembling all over and fell on the floor . . . fell all of a heap. Alyosha, Alyosha, what's the matter?"

The old man jumped up in alarm. From the time he had begun speaking about his mother, a change had gradually come over Alyosha's face. He flushed crimson, his eyes glowed, his lips quivered. The old sot had gone spluttering on, noticing nothing, till the moment when something very strange happened to Alyosha. Precisely what he was describing in the crazy woman was suddenly repeated with Alyosha. He jumped up from his seat exactly as his mother was said to have done, wrung his hands, his face in them, and fell back in his chair, shaking all over in an hysterical paroxysm of sudden violent, silent weeping. His extraordinary resemblance to his mother particularly impressed the old man.

"Ivan, Ivan! Water, quickly! It's like her, exactly as she used to be then, his mother. Spurt some water on him from your mouth, that's what I used to do to her. He's upset about his mother, his mother," he muttered to Ivan.

"But she was my mother, too, I believe, his mother. Was she not?" said Ivan, with uncontrolled anger and contempt. The old man shrank before his flashing eyes. But something very strange had happened, though only for a second; it seemed really to have escaped the old man's mind that Alyosha's mother actually was the mother of Ivan too.

"Your mother?" he muttered, not understanding. "What do you mean? What mother are you talking about? Was she? . . . Why, damn it! of course she was yours too! Damn it! My mind has never been so darkened before. Excuse me, why, I was thinking Ivan . . . he, he, he!" He stopped. A broad, drunken, half-senseless grin overspread his face.

At that moment a fearful noise and clamour was heard in the hall, there were violent shouts, the door was flung open, and Dmitri burst into the room. The old man rushed to Ivan in terror.

"He'll kill me! He'll kill me! Don't let him get at me!" he screamed, clinging to the skirt of Ivan's coat.

CHAPTER IX

THE SENSUALISTS

GRIGORY and Smerdyakov ran into the room after Dmitri. They had been struggling with him in the passage, refusing to admit him, acting on instructions given them by Fyodor Pavlovitch some days before. Taking advantage of the fact that Dmitri stopped a moment on entering the room to look about him, Grigory ran round the table, closed the double doors on the opposite side of the room leading to the inner apartments, and stood before the closed doors, stretching wide his arms, prepared to defend the entrance, so to speak, with the last drop of his blood. Seeing this, Dmitri uttered a scream rather than a shout and rushed at Grigory.

"Then she's there! She's hidden there! Out of the way, scoundrel!"

He tried to pull Grigory away, but the old servant pushed him back. Beside himself with fury, Dmitri struck out, and hit Grigory with all his might. The old man fell like a log, and Dmitri, leaping over him, broke in the door. Smerdyakov remained pale and trembling at the other end of the room, huddling close to Fyodor Pavlovitch.

"She's here!" shouted Dmitri. "I saw her turn towards the house just now, but I couldn't catch her. Where is she? Where is she?"

That shout, "She's here!" produced an indescribable effect on Fyodor Pavlovitch. All his terror left him.

"Hold him! Hold him!" he cried, and dashed after Dmitri. Meanwhile Grigory had got up from the floor, but still seemed stunned. Ivan and Alyosha ran after their father. In the third room something was heard to fall on the floor with a ringing crash: it was a large glass vase—not an expensive one—on a marble pedestal which Dmitri had upset as he ran past it.

"At him!" shouted the old man. "Help!"

Ivan and Alyosha caught the old man and were forcibly bringing him back.

"Why do you run after him? He'll murder you outright," Ivan cried wrathfully at his father.

"Ivan! Alyosha! She must be here. Grushenka's here. He said he saw her himself, running."

He was choking. He was not expecting Grushenka at the time, and the sudden news that she was here made him beside himself. He was trembling all over. He seemed frantic.

"But you've seen for yourself that she hasn't come," cried Ivan.

"But she may have come by that other entrance."

"You know that entrance is locked, and you have the key."

Dmitri suddenly reappeared in the drawing-room. He had, of course, found the other entrance locked, and the key actually was in Fyodor Pavlovitch's pocket. The windows of all the rooms were also closed, so Grushenka could not have come in anywhere nor have run out anywhere.

"Hold him!" shrieked Fyodor Pavlovitch, as soon as he saw him again. "He's been stealing money in my bedroom." And tearing himself from Ivan he rushed again at Dmitri. But Dmitri threw up both hands and suddenly clutched the old man by the two tufts of hair that remained on his temples, tugged at them, and flung him with a crash on the floor. He kicked him two or three times with his heel in the face. The old man moaned shrilly. Ivan, though not so strong as Dmitri, threw his arms around him, and with all his might pulled him away. Alyosha helped him with his slender strength, holding Dmitri in front.

"Madman! You've killed him!" cried Ivan.

"Serve him right!" shouted Dmitri breathlessly. "If I haven't killed him, I'll come again and kill him. You can't protect him!"

"Dmitri! Go away at once!" cried Alyosha commandingly.

"Alexey! You tell me. It's only you I can believe; was she here just now, or not? I saw her myself creeping this way by the fence from the lane. I shouted, she ran away."

"I swear she's not been here, and no one expected her."

"But I saw her. . . . So she must . . . I'll find out at once where she is. . . . Good-bye, Alexey! Not a word to Æsop about the money now. But go to Katerina Ivanovna at once and be sure to say: 'He sends his compliments to you!' Compliments, his compliments! Just compliments and farewell! Describe the scene to her."

Meanwhile Ivan and Grigory had raised the old man and seated him in an armchair. His face was covered with blood, but he was conscious and listened greedily to Dmitri's cries. He was still fancying that Grushenka really was somewhere in the house. Dmitri looked at him with hatred as he went out.

"I don't repent shedding your blood!" he cried. "Beware, old man, beware of your dreams, for I have my dreams, too. I curse you, and disown you altogether."

He ran out of the room.

"She's here. She must be here. Smerdyakov! Smerdyakov!" the old man wheezed, scarcely audibly, beckoning to him with his finger.

"No, she's not here, you old lunatic!" Ivan shouted at him angrily. "Here, he's fainting! Water! A towel! Make haste, Smerdyakov!"

Smerdyakov ran for water. At last they got the old man

undressed, and put him to bed. They wrapped a wet towel round his head. Exhausted by the brandy, by his violent emotion, and the blows he had received, he shut his eyes and fell asleep as soon as his head touched the pillow. Ivan and Alyosha went back to the drawing-room. Smerdyakov removed the fragments of the broken vase, while Grigory stood by the table looking gloomily at the floor.

"Shouldn't you put a wet bandage on your head and go to bed, too?" Alyosha said to him. "We'll look after him. My brother gave you a terrible blow—on the head."

"He's insulted me!" Grigory articulated gloomily and distinctly.

"He's 'insulted' his father, not only you," observed Ivan with a forced smile.

"I used to wash him in his tub. He's insulted me," repeated Grigory.

"Damn it all, if I hadn't pulled him away perhaps he'd have murdered him. It wouldn't take much to do for Æsop, would it?" whispered Ivan to Alyosha.

"God forbid!" cried Alyosha.

"Why should He forbid?" Ivan went on in the same whisper, with a malignant grimace. "One reptile will devour the other. And serve them both right, too."

Alyosha shuddered.

"Of course I won't let him be murdered as I didn't just now. Stay here, Alyosha, I'll go for a turn in the yard. My head's begun to ache."

Alyosha went to his father's bedroom and sat by his bedside behind the screen for about an hour. The old man suddenly opened his eyes and gazed for a long while at Alyosha, evidently remembering and meditating. All at once his face betrayed extraordinary excitement.

"Alyosha," he whispered apprehensively, "where's Ivan?"

"In the yard. He's got a headache. He's on the watch."

"Give me that looking-glass. It stands over there. Give it me."

Alyosha gave him a little round folding looking-glass which stood on the chest of drawers. The old man looked at himself in it; his nose was considerably swollen, and on the left side of his forehead there was a rather large crimson bruise.

"What does Ivan say? Alyosha, my dear, my only son, I'm afraid of Ivan. I'm more afraid of Ivan than the other. You're the only one I'm not afraid of. . . ."

"Don't be afraid of Ivan either. He is angry, but he'll defend you."

"Alyosha, and what of the other? He's run to Grushenka. My angel, tell me the truth, was she here just now or not?"

"No one has seen her. It was a mistake. She has not been here."

"You know Mitya wants to marry her, to marry her."

"She won't marry him."

"She won't. She won't. She won't. She won't on any account!"

The old man fairly fluttered with joy, as though nothing more comforting could have been said to him. In his delight he seized Alyosha's hand and pressed it warmly to his heart. Tears positively glittered in his eyes.

"That image of the Mother of God of which I was telling you just now," he said. "Take it home and keep it for yourself. And I'll let you go back to the monastery. . . . I was joking this morning, don't be angry with me. My head aches, Alyosha. . . . Alyosha, comfort my heart. Be an angel and tell me the truth!"

"You're still asking whether she has been here or not?" Alyosha said sorrowfully.

"No, no, no. I believe you. I'll tell you what it is: you go to Grushenka yourself, or see her somehow; make haste and ask her; see for yourself, which she means to choose, him or me? Eh? What? Can you?"

"If I see her I'll ask her," Alyosha muttered embarrassed.

"No, she won't tell you," the old man interrupted, "she's a rogue. She'll begin kissing you and say that it's you she wants. She's a deceitful, shameless hussy. You mustn't go to her, you mustn't!"

"No, father, and it wouldn't be suitable, it wouldn't be right at all."

"Where was he sending you just now? He shouted 'Go!' as he ran away."

"To Katerina Ivanovna."

"For money? To ask her for money?"

"No. Not for money."

"He's no money; not a farthing. I'll settle down for the night, and think things over, and you can go. Perhaps you'll meet her. . . . Only be sure to come to me to-morrow in the morning. Be sure to. I have a word to say to you to-morrow. Will you come?"

143

"Yes."

"When you come, pretend you've come of your own accord to ask after me. Don't tell anyone I told you to. Don't say a word to Ivan."

"Very well."

"Good-bye, my angel. You stood up for me, just now. I shall never forget it. I've a word to say to you to-morrow— but I must think about it."

"And how do you feel now?"

"I shall get up to-morrow and go out, perfectly well, perfectly well!"

Crossing the yard Alyosha found Ivan sitting on the bench at the gateway. He was sitting writing something in pencil in his note-book. Alyosha told Ivan that their father had waked up, was conscious, and had let him go back to sleep at the monastery.

"Alyosha, I should be very glad to meet you to-morrow morning," said Ivan cordially, standing up. His cordiality was a complete surprise to Alyosha.

"I shall be at the Hohlakovs' to-morrow," answered Alyosha. "I may be at Katerina Ivanovna's, too, if I don't find her now."

"But you're going to her now, anyway? For that 'compliments and farewell','' said Ivan, smiling. Alyosha was disconcerted.

"I think I quite understand his exclamations just now, and part of what went before. Dmitri has asked you to go to her and say that he—well, in fact—takes his leaves of her?"

"Brother, how will all this horror end between father and Dmitri?" exclaimed Alyosha.

"One can't tell for certain. Perhaps in nothing: it may all fizzle out. That woman is a beast. In any case we must keep the old man indoors and not let Dmitri in the house."

"Brother, let me ask one thing more: has any man a right to look at other men and decide which is worthy to live?"

"Why bring in the question of worth? The matter is most often decided in men's hearts on other grounds much more natural. And as for rights—who has not the right to wish?"

"Not for another man's death?"

"What even if for another man's death? Why lie to oneself, since all men live so and perhaps cannot help living so? Are you referring to what I said just now—that one reptile will devour the other? In that case let me ask you, do you think me like Dmitri, capable of shedding Æsop's blood, murdering him, eh?"

"What are you saying, Ivan? Such an idea never crossed my mind. I don't think Dmitri is capable of it, either."

"Thanks, if only for that," smiled Ivan. "Be sure, I should always defend him. But in my wishes I reserve myself full latitude in this case. Good-bye till to-morrow. Don't condemn me, and don't look on me as a villain," he added with a smile.

They shook hands warmly as they had never done before. Alyosha felt that his brother had taken the first step towards him, and that he had certainly done this with some definite motive.

CHAPTER X

BOTH TOGETHER

ALYOSHA left his father's house feeling even more exhausted and dejected in spirit than when he had entered it. His mind too seemed shattered and unhinged, while he felt that he was afraid to put together the disjointed fragments and form a general idea from all the agonising and conflicting experiences of the day. He felt something bordering upon despair, which he had never known till then. Towering like a mountain above all the rest stood the fatal insoluble question: How would things end between his father and his brother Dmitri with this terrible woman? Now he had himself been a witness of it, he had been present and seen them face to face. Yet only his brother Dmitri could be made unhappy, terribly, completely unhappy: there was trouble awaiting him. It appeared too that there were other people concerned, far more so than Alyosha could have supposed before. There was something positively mysterious in it, too. Ivan had made a step towards him, which was what Alyosha had been long desiring. Yet now he felt for some reason that he was frightened at it. And these women? Strange to say, that morning he had set out for Katerina Ivanovna's in the greatest embarrassment; now he felt nothing of the kind. On the contrary, he was hastening there as though expecting to find guidance from her. Yet to give her this message was obviously more difficult than before. The matter of the three thousand was decided irrevocably, and Dmitri, feeling himself dishonoured and losing his last hope,

145

might sink to any depth. He had, moreover, told him to describe to Katerina Ivanovna the scene which had just taken place with his father.

It was by now seven o'clock, and it was getting dark as Alyosha entered the very spacious and convenient house in the High Street occupied by Katerina Iyanovna. Alyosha knew that she lived with two aunts. One of them, a woman of little education, was that aunt of her half-sister Agafya Ivanovna who had looked after her in her father's house when she came from boarding-school. The other aunt was a Moscow lady of style and consequence, though in straitened circumstances. It was said that they both gave way in everything to Katerina Ivanovna, and that she only kept them with her as chaperones. Katerina Ivanovna herself gave way to no one but her benefactress, the General's widow, who had been kept by illness in Moscow, and to whom she was obliged to write twice a week a full account of all her doings.

When Alyosha entered the hall and asked the maid who opened the door to him to take his name up, it was evident that they were already aware of his arrival. Possibly he had been noticed from the window. At least, Alyosha heard a noise, caught the sound of flying footsteps and rustling skirts. Two or three women perhaps had run out of the room.

Alyosha thought it strange that his arrival should cause such excitement. He was conducted, however, to the drawing-room at once. It was a large room, elegantly and amply furnished, not at all in provincial style. There were many sofas, lounges, settees, big and little tables. There were pictures on the walls, vases and lamps on the tables, masses of flowers, and even an aquarium in the window. It was twilight and rather dark. Alyosha made out a silk mantel thrown down on the sofa, where people had evidently just been sitting; and on a table in front of the sofa were two unfinished cups of chocolate, cakes, a glass saucer with blue raisins, and another with sweetmeats. Alyosha saw that he had interrupted visitors, and frowned. But at that instant the portière was raised, and with rapid, hurrying footsteps Katerina Ivanovna came in, holding out both hands to Alyosha with a radiant smile of delight. At the same instant a servant brought in two lighted candles and set them on the table.

"Thank God! At last you have come too! I've been simply praying for you all day! Sit down."

Alyosha had been struck by Katerina Ivanovna's beauty

when, three weeks before, Dmitri had first brought him, at Katerina Ivanovna's special request, to be introduced to her. There had been no conversation between them at that interview, however. Supposing Alyosha to be very shy, Katerina Ivanovna had talked all the time to Dmitri to spare him. Alyosha had been silent, but he had seen a great deal very clearly. He was struck by the imperiousness, proud ease, and self-confidence of the haughty girl. And all that was certain, Alyosha felt that he was not exaggerating it. He thought her great glowing black eyes were very fine, especially with her pale, even rather sallow, longish face. But in those eyes and in the lines of her exquisite lips there was something with which his brother might well be passionately in love, but which perhaps could not be loved for long. He expressed this thought almost plainly to Dmitri when, after the visit, his brother besought and insisted that he should not conceal the impressions on seeing his betrothed.

"You'll be happy with her, but perhaps—not tranquilly happy."

"Quite so, brother. Such people remain always the same. They don't yield to fate. So you think I shan't love her for ever?"

"No; perhaps you will love her for ever. But perhaps you won't always be happy with her."

Alyosha had given his opinion at the time, blushing, and angry with himself for having yielded to his brother's entreaties and put such "foolish" ideas into words. For his opinion had struck him as awfully foolish immediately after he had uttered it. He felt ashamed too of having given so confident an opinion about a woman. It was with the more amazement that he felt now, at the first glance at Katerina Ivanovna as she ran in to him, that he had perhaps been utterly mistaken. This time her face was beaming with spontaneous good-natured kindliness and direct warm-hearted sincerity. The "pride and haughtiness", which had struck Alyosha so much before, was only betrayed now in a frank, generous energy and a sort of bright strong faith in herself. Alyosha realised at the first glance, at the first word, that all the tragedy of her position in relation to the man she loved so dearly was no secret to her; that she perhaps already knew everything, positively everything. And yet, in spite of that, there was such brightness in her face, such faith in the future. Alyosha felt at once that he had gravely wronged her in his thoughts. He was conquered and captivated immediately. Besides all this, he noticed at her first words that she was in great excitement, an excitement perhaps quite exceptional and almost approaching ecstasy.

"I was so eager to see you, because I can learn from you the whole truth—from you and no one else."

"I have come," muttered Alyosha confusedly, "I—he sent me."

"Ah, he sent you! I foresaw that. Now I know everything —everything!" cried Katerina Ivanovna, her eyes flashing. "Wait a moment, Alexey Fyodorovitch, I'll tell you why I've been so longing to see you. You see, I know perhaps far more than you do yourself, and there's no need for you to tell me anything. I'll tell you what I want from you. I want to know your own last impression of him. I want you to tell me most directly, plainly, coarsely even (oh, as coarsely as you like!), what you thought of him just now and of his position after your meeting with him to-day. That will perhaps be better than if I had a personal explanation with him, as he does not want to come to me. Do you understand what I want from you? Now, tell me simply, tell me every word of the message he sent you with (I knew he would send you)."

"He told me to give you his compliments—and to say that he would never come again—but to give you his compliments."

"His compliments? Was that what he said—his own expression?"

"Yes."

"Accidentally, perhaps, he made a mistake in the word, perhaps he did not use the right word?"

"No; he told me precisely to repeat the word. He begged me two or three times not to forget to say so."

Katerina Ivanovna flushed hotly.

"Help me now, Alexey Fyodorovitch. Now I really need your help. I'll tell you what I think, and you must simply say whether it's right or not. Listen! If he had sent me his compliments in passing, without insisting on your repeating the words, without emphasising them, that would be the end of everything! But if he particularly insisted on those words, if he particularly told you not to forget to repeat them to me, then perhaps he was in excitement, beside himself. He had made his decision and was frightened at it. He wasn't walking away from me with a resolute step, but leaping headlong. The emphasis on that phrase may have been simply bravado."

"Yes, yes!" cried Alyosha warmly. "I believe that is it."

148

"And, if so, he's not altogether lost. I can still save him. Stay! Did he not tell you anything about money—about three thousand roubles?"

"He did speak about it, and it's that more than anything that's crushing him. He said he had lost his honour and that nothing matters now," Alyosha answered warmly, feeling a rush of hope in his heart and believing that there really might be a way of escape and salvation for his brother. "But do you know about the money?" he added, and suddenly broke off.

"I've known of it a long time; I telegraphed to Moscow to inquire, and heard long ago that the money had not arrived. He hadn't sent the money, but I said nothing. Last week I learnt that he was still in need of money. My only object in all this was that he should know to whom to turn, and who was his true friend. No, he won't recognise that I am his truest friend; he won't know me, and looks on me merely as a woman. I've been tormented all the week, trying to think how to prevent him from being ashamed to face me because he spent that three thousand. Let him feel ashamed of himself, let him be ashamed of other people's knowing, but not of my knowing. He can tell God everything without shame. Why is it he still does not understand how much I am ready to bear for his sake? Why, why doesn't he know me? How dare he not know me after all that has happened? I want to save him for ever. Let him forget me as his betrothed. And here he fears that he is dishonoured in my eyes. Why, he wasn't afraid to be open with you, Alexey Fyodorovitch. How is it that I don't deserve the same?"

The last words she uttered in tears. Tears gushed from her eyes.

"I must tell you," Alyosha began, his voice trembling too, "what happened just now between him and my father."

And he described the whole scene: how Dmitri had sent him to get the money, how he had broken in, knocked his father down, and after that had again specially and emphatically begged him to take his compliments and farewell. "He went to that woman," Alyosha added softly.

"And do you suppose that I can't put up with that woman? Does he think I can't? But he won't marry her," she suddenly laughed nervously. "Could such a passion last for ever in a Karamazov? It's passion, not love. He won't marry her because she won't marry him." Again Katerina Ivanovna laughed strangely.

149

"He may marry her," said Alyosha mournfully, looking down.

"He won't marry her, I tell you. That girl is an angel. Do you know that? Do you know that?" Katerina Ivanovna exclaimed suddenly with extraordinary warmth. "She is one of the most fantastic of fantastic creatures. I know how bewitching she is, but I know too that she is kind, firm and noble. Why do you look at me like that, Alexey Fyodorovitch? Perhaps you are wondering at my words, perhaps you don't believe me? Agrafena Alexandrovna, my angel!" she cried suddenly to someone, peeping into the next room, "come in to us. This is a friend. This is Alyosha. He knows all about our affairs. Show yourself to him."

"I've only been waiting behind the curtain for you to call me," said a soft, one might even say sugary, feminine voice.

The portière was raised and Grushenka herself, smiling and beaming, came up to the table. A violent revulsion passed over Alyosha. He fixed his eyes on her and could not take them off. Here she was, that awful woman, the "beast", as Ivan had called her half an hour before. And yet one would have thought the creature standing before him most simple and ordinary, a good-natured, kind woman, handsome certainly, but so like other handsome ordinary women! It is true she was very, very good-looking, with that Russian beauty so passionately loved by many men. She was a rather tall woman, though a little shorter than Katerina Ivanovna, who was exceptionally tall. She had a full figure, with soft, as it were noiseless, movements, softened to a peculiar over-sweetness, like her voice. She moved, not like Katerina Ivanovna, with a vigorous, bold step, but noiselessly. Her feet made absolutely no sound on the floor. She sank softly into a low chair, softly rustling her sumptuous black silk dress, and delicately nestling her milk-white neck and broad shoulders in a costly black cashmere shawl. She was twenty-two years old, and her face looked exactly that age. She was very white in the face, with a pale pink tint on her cheeks. The modelling of her face might be said to be too broad, and the lower jaw was set a trifle forward. Her upper lip was thin, but the slightly prominent lower lip was at least twice as full, and looked pouting. But her magnificent, abundant dark brown hair, her sable-coloured eyebrows and charming grey-blue eyes with their long lashes would have made the most indifferent person, meeting her

150

casually in a crowd in the street, stop at the sight of her face and remember it long after. What struck Alyosha most in that face was its expression of child-like good-nature. There was a child-like look in her eyes, a look of childish delight. She came up to the table, beaming with delight and seeming to expect something with childish, impatient, and confiding curiosity. The light in her eyes gladdened the soul—Alyosha felt that. There was something else in her which he could not understand, or would not have been able to define, and which yet perhaps unconsciously affected him. It was that softness, the voluptuousness of her bodily movements, that catlike noiselessness. Yet it was a vigorous, ample body. Under the shawl could be seen full broad shoulders, a high, still quite girlish bosom. Her figure suggested the lines of the Venus of Milo, though already in somewhat exaggerated proportions. That could be divined. Connoisseurs of Russian beauty could have foretold with certainty that this fresh, still youthful, beauty would lose its harmony by the age of thirty, would "spread"; that the face would become puffy, and that wrinkles would very soon appear upon her forehead and round the eyes; the complexion would grow coarse and red perhaps—in fact, that it was the beauty of the moment, the fleeting beauty which is so often met with in Russian women. Alyosha, of course, did not think of this; but though he was fascinated, yet he wondered with an unpleasant sensation, and as it were regretfully, why she drawled in that way and could not speak naturally. She did so evidently feeling there was a charm in the exaggerated, honeyed modulation of the syllables. It was, of course, only a bad, underbred habit that showed bad education and a false idea of good manners. And yet this intonation and manner of speaking impressed Alyosha as almost incredibly incongruous with the childishly simple and happy expression of her face, the soft, babyish joy in her eyes. Katerina Ivanovna at once made her sit down in an armchair facing Alyosha, and ecstatically kissed her several times on her smiling lips. She seemed quite in love with her.

"This is the first time we've met, Alexey Fyodorovitch," she said rapturously. "I wanted to know her, to see her. I wanted to go to her, but I'd no sooner expressed the wish than she came to me. I knew we should settle everything together—everything. My heart told me so—I was begged not to take the step, but I foresaw it would be a way out of the difficulty, and I was not mistaken. Grushenka has explained everything to me, told me all she means to do. She flew here like an angel of goodness and brought us peace and joy."

"You did not disdain me, sweet, excellent young lady," drawled Grushenka in her sing-song voice, still with the same charming smile of delight.

"Don't dare to speak to me like that, you sorceress, you witch! Disdain you! Here I must kiss your lower lip once more. It looks as though it were swollen, and now it will be more so, and more and more. Look how she laughs, Alexey Fyodorovitch! It does one's heart good to see the angel."

Alyosha flushed, and faint, imperceptible shivers kept running down him.

"You make so much of me, dear young lady, and perhaps I am not at all worthy of your kindness."

"Not worthy! She's not worthy of it!" Katerina Ivanovna cried again with the same warmth. "You know, Alexey Fyodorovitch, we're fanciful, we're self-willed, but proudest of the proud in our little heart. We're noble, we're generous, Alexey Fyodorovitch, let me tell you. We have only been unfortunate. We were too ready to make every sacrifice for an unworthy, perhaps, or fickle man. There was one man—one, an officer too, we loved him, we sacrificed everything to him. That was long ago, five years ago, and he has forgotten us, he has married. Now he is a widower, he has written, he is coming here, and, do you know, we've loved him, none but him, all this time, and we've loved him all our life! He will come, and Grushenka will be happy again. For the last five years she's been wretched. But who can reproach her, who can boast of her favour? Only that bedridden old merchant, but he is more like her father, her friend, her protector. He found her then in despair, in agony, deserted by the man she loved. She was ready to drown herself then, but the old merchant saved her—saved her!"

"You defend me very kindly, dear young lady. You are in a great hurry about everything," Grushenka drawled again.

"Defend her! Is it for me to defend you? Should I dare to defend you? Grushenka, angel, give me your hand. Look at that charming soft little hand, Alexey Fyodorovitch! Look at it! It has brought me happiness and has lifted me up, and I'm going to kiss it, outside and inside, here, here, here!"

And three times she kissed the certainly charming, though rather fat, hand of Grushenka in a sort of rapture. She held out her hand with a charming musical, nervous little laugh, watched the "sweet young lady", and obviously liked having her hand kissed.

"Perhaps there's rather too much rapture," thought Alyosha. He blushed. He felt a peculiar uneasiness at heart the whole time.

"You won't make me blush, dear young lady, kissing my hand like this before Alexey Fyodorovitch."

"Do you think I meant to make you blush?" said Katerina Ivanovna, somewhat surprised. "Ah, my dear, how little you understand me!"

"Yes, and you too perhaps quite misunderstand me, dear young lady. Maybe I'm not so good as I seem to you. I've a bad heart; I will have my own way. I fascinated poor Dmitri Fyodorovitch that day simply for fun."

"But now you'll save him. You've given me your word. You'll explain it all to him. You'll break to him that you have long loved another man, who is now offering you his hand."

"Oh, no! I didn't give you my word to do that. It was you kept talking about that. I didn't give you my word."

"Then I didn't quite understand you," said Katerina Ivanovna slowly, turning a little pale. "You promised . . ."

"Oh no, angel lady, I've promised nothing," Grushenka interrupted softly and evenly, still with the same gay and simple expression. "You see at once, dear young lady, what a wilful wretch I am compared with you. If I want to do a thing I do it. I may have made you some promise just now. But now again I'm thinking: I may take to Mitya again. I liked him very much once—liked him for almost a whole hour. Now maybe I shall go and tell him to stay with me from this day forward. You see, I'm so changeable."

"Just now you said—something quite different," Katerina Ivanovna whispered faintly.

"Ah, just now! But, you know, I'm such a soft-hearted, silly creature. Only think what he's gone through on my account! What if when I go home I feel sorry for him? What then?"

"I never expected——"

"Ah, young lady, how good and generous you are compared with me! Now perhaps you won't care for a silly creature like me, now you know my character. Give me your sweet little hand, angelic lady," she said tenderly, and with a sort of reverence took Katerina Ivanovna's hand.

"Here, dear young lady, I'll take your hand and kiss it as

you did mine. You kissed mine three times, but I ought to kiss yours three hundred times to be even with you. Well, but let that pass. And then it shall be as God wills. Perhaps I shall be your slave entirely and want to do your bidding like a slave. Let it be as God wills, without any agreements and promises. What a sweet hand—what a sweet hand you have! You sweet young lady, you incredible beauty!"

She slowly raised the hands to her lips, with the strange object indeed of ''being even'' with her in kisses.

Katerina Ivanovna did not take her hand away. She listened with timid hope to the last words, though Grushenka's promise to do her bidding like a slave was very strangely expressed. She looked intently into her eyes; she still saw in those eyes the same simple-hearted, confiding expression, the same bright gaiety.

"She's perhaps too naïve," thought Katerina Ivanovna, with a gleam of hope.

Grushenka meanwhile seemed enthusiastic over the "sweet hand". She raised it deliberately to her lips. But she held it for two or three minutes near her lips, as though reconsidering something.

"Do you know, angel lady," she suddenly drawled in an even more soft and sugary voice, "do you know, after all, I think I won't kiss your hand?" And she laughed a little merry laugh.

"As you please. What's the matter with you?" said Katerina Ivanovna, starting suddenly.

"So that you may be left to remember that you kissed my hand but I didn't kiss yours."

There was a sudden gleam in her eyes. She looked with awful intentness at Katerina Ivanovna.

"Insolent creature!" cried Katerina Ivanovna, as though suddenly grasping something. She flushed all over and leapt up from her seat.

Grushenka too got up, but without haste.

"So I shall tell Mitya how you kissed my hand but I didn't kiss yours at all. And how he will laugh!"

"Vile slut! Go away!"

"Ah, for shame, young lady! Ah, for shame! That's unbecoming for you, dear young lady, a word like that."

"Go away! You're a creature for sale!" screamed Katerina Ivanovna. Every feature was working in her utterly distorted face.

"For sale indeed! You used to visit gentlemen in the dusk for money once; you brought your beauty for sale. You see, I know."

Katerina Ivanovna shrieked, and would have rushed at her, but Alyosha held her with all his strength.

"Not a step, not a word! Don't speak, don't answer her. She'll go away—she'll go at once."

At that instant Katerina Ivanovna's two aunts ran in at her cry, and with them a maidservant. All hurried to her.

"I will go away," said Grushenka, taking up her mantle from the sofa. "Alyosha darling, see me home!"

"Go away, go away, make haste!" cried Alyosha, clasping his hands imploringly.

"Dear little Alyosha, see me home! I've got a pretty little story to tell you on the way. I got up this scene for your benefit, Alyosha. See me home, dear, you'll be glad of it afterwards."

Alyosha turned away, wringing his hands. Grushenka ran out of the house, laughing musically.

Katerina Ivanovna went into a fit of hysterics. She sobbed, and was shaken with convulsions. Everyone fussed round her.

"I warned you," said the elder of her aunts. "I tried to prevent your doing this. You're too impulsive. How could you do such a thing? You don't know these creatures, and they say she's worse than any of them. You are too self-willed."

"She's a tigress!" yelled Katerina Ivanovna. "Why did you hold me, Alexey Fyodorovitch? I'd have beaten her—beaten her!"

She could not control herself before Alyosha; perhaps she did not care to, indeed.

"She ought to be flogged in public on a scaffold!"

Alyosha withdrew towards the door.

"But, my God!" cried Katerina Ivanovna, clasping her hands. "He! He! He could be so dishonourable, so inhuman! Why, he told that creature what happened on that fatal, accursed day! 'You brought your beauty for sale, dear young lady.' She knows it! Your brother's a scoundrel, Alexey Fyodorovitch."

Alyosha wanted to say something, but he couldn't find a word. His heart ached.

"Go away, Alexey Fyodorovitch! It's shameful, it's awful for me. To-morrow, I beg you on my knees, come to-morrow.

Don't condemn me. Forgive me. I don't know what I shall do with myself now!"

Alyosha walked out into the street reeling. He could have wept as she did. Suddenly he was overtaken by the maid.

"The young lady forgot to give you this letter from Madame Hohlakov; it's been left with us since dinner-time."

Alyosha took the little pink envelope mechanically and put it, almost unconsciously, into his pocket.

CHAPTER XI

ANOTHER REPUTATION RUINED

IT was not much more than three-quarters of a mile from the town to the monastery. Alyosha walked quickly along the road, at that hour deserted. It was almost night, and too dark to see anything clearly at thirty paces ahead. There were cross-roads half-way. A figure came into sight under a solitary willow at the cross-roads. As soon as Alyosha reached the cross-roads the figure moved out and rushed at him, shouting savagely:

"Your money or your life!"

"So it's you, Mitya," cried Alyosha, in surprise, violently startled, however.

"Ha, ha, ha! You didn't expect me? I wondered where to wait for you. By her house? There are three ways from it, and I might have missed you. At last I thought of waiting here, for you had to pass here, there's no other way to the monastery. Come, tell me the truth. Crush me like a beetle. But what's the matter?"

"Nothing, brother—it's the fright you gave me. Oh, Dmitri! Father's blood just now." (Alyosha began to cry, he had been on the verge of tears for a long time, and now something seemed to snap in his soul.) "You almost killed him—cursed him—and now—here—you're making jokes—— Your money or your life!"

"Well, what of that? It's not seemly—is that it? Not suitable in my position?"

"No—I only——"

"Stay. Look at the night. You see what a dark night, what clouds, what a wind has risen. I hid here under the willow waiting for you. And, as God's above, I suddenly thought, why go on in misery any longer, what is there to wait for? Here I have a willow, a handkerchief, a shirt, I can twist them into a rope in a minute, and braces besides, and why go on burdening the earth, dishonouring it with my vile presence. And then I heard you coming—Heavens, it was as though something flew down to me suddenly. So there is a man, then, whom I love. Here he is, that man, my dear little brother, whom I love more than anyone in the world, the only one I love in the world. And I loved you so much, so much at that moment that I thought, 'I'll fall on his neck at once'. Then a stupid idea struck me, to have a joke with you and scare you. I shouted, like a fool, "Your money! Forgive my foolery—it was only nonsense, and there's nothing unseemly in my soul. . . . Damn it all, tell me what's happened. What did she say? Strike me, crush me, don't spare me! Was she furious?"

"No, not that. . . . There was nothing like that, Mitya. There—I found them both there."

"Both? Whom?"

"Grushenka at Katerina Ivanovna's."

Dmitri was struck dumb.

"Impossible!" he cried. "You're raving! Grushenka with her?"

Alyosha described all that had happened from the moment he went in to Katerina Ivanovna's. He was ten minutes telling his story. He can't be said to have told it fluently and consecutively, but he seemed to make it clear, not omitting any word or action of significance, and vividly describing, often in one word, his own sensations. Dmitri listened in silence, gazing at him with a terrible fixed stare, but it was clear to Alyosha that he understood it all, and had grasped every point. But as the story went on, his face became not merely gloomy but menacing. He scowled, he clenched his teeth, and his fixed stare became still more rigid, more concentrated, more terrible, when suddenly, with incredible rapidity, his wrathful, savage face changed, his tightly compressed lips parted, and Dmitri Fyodorovitch broke into uncontrolled, spontaneous laughter. He literally shook with laughter. For a long time he could not speak.

"So she wouldn't kiss her hand! So she didn't kiss it; so she ran away!" he kept exclaiming with hysterical delight; insolent delight it might have been called, if it had not been so spontaneous. "So the other one called her tigress! And a tigress she is! So she ought to be flogged on a scaffold? Yes,

157

yes, so she ought. That's just what I think; she ought to have been long ago. It's like this, brother, let her be punished, but I must get better first. I understand the queen of impudence. 'That's her all over! You saw her all over in that hand-kissing, the she-devil! She's the queen of all she-devils you can imagine in the world! She's magnificent in her own line! So she ran home? I'll go—ah—— I'll run to her! Alyosha, don't blame me, I agree that hanging is too good for her."

"But Katerina Ivanovna!" exclaimed Alyosha sorrowfully.

"I see her, too! I see right through her, as I've never done before! It's a regular discovery of the four continents of the world, that is, of the five! What a thing to do! That's just like Katya, who was not afraid to face a coarse, unmannerly officer and risk a deadly insult on a generous impulse to save her father! But the pride, the recklessness, the defiance of fate, the unbounded defiance! You say that aunt tried to stop her? That aunt, you know, is overbearing, herself. She's the sister of the General's widow in Moscow, and even more stuck-up than she. But her husband was caught stealing government money. He lost everything, his estate and all, and the proud wife had to lower her colours, and hasn't raised them since. So she tried to prevent Katya, but she wouldn't listen to her! She thinks she can overcome everything, that everything will give way to her. She thought she could bewitch Grushenka if she liked, and she believed it herself; she plays a part to herself, and whose fault is it? Do you think she kissed Grushenka's hand first, on purpose, with a motive? No, she really was fascinated by Grushenka, that's to say, not by Grushenka but by her own dream, her own delusion—because it was *her* dream, *her* delusion! Alyosha darling, how did you escape from them, those women? Did you pick up your cassock and run? Ha, ha, ha!"

"Brother, you don't seem to have noticed how you've insulted Katerina Ivanovna by telling Grushenka about that day. And she flung it in her face just now that she had gone to gentlemen in secret to sell her beauty! Brother, what could be worse than that insult?"

What worried Alyosha more than anything was that, incredible as it seemed, his brother appeared pleased at Katerina Ivanovna's humiliation.

"Bah!" Dmitri frowned fiercely, and struck his forehead with his hand. He only now realised it, though Alyosha had just told him of the insult, and Katerina Ivanovna's cry: "Your brother is a scoundrel!"

"Yes, perhaps I really did tell Grushenka about that 'fatal day', as Katya calls it. Yes, I did tell her, I remember! It was that time at Mokroe. I was drunk, the gypsies were singing . . . But I was sobbing. I was sobbing then, kneeling and praying to Katya's image, and Grushenka understood it. She understood it all then. I remember, she cried herself. . . . Damn it all! But it's bound to be so now. . . . Then she cried, but now 'the dagger in the heart'! That's how women are."

He looked down and sank into thought.

"Yes, I am a scoundrel, a thorough scoundrel!" he said suddenly, in a gloomy voice. "It doesn't matter whether I cried or not, I'm a scoundrel! Tell her I accept the name, if that's any comfort. Come, that's enough. Good-bye. It's no use talking! It's not amusing. You go your way and I mine. And I don't want to see you again except as a last resource. Good-bye, Alexey!"

He warmly pressed Alyosha's hand, and still looking down, without raising his head, as though tearing himself away, turned rapidly towards the town.

Alyosha looked after him, unable to believe he would go away so abruptly.

"Stay, Alexey, one more confession to you alone!" cried Dmitri, suddenly turning back. "Look at me. Look at me well. You see here, here—there's terrible disgrace in store for me." (As he said "here", Dmitri struck his chest with his fist with a strange air, as though the dishonour lay precisely on his chest, in some spot, in a pocket, perhaps, or hanging round his neck.) "You know me now, a scoundrel, an avowed scoundrel, but let me tell you that I've never done anything before and never shall again, anything that can compare in baseness with the dishonour which I bear now at this very minute on my breast, here, here, which will come to pass, though I'm perfectly free to stop it. I can stop it or carry it through, note that. Well, let me tell you, I shall carry it through. I shan't stop it. I told you everything just now, but I didn't tell you this, because even I had not brass enough for it. I can still pull up; if I do, I can give back the full half of my lost honour to-morrow. But I shan't pull up. I shall carry out my base plan, and you can bear witness that I told you so beforehand. Darkness and destruction! No need to explain. You'll find out in due time. The filthy back-alley and the she-devil. Good-bye. Don't pray

for me, I'm not worth it. And there's no need, no need at all.
. . . I don't need it! Away!"

And he suddenly retreated, this time finally. Alyosha went
towards the monastery.,

"What? I shall never see him again! What is he saying?"
he wondered wildly. "Why, I shall certainly see him to-morrow.
I shall look him up. I shall make a point of it. What does he
mean?"

He went round the monastery, and crossed the pine-wood to
the hermitage. The door was opened to him, though no one was
admitted at that hour. There was a tremor in his heart as he
went into Father Zossima's cell.

"Why, why, had he gone forth? Why had he sent him into
the world? Here was peace. Here was holiness. But there
was confusion, there was darkness in which one lost one's way
and went astray at once. . . ."

In the cell he found the novice Porfiry and Father Païssy,
who came every hour to inquire after Father Zossima. Alyosha
learnt with alarm that he was getting worse and worse. Even
his usual discourse with the brothers could not take place that
day. As a rule every evening after service the monks flocked
into Father Zossima's cell, and all confessed aloud their sins of
the day, their sinful thoughts and temptations; even their dis-
putes, if there had been any. Some confessed kneeling. The
elder absolved, reconciled, exhorted, imposed penance, blessed,
and dismissed them. It was against this general "confession"
that the opponents of "elders" protested, maintaining that it
was a profanation of the sacrament of confession, almost a
sacrilege, though this was quite a different thing. They even
represented to the diocesan authorities that such confessions
attained no good object, but actually to a large extent led to
sin and temptation. Many of the brothers disliked going to the
elder, and went against their own will because everyone went, and
for fear they should be accused of pride and rebellious ideas.
People said that some of the monks agreed beforehand, saying:
"I'll confess I lost my temper with you this morning, and you
confirm it," simply in order to have something to say. Alyosha
knew that this actually happened sometimes. He knew, too,
that there were among the monks some who deeply resented the
fact that letters from relations were habitually taken to the elder,
to be opened and read by him before those to whom they were
addressed.

It was assumed, of course, that all this was done freely, and in good faith, by way of voluntary submission and salutary guidance. But, in fact, there was sometimes no little insincerity, and much that was false and strained in this practice. Yet the older and more experienced of the monks adhered to their opinion, arguing that "for those who have come within these walls sincerely seeking salvation, such obedience and sacrifice will certainly be salutary and of great benefit; those, on the other hand, who find it irksome, and repine, are no true monks, and have made a mistake in entering the monastery—their proper place is in the world. Even in the temple one cannot be safe from sin and the devil. So it was no good taking it too much into account."

"He is weaker, a drowsiness has come over him. Father Païssy whispered to Alyosha, as he blessed him. "It's difficult to rouse him. And he must not be roused. He waked up for five minutes, sent his blessing to the brothers, and begged their prayers for him at night. He intends to take the sacrament again in the morning. He remembered you, Alexey. He asked whether you had gone away, and was told that you were in the town. 'I blessed him for that work,' he said, 'his place is there, not here, for a while.' Those were his words about you. He remembered you lovingly, with anxiety; do you understand how he honoured you? But how is it that he has decided that you shall spend some time in the world? He must have foreseen something in your destiny! Understand, Alexey, that if you return to the world, it must be to do the duty laid upon you by your elder, and not for frivolous vanity and worldly pleasures."

Father Païssy went out. Alyosha had no doubt that Father Zossima was dying, though he might live another day or two. Alyosha firmly and ardently resolved that in spite of his promises to his father, the Hohlakovs, and Katerina Ivanovna, he would not leave the monastery next day but would remain with his elder to the end. His heart glowed with love, and he reproached himself bitterly for having been able for one instant to forget him whom he had left in the monastery on his death-bed, and whom he honoured above everyone in the world. He went into Father Zossima's bedroom, knelt down, and bowed to the ground before the elder, who slept quietly without stirring, with regular, hardly audible breathing and a peaceful face.

Alyosha returned to the other room, where Father Zossima had received his guests in the morning. Taking off his boots, he lay down on the hard, narrow, leathern sofa, which he had long used as a bed, bringing nothing but a pillow. The mattress, about which his father had shouted to him that morning, he had long forgotten to lay on. He took off his cassock, which he used as a covering. But before going to bed he fell on his knees and prayed a long time. In his fervent prayer he did not beseech God to lighten his darkness but only thirsted for the joyous emotion which always visited his soul after the praise and adoration of which his evening prayer usually consisted. That joy always brought him light untroubled sleep. As he was praying, he suddenly felt in his pocket the little pink note the servant had handed him as he left Katerina Ivanovna's. He was disturbed, but finished his prayer. Then, after some hesitation, he opened the envelope. In it was a letter to him, signed by Lise, the young daughter of Madame Hohlakov, who had laughed at him before the elder in the morning.

"Alexey Fyodorovitch," she wrote, "I am writing to you without anyone's knowledge, even mama's, and I know how wrong it is. But I cannot live without telling you the feeling that has sprung up in my heart, and this no one but us two must know for a time. But how am I to say what I want so much to tell you? Paper, they say, does not blush, but I assure you it's not true, and that it's blushing just as I am now, all over. Dear Alyosha, I love you, I've loved you from my childhood, since our Moscow days, when you were very different from what you are now, and I shall love you all my life. My heart has chosen you, to unite our lives, and pass them together till our old age. Of course, on condition that you will leave the monastery. As for our age we will wait for the time fixed by the law. By that time I shall certainly be quite strong, I shall be walking and dancing. There can be no doubt of that.

"You see how I've thought of everything. There's only one thing I can't imagine: what you'll think of me when you read this. I'm always laughing and being naughty. I made you angry this morning, but I assure you before I took up my pen I prayed before the Image of the Mother of God, and now I'm praying, and almost crying.

"My secret is in your hands. When you come to-morrow, I don't know how I shall look at you. Ah, Alexey Fyodorovitch, what if I can't restrain myself like a silly and laugh when I look at you as I did to-day? You'll think I'm a nasty girl making fun of you, and you won't believe my letter. And so I beg you, dear one, if you've any pity for me, when you come to-morrow, don't look me straight in the face, for if I meet your eyes it will be sure to make me laugh, especially as you'll be in that long gown. I feel cold all over when I think of it, so when you come, don't look at me at all for a long time, look at mamma or at the window. . . .

"Here I've written you a love-leter. Oh dear, what have I done? Alyosha, don't despise me, and if I've done something very horrid and wounded you, forgive me. Now the secret of my reputation, ruined perhaps for ever, is in your hands.

"I shall certainly cry to-day. Good-bye till our meeting, our *awful* meeting.—LISE.

"PS.—Alyosha! You must, must, must come!—LISE."

Alyosha read the note in amazement, read it through twice, thought a little, and suddenly laughed a soft, sweet laugh. He started. That laugh seemed to him sinful. But a minute later he laughed again just as softly and happily. He slowly replaced the note in the envelope, crossed himself and lay down. The agitation in his heart passed at once. "God have mercy upon all of them, have all these unhappy and turbulent souls in Thy keeping, and set them in the right path. All ways are Thine. Save them according to Thy wisdom. Thou art love. Thou wilt send joy to all!" Alyosha murmured, crossing himself, and falling into peaceful sleep.

PART II

BOOK IV: LACERATIONS

CHAPTER I

FATHER FERAPONT

ALYOSHA was roused early, before daybreak. Father Zossima woke up feeling very weak, though he wanted to get out of bed and sit up in a chair. His mind was quite clear; his face looked very tired, yet bright and almost joyful. It wore an expression of gaiety, kindness and cordiality. "Maybe I shall not live through the coming day," he said to Alyosha. Then he desired to confess and take the sacrament at once. He always confessed to Father Païssy. After taking the communion, the service of extreme unction followed. The monks assembled and the cell was gradually filled up by the inmates of the hermitage. Meantime it was daylight. People began coming from the monastery. After the service was over the elder desired to kiss and take leave of everyone. As the cell was so small the earlier visitors withdrew to make room for others. Alyosha stood beside the elder, who was seated again in his arm-chair. He talked as much as he could. Though his voice was weak, it was fairly steady.

"I've been teaching you so many years, and therefore I've been talking aloud so many years, that I've got into the habit of talking, and so much so that it's almost more difficult for me to hold my tongue than to talk, even now, in spite of my weakness, dear fathers and brothers," he jested, looking with emotion at the group around him.

Alyosha remembered afterwards something of what he said to them. But though he spoke out distinctly and his voice was fairly steady, his speech was somewhat disconnected. He spoke of many things, he seemed anxious before the moment of death to say everything he had not said in his life, and not simply for the sake of instructing them but as though thirsting to share with all men and all creation his joy and ecstasy, and once more in his life to open his whole heart.

164

"Love one another, Fathers," said Father Zossimov, as far as Alyosha could remember afterwards. "Love God's people. Because we have come here and shut ourselves within these walls, we are no holier than those that are outside, but, on the contrary, from the very fact of coming here each of us has confessed to himself that he is worse than others, than all men on earth. . . . And the longer the monk lives in his seclusion, the more keenly he must recognise that. Else he would have had no reason to come here. When he realises that he is not only worse than others but that he is responsible to all men for all and everything, for all human sins, national and individual, only then the aim of our seclusion is attained. For know, dear ones, that every one of us is undoubtedly responsible for all men and everything on earth, not merely through the general sinfulness of creation, but each one personally for all mankind and every individual man. This knowledge is the crown of life for the monk and for every man. For monks are not a special sort of men, but only what all men ought to be. Only through that knowledge, our heart grows soft with infinite, universal, inexhaustible love. Then every one of you will have the power to win over the whole world by love and to wash away the sins of the world with your tears. . . . Each of you keep watch over your heart and confess your sins to yourself unceasingly. Be not afraid of your sins, even when perceiving them, if only there be penitence, but make no conditions with God. Again I say, Be not proud. Be proud neither to the little nor to the great. Hate not those who reject you, who insult you, who abuse and slander you. Hate not the atheists, the teachers of evil, the materialists—and I mean not only the good ones—for there are many good ones among them, especially in our day—hate not even the wicked ones. Remember them in your prayers thus: Save, O Lord, all those who have none to pray for them, save too all those who will not pray. And add: it is not in pride that I make this prayer, O Lord, for I am lower than all men. . . . Love God's people, let not strangers draw away the flock, for if you slumber in your slothfulness and disdainful pride, or, worse still, in covetousness, they will come from all sides and draw away your flock. Expound the Gospel to the people unceasingly . . . be not extortionate. . . . Do not love gold or silver, do not hoard them. . . . Have faith. Cling to the banner and raise it on high."

But the elder spoke more disconnectedly than Alyosha reported his words afterwards. Sometimes he broke off altogether,

165

as though to take breath and recover his strength, but he was in a sort of ecstasy. They heard him with emotion, though many wondered at his words and found them obscure. . . . Afterwards all remembered those words.

When Alyosha happened for a moment to leave the cell, he was struck by the general excitement and suspense in the monks who were crowding about it. This anticipation showed itself in some by anxiety, in others by devout solemnity. All were expecting that some marvel would happen immediately after the elder's death. Their suspense was, from one point of view, almost frivolous, but even the most austere of the monks were affected by it. Father Païssy's face looked the gravest of all.

Alyosha was mysteriously summoned by a monk to see Rakitin, who had arrivel from town with a singular letter for him from Madame Hohlakov. In it she informed Alyosha of a strange and very opportune incident. It apeared that among the women who had come on the previous day to receive Father Zossima's blessing, there had been an old woman from the town, a sergeant's widow, called Prohorovna. She had inquired whether she might pray for the rest of the soul of her son Vassenka, who had gone to Irkutsk, and had sent her no news for over a year. To which Father Zossima had answered sternly, forbidding her to do so, and saying that to pray for the living as though they were dead was a kind of sorcery. He afterwards forgave her on account of her ignorance, and added "as though reading the book of the future" (this was Madame Hohlakov's expression) words of comfort: "that her son Vassya was certainly alive and he would either come himself very shortly or send a letter, and that she was to go home and expect him." And "would you believe it", exclaimed Madame Hohlakov enthusiastically, "the prophecy has been fulfilled literally indeed and more than that". Scarcely had the old woman reached home when they gave her a letter from Siberia which had been awaiting her. But that was not all; in the letter written on the road from Ekaterinenburg, Vassya informed his mother that he was returning to Russia with an official, and that three weeks after her receiving the letter he hoped "to embrace his mother".

Madame Hohlakov warmly entreated Alyosha to report this new "miracle of prediction" to the superior and all the brotherhood. "All, all, ought to know of it!" she concluded. The letter had been written in haste, the excitement of the writer was apparent in every line of it. But Alyosha had no need to tell the monks, for all knew of it already. Rakitin had commissioned the monk who brought his message "to inform most respectfully his reverence Father Païssy, that he, Rakitin, has a matter to speak of with him, of such gravity that he dare not defer it for a moment; and humbly beg forgiveness for his presumption". As the monk had given the message to Father Païssy before that to Alyosha, the latter found, after reading the letter there was nothing left for him to do but to hand it to Father Païssy in confirmation of the story.

And even that austere and cautious man, though he frowned as he read the news of the "miracle", could not completely restrain some inner emotion. His eyes gleamed, and a grave and solemn smile came into his lips.

"We shall see greater things!" broke from him.

"We shall see greater things, greater things yet!" the monks around repeated.

But Father Païssy, frowning again, begged all of them, at least for a time, not to speak of the matter "till it be more fully confirmed, seeing there is so much credulity among those of this world, and indeed this might well have chanced naturally", he added, prudently, as it were to satisfy his conscience, though scarcely believing his own disavowal, a fact his listeners very clearly perceived.

Within the hour the "miracle" was, of course, known to the whole monastery, and many visitors who had come for the mass. No one seemed more impressed by it than the monk who had come the day before from St. Sylvester, from the little monastery of Obdorsk in the far North. It was he who had been standing near Madame Hohlakov the previous day and had asked Father Zossima earnestly, referring to the "healing" of the lady's daughter, "how can you presume to do such things?"

He was now somewhat puzzled and did not know whom to believe. The evening before he had visited Father Ferapont in his cell apart, behind the apiary, and had been greatly impressed and overawed by the visit. This Father Ferapont was that aged monk so devout in fasting and observing silence who has been mentioned already, as antagonistic to Father Zossima and the whole institution of "elders", which he regarded as a pernicious and frivolous innovation. He was a very formidable opponent, although from his practice of silence he scarcely spoke a word to anyone. What made him formidable was that a number of monks fully shared his feeling, and many of the visitors looked upon him as a great saint and ascetic, although they had no doubt that he was crazy. But it was just his craziness attracted them.

Father Ferapont never went to see the elder. Though he lived in the hermitage they did not worry him to keep its regulations, and this too because he behaved as though he were crazy. He was seventy-five or more, and he lived in a corner beyond the apiary in an old decaying wooden cell which had been built long ago for another great ascetic, Father Iona, who had lived to be a hundred and five, and of whose saintly doings many curious stories were still extant in the monastery and the neighbourhood.

Father Ferapont had succeeded in getting himself installed in this same solitary cell seven years previously. It was simply a peasant's hut, though it looked like a chapel, for it contained an extraordinary number of ikons with lamps perpetually burning before them—which men brought to the monastery as offerings to God. Father Ferapont had been appointed to look after them and keep the lamps burning. It was said (and indeed it was true) that he ate only two pounds of bread in three days. The beekeeper, who lived close by the apiary, used to bring him the bread every three days, and even to this man who waited upon him Father Ferapont rarely uttered a word. The four pounds of bread, together with the sacrament bread, regularly sent him on Sundays after the late mass by the Father Superior, made up his weekly rations. The water in his jug was changed every day. He rarely appeared at mass. Visitors who came to do him homage saw him sometimes kneeling all day long at prayer without looking round. If he addressed them, he was brief, abrupt, strange, and almost always rude. On very rare occasions, however, he would talk to visitors, but for the most part he would utter some one strange saying which was a complete riddle, and no entreaties would induce him to pronounce a word in explanation. He was not a priest but a simple monk. There was a strange belief, chiefly, however, among the most ignorant, that Father Ferapont had communication with heavenly spirits and would only converse with them, and so was silent with men.

The monk from Obdorsk, having been directed to the apiary by the beekeeper, who was also a very silent and surly monk, went to the corner where Father Ferapont's cell stood. "Maybe he will speak as you are a stranger and maybe you'll get nothing out of him," the beekeeper had warned him. The monk, as he related afterwards, approached in the utmost apprehension. It was rather late in the evening. Father Ferapont was sitting at the door of his cell on a low bench. A huge old elm was lightly rustling overhead. There was an evening freshness in the air. The monk from Obdorsk bowed down before the saint and asked his blessing.

"Do you want me to bow down to you, monk?" said Father Ferapont. "Get up!"

The monk got up.

"Blessing, be blessed! Sit beside me. Where have you come from?"

What most struck the poor monk was the fact that, in spite of his strict fasting and great age, Father Ferapont still looked a vigorous old man. He was tall, held himself erect, and had a thin but fresh and healthy face. There was no doubt he still had considerable strength. He was of athletic build. In spite of his great age he was not even quite grey, and still had very thick hair and a full beard, both of which had once been black. His eyes were grey, large and luminous, but strikingly prominent. He spoke with a broad accent. He was dressed in a peasant's long reddish coat of coarse convict cloth (as it used to be called) and had a stout rope round his waist. His throat and chest were bare. Beneath his coat, his shirt of the coarsest linen showed almost black with dirt, not having been changed for months. They said that he wore irons weighing thirty pounds under his coat. His stockingless feet were thrust in old slippers almost dropping to pieces.

"From the little Obdorsk monastery, from St. Sylvester," the monk answered humbly, whilst his keen and inquisitive but rather frightened little eyes kept watch on the hermit.

"I have been at your Sylvester's. I used to stay there. Is Sylvester well?"

The monk hesitated.

"You are a senseless lot! How do you keep the fasts?"

"Our dietary is according to the ancient conventual rules. During Lent there are no meals provided for Monday, Wednesday, and Friday. For Tuesday and Thursday we have white bread, stewed fruit with honey, wild berries, or salt cabbage and wholemeal stirabout. On Saturday white cabbage soup, noodles with peas, kasha, all with hemp oil. On weekdays we have dried fish and kasha with the cabbage soup. From Monday till Saturday evening, six whole days in Holy Week, nothing is cooked, and we have only bread and water, and that sparingly; if possible not taking food every day, just the same as is ordered for first week in Lent. On Good Friday nothing is eaten. In the same way on the Saturday we have to fast till three o'clock, and then take a little bread and water and drink a single cup of wine. On Holy Thursday we drink wine and have something cooked without oil or not cooked at all. Inasmuch as the Laodicean council lays down for Holy Thursday: "it is unseemly by remitting the fast on the Holy Thursday to dishonour the whole of Lent!" This is how we keep the fast. "But what is that compared with you, holy Father," added the monk, growing more confident, "for all the year round, even at Easter, you take nothing but bread and water, and what we should eat in two days lasts you full seven? It's truly marvellous—your great abstinence."

"And mushrooms?" asked Father Ferapont, suddenly.

"Mushrooms?" repeated the surprised monk.

"Yes. I can give up their bread, not needing it at all, and go away into the forest and live there on the mushrooms or the berries, but they can't give up their bread here, wherefore they are in bondage to the devil. Nowadays the unclean deny that there is need of such fasting. Haughty and unclean is their judgment."

"Och, true," sighed the monk.

"And have you seen devils among them?" asked Ferapont.

"Among them? Among whom?" asked the monk, timidly.

"I went to the Father Superior on Trinity Sunday last year, I haven't been since. I saw a devil sitting on one man's chest hiding under his cassock, only his horns poked out; another had one peeping out of his pocket with such sharp eyes, he was afraid of me; another settled in the unclean belly of one, another was hanging round a man's neck, and so he was carrying him about without seeing him."

"You—can see spirits?" the monk inquired.

"I tell you I can see, I can see through them. When I was coming out from the Superior's I saw one hiding from me behind the door, and a big one, a yard and a half or more high, with a thick long grey tail, and the tip of his tail was in the crack of the door and I was quick and slammed the door, pinching his tail in it. He squealed and began to struggle, and I made the sign of the cross over him three times. And he died on the spot like a crushed spider. He must have rotted there in the corner and be stinking, but they don't see, they don't smell it. It's a year since I have been there. I reveal it to you, as you are a stranger."

"Your words are terrible! But, holy and blessed Father,"

170

said the monk, growing bolder and bolder, "is it true, as they noise abroad even to distant lands about you, that you are in continual communication with the Holy Ghost?"

"He does fly down at times."

"How does he fly down? In what form?"

"As a bird."

"The Holy Ghost in the form of a Dove?"

"There's the Holy Ghost and there's the Holy Spirit. The Holy Spirit can appear as other birds—sometimes as a swallow, sometimes a goldfinch and sometimes a blue-tit."

"How do you know him from an ordinary tit?"

"He speaks."

"How does he speak, in what language?"

"Human language."

"And what does he tell you?"

"Why, to-day he told me that a fool would visit me and would ask me unseemly questions. You want to know too much, monk."

"Terrible are your words, most holy and blessed Father." The monk shook his head. But there was a doubtful look in his frightened little eyes.

"Do you see this tree?" asked Father Ferapont, after a pause.

"I do, blessed Father."

"You think it's an elm, but for me it has another shape."

"What sort of shape?" inquired the monk, after a pause of vain expectation.

"It happens at night. You see those two branches? In the night it is Christ holding out His arms to me and seeking me with those arms, I see it clearly and tremble. It's terrible, terrible!"

"What is there terrible if it's Christ Himself?"

"Why, He'll snatch me up and carry me away."

"Alive?"

"In the spirit and glory of Elijah, haven't you heard? He will take me in His arms and bear me away."

Though the monk returned to the cell he was sharing with one of the brothers, in considerable perplexity of mind, he still cherished at heart a greater reverence for Father Ferapont than for Father Zossima. He was strongly in favour of fasting, and it was not strange that one who kept so rigid a fast as Father Ferapont should "see marvels". His words seemed certainly queer, but God only could tell what was hidden in those words,

171

and were not worse words and acts commonly seen in those who have sacrificed their intellects for the glory of God? The pinching of the devil's tail he was ready and eager to believe, and not only in the figurative sense. Besides he had, before visiting the monastery, a strong prejudice against the institution of "elders", which he only knew of by hearsay and believed to be a pernicious innovation. Before he had been long at the monastery, he had detected the secret murmurings of some shallow brothers who disliked the institution. He was, besides, a meddlesome, inquisitive man, who poked his nose into everything. This was why the news of the fresh "miracle" performed by Father Zossima reduced him to extreme perplexity. Alyosha remembered afterwards how their inquisitive guest from Obdorsk had been continually flitting to and fro from one group to another, listening and asking questions among the monks that were crowding within and without the elder's cell. But he did not pay much attention to him at the time, and only recollected it afterwards.

He had no thought to spare for it, indeed, for when Father Zossima, feeling tired again, had gone back to bed, he thought of Alyosha as he was closing his eyes, and sent for him. Alyosha ran at once. There was no one else in the cell but Father Païssy, Father Iosif, and the novice Porfiry. The elder, opening his weary eyes and looking intently at Alyosha, asked him suddenly:

"Are your people expecting you, my son?"

Alyosha hesitated.

"Haven't they need of you? Didn't you promise someone yesterday to see them to-day?"

"I did promise—to my father—my brothers—others too."

"You see, you must go. Don't grieve. Be sure I shall not die without your being by to hear my last word. To you I will say that word, my son, it will be my last gift to you. To you, dear son, because you love me. But now go to keep your promise."

Alyosha immediately obeyed, though it was hard to go. But the promise that he should hear his last word on earth, that it should be the last gift to him, Alyosha, sent a thrill of rapture through his soul. He made haste that he might finish what he had to do in the town and return quickly. Father Païssy, too, uttered some words of exhortation which moved and surprised him greatly. He spoke as they left the cell together.

"Remember, young man, unceasingly," Father Païssy began,

172

without preface, "that the science of this world, which has become a great power, has, especially in the last century, analysed everything divine handed down to us in the holy books. After this cruel analysis the learned of this world have nothing left of all that was sacred of old. But they have only analysed the parts and overlooked the whole, and indeed their blindness is marvellous. Yet the whole still stands steadfast before their eyes, and the gates of hell shall not prevail against it. Has it not lasted nineteen centuries, is it not still a living, a moving power in the individual soul and in the masses of people? It is still as strong and living even in the souls of atheists, who have destroyed everything! For even those who have renounced Christianity and attack it, in their inmost being still follow the Christian ideal, for hitherto neither their subtlety nor the ardour of their hearts has been able to create a higher ideal of man and of virtue than the ideal given by Christ of old. When it has been attempted, the result has been only grotesque. Remember this especially, young man, since you are being sent into the world by your departing elder. Maybe, remembering this great day, you will not forget my words, uttered from the heart for your guidance, seeing you are young, and the temptations of the world are great and beyond your strength to endure. Well, now go, my orphan."

With these words Father Païssy blessed him. As Alyosha left the monastery and thought them over, he suddenly realised that he had met a new and unexpected friend, a warmly loving teacher, in this austere monk who had hitherto treated him sternly. It was as though Father Zossima had bequeathed him to him at his death, and "perhaps that's just what had passed between them", Alyosha thought suddenly. The philosophic reflections he had just heard so unexpectedly testified to the warmth of Father Païssy's heart. He was in haste to arm the boy's mind for conflict with temptation and to guard the young soul left in his charge with the strongest defence he could imagine.

CHAPTER II

AT HIS FATHER'S

FIRST of all, Alyosha went to his father. On the way he remembered that his father had insisted the day before that he should come without his brother Ivan seeing him. "Why so?'' Alyosha wondered suddenly. "Even if my father has something to say to me alone, why should I go in unseen? Most likely in his excitement yesterday he meant to say something different," he decided. Yet he was very glad when Marfa Ignatyevna, who opened the garden gate to him (Grigory, it appeared, was ill in bed in the lodge), told him in answer to his question that Ivan Fyodorovitch had gone out two hours ago.

"And my father?"

"He is up, taking his coffee," Marfa answered somewhat dryly.

Alyosha went in. The old man was sitting alone at the table, wearing slippers and a little old overcoat. He was amusing himself by looking through some accounts, rather inattentively, however. He was quite alone in the house, for Smerdyakov too had gone out marketing. Though he had got up early and was trying to put a bold face on it, he looked tired and weak. His forehead, upon which huge purple bruises had come out during the night, was bandaged with a red handkerchief; his nose too had swollen terribly in the night, and some smaller bruises covered it in patches, giving his whole face a peculiarly spiteful and irritable look. The old man was aware of this, and turned a hostile glance on Alyosha as he came in.

"The coffee is cold," he cried harshly; "I won't offer you any. I've ordered nothing but a Lenten fish soup to-day, and I don't invite anyone to share it. Why have you come?"

"To find out how you are," said Alyosha.

"Yes. Besides, I told you to come yesterday. It's all of no consequence. You need not have troubled. But I knew you'd come poking in directly."

He said this with almost hostile feeling. At the same time he got up and looked anxiously in the looking-glass (perhaps for the fortieth time that morning) at his nose. He began, too, binding his red handkerchief more becomingly on his forehead.

"Red's better. It's just like the hospital in a white one," he observed sententiously. "Well, how are things over there? How is your elder?"

"He is very bad; he may die to-day," answered Alyosha. But his father had not listened, and had forgotten his own question at once.

"Ivan's gone out," he said suddenly. "He is doing his utmost to carry off Mitya's betrothed. That's what he is stay-

174

ing here for," he added maliciously, and, twisting his mouth, looked at Alyosha.

"Surely he did not tell you so?" asked Alyosha.

"Yes, he did, long ago. Would you believe it, he told me three weeks ago? You don't suppose he too came to murder me, do you? He must have had some object in coming."

"What do you mean? Why do you say such things?" said Alyosha, troubled.

"He doesn't ask for money, it's true, but yet he won't get a farthing from me. I intend living as long as possible, you may as well know, my dear Alexey Fyodorovitch, and so I need every farthing, and the longer I live, the more I shall need it," he continued, pacing from one corner of the room to the other, keeping his hands in the pockets of his loose greasy overcoat made of yellow cotton material. "I can still pass for a man at five-and-fifty, but I want to pass for one for another twenty years. As I get older, you know, I shan't be a pretty object. The wenches won't come to me of their own accord, so I shall want my money. So I am saving up more and more, simply for myself, my dear son Alexey Fyodorovitch. You may as well know. For I mean to go on in my sins to the end, let me tell you. For sin is sweet; all abuse it, but all men live in it, only others do it on the sly, and I openly. And so all the other sinners fall upon me for being so simple. And your paradise, Alexey Fyodorovitch, is not to my taste, let me tell you that; and it's not the proper place for a gentleman, your paradise, even if it exists. I believe that I fall asleep and don't wake up again, and that's all. You can pray for my soul if you like. And if you don't want to, don't, damn you! That's my philosophy. Ivan talked well here yesterday, though we were all drunk. Ivan is a conceited coxcomb, but he has no particular learning . . . nor education either. He sits silent and smiles at one without speaking—that's what pulls him through."

Alyosha listened to him in silence.

"Why won't he talk to me? If he does speak, he gives himself airs. Your Ivan is a scoundrel! And I'll marry Grushenka in a minute if I want to. For if you've money, Alexey Fyodorovitch, you have only to want a thing and you can have it. That's what Ivan is afraid of, he is on the watch to prevent me getting married and that's why he is egging on Mitya to marry Grushenka himself. He hopes to keep me from Grushenka by that (as though I should leave him my money if I don't marry her!). Besides if Mitya marries Grushenka, Ivan

175

will carry off his rich betrothed, that's what he's reckoning on! He is a scoundrel, your Ivan!"

"How cross you are. It's because of yesterday; you had better lie down," said Alyosha.

"There! you say that," the old man observed suddenly, as though it had struck him for the first time, "and I am not angry with you. But if Ivan said it, I should be angry with him. It is only with you I have good moments, else you know I am an ill-natured man."

"You are not ill-natured, but distorted," said Alyosha, with a smile.

"Listen. I meant this morning to get that ruffian Mitya locked up and I don't know now what I shall decide about it. Of course in these fashionable days fathers and mothers are looked upon as a prejudice, but even now the law does not allow you to drag your old father about by the hair, to kick him in the face in his own house, and brag of murdering him outright—all in the presence of witnesses. If I liked, I could crush him and could have him locked up at once for what he did yesterday."

"Then you don't mean to take proceedings?"

"Ivan has dissuaded me. I shouldn't care about Ivan, but there's another thing."

And bending down to Alyosha, he went on in a confidential half-whisper:

"If I send the ruffian to prison, she'll hear of it and run to see him at once. But if she hears that he has beaten me, a weak old man, within an inch of my life, she may give him up and come to me. . . . For that's her way, everything by contraries. I know her through and through! Won't you have a drop of brandy? Take some cold coffee and I'll pour a quarter of a glass of brandy into it, it's delicious, my boy."

"No, thank you. I'll take that roll with me if I may," said Alyosha, and taking a halfpenny French roll he put it in the pocket of his cassock. "And you'd better not have brandy, either," he suggested apprehensively, looking into the old man's face.

"You are quite right, it irritates my nerves instead of soothing them. Only one little glass. I'll get it out of the cupboard."

He unlocked the cupboard, poured out a glass, drank it, then locked the cupboard and put the key back in his pocket.

"That's enough. One glass won't kill me."

"You see, you are in a better humour now," said Alyosha, smiling.

"Um! I love you even without the brandy, but with scoundrels I am a scoundrel. Ivan is not going to Tchermashnya —why is that? He wants to spy how much I give Grushenka if she comes. They are all scoundrels! But I don't recognise Ivan, I don't know him at all. Where does he come from? He is not one of us in soul. As though I'd leave him anything! I shan't leave a will at all, you may as well know. And I'll crush Mitya like a beetle. I squash black-beetles at night with my slipper; they squelch when you tread on them. And your Mitya will squelch too. *Your* Mitya, for you love him. Yes, you love him and I am not afraid of your loving him. But if Ivan loved him I should be afraid for myself at his loving him. But Ivan loves nobody. Ivan is not one of us. People like Ivan are not our sort, my boy. They are like a cloud of dust. When the wind blows, the dust will be gone . . . I had a silly idea in my head when I told you to come to-day; I wanted to find out from you about Mitya. If I were to hand him over a thousand or maybe two now, would the beggarly wretch agree to take himself off altogether for five years or, better still, thirty-five, and without Grushenka, and give her up once for all, eh?"

"I—I'll ask him," muttered Alyosha. "If you would give him three thousand, perhaps he——"

"That's nonsense! You needn't ask him now, no need! I've changed my mind. It was a nonsensical idea of mine. I won't give him anything, not a penny, I want my money myself," cried the old man, waving his hand. "I'll crush him like a beetle without it. Don't say anything to him or else he will begin hoping. There's nothing for you to do here, you needn't stay. Is that betrothed of his, Katerina Ivanovna, whom he has kept so carefully hidden from me all this time, going to marry him or not? You went to see her yesterday, I believe?"

"Nothing will induce her to abandon him."

"There you see how dearly these fine young ladies love a rake and a scoundrel. They are poor creatures I tell you, those pale young ladies, very different from . . . Ah, if I had his youth and the looks I had then (for I was better-looking than he at eight-and-twenty) I'd have been a conquering hero just as he is. He is a low cad! But he shan't have Grushenka, anyway, he shan't! I'll crush him!"

His anger had returned with the last words.

"You can go. There's nothing for you to do here to-day," he snapped harshly.

Alyosha went up to say good-bye to him, and kissed him on the shoulder.

"What's that for?" The old man was a little surprised. "We shall see each other again, or do you think we shan't?"

"Not at all, I didn't mean anything."

"Nor did I, I did not mean anything," said the old man, looking at him. "Listen, listen," he shouted after him, "make haste and come again and I'll have a fish soup for you, a fine one, not like to-day. Be sure to come! Come to-morrow, do you hear, to-morrow!"

And as soon as Alyosha had gone out of the door, he went to the cupboard again and poured out another half-glass.

"I won't have more!" he muttered, clearing his throat, and again he locked the cupboard and put the key in his pocket. Then he went into his bedroom, lay down on the bed, exhausted, and in one minute he was asleep.

CHAPTER III

A MEETING WITH THE SCHOOLBOYS

"THANK goodness he did not ask me about Grushenka," thought Alyosha, as he left his father's house and turned towards Madame Hohlakov's, "or I might have to tell him of my meeting with Grushenka yesterday."

Alyosha felt painfully that since yesterday both combatants had renewed their energies, and that their hearts had grown hard again. "Father is spiteful and angry, he's made some plan and will stick to it. And what of Dmitri? He too will be harder than yesterday, he too must be spiteful and angry, and he too, no doubt, has made some plan. Oh, I must succeed in finding him to-day, whatever happens."

But Alyosha had not long to meditate. An incident occurred on the road which, though apparently of little consequence, made a great impression on him. Just after he had crossed the square and turned the corner coming out into Mihailovsky Street, which is divided by a small ditch from the High Street (our whole town is intersected by ditches), he saw a group of schoolboys, between the ages of nine and twelve, at the bridge. They were going home from school, some with their bags on their shoulders, others with leather satchels slung across them, some in short jackets, others in little overcoats. Some even had those high boots with creases round the ankles, such as little boys spoilt by rich fathers love to wear. The whole group was talking eagerly about something, apparently holding a council. Alyosha had never from his Moscow days been able to pass children without taking notice of them, and although he was particularly fond of children of three or thereabout, he liked schoolboys of ten and eleven too. And so, anxious as he was to-day, he wanted at once to turn aside to talk to them. He looked into their excited rosy faces, and noticed at once that all the boys had stones in their hands. Behind the ditch, some thirty paces away, there was another schoolboy standing by a fence. He too had a satchel at his side. He was about ten years old, pale, delicate-looking and with sparkling black eyes. He kept an attentive and anxious watch on the other six, obviously his schoolfellows with whom he had just come out of school, but with whom he had evidently had a feud.

Alyosha went up and addressing a fair, curly-headed, rosy boy in a black jacket observed:

"When I used to wear a satchel like yours, I always used to carry it on my left side, so as to have my right hand free, but you've got yours on your right side. So it will be awkward for you to get at it."

Alyosha had no art or premeditation in beginning with this practical remark. But it is the only way for a grown-up person to get at once into confidential relations with a child, or still more with a group of children. One must begin in a serious business-like way so as to be on a perfectly equal footing. Alyosha understood it by instinct.

"But he is left-handed," another, a fine healthy-looking boy of eleven, answered promptly. All the others stared at Alyosha.

"He even throws stones with his left hand," observed a third.

At that instant a stone flew into the group, but only just grazed the left-handed boy, though it was well and vigorously thrown by the boy standing the other side of the ditch.

"Give it him, hit him back, Smurov," they all shouted. But Smurov, the left-handed boy, needed no telling, and at once avenged himself; he threw a stone, but it missed the boy and hit the ground. The boy the other side of the ditch, the pocket of whose coat was visibly bulging with stones, flung another stone at the group; this time it flew straight at Alyosha and hit him painfully on the shoulder.

"He aimed it at you, he meant it for you. You are Kara-mazov, Karamazov?" the boys shouted, laughing. "Come, all throw at him at once!" and six stones flew at the boy. One struck the boy on the head and he fell down, but at once leapt up and began ferociously returning their fire. Both sides threw stones incessantly. Many of the group had their pockets full too.

"What are you about? Aren't you ashamed? Six against one! Why, you'll kill him," cried Alyosha.

He ran forward and met the flying stones to screen the solitary boy. Three or four ceased throwing for a minute.

"He began first!" cried a boy in a red shirt in an angry childish voice. "He is a beast, he stabbed Krassotkin in class the other day with a penknife. It bled. Krassotkin wouldn't tell tales, but he must be thrashed."

"But what for? I suppose you tease him."

"There, he sent a stone in your back again, he knows you," cried the children. "It's you he is throwing at now, not us. Come, all of you, at him again, don't miss, Smurov!" and again a fire of stones, and a very vicious one, began. The boy the other side of the ditch was hit in the chest; he screamed, began to cry and ran away uphill towards Mihailovsky Street. They all shouted: "Aha, he is funking, he is running away. Wisp of tow!"

"You don't know what a beast he is, Karamazov, killing is too good for him," said the boy in the jacket, with flashing eyes. He seemed to be the eldest.

"What's wrong with him?" asked Alyosha, "is he a tell-tale or what?"

The boys looked at one another as though derisively.

"Are you going that way, to Mihailovsky?" the same boy went on. "Catch him up . . . You see he's stopped again, he is waiting and looking at you."

"He is looking at you," the other boys chimed in.

"You ask him, does he like a dishevelled wisp of tow? Do you hear, ask him that!"

There was a general burst of laughter. Alyosha looked at them, and they at him.

"Don't go near him, he'll hurt you," cried Smurov in a warning voice.

"I shan't ask him about the wisp of tow, for I expect you tease him with that question somehow. But I'll find out from him why you hate him so."

"Find out then, find out," cried the boys, laughing.

Alyosha crossed the bridge and walked uphill by the fence, straight towards the boy.

"You'd better look out," the boys called after him; "he won't be afraid of you. He will stab you in a minute, on the sly, as he did Krassotkin." ·

The boy waited for him without budging. Coming up to him, Alyosha saw facing him a child of about nine years old. He was an undersized weakly boy with a thin long pale face, with large dark eyes that gazed at him vindictively. He was dressed in a rather shabby old overcoat, which he had monstrously outgrown. His bare arms stuck out beyond his sleeves. There was a large patch on the right knee of his trousers, and in his right boot just at the toe there was a big hole in the leather, carefully blackened with ink. Both the pockets of his greatcoat were weighed down with stones. Alyosha stopped two steps in front of him, looking inquiringly at him. The boy, seeing at once from Alyosha's eyes that he wouldn't beat him, became less defiant, and addressed him first.

"I am alone, and there are six of them. I'll beat them all, alone!" he said suddenly, with flashing eyes.

"I think one of the stones must have hurt you badly," observed Alyosha.

"But I hit Smurov on the head!" cried the boy.

"They told me that you know me, and that you threw a stone at me on purpose," said Alyosha.

The boy looked darkly at him.

"I don't know you. Do you know me?" Alyosha continued.

"Let me alone!" the boy cried irritably; but he did not move, as though he were expecting something, and again there was a vindictive light in his eyes.

"Very well, I am going," said Alyosha; "only I don't know you and I don't tease you. They told me how they tease you, but I don't want to tease you. Good-bye!"

"Monk in silk trousers!" cried the boy, following Alyosha with the same vindictive and defiant expression, and he threw himself into an attitude of defence, feeling sure that now Alyosha would fall upon him; but Alyosha turned, looked at him, and walked away. He had not gone three steps before the biggest stone the boy had in his pocket hit him a painful blow in the back.

"So you'll hit a man from behind! They tell the truth, then, when they say that you attack on the sly," said Alyosha, turning round again. This time the boy threw a stone savagely right into Alyosha's face; but Alyosha just had time to guard himself, and the stone struck him on the elbow.

"Aren't you ashamed? What have I done to you?" he cried.

The boy waited in silent defiance, certain that now Alyosha would attack him. Seeing that even now he would not, his rage was like a little wild beast's; he flew at Alyosha himself, and before Alyosha had time to move, the spiteful child had seized his left hand with both of his and bit his middle finger. He fixed his teeth in it and it was ten seconds before he let go. Alyosha cried out with pain and pulled his finger away with all his might. The child let go at last and retreated to his former distance. Alyosha's finger had been badly bitten to the bone, close to the nail; it began to bleed. Alyosha took out his handkerchief and bound it tightly round his injured hand. He was a full minute bandaging it. The boy stood waiting all the time. At last Alyosha raised his gentle eyes and looked at him.

"Very well," he said, "you see how badly you've bitten me. That's enough, isn't it? Now tell me what have I done to you?"

The boy stared in amazement.

"Though I don't know you and it's the first time I've seen you," Alyosha went on with the same serenity, "yet I must have done something to you—you wouldn't have hurt me like this for nothing. So what have I done? How have I wronged you, tell me?"

Instead of answering, the boy broke into a loud tearful wail and ran away. Alyosha walked slowly after him towards Mihailovsky Street, and for a long time he saw the child running in the distance as fast as ever, not turning his head, and no doubt still keeping up his tearful wail. He made up his mind to find him out as soon as he had time, and to solve the mystery. Just now he had not the time.

CHAPTER IV

AT THE HOHLAKOVS'

ALYOSHA soon reached Madame Hohlakov's house, a handsome stone house of two storeys, one of the finest in our town. Though Madame Hohlakov spent most of her time in another province where she had an estate, or in Moscow, where she had a house of her own, yet she had a house in our town too, inherited from her forefathers. The estate in our district was the largest of her three estates, yet she had been very little in our province before this time. She ran out to Alyosha in the hall.

"Did you get my letter about the new miracle?" She spoke rapidly and nervously.

"Yes."

"Did you show it to everyone? He restored the son to his mother!"

"He is dying to-day," said Alyosha.

"I have heard, I know, oh, how I long to talk to you, to you, or someone about all this. No, to you, to you! And how sorry I am I can't see him! The whole town is in excitement, they are all suspense. But now—do you know Katerina Ivanovna is here now?"

"Ah, that's lucky," cried Alyosha. "Then I shall see her here. She told me yesterday to be sure to come and see her to-day."

"I know, I know all. I've heard exactly what happened yesterday—and the atrocious behaviour of that—creature. *C'est tragique,* and if I'd been in her place I don't know what I should have done. And your brother Dmitri Fyodorovitch, what do you think of him?—my goodness! Alexey Fyodorovitch, I am forgetting, only fancy; your brother is in there with her, not that dreadful brother who was so shocking yesterday, but the other, Ivan Fyodorovitch, he is sitting with her talking; they are having a serious conversation. If you could only imagine what's passing between them now—it's awful, I tell you it's lacerating, it's like some incredible tale of horror. They are ruining their lives for no reason anyone can see. They both recognise it and revel in it. I've been watching for you! I've been thirsting for you! It's too much for me, that's the worst of it. I'll tell you all about it presently, but now I must speak of something else, the most important thing—I had quite forgotten what's most important. Tell me, why has Lise been in hysterics? As soon as she heard you were here, she began to be hysterical!"

"*Maman,* it's you who are hysterical now, not I." Lise's voice carolled through a tiny crack of the door at the side. Her voice sounded as though she wanted to laugh, but was doing her utmost to control it. Alyosha at once noticed the crack, and no doubt Lise was peeping through it, but that he could not see.

"And no wonder, Lise, no wonder . . . your caprices will make me hysterical too. But she is so ill, Alexey Fyodorovitch, she has been so ill all night, feverish and moaning! I could hardly wait for the morning and for Herzenstube to come. He says that he can make nothing of it, that we must wait. Herzenstube always comes and says that he can make nothing of it. As soon as you approached the house, she screamed, fell into hysterics, and insisted on being wheeled back into this room here."

"Mamma, I didn't know he had come. It wasn't on his account I wanted to be wheeled into this room."

"That's not true, Lise. Yulia ran to tell that Alexey Fyodorovitch was coming. She was on the look-out for you."

"My darling mamma, it's not at all clever of you. But if you want to make up for it and say something very clever, dear mamma, you'd better tell our honoured visitor, Alexey Fyodorovitch, that he has shown his want of wit by venturing to us after what happened yesterday and although everyone is laughing at him."

"Lise, you go too far. I declare I shall have to be severe. Who laughs at him? I am so glad he has come, I need him, I can't do without him. Oh, Alexey Fyodorovitch, I am exceedingly unhappy!"

"But what's the matter with you, mamma darling?"

"Ah, your caprices, Lise, your fidgetiness, your illness, that awful night of fever, that awful everlasting Herzenstube, ever-lasting, everlasting, that's the worst of it! Everything, in fact, everything. . . . Even that miracle, too! Oh, how it has up-set me, how it has shattered me, that miracle, dear Alexey Fyodorovitch! And that tragedy in the drawing-room, it's more than I can bear, I warn you. I can't bear it. A comedy, perhaps, not a tragedy. Tell me, will Father Zossima live till to-morrow, will he? Oh, my God! What is happening to me? Every minute I close my eyes and see that it's all nonsense, all nonsense."

"I should be very grateful," Alyosha interrupted suddenly, "if you could give me a clean rag to bind up my finger with. I have hurt it, and it's very painful."

Alyosha unbound his bitten finger. The handkerchief was soaked with blood. Madame Hohlakov screamed and shut her eyes.

"Good heavens, what a wound, how awful!"

184

But as soon as Lise saw Alyosha's finger through the crack, she flung the door wide open.

"Come, come here," she cried, imperiously. "No nonsense now! Good heavens, why did you stand there saying nothing about it all this time? He might have bled to death, mamma! How did you do it? Water, water! You must wash it first of all, simply hold it in cold water to stop the pain, and keep it there, keep it there. . . . Make haste, mamma, some water in a slop basin. But do make haste," she finished nervously. She was quite frightened at the sight of Alyosha's wound.

"Shouldn't we send for Herzenstube?" cried Madame Hohlakov.

"Mamma, you'll be the death of me. Your Herzenstube will come and say that he can make nothing of it! Water, water! Mamma, for goodness' sake go yourself and hurry Yulia, she is such a slow-coach and never can come quickly! Make haste, mamma, or I shall die."

"Why, it's nothing much," cried Alyosha, frightened at this alarm.

Yulia ran in with water and Alyosha put his finger in it.

"Some lint, mamma, for mercy's sake, bring some lint and that muddy caustic lotion for wounds, what's it called? We've got some. You know where the bottle is, mamma; it's in your bedroom in the right-hand cupboard, there's a big bottle of it there with the lint."

"I'll bring everything in a minute, Lise, only don't scream and don't fuss. You see how bravely Alexey Fyodorovitch bears it. Where did you get such a dreadful wound, Alexey Fyodorovitch?"

Madame Hohlakov hastened away. This was all Lise was waiting for.

"First of all, answer the question, where did you get hurt like this?" she asked Alyosha quickly. "And then I'll talk to you about something quite different. Well?"

Instinctively feeling that the time of her mother's absence was precious for her, Alyosha hastened to tell her of his enigmatic meeting with the schoolboys in the fewest words possible. Lise clasped her hands at his story.

"How can you, and in that dress too, associate with school-boys!" she cried angrily, as though she had a right to control him. "You are nothing but a boy yourself if you can do that, a perfect boy! But you must find out for me about that horrid boy and tell me all about it, for there's some mystery in it.

Now for the second thing, but first a question: does the pain prevent you talking about utterly unimportant things, but talking sensibly?"

"Of course not, and I don't feel much pain now."

"That's because your finger is in the water. It must be changed directly, for it will get warm in a minute. Yulia, bring some ice from the cellar and another basin of water. Now she is gone, I can speak; will you give me the letter I sent you yesterday, dear Alexey Fyodorovitch—be quick, for mamma will be back in a minute and I don't want——"

"I haven't got the letter."

"That's not true, you have. I knew you would say that. You've got it in that pocket. I've been regretting that joke all night. Give me back the letter at once, give it me."

"I've left it at home."

"But you can't consider me as a child, a little girl, after that silly joke! I beg your pardon for that silliness, but you must bring me the letter, if you really haven't got it—bring it to-day, you must, you must."

"To-day I can't possibly, for I am going back to the monastery and I shan't come and see you for the next two days—three or four perhaps—for Father Zossima——"

"Four days, what nonsense! Listen. Did you laugh at me very much?"

"I didn't laugh at all."

"Why not?"

"Because I believed all you said."

"You are insulting me!"

"Not at all. As soon as I read it I thought that all that would come to pass, for as soon as Father Zossima dies I am to leave the monastery. Then I shall go back and finish my studies, and when you reach the legal age we will be married. I shall love you. Though I haven't had time to think about it, I believe I couldn't find a better wife than you, and Father Zossima tells me I must marry."

"But I am a cripple, wheeled about in a chair," laughed Lise, flushing crimson.

"I'll wheel you about myself, but I'm sure you'll get well by then."

"But you are mad," said Lise nervously, "to make all this nonsense out of a joke! Here's mamma, very à propos, perhaps. Mamma, how slow you always are, how can you be so long! And here's Yulia with the ice!"

"Oh, Lise, don't scream, above all things don't scream. That scream drives me . . . How can I help it when you put the lint in another place? I've been hunting and hunting—I do believe you did it on purpose."

"But I couldn't tell that he would come with a bad finger, or else perhaps I might have done it on purpose. My darling mamma, you begin to say really witty things."

'Never mind my being witty, but I must say you show nice feeling for Alexey Fyodorovitch's sufferings! Oh, my dear Alexey Fyodorovitch, what's killing me is no one thing in particular, not Herzenstube, but everything together, that's what is too much for me."

"That's enough, mamma, enough about Herzenstube," Lise laughed gaily. "Make haste with the lint and the lotion, mamma. That's simply Goulard's water, Alexey Fyodorovitch, I remember the name now, but it's a splendid lotion. Would you believe it, mamma, on the way here he had a fight with the boys in the street, and it was a boy bit his finger! Isn't he a child, a child himself? Is he fit to be married after that? For, only fancy, he wants to be married, mamma. Just think of him married, wouldn't it be funny, wouldn't it be awful?"

And Lise kept laughing her thin hysterical giggle, looking shyly at Alyosha.

"But why married, Lise? What makes you talk of such a thing? It's quite out of place—and perhaps the boy was rabid."

"Why, mamma! As though there were rabid boys!"

"Why not, Lise, as though I had said something stupid! Your boy might have been bitten by a mad dog and he would become mad and bite anyone near him. How well she has bandaged it, Alexey Fyodorovitch. I couldn't have done it. Do you still feel the pain?"

"It's nothing much now."

"You don't feel afraid of water?" asked Lise.

"Come, that's enough, Lise, perhaps I really was rather too quick talking of the boy being rabid, and you pounced upon it at once. Katerina Ivanovna has only just heard that you are here, Alexey Fyodorovitch, she simply rushed at me, she's dying to see you, dying!"

"Ach, mamma, go to them yourself. He can't go just now, he is in too much pain."

"Not at all, I can go quite well," said Alyosha.

·"What! You are going away? Is that what you say?"

"Well, when I've seen them I'll come back here and we can talk as much as you like. But I should like to see Katerina Ivanovna at once, for I am very anxious to be back at the monastery as soon as I can."

"Mamma, take him away quickly. Alexey Fyodorovitch, don't trouble to come and see me afterwards, but go straight back to your monastery and a good riddance. I want to sleep, I didn't sleep all night."

"Ah, Lise, you are only making fun, but how I wish you would sleep!" cried Madame Hohlakov.

"I don't know what I've done. . . . I'll stay another three minutes, five if you like," muttered Alyosha.

"Even five! Do take him away quickly, mamma, he is a monster."

"Lise, you are crazy. Let us go, Alexey Fyodorovitch, she is too capricious to-day. I am afraid to cross her. Oh, the trouble one has with nervous girls! Perhaps she really will be able to sleep after seeing you. How quickly you have made her sleepy, and how fortunate it is."

"Ah, mamma, how sweetly you talk. I must kiss you for it, mamma."

"And I kiss you too, Lise. Listen, Alexey Fyodorovitch," Madame Hohlakov began mysteriously and importantly, speaking in a rapid whisper. "I don't want to suggest anything, I don't want to lift the veil, you will see for yourself what's going on. It's appalling. It's the most fantastic farce. She loves your brother Ivan, and she is doing her utmost to persuade herself she loves your brother Dmitri. It's appalling! I'll go in with you, and if they don't turn me out, I'll stay to the end.

CHAPTER V

A LACERATION IN THE DRAWING-ROOM

BUT in the drawing-room the conversation was already over. Katerina Ivanovna was greatly excited, though she looked resolute. At the moment Alyosha and Madame Hohlakov entered Ivan Fyodorovitch stood up to take leave. His face was rather pale, and Alyosha looked at him anxiously. For this moment was to solve a doubt, a harassing enigma which had for some time haunted Alyosha. During the preceding month it had been several times suggested to him that his brother Ivan was in love with Katerina Ivanovna, and, what was more, than he meant "to carry her off" from Dmitri. Until quite lately the idea seemed to Alyosha monstrous, though it worried him extremely. He loved both his brothers, and dreaded such rivalry between them. Meantime, Dmitri had said outright on the previous day that he was glad that Ivan was his rival, and that it was a great assistance to him, Dmitri. In what way did it assist him? To marry Grushenka? But that Alyosha considered the worst thing possible. Besides all this, Alyosha had till the evening before implicitly believed that Katerina Ivanovna had a steadfast and passionate love for Dmitri; but he had only believed it till the evening before. He had fancied, too, that she was incapable of loving a man like Ivan, and that she did love Dmitri, and loved him just as he was, in spite of all the strangeness of such a passion.

But during yesterday's scene with Grushenka another idea had struck him. The word "lacerating", which Madame Hohlakov had just uttered, almost made him start, because half waking up towards daybreak that night he had cried out, "Laceration, laceration!" probably applying it to his dream. He had been dreaming all night of the previous day's scene at Katerina Ivanovna's. Now Alyosha was impressed by Madame Hohlakov's blunt and persistent assertion that Katerina Ivanovna was in love with Ivan, and only deceived herself through some sort of pose, from "self-laceration", and tortured herself by her pretended love for Dmitri from some fancied duty of gratitude. "Yes," he thought, "perhaps the whole truth lies in those words." But in that case what was Ivan's position? Alyosha felt instinctively that a character like Katerina Ivanovna's must dominate, and she could only dominate someone like Dmitri, and never a man like Ivan. For Dmitri might at last submit to her domination "to his own happiness" (which was what Alyosha would have desired), but Ivan—no, Ivan could not submit to her, and such submission would not give him happiness. Alyosha could not help believing that of Ivan. And now all these doubts and reflections flitted through his mind as he entered the drawing-room. Another idea, too, forced itself upon him: "What if she loved neither of them—neither Ivan nor Dmitri?"

It must be noted that Alyosha felt, as it were, ashamed of his own thoughts and blamed himself when they kept recurring to him during the last month. "What do I know about love and women and how can I decide such questions?" he thought reproachfully, after some doubts and surmises. And yet it was impossible not to think about it. He felt instinctively that this rivalry was of immense importance in his brothers' lives and that a great deal depended upon it.

"One reptile will devour the other," Ivan had pronounced the day before, speaking in anger of his father and Dmitri. So Ivan looked upon Dmitri as a reptile, and perhaps had long done so. Was it perhaps since he had known Katerina Ivanovna? That phrase had, of course, escaped Ivan unawares yesterday, but that only made it more important. If he felt like that, what chance was there of peace? Were there not, on the contrary, new grounds for hatred and hostility in their family? And with which of them was Alyosha to sympathise? And what was he to wish for each of them? He loved them both, but what could he desire for each in the midst of these conflicting interests? He might go quite astray in this maze, and Alyosha's heart could not endure uncertainty, because his love was always of an active character. He was incapable of passive love. If he loved anyone, he set to work at once to help him. And to do so he must know what he was aiming at; he must know for certain what was best for each, and having ascertained this it was natural for him to help them both. But instead of a definite aim, he found nothing but uncertainty and perplexity on all sides. "It was lacerating," as was said just now. But what could he understand even in this "laceration"? He did not understand the first word in this perplexing maze.

Seeing Alyosha, Katerina Ivanovna said quickly and joyfully to Ivan, who had already got up to go: "A minute! Stay another minute! I want to hear the opinion of this person here whom I trust absolutely. Don't go away," she added, addressing Madame Hohlakov. She made Alyosha sit down beside her, and Madame Hohlakov sat opposite, by Ivan.

"You are all my friends here, all I have in the world, my dear friends," she began warmly, in a voice which quivered with genuine tears of suffering, and Alyosha's heart warmed to her at once. "You, Alexey Fyodorovitch, were witness yesterday of that abominable scene, and saw what I did. You did not see it, Ivan Fyodorovitch; he did. What he thought of me yesterday I don't know. I only know one thing, that if it were repeated to-day, this minute, I should express the same feelings again as yesterday—the same feelings, the same words, the same actions. You remember my actions, Alexey Fyodorovitch;

you checked me in one of them" . . . (as she said that, she flushed and her eyes shone). "I must tell you that I can't get over it. Listen, Alexey Fyodorovitch. I don't even know whether I still love *him*. I feel *pity* for him, and that is a poor sign of love. If I loved him, if I still loved him, perhaps I shouldn't be sorry for him now, but should hate him."

Her voice quivered, and tears glittered on her eyelashes. Alyosha shuddered inwardly. "That girl is truthful and sincere," he thought, "and she does not love Dmitri any more."

"That's true, that's true," cried Madame Hohlakov.

"Wait, dear. I haven't told you the chief, the final decision I came to during the night. I feel that perhaps my decision is a terrible one—for me—but I foresee that nothing will induce me to change it—nothing. It will be so all my life. My dear, kind, ever-faithful and generous adviser, the one friend I have in the world, Ivan Fyodorovitch, with his deep insight into the heart, approves and commends my decision. He knows it."

"Yes, I approve of it," Ivan assented, in a subdued but firm voice.

"But I should like Alyosha, too (Ah! Alexey Fyodorovitch, forgive my calling you simply Alyosha), I should like Alexey Fyodorovitch, too, to tell me before my two friends whether I am right. I feel instinctively that you, Alyosha, my dear brother (for you are a dear brother to me)," she said again ecstatically, taking his cold hand in her hot one, "I foresee that your decision, your approval, will bring me peace, in spite of all my sufferings, for, after your words, I shall be calm and submit—I feel that."

"I don't know what you are asking me," said Alyosha, flushing. "I only know that I love you and at this moment wish for your happiness more than my own! . . . But I know nothing about such affairs," something impelled him to add hurriedly.

"In such affairs, Alexey Fyodorovitch, in such affairs, the chief thing is honour and duty and something higher—I don't know what—but higher perhaps even than duty. I am conscious of this irresistible feeling in my heart, and it compels me irresistibly. But it may be all put in two words. I've already decided, even if he marries that—creature (she began solemnly), whom I never, never can forgive, *even then I will not abandon him.* Henceforward I will never, never abandon him!" she cried, breaking into a sort of pale, hysterical ecstasy. "Not that I would run after him continually, get in

191

his way and worry him. Oh, no! I will go away to another town—where you like—but I will watch over him all my life— I will watch over him all my life unceasingly. When he becomes unhappy with that woman, and that is bound to happen quite soon, let him come to me and he will find a friend, a sister. . . . Only a sister, of course, and so for ever; but he will learn at least that that sister is really his sister, who loves him and has sacrificed all her life to him. I will gain my point. I will insist on his knowing me and confiding entirely in me, without reserve," she cried, in a sort of frenzy. "I will be a god to whom he can pray—and that, at least, he owes me for his treachery and for what I suffered yesterday through him. And let him see that all my life I will be true to him and the promise I gave him, in spite of his being untrue and betraying me. I will—I will become nothing but a means for his happiness, or—how shall I say?—an instrument, a machine for his happiness, and that for my whole life, my whole life, and that he may see that all his life! That's my decision. Ivan Fyodorovitch fully approves me."

She was breathless. She had perhaps intended to express her idea with more dignity, art and naturalness, but her speech was too hurried and crude. It was full of youthful impulsiveness, it betrayed that she was still smarting from yesterday's insult, and that her pride craved satisfaction. She felt this herself. Her face suddenly darkened, an unpleasant look came into her eyes. Alyosha at once saw it and felt a pang of sympathy. His brother Ivan made it worse by adding:

"I've only expressed my own view," he said. "From anyone else this would have been affected and overstrained, but from you—no. Any other woman would have been wrong, but you are right. I don't know how to explain it, but I see that you are absolutely genuine and, therefore, you are right."

"But that's only for the moment. And what does this moment stand for? Nothing but yesterday's insult." Madame Hohlakov obviously had not intended to interfere, but she could not refrain from this very just comment.

"Quite so, quite so," cried Ivan, with peculiar eagerness, obviously annoyed at being interrupted. "In anyone else this moment would be only due to yesterday's impression and would be only a moment. But with Katerina Ivanovna's character, that moment will last all her life. What for anyone else would be only a promise is for her an everlasting, burdensome, grim perhaps, but unflagging duty. And she will be sustained by the feeling of this duty being fulfilled. Your life, Katerina Ivanovna, will henceforth be spent in painful brooding over your own feelings, your own heroism, and your own suffering; but in the end that suffering will be softened and will pass into sweet contemplation of the fulfilment of a bold and proud design. Yes, proud it certainly is, and desperate in any case, but a triumph for you. And the consciousness of it will at last be a source of complete satisfaction and will make you resigned to everything else."

This was unmistakably said with some malice and obviously with intention; even perhaps with no desire to conceal that he spoke ironically and with intention.

"Oh dear, how mistaken it all is!" Madame Hohlakov cried again.

"Alexey Fyodorovitch, you speak. I want dreadfully to know what you will say!" cried Katerina Ivanovna, and burst into tears. Alyosha got up from the sofa.

"It's nothing, nothing!" she went on through her tears. "I'm upset, I didn't sleep last night. But by the side of two such friends as you and your brother I still feel strong—for I know—you two will never desert me."

"Unluckily I am obliged to return to Moscow—perhaps to-morrow—and to leave you for a long time—— And, unluckily, it's unavoidable," Ivan said suddenly.

"To-morrow—to Moscow!" her face was suddenly contorted; "but—but, dear me, how fortunate," she cried in a voice suddenly changed. In one instant there was no trace left of her tears. She underwent an instantaneous transformation, which amazed Alyosha. Instead of a poor, insulted girl, weeping in a sort of "laceration", he saw a woman completely self-possessed and even exceedingly pleased, as though something agreeable had just happened.

"Oh, not fortunate that I am losing you, of course not," she corrected herself suddenly, with a charming society smile. "Such a friend as you are could not suppose that. I am only too unhappy at losing you." She rushed impulsively at Ivan, and seizing both his hands, pressed them warmly. "But what is fortunate is that you will be able in Moscow to see auntie and Agafya and to tell them all the horror of my present position. You can speak with complete openness to Agafya, but spare dear auntie. You will know how to do that. You can't think how wretched I was yesterday and this morning, wondering how I could write them that dreadful letter—for one can never tell such things in a letter. . . . Now it will be easy for me to write, for you will see them and explain everything. Oh, how glad I am! But I am only glad of that, believe me. Of course, no one can take your place. . . . I will run at once to write the letter," she finished suddenly, and took a step as though to go out of the room.

"And what about Alyosha and his opinion, which you were so desperately anxious to hear?" cried Madame Hohlakov. There was a sarcastic, angry note in her voice.

"I had not forgotten that," cried Katerina Ivanovna, coming to a sudden standstill, "and why are you so antagonistic at such a moment?" she added, with warm and bitter reproachfulness. "What I said, I repeat. I must have his opinion. More than that, I must have his decision! As he says, so it shall be. You see how anxious I am for your words, Alexey Fyodorovitch. . . . But what's the matter?"

"I couldn't have believed it. I can't understand it!" Alyosha cried suddenly in distress.

"What? what?"

"He is going to Moscow, and you cry out that you are glad. You said that on purpose! And you begin explaining that you are not glad of that but sorry to be—losing a friend. But that was acting, too—you were playing a part—as in a theatre!"

"In a theatre? What? What do you mean?" exclaimed Katerina Ivanovna, profoundly astonished, flushing crimson, and frowning.

"Though you assure him you are sorry to lose a friend in him, you persist in telling him to his face that it's fortunate he is going," said Alyosha breathlessly. He was standing at the table and did not sit down.

"What are you talking about? I don't understand?"

"I don't understand myself. . . . I seemed to see in a flash . . . I know I am not saying it properly, but I'll say it all the same," Alyosha went on in the same shaking and broken voice. "What I see is that perhaps you don't love Dmitri at all . . . and never have, from the beginning. . . . And Dmitri, too, has never loved you . . . and only esteems you. . . . I really don't know how I dare to say all this, but somebody must tell the truth . . . for nobody here will tell the truth."

"What truth?" cried Katerina Ivanovna, and there was an hysterical ring in her voice.

"I'll tell you," Alyosha went on with desperate haste, as

though he were jumping from the top of a house. "Call Dmitri; I will fetch him—and let him come here and take your hand and take Ivan's and join your hands. For you're torturing Ivan, simply because you love him—and torturing him, because you love Dmitri through 'self-laceration'—with an unreal love—because you've persuaded yourself."

Alyosha broke off and was silent.

"You . . . you . . . you are a little religious idiot—that's what you are!" Katerina Ivanovna snapped. Her face was white and her lips were moving with anger.

Ivan suddenly laughed and got up. His hat was in his hand.

"You are mistaken, my good Alyosha," he said, with an expression Alyosha had never seen in his face before—an expression of youthful sincerity and strong, irresistibly frank feeling. "Katerina Ivanovna has never cared for me! She has known all the time that I cared for her—though I never said a word of my love to her—she knew, but she didn't care for me. I have never been her friend either, not for one moment; she is too proud to need my friendship. She kept me at her side as a means of revenge. She avenged with me and on me all the insults which she has been continually receiving from Dmitri ever since their first meeting. For even that first meeting has rankled in her heart as an insult—that's what her heart is like! She has talked to me of nothing but her love for him. I am going now; but, believe me, Katerina Ivanovna, you really love him. And the more he insults you, the more you love him—that's your 'laceration'. You love him just as he is; you love him for insulting you. If he reformed, you'd give him up at once and cease to love him. But you need him so as to contemplate continually your heroic fidelity and to reproach him for infidelity. And it all comes from your pride. Oh, there's a great deal of humiliation and self-abasement about it, but it all comes from pride. . . . I am too young and I've loved you too much. I know that I ought not to say this, that it would be more dignified on my part simply to leave you, and it would be less offensive for you. But I am going far away, and shall never come back. . . . It is for ever. I don't want to sit beside a 'laceration'. . . . But I don't know how to speak now. I've said everything. . . . Good-bye, Katerina Ivanovna; you can't be angry with me, for I am a hundred times more severely punished than you, if only by the fact that I shall never see you again. Good-bye! I don't want your hand. You have tortured me too deliberately for me to be able to forgive you at this moment. I shall forgive you later, but now I don't want your hand. *'Den Dank, Dame, begehr ich nicht,'* " he added, with a forced smile, showing, however, that he could read Schiller, and read him till he knew him by heart—which Alyosha would never have believed. He went out of the room without saying good-bye even to his hostess, Madame Hohlakov. Alyosha clasped his hands.

"Ivan!" he cried desperately after him. "Come back, Ivan! No, nothing will induce him to come back now!" he cried again, regretfully realising it; "but it's my fault, my fault. I began it! Ivan spoke angrily, wrongly. Unjustly and angrily. He must come back here, come back!" Alyosha kept exclaiming frantically.

Katerina Ivanovna went suddenly into the next room.

"You have done no harm. You behaved beautifully, like an angel," Madame Hohlakov whispered rapidly and ecstatically to Alyosha. "I will do my utmost to prevent Ivan Fyodorovitch from going.

Her face beamed with delight, to the great distress of Alyosha, but Katerina Ivanovna suddenly returned. She had two hundred-rouble notes in her hand.

"I have a great favour to ask you, Alexey Fyodorovitch," she began, addressing Alyosha with an apparently calm and even voice, as though nothing had happened. "A week—yes, I think it was a week ago—Dmitri Fyodorovitch was guilty of a hasty and unjust action—a very ugly action. There is a low tavern here and in it he met that discharged officer, that captain, whom your father used to employ in some business. Dmitri Fyodorovitch somehow lost his temper with this captain, seized him by the beard and dragged him out into the street and for some distance along it, in that insulting fashion. And I am told that his son, a boy, quite a child, who is at the school here, saw it and ran beside them crying and begging for his father, appealing to everyone to defend him, while everyone laughed. You must forgive me, Alexey Fyodorovitch, I cannot think without indignation of that disgraceful action of *his* . . . one of those actions of which only Dmitri Fyodorovitch would be capable in his anger . . . and in his passions! I can't describe it even. . . . I can't find my words. I've made inquiries about his victim, and find he is quite a poor man. His name is Snegiryov. He did something wrong in the army and was discharged. I can't tell you what. And now he has sunk into terrible destitution, with his family—an unhappy family of sick children, and, I believe, an insane wife. He has been living here a long time; he used to work as a copying clerk, but now he is getting nothing. I thought of you . . . that is, I thought . . . I don't know. I am so confused. You see, I wanted to ask you, my dear Alexey Fyodorovitch, to go to him, to find some excuse to go to them—I mean to that captain—oh, goodness, how badly I explain it!—and delicately, carefully, as only you know how to" (Alyosha blushed), "manage to give him this assistance, these two hundred roubles. He will be sure to take it. . . . I mean, persuade him to take it. . . . Or, rather, what do I mean? You see it's not by way of compensation to prevent him from taking proceedings (for I believe he meant to), but simply a token of sympathy, of a desire to assist him from me, Dmitri Fyodorovitch's betrothed, not from himself. . . . But you know. . . . I would go myself, but you'll know how to do it ever so much better. He lives in Lake Street, in the house of a woman called Kalmikov. . . . For God's sake, Alexey Fyodorovitch, do it for me, and now . . . now I am rather . . . tired. Good-bye!"

She turned so quickly and disappeared behind the portière that Alyosha had not time to utter a word, though he wanted to speak. He longed to beg her pardon, to blame himself, to say something, for his heart was full and he could not bear to go out of the room without it. But Madame Hohlakov took him by the hand and drew him along with her. In the hall she stopped him again as before.

"She is proud, she is struggling with herself; but kind, charming, generous," she exclaimed, in a half-whisper. "Oh, how I love her, especially sometimes, and how glad I am again of everything! Dear Alexey Fyodorovitch, you didn't know, but I must tell you, that we all, all—both her aunts, I and all of us, Lise, even—have been hoping and praying for nothing for the last month but that she may give up your favourite Dmitri, who takes no notice of her and does not care for her, and may marry Ivan Fyodorovitch—such an excellent and cultivated young man, who loves her more than anything in the world. We are in a regular plot to bring it about, and I am even staying on here perhaps on that account."

"But she has been crying—she has been wounded again," cried Alyosha.

"Never trust a woman's tears, Alexey Fyodorovitch. I am

never for the women in such cases. I am always on the side of the men."

"Mamma, you are spoiling him," Lise's little voice cried from behind the door.

"No, it was all my fault. I am horribly to blame," Alyosha repeated unconsoled, hiding his face in his hands in an agony of remorse for his indiscretion.

"Quite the contrary; you behaved like an angel, like an angel. I am ready to say so a thousand times over."

"Mamma, how has he behaved like an angel?" Lise's voice was heard again.

"I somehow fancied all at once," Alyosha went on as though he had not heard Lise, "that she loved Ivan, and so I said that stupid thing. . . . What will happen now?"

"To whom, to whom?" cried Lise. "Mamma, you really want to be the death of me. I ask you and you don't answer."

At the moment the maid ran in.

"Katerina Ivanovna is ill. . . . She is crying, struggling . . . hysterics."

"What is the matter?" cried Lise, in a tone of real anxiety. "Mamma, I shall be having hysterics, and not she!"

"Lise, for mercy's sake, don't scream, don't persecute me. At your age one can't know everything that grown-up people know. I'll come and tell you everything you ought to know. Oh, mercy on us! I am coming, I am coming . . . Hysterics is a good sign, Alexey Fyodorovitch; it's an excellent thing that she is hysterical. That's just as it ought to be. In such cases I am always against the woman, against all these feminine tears and hysterics. Run and say, Yulia, that I'll fly to her. As for Ivan Fyodorovitch's going away like that, it's her own fault. But he won't go away. Lise, for mercy's sake, don't scream! Oh, yes; you're not screaming. It's I who am screaming. Forgive your mamma; but I am delighted, delighted, delighted! Did you notice, Alexey Fyodorovitch, how young, how young Ivan Fyodorovitch was just now when he went out, when he said all that and went out? I thought he was so learned, such a *savant,* and all of a sudden he behaved so warmly, openly, and youthfully, with such youthful inexperience, and it was all so fine, like you. . . . And the way he repeated that German verse, it was just like you! But I must fly, I must fly! Alexey Fyodorovitch, make haste to carry out her commission, and then make haste back. Lise, do you want anything now? For mercy's sake, don't keep Alexey

Fyodorovitch a minute. He will come back to you at once."

Madame Hohlakov at last ran off. Before leaving, Alyosha would have opened the door to see Lise.

"On no account," cried Lise. "On no account now. Speak through the door. How have you come to be an angel? That's the only thing I want to know."

"For an awful piece of stupidity, Lise! Good-bye!"

"Don't dare to go away like that!" Lise was beginning.

"Lise, I have a real sorrow! I'll be back directly, but I have a great, great sorrow!"

And he ran out of the room.

CHAPTER VI

A LACERATION IN THE COTTAGE

HE certainly was really grieved in a way he had seldom been before. He had rushed in like a fool, and meddled in what? In a love-affair. "But what do I know about it? What can I tell about such things?" he repeated to himself for the hundredth time, flushing crimson. "Oh, being ashamed would be nothing; shame is only the punishment I deserve. The trouble is I shall certainly have caused more unhappiness. . . . And Father Zossima sent me to reconcile and bring them together. Is this the way to bring them together?" Then he suddenly remembered how he had tried to join their hands, and he felt fearfully ashamed again. "Though I acted quite sincerely, I must be more sensible in the future," he concluded suddenly, and did not even smile at his conclusion.

Katerina Ivanovna's commission took him to Lake Street, and his brother Dmitri lived close by, in a turning out of Lake Street. Alyosha decided to go to him in any case before going to the captain, though he had a presentiment that he would not find his brother. He suspected that he would intentionally keep out of his way now, but he must find him, anyhow. Time was passing: the thought of his dying elder had not left Alyosha for one minute from the time he set off from the monastery.

There was one point which interested him particularly about Katerina Ivanovna's commission; when she had mentioned the captain's son, the little schoolboy who had run beside his father crying, the idea had at once struck Alyosha that this must be the schoolboy who had bitten his finger when he, Alyosha, asked him what he had done to hurt him. Now Alyosha felt practically certain of this, though he could not have said why. Thinking of another subject was a relief, and he resolved to think no more about the "mischief" he had done, and not to torture himself with remorse, but to do what he had to do, let come what would. At that thought he was completely comforted. Turning to the street where Dmitri lodged, he felt hungry, and taking out of his pocket the roll he had brought from his father's, he ate it. It made him feel stronger.

Dmitri was not at home. The people of the house, an old cabinet-maker, his son, and his old wife, looked with positive suspicion at Alyosha. "He hasn't slept here for the last three nights. Maybe he has gone away," the old man said in answer to Alyosha's persistent inquiries. Alyosha saw that he was answering in accordance with instructions. When he asked whether he were not at Grushenka's or in hiding at Foma's (Alyosha spoke so freely on purpose), all three looked at him in alarm. "They are fond of him, they are doing their best for him," thought Alyosha. "That's good."

At last he found the house in Lake Street. It was a decrepit little house, sunk on one side, with three windows looking into the street, and with a muddy yard, in the middle of which stood a solitary cow. He crossed the yard and found the door opening into the passage. On the left of the passage lived the old woman of the house with her old daughter. Both seemed to be deaf. In answer to his repeated inquiry for the captain, one of them at last understood that he was asking for their lodgers, and pointed to a door across the passage. The captain's lodging turned out to be a simple cottage room. Alyosha had his hand on the iron latch to open the door when he was struck by the strange hush within. Yet he knew from Katerina Ivanovna's words that the man had a family. "Either they are all asleep or perhaps they have heard me coming and are waiting for me to open the door. I'd better knock first," and he knocked. An answer came, but not at once, after an interval of perhaps ten seconds.

"Who's there?" shouted someone in a loud and very angry voice.

Then Alyosha opened the door and crossed the threshold. He found himself in a regular peasant's room. Though it was large, it was cumbered up with domestic belongings of all sorts, and there were several people in it. On the left was a large

Russian stove. From the stove to the window on the left was a string running across the room, and on it there were rags hanging. There was a bedstead against the wall on each side, right and left, covered with knitted quilts. On the one on the left was a pyramid of four print-covered pillows, each smaller than the one beneath. On the other there was only one very small pillow. The opposite corner was screened off by a curtain or a sheet hung on a string. Behind this curtain could be seen a bed made up on a bench and a chair. The rough square table of plain wood had been moved into the middle window. The three windows, which consisted each of four tiny greenish mildewy panes, gave little light, and were close-shut, so that the room was not very light and rather stuffy. On the table were a frying-pan with the remains of some fried eggs, a half-eaten piece of bread, and a small bottle with a few drops of vodka.

A woman of genteel appearance, wearing a cotton gown, was sitting on a chair by the bed on the left. Her face was thin and yellow, and her sunken cheeks betrayed at the first glance that she was ill. But what struck Alyosha most was the expression of the poor woman's eyes—a look of surprised inquiry and yet of haughty pride. And while he was talking to her husband, her big brown eyes moved from one speaker to the other with the same haughty and questioning expression. Beside her at the window stood a young girl, rather plain, with scanty reddish hair, poorly but very neatly dressed. She looked disdainfully at Alyosha as he came in. Beside the other bed was sitting another female figure. She was a very sad sight, a young girl of about twenty, but hunchback and crippled "with withered legs", as Alyosha was told afterwards. Her crutches stood in the corner close by. The strikingly beautiful and gentle eyes of this poor girl looked with mild serenity at Alyosha. A man of forty-five was sitting at the table, finishing the fried eggs. He was spare, small and weakly built. He had reddish-brown hair and a scanty light-coloured beard, very much like a wisp of tow (this comparison and the phrase "a wisp of tow" flashed at once into Alyosha's mind for some reason, he remembered it afterwards). It was obviously this gentleman who had shouted at him, as there was no other man in the room. But when Alyosha went in, he leapt up from the bench on which he was sitting, and, hastily wiping his mouth with a ragged napkin, darted up to Alyosha.

"It's a monk come to beg for the monastery. A nice place to come to!" the girl standing in the left corner said aloud.

The man spun round instantly towards her and answered her in an excited and breaking voice.

"No, Varvara, you are wrong. Allow me to ask," he turned again to Alyosha, "what has brought you to—our retreat?"

Alyosha looked attentively at him. It was the first time he had seen him. There was something angular, flurried and irritable about him. Though he had obviously just been drinking, he was not drunk. There was extraordinary impudence in his expression, and yet, strange to say, at the same time there was fear. He looked like a man who had long been kept in subjection and had submitted to it, and now had suddenly turned and was trying to assert himself. Or, better still, like a man who wants dreadfully to hit you but is horribly afraid you will hit him. In his words and in the intonation of his shrill voice there was a sort of crazy humour, at times spiteful and at times cringing, and continually shifting from one tone to another. The question about "our retreat" he had asked as it were quivering all over, rolling his eyes, and skipping up so close to Alyosha that he instinctively drew back a step. He was dressed in a very shabby dark cotton coat, patched and spotted. He wore checked trousers of an extremely light colour, long out of fashion, and of very thin material. They were so crumpled and so short that he looked as though he had grown out of them like a boy.

"I am Alexey Karamazov," Alyosha began in reply.

"I quite understand that, sir," the gentleman snapped out at once to assure him that he knew who he was already. "I am Captain Snegiryov, sir, but I am still desirous to know precisely what has led you——"

"Oh, I've come for nothing special. I wanted to have a word with you—if only you allow me."

"In that case, here is a chair, sir; kindly be seated. That's what they used to say in the old comedies, 'kindly be seated'," and with a rapid gesture he seized an empty chair (it was a rough wooden chair, not upholstered) and set it for him almost in the middle of the room; then, taking another similar chair for himself, he sat down facing Alyosha, so close to him that their knees almost touched.

"Nikolay Ilyitch Snegiryov, sir, formerly a captain in the Russian infantry, put to shame for his vices, but still a captain. Though I might not be one now for the way I talk; for the last half of my life I've learnt to say 'sir'. It's a word you use when you've come down in the world."

"That's very true," smiled Alyosha. "But is it used involuntarily or on purpose?"

"As God's above, it's involuntary, and I usen't to use it! I didn't use the word 'sir' all my life, but as soon as I sank into low water I began to say 'sir'. It's the work of a higher power. I see you are interested in contemporary questions, but how can I have excited your curiosity, living as I do in surroundings impossible for the exercise of hospitality?"

"I've come—about that business."

"About what business?" the captain interrupted impatiently.

"About your meeting with my brother, Dmitri Fyodorovitch," Alyosha blurted out awkwardly.

"What meeting, sir? You don't mean that meeting? About my 'wisp of tow', then?" He moved closer so that his knees positively knocked against Alyosha. His lips were strangely compressed like a thread.

"What wisp of tow?" muttered Alyosha.

"He is come to complain of me, father!" cried a voice familiar to Alyosha—the voice of the schoolboy—from behind the curtain. "I bit his finger just now." The curtain was pulled, and Alyosha saw his assailant lying on a little bed made up on the bench and the chair in the corner under the ikons. The boy lay covered by his coat and an old wadded quilt. He was evidently unwell, and, judging by his glittering eyes, he was in a fever. He looked at Alyosha without fear, as though he felt he was at home and could not be touched.

"What! Did he bite your finger?" The captain jumped up from his chair. "Was it your finger he bit?"

"Yes. He was throwing stones with other schoolboys. There were six of them against him alone. I went up to him, and he threw a stone at me and then another at my head. I asked him what I had done to him. And then he rushed at me and bit my finger badly, I don't know why."

"I'll thrash him, sir, at once—this minute!" The captain jumped up from his seat.

"But I am not complaining at all, I am simply telling you. . . . I don't want him to be thrashed. Besides, he seems to be ill."

"And do you suppose I'd thrash him? That I'd take my Ilusha and thrash him before you for your satisfaction? Would you like it done at once, sir?" said the captain, suddenly turning to Alyosha, as though he were going to attack him. "I am sorry about your finger, sir; but instead of thrashing Ilusha, would you like me to chop off my four fingers with this knife here before your eyes to satisfy your just wrath? I should think four fingers would be enough to satisfy your thirst for vengeance. You won't ask for the fifth one too?" He stopped short with a catch in his throat. Every feature in his face was twitching and working; he looked extremely defiant. He was in a sort of frenzy.

"I think I understand it all now," said Alyosha gently and sorrowfully, still keeping his seat. "So your boy is a good boy, he loves his father, and he attacked me as the brother of your assailant. . . . Now I understand it," he repeated thoughtfully. "But my brother Dmitri Fyodorovitch regrets his action, I know that, and if only it is possible for him to come to you, or better still, to meet you in that same place, he will ask your forgiveness before everyone—if you wish it."

"After pulling out my beard, you mean, he will ask my forgiveness? And he thinks that will be a satisfactory finish, doesn't he?"

"Oh, no! On the contrary, he will do anything you like and in any way you like."

"So if I were to ask his highness to go down on his knees before me in that very tavern—'The Metropolis' it's called—or in the market-place, he would do it?"

"Yes, he would even go down on his knees."

"You've pierced me to the heart, sir. Touched me to tears and pierced me to the heart! I am only too sensible of your brother's generosity. Allow me to introduce my family, my two daughters and my son—my litter. If I die, who will care for them, and while I live who but they will care for a wretch like me? That's a great thing the Lord has ordained for every man of my sort, sir. For there must be someone able to love even a man like me."

"Ah, that's perfectly true!" exclaimed Alyosha.

"Oh, do leave off playing the fool! Some idiot comes in, and you put us to shame!" cried the girl by the window, suddenly turning to her father with a disdainful and contemptuous air.

"Wait a little, Varvara!" cried her father, speaking peremptorily but looking at her quite approvingly. "That's her character," he said, addressing Alyosha again.

> *"And in all nature there was naught*
> *That could find favour in his eyes*

or rather in the feminine: 'that could find favour in *her* eyes.'

But now let me present you to my wife, Arina Petrovna. She is crippled, she is forty-three; she can move, but very little. She is of humble origin. Arina Petrovna, compose your countenance. This is Alexey Fyodorovitch Karamazov. Get up, Alexey Fyodorovitch.'' He took him by the hand and with unexpected force pulled him up. "You must stand up to be introduced to a lady. It's not the Karamazov, mamma, who . . . h'm . . . etcetera, but his brother, radiant with modest virtues. Come, Arina Petrovna, come, mamma, first your hand to be kissed.''

And he kissed his wife's hand respectfully and even tenderly. The girl at the window turned her back indignantly on the scene; an expression of extraordinary cordiality came over the haughtily inquiring face of the woman.

"Good morning! Sit down, Mr. Tchernomazov,'' she said.

"Karamazov, mamma, Karamazov (we are of humble origin),'' he whispered again.

"Well, Karamazov, or whatever it is, but I always think of Tchernomazov. . . . Sit down. Why has he pulled you up? He calls me crippled but I am not, only my legs are swollen like barrels, and I am shrivelled up myself. Once I used to be so fat, but now it's as though I had swallowed a needle.''

"We are of humble origin,'' the captain muttered again.

"Oh, father, father!'' the hunchback girl, who had till then been silent in her chair, said suddenly, and she hid her eyes in her handkerchief.

"Buffoon!'' blurted out the girl at the window.

"Have you heard our news?'' said the mother, pointing at her daughters. "It's like clouds coming over; the clouds pass and we have music again. When we were with the army, we used to have many such guests. I don't mean to make any comparisons; everyone to their taste. The deacon's wife used to come then and say, 'Alexandr Alexandrovitch is a man of the noblest heart, but Nastasya Petrovna,' she would say, 'is of the brood of hell'. 'Well,' I said, 'that's a matter of taste; but you are a little spitfire.' 'And you want keeping in your place,' says she. 'You black sword,' said I, 'who asked you to teach me?' 'But my breath,' says she, 'is clean, and yours is unclean.' 'You ask all the officers whether my breath is unclean.' And ever since then I had it in my mind. Not long ago I was sitting here as I am now, when I saw that very General come in who came here for Easter, and I asked him: 'Your Excellency,' said I, 'can a lady's breath be unpleasant?' 'Yes.' he answered; 'you ought to open a window-pane or open the door, for the air is not fresh here.' And they all go on like that! And what is my breath to them? The dead smell worse still! 'I won't spoil the air,' said I, 'I'll order some slippers and go away.' My darlings, don't blame your own mother! Nikolay. Ilyitch, how is it I can't please you? There's only Ilusha who comes home from school and loves me. Yesterday he brought me an apple. Forgive your own mother—forgive a poor lonely creature! Why has my breath become unpleasant to you?"

And the poor mad woman broke into sobs, and tears streamed down her cheeks. The captain rushed up to her.

"Mamma, mamma, my dear, give over! You are not lonely. Everyone loves you, everyone adores you." He began kissing both her hands again and tenderly stroking her face; taking the dinner-napkin, he began wiping away her tears. Alyosha fancied that he too had tears in his eyes. "There, you see, you hear?" he turned with a sort of fury to Alyosha, pointing to the poor imbecile.

"I see and hear," muttered Alyosha.

"Father, father, how can you—with him! Let him alone!" cried the boy, sitting up in his bed and gazing at his father with glowing eyes.

"Do give over fooling, showing off your silly antics which never lead to anything!" shouted Varvara, stamping her foot with passion.

"Your anger is quite just this time, Varvara, and I'll make haste to satisfy you. Come, put on your cap, Alexey Fyodorovitch, and I'll put on mine. We will go out. I have a word to say to you in earnest, but not within these walls. This girl sitting here is my daughter Nina; I forgot to introduce her to you. She is a heavenly angel incarnate . . . who has flown down to us mortals . . . if you can understand."

"There he is shaking all over, as though he is in convulsions!" Varvara went on indignantly.

"And she there stamping her foot at me and calling me a fool just now, she is a heavenly angel incarnate too, and she has good reason to call me so. Come along, Alexey Fyodorovitch, we must make an end."

And, snatching Alyosha's hand, he drew him out of the room into the street.

CHAPTER VII

AND IN THE OPEN AIR

"THE air is fresh, but in my apartment it is not so in any sense of the word. Let us walk slowly, sir. I should be glad of your kind interest."

"I too have something important to say to you," observed Alyosha, "only I don't know how to begin."

"To be sure you must have business with me. You would never have looked in upon me without some object. Unless you come simply to complain of the boy, and that's hardly likely. And, by the way, about the boy: I could not explain to you in there, but here I will describe that scene to you. My tow was thicker a week ago—I mean my beard. That's the nickname they give to my beard, the schoolboys most of all. Well, your brother Dmitri Fyodorovitch was pulling me by my beard. I'd done nothing, he was in a towering rage and happened to come upon me. He dragged me out of the tavern into the market-place; at that moment the boys were coming out of school, and with them Ilusha. As soon as he saw me in such a state he rushed up to me. 'Father,' he cried, 'father!' He caught hold of me, hugged me, tried to pull me away, crying to my assailant: 'Let go, let go, it's my father, forgive him!'—yes, he actually cried 'forgive him'; He clutched at that hand, that very hand, in his little hands and kissed it. . . . I remember his little face at that moment, I haven't forgotten it and I never shall!"

"I swear," cried Alyosha, "that my brother will express his most deep and sincere regret, even if he has to go down on his knees in that same market-place. . . . I'll make him or he is no brother of mine."

"Aha, then it's only a suggestion! And it does not come from him but simply from the generosity of your own warm heart. You should have said so. No, in that case allow me to tell you of your brother's highly chivalrous soldierly generosity, for he did give expression to it at the time. He left off dragging me by my beard and released me: 'You are an officer,' he said, 'and I am an officer, if you can find a decent man to be your second send me your challenge. I will give you satisfaction, though you are a scoundrel.' That's what he said. A chivalrous spirit indeed! I retired with Ilusha, and that scene is a family record imprinted for ever on Ilusha's soul. No, it's not for us

to claim the privileges of noblemen. Judge for yourself.
You've just been in our mansion, what did you see there?
Three ladies, one a cripple and weak-minded, another a cripple
and hunchback and the third not crippled but far too clever.
She is a student, dying to get back to Petersburg, to work for
the emancipation of the Russian woman on the banks of the
Neva. I won't speak of Ilusha, he is only nine. I am alone in
the world, and if I die, what will become of all of them, I simply
ask you that. And if I challenge him and he kills me on the
spot, what then? What will become of them? And worse still,
if he doesn't kill me but only cripples me: I couldn't work,
but I should still be a mouth to feed. Who would feed it and
who would feed them all? Must I take Ilusha from school and
send him to beg in the streets? That's what it means for me to
challenge him to a duel. It's silly talk and nothing else."

"He will beg your forgiveness, he will bow down at your feet
in the middle of the market-place," cried Alyosha again, with
glowing eyes.

"I did think of prosecuting him," the captain went on, "but
look in our code, could I get much compensation for a personal
injury. And then Agafena Alexandrovna* sent for me and
shouted at me: 'Don't dare to dream of it! If you proceed
against him, I'll publish it to all the world that he beat you for
your dishonesty, and then you will be prosecuted.' I call God
to witness whose was the dishonesty and by whose commands I
acted, wasn't it by her own and Fyodor Pavlovitch's? 'And
what's more,' she went on, 'I'll dismiss you for good and you'll
never earn another penny from me. I'll speak to my merchant
too (that's what she calls her old man), and he will dismiss you!'
And if he dismisses me, what can I earn then from anyone?
Those two are all I have to look to, for your Fyodor Pavlovitch
has not only given over employing me, for another reason, but
he means to make use of papers I've signed to go to law against
me. And so I kept quiet, and you have seen our retreat. But
now let me ask you: did Ilusha hurt your finger much? I
didn't like to go into it in our mansion before him."

"Yes, very much, and he was in a great fury. He was
avenging you on me as a Karamazov, I see that now. But if
only you had seen how he was throwing stones at his schoolfellows! It's very dangerous. They might kill him. They are
children and stupid. A stone may be thrown and break somebody's head."

* Grushenka

208

"That's just what has happened. He has been bruised by a stone to-day. Not on the head but on the chest, just above the heart. He came home crying and groaning and now he is ill."

"And you know he attacks them first. He is bitter against them on your account. They say he stabbed a boy called Krassotkin with a penknife not long ago."

"I've heard about that too, it's dangerous. Krassotkin is an official here, we may hear more about it."

"I would advise you," Alyosha went on warmly, "not to send him to school at all for a time till he is calmer . . . and his anger is passed."

"Anger!" the captain repeated, "that's just what it is. He is a little creature, but it's a mighty anger. You don't know all, sir. Let me tell you more. Since that incident all the boys have been teasing him about the 'wisp of tow'. Schoolboys are a merciless race, individually they are angels, but together, especially in schools, they are often merciless. Their teasing has stirred up a gallant spirit in Ilusha. An ordinary boy, a weak son, would have submitted, have felt ashamed of his father, sir, but he stood up for his father against them all. For his father and for truth and justice. For what he suffered when he kissed your brother's hand and cried to him, 'Forgive father, forgive him'—that only God knows—and I, his father. For our children—not your children, but ours—the children of the poor gentlemen looked down upon by everyone—know what justice means, sir, even at nine years old. How should the rich know? They don't explore such depths once in their lives. But at that moment in the square when he kissed his hand, at that moment my Ilusha had grasped all that justice means. That truth entered into him and crushed him for ever, sir," the captain said hotly again with a sort of frenzy, and he struck his right fist against his left palm as though he wanted to show how "the truth" crushed Ilusha. "That very day, sir, he fell ill with fever and was delirious all night. All that day he hardly said a word to me, but I noticed he kept watching me from the corner, though he turned to the window and pretended to be learning his lessons. But I could see his mind was not on his lessons. Next day I got drunk to forget my troubles, sinful man as I am, and I don't remember much. Mamma began crying, too—I am very fond of mamma—well, I spent my last penny drowning my troubles. Don't despise me for that, sir, in Russia men who drink are the best. The best men amongst us are the greatest drunkards. I lay down and I don't remember about Ilusha, though all that day the boys had been jeering at him at school. 'Wisp of tow!' they shouted, 'your father was pulled out of the tavern by his wisp of tow, you ran by and begged forgiveness.'

"On the third day when he came back from school, I saw he looked pale and wretched. 'What is it?' I asked. He wouldn't answer. Well, there's no talking in our mansion without mamma and the girls taking part in it. What's more, the girls had heard about it the very first day. Varvara had begun snarling. 'You fools and buffoons, can you ever do anything rational?' 'Quite so,' I said, 'can we ever do anything rational?' For the time I turned it off like that. So in the evening I took the boy out for a walk, for you must know we go for a walk every evening, always the same way, along which we are going now—from our gate to that great stone which lies alone in the road under the hurdle, which marks the beginning of the town pasture. A beautiful and lonely spot, sir. Ilusha and I walked along hand in hand as usual. He has a little hand, his fingers are thin and cold—he suffers with his chest, you know. 'Father,' said he, 'father!' 'Well?' said I. I saw his eyes flashing. 'Father, how he treated you then!' 'It can't be helped, Ilusha,' I said. 'Don't forgive him, father, don't forgive him! At school they say that he has paid you ten roubles for it.' 'No, Ilusha,' said I, 'I would not take money from him for anything.' Then he began trembling all over, took my hand in both his and kissed it again. 'Father,' he said, 'father, challenge him to a duel, at school they say you are a coward and won't challenge him, and that you'll accept ten roubles from him.' 'I can't challenge him to a duel, Ilusha,' I answered. And I told briefly what I've just told you. He listened. 'Father,' he said, 'anyway, don't forgive it. When I grow up I'll call him out myself and kill him.' His eyes shone and glowed. And of course I am his father, and I had to put in a word: 'It's a sin to kill,' I said, 'even in a duel.' 'Father,' he said, 'when I grow up, I'll knock him down, knock the sword out of his hand, I'll fall on him, wave my sword over him and say: "I could kill you, but I forgive you, so there!"' You see what the workings of his little mind have been during these two days; he must have been planning that vengeance all day, and raving about it at night.

"But he began to come home from school badly beaten. I found out about it the day before yesterday, and you are right.

I won't send him to that school any more. I heard that he was standing up against all the class alone and defying them all, that his heart was full of resentment, of bitterness—I was alarmed about him. We went for another walk. 'Father,' he asked, 'are the rich people stronger than anyone else on earth?' 'Yes, Ilusha,' I said, 'there are no people on earth stronger than the rich.' 'Father,' he said, 'I will get rich, I will become an officer and conquer everybody. The Tsar will reward me, I will come back here and then no one will dare.' . . . Then he was silent and his lips still kept trembling. 'Father,' he said, 'what a horrid town this is.' 'Yes, Ilusha,' I said, 'it isn't a very nice town.' 'Father, let us move into another town, a nice one,' he said, 'where people don't know about us.' 'We will move, we will, Ilusha,' said I, 'only I must save up for it.' I was glad to be able to turn his mind from painful thoughts, and we began to dream of how we would move to another town, how we would buy a horse and cart. 'We will put mamma and your sisters inside, we will cover them up and we'll walk, you shall have a lift now and then, and I'll walk beside, for we must take care of our horse, we can't all ride. That's how we'll go.' He was enchanted at that, most of all at the thought of having a horse and driving him. For of course a Russian boy is born among horses. We chattered a long while. Thank God, I thought, I have diverted his mind and comforted him.

"That was the day before yesterday, in the evening, but last night everything was changed. He had gone to school in the morning, he came back depressed, terribly depressed. In the evening I took him by the hand and we went for a walk; he would not talk. There was a wind blowing and no sun, and a feeling of autumn; twilight was coming on. We walked along, both of us depressed. 'Well, my boy,' said I, 'how about our setting off on our travels?' I thought I might bring him back to our talk of the day before. He didn't answer, but I felt his fingers trembling in my hand. Ah, I thought, it's a bad job; there's something fresh. We had reached the stone where we are now. I sat down on the stone. And in the air there were lots of kites flapping and whirling. There were as many as thirty in sight. Of course, it's just the season for the kites. 'Look, Ilusha,' said I, 'it's time we got out our last year's kite again. I'll mend it, where have you put it away?' My boy made no answer. He looked away and turned sideways to me. And then a gust of wind blew up the sand. He suddenly fell on me, threw both his little arms round my neck and held me tight. You know, when children are silent and proud, and try to keep back their tears when they are in great trouble and suddenly break down, their tears fall in streams. With those warm streams of tears, he suddenly wetted my face. He sobbed and shook as though he were in convulsions, and squeezed up against me as I sat on the stone. 'Father,' he kept crying, 'dear father, how he insulted you!' And I sobbed too. We sat shaking in each other's arms. 'Ilusha,' I said to him, 'Ilusha darling.' No one saw us then. God alone saw us, I hope he will record it to my credit. You must thank your brother, Alexey Fyodorovitch. No, sir, I won't thrash my boy for your satisfaction."

He had gone back to his original tone of resentful buffoonery. Alyosha felt, though, that he trusted him, and that if there had been someone else in his, Alyosha's, place the man would not have spoken so openly and would not have told what he had just told. This encouraged Alyosha, whose heart was trembling on the verge of tears.

"Ah, how I would like to make friends with your boy!" he cried. "If you could arrange it——"

"Certainly, sir," muttered the captain.

"But now listen to something quite different!" Alyosha went on. "I have a message for you. That same brother of mine, Dmitri, has insulted his betrothed, too, a noble-hearted girl of whom you have probably heard. I have a right to tell you of her wrong; I ought to do so, in fact, for hearing of the insult done to you and learning all about your unfortunate position, she commissioned me at once—just now—to bring you this help from her—but only from her alone, not from Dmitri, who has abandoned her. Nor from me, his brother, nor from anyone else, but from her, only from her! She entreats you to accept her help. . . . You have both been insulted by the same man. She thought of you only when she had just received a similar insult from him—similar in its cruelty, I mean. She comes like a sister to help a brother in misfortune. . . . She told me to persuade you to take these two hundred roubles from her, as from a sister, knowing that you are in such need. No one will know of it, it can give rise to no unjust slander. There are the two hundred roubles, and I swear you must take them unless—unless all men are to be enemies on earth! But there are brothers even on earth. . . . You have a generous heart . . . you must see that, you must," and Alyosha held out two new rainbow-coloured hundred-rouble notes.

They were both standing at the time by the great stone close to the fence, and there was no one near. The notes seemed to produce a tremendous impression on the captain. He started, but at first only from astonishment. Such an outcome of their conversation was the last thing he expected. Nothing could have been further from his dreams than help from anyone—and such a sum!

He took the notes, and for a minute he was almost unable to answer, quite a new expression came into his face.

"That for me? So much money—two hundred roubles! Good heavens! Why, I haven't seen so much money for the last four years! Mercy on us! And she says she is a sister . . . And is that the truth?"

"I swear that all I told you is the truth," cried Alyosha.

The captain flushed red.

"Listen, my dear, listen. If I take it, I shan't be behaving like a scoundrel? In your eyes, Alexey Fyodorovitch, I shan't be a scoundrel? No, Alexey Fyodorovitch, listen, listen," he hurried, touching Alyosha with both his hands. "You are persuading me to take it, saying that it's a sister sends it, but inwardly, in your heart won't you feel contempt for me if I take it, eh?"

"No, no, on my salvation I swear I shan't! And no one will ever know but me—I, you and she, and one other lady, her great friend."

"Never mind the lady! Listen, Alexey Fyodorovitch, at a moment like this you must listen, for you can't understand what these two hundred roubles mean to me now." The poor fellow went on rising gradually into a sort of incoherent, almost wild enthusiasm. He was thrown off his balance and talked extremely fast, as though afraid he would not be allowed to say all he had to say.

"Besides it's being honestly acquired from a 'sister', so highly respected and revered, do you know that now I can look after mamma and Nina, my hunchback angel daughter? Doctor Herzenstube came to me in the kindness of his heart and was examining them both for a whole hour. 'I can make nothing of it,' said he, but he prescribed a mineral water which is kept at a chemist's here. He said it would be sure to do her good, and he ordered baths, too, with some medicine in them. The mineral water costs thirty copecks, and she'd need to drink forty bottles perhaps; so I took the prescription and laid it on the shelf under the ikons, and there it lies. And he ordered hot baths for Nina with something dissolved in them, morning and evening. But how can we carry out such a cure in our mansion, without servants, without help, without a bath, and without water? Nina is rheumatic all over, I don't think I told you that. All her right side aches at night, she is in agony, and, would you believe it, the angel bears it without groaning for fear of waking us. We eat what we can get, and she'll only take the leavings, what you'd scarcely give to a dog. 'I am not worth it, I am taking it from you, I am a burden on you,' that's what her angel eyes try to express. We wait on her, but she doesn't like it. 'I am a useless cripple, no good to anyone.' As though she were not worth it, when she is the saving of all of us with her angelic sweetness. Without her, without her gentle word it would be hell among us! She softens even Varvara. And don't judge Varvara harshly either, she is an angel too, she, too, has suffered wrong. She came to us for the summer, and she brought sixteen roubles she had earned by lessons and saved up, to go back with to Petersburg in September, that is now. But we took her money and lived on it, so now she has nothing to go back with. Though indeed she couldn't go back, for she has to work for us like a slave. She is like an over-driven horse with all of us on her back. She waits on us all, mends and washes, sweeps the floor, puts mamma to bed. And mamma is capricious and tearful and insane! And now I can get a servant with this money, you understand, Alexey Fyodoro-vitch, I can get medicines for the dear creatures, I can send my student to Petersburg, I can buy beef, I can feed them properly. Good Lord, but it's a dream!"

Alyosha was delighted that he had brought him such happi-ness and that the poor fellow had consented to be made happy.

"Stay, Alexey Fyodorovitch, stay," the captain began to talk with frenzied rapidity carried away by a new day-dream. "Do you know that Ilusha and I will perhaps really carry out our dream. We will buy a horse and cart, a black horse, he insists on its being black, and we will set off as we pretended the other day. I have an old friend, a lawyer in K. province, and I heard through a trustworthy man that if I were to go he'd give me a place as clerk in his office, so, who knows, maybe he would. So I'd just put mamma and Nina in the cart, and Ilusha could drive, and I'd walk, I'd walk. . . . Why, if I only succeed in getting one debt paid that's owing me, I should have perhaps enough for that too!"

"There would be enough!" cried Alyosha. "Katerina Ivanovna will send you as much more as you need, and you

know, I have money too, take what you want, as you would from a brother, from a friend, you can give it back later. . . . (You'll get rich, you'll get rich!) And you know you couldn't have a better idea than to move to another province! It would be the saving of you, especially of your body—and you ought to go quickly, before the winter, before the cold. You must write to us when you are there, and we will always be brothers. . . . No, it's not a dream!"

Alyosha could have hugged him, he was so pleased. But glancing at him he stopped short. The man was standing with his neck outstretched and his lips protruding, with a pale and frenzied face. His lips were moving as though trying to articulate something; no sound came, but still his lips moved. It was uncanny.

"What is it?" asked Alyosha, startled.

"Alexey Fyodorovitch . . . I . . . you," muttered the captain, faltering, looking at him with a strange, wild, fixed stare, and an air of desperate resolution. At the same time there was a sort of grin on his lips. "I . . . you, sir . . . wouldn't you like me to show you a little trick I know?" he murmured, suddenly, in a firm rapid whisper, his voice no longer faltering.

"What trick?"

"A pretty trick," whispered the captain. His mouth was twisted on the left side, his left eye was screwed up. He still stared at Alyosha.

"What is the matter, what trick?" Alyosha cried, now thoroughly alarmed.

"Why, look," squealed the captain suddenly, and showing him the two notes which he had been holding by one corner between his thumb and forefinger during the conversation, he crumpled them up savagely and squeezed them tight in his right hand. "Do you see, do you see?" he shrieked, pale and infuriated. And suddenly flinging up his hand, he threw the crumpled notes on the sand. "Do you see?" he shrieked again, pointing to them. "Look there!"

And with wild fury he began crumpling them under his heel, gasping and exclaiming as he did so:

"So much for your money! So much for your money! So much for your money! So much for your money!"

Suddenly he darted back and drew himself up before Alyosha, and his whole figure expressed unutterable pride.

"Tell those who sent you that the wisp of tow does not sell his honour," he cried, raising his arm in the air. Then he turned

215

quickly and began to run; but he had not run five steps before he turned completely round and kissed his hand to Alyosha. He ran another five paces and then turned round for the last time. This time his face was not contorted with laughter but quivering all over with tears. In a tearful, faltering, sobbing voice he cried:

"What should I say to my boy if I took money from you for our shame?"

And then he ran on without turning. Alyosha looked after him, inexpressibly grieved. Oh, he saw that till the very last moment the man had known he would crumple up and fling away the notes. He did not turn back. Alyosha knew he would not. He would not follow him and call him back, he knew why. When he was out of sight, Alyosha picked up the two notes. They were very much crushed and crumpled, and had been pressed into the sand, but were uninjured and even rustled like new ones when Alyosha unfolded them and smoothed them out. After smoothing them out, he folded them up, put them in his pocket and went to Katerina Ivanovna to report on the success of her commission.

BOOK V: PRO AND CONTRA

CHAPTER I

THE ENGAGEMENT

M ADAME HOHLAKOV was again the first to meet Alyosha. She was flustered; something important had happened. Katerina Ivanovna's hysterics had ended in a fainting fit, and then "a terrible, awful weakness had followed, she lay with her eyes turned up and was delirious. Now she was in a fever. They had sent for Herzenstube; they had sent for the aunts. The aunts were already here, but Herzenstube had not yet come. They were all sitting in her room, waiting. She was unconscious now, and what if it turned to brain fever!"

Madame Hohlakov looked gravely alarmed. "This is serious, serious," she added at every word, as though nothing that had happened to her before had been serious. Alyosha listened with distress, and was beginning to describe his adventures, but she interrupted him at the first words. She had not time to listen. She begged him to sit with Lise and wait for her there.

"Lise," she whispered almost in his ear, "Lise has greatly surprised me just now, dear Alexey Fyodorovitch. She touched me, too, and so my heart forgives her everything. Only fancy, as soon as you had gone, she began to be truly remorseful for having laughed at you to-day and yesterday, though she was not laughing at you, but only joking. But she was seriously sorry for it, almost ready to cry, so that I was quite surprised. She has never been really sorry for laughing at me, but has only made a joke of it. And you know she is laughing at me every minute. But this time she was in earnest. She thinks a great deal of your opinion, Alexey Fyodorovitch, and don't take offence or be wounded by her if you can help it. I am never hard upon her, for she's such a clever little thing—would you believe it? She said just now that you were a friend of her childhood, 'the greatest friend of her childhood'—just think of that—'greatest friend'—and what about me? She has very strong feelings and memories, and, what's more, she uses these phrases, most unexpected words, which come out all of a sudden when you least expect them. She spoke lately about a pine-tree, for instance: there used to be a pine-tree standing in our garden in her early childhood. Very likely it's standing there still; so there's no need to speak in the past tense. Pine-trees are not like people, Alexey Fyodorovitch, they don't change quickly. 'Mamma,' she said, 'I remember this pine-tree as in a dream,' only she said something so original about it that I can't repeat it. Besides, I've forgotten it. Well, good-bye! I am so worried I feel I shall go out of my mind. Ah! Alexey Fyodorovitch, I've been out of my mind twice in my life. Go to Lise, cheer her up, as you always can so charmingly. Lise," she cried, going to her door, "here I've brought you Alexey Fyodorovitch, whom you insulted so. He is not at all angry, I assure you; on the contrary, he is surprised that you could suppose so."

"Merci, maman. Come in, Alexey Fyodorovitch."

Alyosha went in. Lise looked rather embarrassed, and at once flushed crimson. She was evidently ashamed of something, and, as people always do in such cases, she began immediately talking of other things, as though they were of absorbing interest to her at the moment.

217

"Mamma has just told me all about the two hundred roubles, Alexey Fyodorovitch, and your taking them to that poor officer . . . and she told me all the awful story of how he had been insulted . . . and you know, although mamma muddles things . . . she always rushes from one thing to another . . . I cried when I heard. Well, did you give him the money and how is that poor man getting on?"

"The fact is I didn't give it to him, and it's a long story," answered Alyosha, as though he, too, could think of nothing but his regret at having failed, yet Lise saw perfectly well that he, too, looked away, and that he, too, was trying to talk of other things.

Alyosha sat down at the table and began to tell his story, but at the first words he lost his embarrassment and gained the whole of Lise's attention as well. He spoke with deep feeling, under the influence of the strong impression he had just received, and he succeeded in telling his story well and circumstantially. In old days in Moscow he had been fond of coming to Lise and describing to her what had just happened to him, what he had read, or what he remembered of his childhood. Sometimes they had made day-dreams and woven whole romances together—generally cheerful and amusing ones. Now they both felt suddenly transported to the old days in Moscow, two years before. Lise was extremely touched by his story. Alyosha described Ilusha with warm feeling. When he finished describing how the luckless man trampled on the money, Lise could not help clasping her hands and crying out:

"So you didn't give him the money! So you let him run away! Oh dear, you ought to have run after him!"

"No, Lise! it's better I didn't run after him," said Alyosha, getting up from his chair and walking thoughtfully across the room.

"How so? How is it better? Now they are without food and their case is hopeless."

"Not hopeless, for the two hundred roubles will still come to them. He'll take the money to-morrow. To-morrow he will be sure to take it," said Alyosha, pacing up and down, pondering. "You see, Lise," he went on, stopping suddenly before her, "I made one blunder, but that, even that, is all for the best."

"What blunder, and why is it for the best?"

"I'll tell you. He is a man of weak and timorous character; he has suffered so much and is very good-natured. I keep wondering why he took offence so suddenly, for I assure you, up to the last minute, he did not know that he was going to trample on the notes. And I think now that there was a great deal to offend him . . . and it could not have been otherwise in his position. . . . To begin with, he was sore at having been so glad of the money in my presence and not having concealed it from me. If he had been pleased, but not so much; if he had not shown it; if he had begun affecting scruples and difficulties, as other people do when they take money, he might still endure to take it. But he was too genuinely delighted, and that was mortifying. Ah, Lise, he is a good and truthful man—that's the worst of the whole business. All the while he talked, his voice was so weak, so broken, he talked so fast, so fast, he kept laughing such a laugh, or perhaps he was crying—yes, I am sure he was crying, he was so delighted—and he talked about his daughters—and about the situation he could get in another town. . . . And when he had poured out his heart, he felt ashamed at having shown me his inmost soul like that. So he began to hate me at once. He is one of those awfully sensitive poor people. What had made him feel most ashamed was that he had given in too soon and accepted me as a friend, you see. At first he almost flew at me and tried to intimidate me, but as soon as he saw the money he had begun embracing me; he kept touching me with his hands. This must have been how he came to feel it all so humiliating, and then I made that blunder, a very important one. I suddenly said to him that if he had not money enough to move to another town, we would give it to him, and, indeed, I myself would give him as much as he wanted out of my own money. That struck him all at once. Why, he thought, did I put myself forward to help him? You know, Lise, it's awfully hard for a man who has been injured, when other people look at him as though they were his bene-factors. . . . I've heard that; Father Zossima told me so. I don't know how to put it, but I have often seen it myself. And I feel like that myself, too. And the worst of it was that though he did not know, up to the very last minute, that he would trample on the notes, he had a kind of presentiment of it, I am sure of that. That's just what made him so ecstatic, that he had that presentiment. . . . And though it's so dreadful, it's all for the best. In fact, I believe nothing better could have happened."

"Why, why could nothing better have happened?" cried Lise, looking with great surprise at Alyosha.

"Because if he had taken the money, in an hour after getting home, he would be crying with mortification, that's just what would have happened And most likely he would have come to me early to-morrow, and perhaps have flung the notes at me and trampled upon them as he did just now. But now he has gone home awfully proud and triumphant, though he knows he has 'ruined himself'. So now nothing could be easier than to make him accept the two hundred roubles by to-morrow, for he has already vindicated his honour, tossed away the money, and trampled it under foot. . . . He couldn't know when he did it that I should bring it to him again to-morrow, and yet he is in terrible need of that money. Though he is proud of himself now, yet even to-day he'll be thinking what a help he has lost. He will think of it more than ever at night, will dream of it, and by to-morrow morning he may be ready to run to me to ask forgiveness. It's just then that I'll appear. 'Here, you are a proud man,' I shall say: 'you have shown it; but now take the money and forgive us!' And then he will take it!"

Alyosha was carried away with joy as he uttered the last words. "And then he will take it!" Lise clapped her hands.

"Ah, that's true! I understand that perfectly now. Ah, Alyosha, how do you know all this? So young and yet he knows what's in the heart. . . . I should never have worked it out."

"The great thing now is to persuade him that he is on an equal footing with us, in spite of his taking money from us," Alyosha went on in his excitement, "and not only on an equal but even on a higher footing."

" 'On a higher footing' is charming, Alexey Fyodorovitch; but go on, go on!"

"You mean there isn't such an expression as 'on a higher footing'? but that doesn't matter because——"

"Oh, no, of course it doesn't matter. Forgive me, Alyosha dear. . . . You know, I scarcely respected you till now—that is I respected you but on an equal footing; but now I shall begin to respect you on a higher footing. Don't be angry, dear, at my joking," she put in at once, with strong feeling. "I am absurd and small, but you, you! Listen, Alexey Fyodorovitch. Isn't there in all our analysis—I mean your analysis. . . . No, better call it 'ours'—aren't we showing contempt for him, for that poor man—in analysing his soul like this, as it were, from above, eh? In deciding so certainly that he will take the money?"

"No, Lise, ít's not contempt," Alyosha answered, as though

he had prepared himself for the question. "I was thinking of that on the way here. How can it be contempt when we are all like him, when we are all just the same as he is. For you know we are just the same, no better. If we are better, we should have been just the same in his place. . . . I don't know about you, Lise, but I consider that I have a sordid soul in many ways, and his soul is not sordid; on the contrary, full of fine feeling. . . . No, Lise, I have no contempt for him. Do you know, Lise, my elder told me once to care for most people exactly as one would for children, and for some of them as one would for the sick in hospitals."

"Ah, Alexey Fyodorovitch, dear, let us care for people as we would for the sick!"

"Let us, Lise; I am ready. Though I am not altogether ready in myself. I am sometimes very impatient and at other times I don't see things. It's different with you."

"Ah, I don't believe it! Alexey Fyodorovitch, how happy ı am."

"I am so glad you say so, Lise."

"Alexey Fyodorovitch, you are wonderfully good, but you are sometimes sort of formal. . . . And yet you are not a bit formal really. Go to the door, open it gently, and see whether mamma is listening," said Lise, in a nervous, hurried whisper.

Alyosha went, opened the door, and reported that no one was listening.

"Come here, Alexey Fyodorovitch," Lise went on, flushing redder and redder. "Give me your hand—that's right. I have to make a great confession, I didn't write to you yesterday in joke but in earnest," and she hid her eyes with her hand. It was evident that she was greatly ashamed of the confession.

Suddenly she snatched his hand and impulsively kissed it three times.

"Ah, Lise, what a good thing!" cried Alyosha joyfully. "You know, I was perfectly sure you were in earnest."

"Sure? Upon my word!" She put aside his hand, but did not leave go of it, blushing hotly, and laughing a little happy laugh. "I kiss his hand and he says: 'What a good thing!'"

But her reproach was undeserved: Alyosha, too, was greatly overcome.

"I should like to please you always, Lise, but I don't know how to do it," he muttered, blushing too.

"Alyosha dear, you are cold and rude. Do you see? He has chosen me as his wife and is quite settled about it. He is

221

sure I was in earnest. What a thing to say! Why, that's impertinence—that's what it is."

"Why, was it wrong of me to feel sure?" Alyosha asked, laughing suddenly.

"Ah, Alyosha, on the contrary, it was delightfully right," cried Lise, looking tenderly and happily at him.

Alyosha stood still, holding her hand in his. Suddenly he stooped down and kissed her on her lips.

"Oh, what are you doing?" cried Lise. Alyosha was terribly abashed.

"Oh, forgive me if I shouldn't. . . . Perhaps I'm awfully stupid. . . . You said I was cold, so I kissed you. . . . But I see it was stupid."

Lise laughed, and hid her face in her hands. "And in that dress!" she ejaculated in the midst of her mirth. But she suddenly ceased laughing and became serious, almost stern.

"Alyosha, we must put off kissing. We are not ready for that yet, and we shall have a long time to wait," she ended suddenly. "Tell me rather why you who are so clever, so intellectual, so observant, choose a little idiot, an invalid like me? Ah, Alyosha, I am awfully happy, for I don't deserve you a bit."

"You do, Lise. I shall be leaving the monastery altogether in a few days. If I go into the world I must marry. I know that. *He* told me to marry, too. Whom could I marry better than you—and who would have me except you? I have been thinking it over. In the first place, you've known me from a child and you've a great many qualities I haven't. You are more light-hearted than I am; above all, you are more innocent than I am. I have been brought into contact with many, many things already. . . . Ah, you don't know, but I, too, am a Karamazov. What does it matter if you do laugh and make jokes, and at me, too? Go on laughing. I am so glad you do. You laugh like a little child, but you think like a martyr."

"Like a martyr? How?"

"Yes, Lise, your question just now: whether we weren't showing contempt for that poor man by dissecting his soul—that was the question of a sufferer. . . . You see, I don't know how to express it, but anyone who thinks of such questions is capable of suffering. Sitting in your invalid chair you must have thought over many things already."

"Alyosha, give me your hand. Why are you taking it away?" murmured Lise in a failing voice, weak with happiness. "Listen, Alyosha. What will you wear when you come out of the monastery? What sort of suit? Don't laugh, don't be angry, it's very, very important to me."

"I haven't thought about the suit, Lise; but I'll wear whatever you like."

"I should like you to have a dark blue velvet coat, a white piqué waistcoat, and a soft grey felt hat. . . . Tell me, did you believe that I didn't care for you when I said I didn't mean what I wrote?"

"No, I didn't believe it."

"Oh, you insupportable person, you are incorrigible."

"You see, I knew that you—seemed to care for me, but I pretended to believe that you didn't care for me to make it—easier for you."

"That makes it worse! Worse and better than all! Alyosha, I am awfully fond of you. Just before you came this morning I tried my fortune. I decided I would ask you for my letter, and if you brought it out calmly and gave it to me (as might have been expected from you) it would mean that you did not love me at all, that you felt nothing, and were simply a stupid boy, good for nothing, and that I am ruined. But you left the letter at home and that cheered me. You left it behind you on purpose, so as not to give it back, because you knew I would ask for it? That was it, wasn't it?"

"Ah, Lise, it was not so a bit. The letter is with me now, and it was this morning, in this pocket. Here it is."

Alyosha pulled the letter out laughing, and showed it her at a distance.

"But I am not going to give it to you. Look at it from here."

"Why, then you told a lie? You, a monk, told a lie!"

"I told a lie if you like," Alyosha laughed, too. "I told a lie so as not to give you back the letter. It's very precious to me," he added suddenly, with strong feeling, and again he flushed. "It always will be, and I won't give it up to anyone!"

Lise looked at him joyfully. "Alyosha," she murmured again, "look at the door. Isn't mamma listening?"

"Very well, Lise, I'll look; but wouldn't it be better not to look? Why suspect your mother of such meanness?"

"What meanness? As for her spying on her daughter, it's her right, it's not meanness!" cried Lise, firing up. "You may be sure, Alexey Fyodorovitch, that when I am a mother, if I have a daughter like myself I shall certainly spy on her!"

"Really, Lise? That's not right."

"Oh, my goodness! What has meanness to do with it? If she were listening to some ordinary worldly conversation, it would be meanness, but when her own daughter is shut up with a young man . . . Listen, Alyosha, do you know I shall spy upon you as soon as we are married, and let me tell you I shall open all your letters and read them, so you may as well be prepared."

"Yes, of course, if so——" muttered Alyosha, "only it's not right."

"Ah, how contemptuous! Alyosha dear, we won't quarrel the very first day. I'd better tell you the whole truth. Of course, it's very wrong to spy on people, and, of course, I am not right and you are, only I shall spy on you all the same."

"Do, then; you won't find out anything," laughed Alyosha.

"And, Alyosha, will you give in to me? We must decide that too."

"I shall be delighted to, Lise, and certain to, only not in the most important things. Even if you don't agree with me, I shall do my duty in the most important things."

"That's right; but let me tell you I am ready to give in to you not only in the most important matters but in everything. And I am ready to vow to do so now—in everything, and for all my life!" cried Lise fervently, "and I'll do it gladly, gladly! What's more, I'll swear never to spy on you, never once, never to read one of your letters. For you are right and I am not. And though I shall be awfully tempted to spy, I know that I won't do it since you consider it dishonourable. You are my conscience now. . . . Listen, Alexey Fyodorovitch, why have you been so sad lately—both yesterday and to-day? I know you have a lot of anxiety and trouble, but I see you have some special grief besides, some secret one, perhaps?"

"Yes, Lise, I have a secret one, too," answered Alyosha mournfully. "I see you love me, since you guessed that."

"What grief? What about? Can you tell me?" asked Lise, with timid entreaty.

"I'll tell you later, Lise—afterwards," said Alyosha, confused. "Now you wouldn't understand it, perhaps—and perhaps I couldn't explain it."

"I know your brothers and your father are worrying you, too?"

"Yes, my brothers too," murmured Alyosha, pondering.

"I don't like your brother Ivan, Alyosha," said Lise suddenly.

He noticed this remark with some surprise, but did not answer it.

"My brothers are destroying themselves," he went on, "my father, too. And they are destroying others with them. It's 'the primitive force of the Karamazovs', as Father Païssy said the other day, a crude, unbridled, earthly force. Does the spirit of God move above that force? Even that I don't know. I only know that I, too, am a Karamazov. . . . Me a monk, a monk! Am I a monk, Lise? You said just now that I was."

"Yes, I did."

"And perhaps I don't even believe in God."

"You don't believe? What is the matter?" said Lise quietly and gently. But Alyosha did not answer. There was something too mysterious, too subjective in these last words of his, perhaps obscure to himself, but yet torturing him.

"And now on the top of it all, my friend, the best man in the world, is going, is leaving the earth! If you knew, Lise, how bound up in soul I am with him! And then I shall be left alone. . . . I shall come to you, Lise. . . . For the future we will be together."

"Yes, together, together! Henceforward we shall be always together, all our lives! Listen, kiss me, I allow you."

Alyosha kissed her.

"Come, now go. Christ be with you!" and she made the sign of the cross over him. "Make haste back to *him* while he is alive. I see I've kept you cruelly. I'll pray to-day for him and you. Alyosha, we shall be happy! Shall we be happy, shall we?"

"I believe we shall, Lise."

Alyosha thought it better not to go in to Madame Hohlakov and was going out of the house without saying good-bye to her. But no sooner had he opened the door than he found Madame Hohlakov standing before him. From the first word Alyosha guessed that she had been waiting on purpose to meet him.

"Alexey Fyodorovitch, this is awful. This is all childish nonsense and ridiculous. I trust you won't dream . . . It's foolishness, nothing but foolishness!" she said, attacking him at once.

"Only don't tell her that," said Alyosha, "or she will be upset, and that's bad for her now."

"Sensible advice from a sensible young man. Am I to understand that you only agreed with her from compassion for her invalid state, because you didn't want to irritate her by contradiction?"

"Oh no, not at all. I was quite serious in what I said," Alyosha declared stoutly.

"To be serious about it is impossible, unthinkable, and in the first place I shall never be at home to you again, and I shall take her away, you may be sure of that."

"But why?" asked Alyosha. "It's all so far off. We may have to wait another year and a half."

"Ah, Alexey Fyodorovitch, that's true, of course, and you'll have time to quarrel and separate a thousand times in a year and a half. But I am so unhappy! Though it's such nonsense, it's a great blow to me. I feel like Famusov in the last scene of *Sorrow from Wit*. You are Tchatsky and she is Sofya, and, only fancy, I've run down to meet you on the stairs, and in the play the fatal scene takes place on the staircase. I heard it all; I almost dropped. So this is the explanation of her dreadful night and her hysterics of late! It means love to the daughter but death to the mother. I might as well be in my grave at once. And, a more serious matter still, what is this letter she has written? Show it me at once, at once!"

"No, there's no need. Tell me, how is Katerina Ivanovna now? I must know."

"She still lies in delirium; she has not regained consciousness. Her aunts are here; but they do nothing but sigh and give themselves airs. Herzenstube came, and he was so alarmed that I didn't know what to do for him. I nearly sent for a doctor to look after him. He was driven home in my carriage. And on the top of it all, you and this letter! It's true nothing can happen for a year and a half. In the name of all that's holy, in the name of your dying elder, show me that letter, Alexey Fyodorovitch. I'm her mother. Hold it in your hand, if you like, and I will read it so."

"No, I won't show it to you. Even if she sanctioned it, I wouldn't. I am coming to-morrow, and if you like, we can talk over many things, but now good-bye!"

And Alyosha ran downstairs and into the street.

CHAPTER II

SMERDYAKOV WITH A GUITAR

HE had no time to lose indeed. Even while he was saying good-bye to Lise, the thought had struck him that he must attempt some stratagem to find his brother Dmitri, who was evidently keeping out of his way. It was getting late, nearly three o'clock. Alyosha's whole soul turned to the monastery, to his dying saint, but the necessity of seeing Dmitri outweighed everything. The conviction that a great inevitable catastrophe was about to happen grew stronger in Alyosha's mind with every hour. What that catastrophe was, and what he would say at that moment to his brother, he could perhaps not have said definitely. "Even if my benefactor must die without me, anyway I won't have to reproach myself all my life with the thought that I might have saved something and did not, but passed by and hastened home. If I do as I intend, I shall be following his great precept."

His plan was to catch his brother Dmitri unawares, to climb over the fence, as he had the day before, get into the garden and sit in the summer-house. If Dmitri were not there, thought Alyosha, he would not announce himself to Foma or the women of the house, but would remain hidden in the summer-house, even if he had to wait there till evening. If, as before, Dmitri were lying in wait for Grushenka to come, he would be very likely to come to the summer-house. Alyosha did not, however, give much thought to the details of his plan, but resolved to act upon it, even if it meant not getting back to the monastery that day.

Everything happened without hindrance, he climbed over the hurdle almost in the same spot as the day before, and stole into the summer-house unseen. He did not want to be noticed. The woman of the house and Foma too, if he were here, might be loyal to his brother and obey his instructions, and so refuse to let Alyosha come into the garden, or might warn Dmitri that he was being sought and inquired for.

There was no one in the summer-house. Alyosha sat down and began to wait. He looked round the summer-house, which somehow struck him as a great deal more ancient than before. Though the day was just as fine as yesterday, it seemed a wretched little place this time. There was a circle on the table, left no doubt from the glass of brandy having been spilt the day before. Foolish and irrelevant ideas strayed about his mind, as they always do in a time of tedious waiting. He wondered, for instance, why he had sat down precisely in the same place as before, why not in the other seat. At last he felt very depressed—depressed by suspense and uncertainty. But he had not sat there more than a quarter of an hour when he suddenly heard the thrum of a guitar somewhere quite close. People were sitting, or had only just sat down, somewhere in the bushes not more than twenty paces away. Alyosha suddenly recollected that on coming out of the summer-house the day before, he had caught a glimpse of an old green low garden-seat among the bushes on the left, by the fence. The people must be sitting on it now. Who were they?

A man's voice suddenly began singing in a sugary falsetto, accompanying himself on the guitar:

> *With invincible force*
> *I am bound to my dear.*
> *Oh, Lord, have mercy*
> *On her and on me!*
> *On her and on me!*
> *On her and on me!*

The voice ceased. It was a lackey's tenor and a lackey's song. Another voice, a woman's, suddenly asked insinuatingly and bashfully, though with mincing affectation:

"Why haven't you been to see us for so long, Pavel Fyodorovitch? Why do you always look down upon us?"

"Not at all," answered a man's voice politely but with emphatic dignity. It was clear that the man had the best of the position, and that the woman was making advances. "I believe the man must be Smerdyakov," thought Alyosha, "from his voice. And the lady must be the daughter of the house here, who has come from Moscow, the one who wears the dress with a tail and goes to Marfa for soup."

"I am awfully fond of verses of all kinds, if they rhyme," the woman's voice continued. "Why don't you go on?"

The man sang again:

> *What do I care for royal weaith*
> *If but my dear one be in health?*
> *Lord have mercy*
> *On her and on me!*
> *On her and on me!*
> *On her and on me!*

"It was even better last time," observed the woman's voice. "You sang 'If my darling be in health'; it sounded more tender. I suppose you've forgotten to-day."

"Poetry is rubbish!" said Smerdyakov curtly.

228

"Oh, no! I am very fond of poetry."

"So far as it's poetry, it's essential rubbish. Consider yourself, whoever talks in rhyme? And if we were all to talk in rhyme, even though it were decreed by government, we shouldn't say much, should we? Poetry is no good, Marya Kondratyevna."

"How clever you are! How is it you've gone so deep into everything?" The woman's voice was more and more insinuating.

"I could have done better than that. I could have known more than that, if it had not been for my destiny from my childhood up. I would have shot a man in a duel if he called me names because I am descended from a filthy beggar and have no father. And they used to throw it in my teeth in Moscow. It had reached them from here, thanks to Grigory Vassilyevitch. Grigory Vassilyevitch blames me for rebelling against my birth, but I would have sanctioned their killing me before I was born that I might not have come into the world at all. They used to say in the market, and your mamma too, with great lack of delicacy, set off telling me that her hair was like a mat on her head, and that she was short of five foot by a wee bit. Why talk of a wee bit while she might have said 'a little bit', like everyone else? She wanted to make it touching, a regular peasant's feeling. Can a Russian peasant be said to feel, in comparison with an educated man? He can't be said to have feeling at all, in his ignorance. From my childhood up, when I hear 'a wee bit', I am ready to burst with rage. I hate all Russia, Marya Kondratyevna."

"If you'd been a cadet in the army, or a young hussar, you wouldn't have talked like that, but would have drawn your sabre to defend all Russia."

"I don't want to be a hussar, Marya Kondratyevna, and, what's more, I should like to abolish all soldiers."

"And when an enemy comes, who is going to defend us?"

"There's no need of defence. In 1812 there was a great invasion of Russia by Napoleon, first Emperor of the French, father of the present one, and it would have been a good thing if they had conquered us. A clever nation would have conquered a very stupid one and annexed it. We should have had quite different institutions."

"Are they so much better in their own country than we are? I wouldn't change a dandy I know of for three young Englishmen," observed Marya Kondratyevna tenderly, doubtless accompanying her words with a most languishing glance.

"That's as one prefers."

"But you are just like a foreigner—just like a most gentlemanly foreigner. I tell you that, though it makes me bashful."

"If you care to know, the folks there and ours here are just alike in their vice. They are swindlers, only there the scoundrel wears polished boots and here he grovels in filth and sees no harm in it. The Russian people want thrashing, as Fyodor Pavlovitch said very truly yesterday, though he is mad, and all his children."

"You said yourself you had such a respect for Ivan Fyodorovitch."

"But he said I was a stinking lackey. He thinks that I might be unruly. He is mistaken there. If I had a certain sum in my pocket I would have left here long ago. Dmitri Fyodorovitch is lower than any lackey in his behaviour in his mind, and in his poverty. He doesn't know how to do anything, and yet he is respected by everyone. I may be only a soup-maker, but with luck I could open a café restaurant in Petrovka, in Moscow, for my cookery is something special, and there's no one in Moscow, except the foreigners, whose cookery is anything special. Dmitri Fyodorovitch is a beggar, but if he were to challenge the son of the first count in the country, he'd fight him. Though in what way is he better than I am? For he is ever so much stupider than I am. Look at the money he has wasted without any need!"

"It must be lovely, a duel," Marya Kondratyevna observed suddenly.

"How so?"

"It must be so dreadful and so brave, especially when young officers with pistols in their hands pop at one another for the sake of some lady. A perfect picture! Ah, if only girls were allowed to look on, I'd give anything to see one!"

"It's all very well when you are firing at someone, but when he is firing straight in your mug you must feel pretty silly. You'd be glad to run away, Marya Kondratyevna."

"You don't mean you would run away?" But Smerdyakov did not deign to reply. After a moment's silence the guitar tinkled again, and he sang again in the same falsetto:

Whatever you may say,
I shall go far away.

Life will be bright and gay
In the city far away.
I shall not grieve,
I shall not grieve at all,
I don't intend to grieve at all.

Then something unexpected happened. Alyosha suddenly sneezed. They were silent. Alyosha got up and walked towards them. He found Smerdyakov dressed up and wearing polished boots, his hair pomaded, and perhaps curled. The guitar lay on the garden-seat. His companion was the daughter of the house, wearing a light blue dress with a train two yards long. She was young and would not have been bad-looking but that her face was so round and terribly freckled.

"Will my brother Dmitri soon be back?" asked Alyosha, with as much composure as he could.

Smerdyakov got up slowly; Marya Kondratyevna rose too.

"How am I to know about Dmitri Fyodorovitch? It's not as if I were his keeper," answered Smerdyakov quietly, distinctly, and superciliously.

"But I simply asked whether you do know?" Alyosha explained.

"I know nothing of his whereabouts and don't want to."

"But my brother told me that you let him know all that goes on in the house, and promised to let him know when Agrafena Alexandrovna comes."

Smerdyakov turned a deliberate, unmoved glance upon him.

"And how did you get in this time, since the gate was bolted an hour ago?" he asked, looking at Alyosha.

"I came in from the back-alley, over the fence, and went straight to the summer-house. I hope you'll forgive me," he added, addressing Marya Kondratyevna. "I was in a hurry to find my brother."

"Ach, as though we could take it amiss in you!" drawled Marya Kondratyevna, flattered by Alyosha's apology. "For Dmitri Fyodorovitch often goes to the summer-house in that way. We don't know he is here and he is sitting in the summer-house."

"I am very anxious to find him, or to learn from you where he is now. Believe me, it's on business of great importance to him."

"He never tells us," lisped Marya Kondratyevna.

"Though I used to come here as a friend," Smerdyakov

began again, "Dmitri Fyodorovitch has pestered me in a merciless way even here by his incessant questions about the master. 'What news?' he'll ask. 'What's going on in there now? Who's coming and going,' and can't I tell him something more. Twice already he's threatened me with death."

"With death?" Alyosha exclaimed in surprise.

"Do you suppose he'd think much of that, with his temper, which you had a chance of observing yesterday? He says if I let Agrafena Alexandrovna in and she passes the night there, I'll be the first to suffer for it. I am terribly afraid of him, and if I were not even more afraid of doing so, I ought to let the police know. God only knows what he might not do!"

"His honour said to him the other day: 'I'll pound you in a mortar!'" added Marya Kondratyevna.

"Oh, if it's pounding in a mortar it may be only talk," observed Alyosha. "If I could meet him I might speak to him about that too."

"Well, the only thing I can tell you is this," said Smerdyakov, as though thinking better of it: "I am here as an old friend and neighbour, and it would be odd if I didn't come. On the other hand, Ivan Fyodorovitch sent me first thing this morning to your brother's lodging in Lake Street, without a letter, but with a message to Dmitri Fyodorovitch to go to dine with him at the restaurant here, in the market-place. I went, but didn't find Dmitri Fyodorovitch at home, though it was eight o'clock. 'He's been here, but he is quite gone,' those were the very words of his landlady. It's as though there was an understanding between them. Perhaps at this moment he is in the restaurant with Ivan Fyodorovitch, for Ivan Fyodorovitch has not been home to dinner and Fyodor Pavlovitch dined alone an hour ago and is gone to lie down. But I beg you most particularly not to speak of me and of what I have told you, for he'd kill me for nothing at all."

"Brother Ivan invited Dmitri to the restaurant to-day?" repeated Alyosha quickly.

"That's so."

"The Metropolis tavern in the market-place?"

"The very same."

"That's quite likely," cried Alyosha, much excited. "Thank you, Smerdyakov; that's important. I'll go there at once."

"Don't betray me," Smerdyakov called after him.

"Oh, no, I'll go to the tavern as though by chance. Don't be anxious."

"But wait a minute, I'll open the gate to you," cried Marya Kondratyevna.

"No; it's a short cut, I'll get over the fence again."

What he had heard threw Alyosha into great agitation. He ran to the tavern. It was impossible for him to go into the tavern in his monastic dress, but he could inquire at the entrance for his brothers and call them down. But just as he reached the tavern, a window was flung open, and his brother Ivan called down to him from it.

"Alyosha, can't you come up here to me? I shall be awfully grateful."

"To be sure I can, only I don't quite know whether in this dress . . ."

"But I am in a room apart. Come up the steps; I'll run down to meet you."

A minute later Alyosha was sitting beside his brother. Ivan was alone dining.

CHAPTER III

THE BROTHERS MAKE FRIENDS

IVAN was not, however, in a separate room, but only in a place shut off by a screen, so that it was unseen by other people in the room. It was the first room from the entrance with a buffet along the wall. Waiters were continually darting to and fro in it. The only customer in the room was an old retired military man drinking tea in a corner. But there was the usual bustle going on in the other rooms of the tavern; there were shouts for the waiters, the sounds of popping corks, the click of billiard balls, the drone of the organ. Alyosha knew that Ivan did not usually visit this tavern and disliked taverns in general. So he must have come here, he reflected, simply to meet Dmitri by arrangement. Yet Dmitri was not there.

"Shall I order you fish, soup or anything, you don't live on tea alone, I suppose?" cried Ivan, apparently delighted at having got hold of Alyosha. He had finished dinner and was drinking tea.

"Let me have soup, and tea afterwards, I am hungry," said Alyosha gaily.

"And cherry jam? They have it here. You remember how you used to love cherry jam when you were little?"

233

"You remember that? Let me have jam too, I like it still."

Ivan rang for the waiter and ordered soup, jam and tea.

"I remember everything, Alyosha. I remember you till you were eleven, I was nearly fifteen. There's such a difference between fifteen and eleven that brothers are never companions at those ages. I don't know whether I was fond of you even. When I went away to Moscow for the first few years I never thought of you at all. Then, when you came to Moscow yourself, we only met once somewhere, I believe. And now I've been here more than three months, and so far we have scarcely said a word to each other. To-morrow I am going away, and I was just thinking as I sat here how I could see you to say good-bye and just then you passed."

"Were you very anxious to see me then?"

"Very, I want to get to know you once for all, and I want you to know me. And then to say good-bye. I believe it's always best to get to know people just before leaving them. I've noticed how you've been looking at me these three months. There has been a continual look of expectation in your eyes, and I can't endure that. That's how it is I've kept away from you. But in the end I have learned to respect you. The little man stands firm, I thought. Though I am laughing, I am serious. You do stand firm, don't you? I like people who are firm like that whatever it is they stand by, even if they are such little fellows as you. Your expectant eyes ceased to annoy me, I grew fond of them in the end, those expectant eyes. You seem to love me for some reason, Alyosha?"

"I do love you, Ivan. Dmitri says of you—Ivan is a tomb! I say of you, Ivan is a riddle. You are a riddle to me even now. But I understand something in you, and I did not understand it till this morning."

"What's that?" laughed Ivan.

"You won't be angry?" Alyosha laughed too.

"Well?"

"That you are just as young as other young men of three-and-twenty, that you are just a young and fresh and nice boy, green in fact! Now, have I insulted you dreadfully?"

"On the contrary, I am struck by a coincidence," cried Ivan, warmly and good-humouredly. "Would you believe it that ever since that scene with her I have thought of nothing else but my youthful greenness, and just as though you guessed that, you begin about it. Do you know I've been sitting here thinking to myself: that if I didn't believe in life, if I

234

lost faith in the woman I love, lost faith in the order of things, were convinced in fact that everything is a disorderly, damnable, and perhaps devil-ridden chaos, if I were struck by every horror of man's disillusionment—still I should want to live and, having once tasted of the cup, I would not turn away from it till I had drained it! At thirty, though, I shall be sure to leave the cup, even if I've not emptied it, and turn away— where I don't know. But till I am thirty I knew that my youth will triumph over everything—every disillusionment, every disgust with life. I've asked myself many times whether there is in the world any despair that would overcome this frantic and perhaps unseemly thirst for life in me, and I've come to the conclusion that there isn't, that is, till I am thirty, and then I shall lose it of myself, I fancy. Some drivelling consumptive moralists—and poets especially—often call that thirst for life base. It's a feature of the Karamazovs, it's true, that thirst for life regardless of everything; you have it no doubt too, but why is it base? The centripetal force of our planet is still fearfully strong, Alyosha. I have a longing for life, and I go on living in spite of logic. Though I may not believe in the order of the universe, yet I love the sticky little leaves as they open in spring. I love the blue sky, I love some people, whom one loves, you know, sometimes without knowing why. I love some great deeds done by men, though I've long ceased perhaps to have faith in them, yet from old habit one's heart prizes them. Here they have brought the soup for you, eat it, it will do you good. It's first-rate soup, they know how to make it here. I want to travel in Europe, Alyosha. I shall set off from here. And yet I know that I am only going to a graveyard, but it's a most precious graveyard, that's what it is! Precious are the dead that lie there, every stone over them speaks of such burning life in the past, of such passionate faith in their work, their truth, their struggle and their science, that I know I shall fall on the ground and kiss those stones and weep over them; though I'm convinced in my heart that it's long been nothing but a graveyard. And I shall not weep from despair, but simply because I shall be happy in my tears, I shall steep my soul in my emotion. I love the sticky leaves in spring, the blue sky—that's all it is. It's not a matter of intellect or logic, it's loving with one's inside, with one's stomach. One loves the first strength of one's youth. Do you understand anything of my tirade, Alyosha?" Ivan laughed suddenly.

"I understand too well, Ivan. One longs to love with one's

inside, with one's stomach. You said that so well and I am awfully glad that you have such a longing for life," cried Alyosha. "I think everyone should love life above everything in the world."

"Love life more than the meaning of it?"

"Certainly, love it, regardless of logic, as you say, it must be regardless of logic, and it's only then one will understand the meaning of it. I have thought so a long time. Half your work is done, Ivan, you love life, now you've only to try to do the second half and you are saved."

"You are trying to save me, but perhaps I am not lost! And what does your second half mean?"

"Why, one has to raise up your dead, who perhaps have not died after all. Come, let me have tea. I am so glad of our talk, Ivan."

"I see you are feeling inspired. I am awfully fond of such *professions de foi* from such—novices. You are a steadfast person, Alexey. Is it true that you mean to leave the monastery?"

"Yes, my elder sends me out in the world."

"We shall see each other then in the world. We shall meet before I am thirty, when I shall begin to turn aside from the cup. Father doesn't want to turn aside from his cup till he is seventy, he dreams of hanging on to eighty, in fact, so he says. He means it only too seriously, though he is a buffoon. He stands on a firm rock, too, he stands on his sensuality—though after we are thirty, indeed, there may be nothing else to stand on. . . . But to hang on to seventy is nasty, better only to thirty; one might retain 'a shadow of nobility' by deceiving oneself. Have you see Dmitri to-day?"

"No, but I saw Smerdyakov," and Alyosha rapidly, though minutely, described his meeting with Smerdyakov. Ivan began listening anxiously and questioned him.

"But he begged me not to tell Dmitri that he had told me about him," added Alyosha. Ivan frowned and pondered.

"Are you frowning on Smerdyakov's account?" asked Alyosha.

"Yes, on his account. Damn him, I certainly did want to see Dmitri, but now there's no need," said Ivan reluctantly.

"But are you really going so soon, brother?"

"Yes."

"What of Dmitri and father? how will it end?" asked Alyosha anxiously.

"You are always harping upon it? What have I to do with it? Am I my brother Dmitri's keeper?" Ivan snapped irritably, but then he suddenly smiled bitterly. "Cain's answer about his murdered brother, wasn't it? Perhaps that's what you're thinking at this moment? Well, damn it all, I can't stay here to be their keeper, can I? I've finished what I had to do, and I am going. Do you imagine I am jealous of Dmitri, that I've been trying to steal his beautiful Katerina Ivanovna for the last three months? Nonsense, I had business of my own. I finished it. I am going. I finished it just now, you were witness."

"At Katerina Ivanovna's?"

"Yes, and I've released myself once for all. And after all, what have I to do with Dmitri? Dmitri doesn't come in. I had my own business to settle with Katerina Ivanovna. You know, on the contrary, that Dmitri behaved as though there was an understanding between us. I didn't ask him to do it, but he solemnly handed her over to me and gave us his blessing. It's all too funny. Ah, Alyosha, if you only knew how light my heart is now! Would you believe it, I sat here eating my dinner and was nearly ordering champagne to celebrate my first hour of freedom. Tfoo! It's been going on nearly six months, and all at once I've thrown it off. I could never have guessed, even yesterday, how easy it would be to put an end to it if I wanted."

"You are speaking of your love, Ivan?"

"Of my love, if you like. I fell in love with the young lady, I worried myself over her and she worried me. I sat watching over her . . . and all at once it's collapsed! I spoke this morning with inspiration, but I went away and roared with laughter. Would you believe it? Yes, it's the literal truth."

"You seem very merry about it now," observed Alyosha, looking into his face, which had suddenly grown brighter.

"But how could I tell that I didn't care for her a bit? Ha-ha! It appears, after all, I didn't. And yet how she attracted me! How attractive she was just now when I made my speech! And do you know she attracts me awfully even now, yet how easy it is to leave her. Do you think I am boasting?"

"No, only perhaps it wasn't love."

"Alyosha," laughed Ivan, "don't make reflections about love, it's unseemly for you. How you rushed into the discussion this morning! I've forgotten to kiss you for it. . . . But how she tormented me! It certainly was sitting by a 'laceration'. Ah, she knew how I loved her! She loved me and not Dmitri," Ivan insisted gaily. "Her feeling for Dmitri was simply a self-laceration. All I told her just now was perfectly true, but the worst of it is, it may take her fifteen or twenty years to find out that she doesn't care for Dmitri, and loves me whom she torments, and perhaps she may never find it out at all, in spite of her lesson to-day. Well, it's better so; I can simply go away for good. By the way, how is she now? What happened after I departed?"

Alyosha told him she had been hysterical, and that she was now, he heard, unconscious and delirious.

"Isn't Madame Hohlakov laying it on?"

"I think not."

"I must find out. Nobody dies of hysterics though. They don't matter. God gave woman hysterics as a relief. I won't go to her at all. Why push myself forward again?"

"But you told her that she had never cared for you."

"I did that on purpose. Alyosha, shall I call for some champagne? Let us drink to my freedom. Ah, if only you knew how glad I am!"

"No, brother, we had better not drink," said Alyosha suddenly. "Besides, I feel somehow depressed."

"Yes, you've been depressed a long time, I've noticed it."

"Have you settled to go to-morrow morning then?"

"Morning? I didn't say I should go in the morning. . . . But perhaps it may be the morning. Would you believe it, I dined here to-day only to avoid dining with the old man, I loathe him so. I should have left long ago, so far as he is concerned. But why are you so worried about my going away? We've plenty of time before I go, an eternity!"

"If you are going away to-morrow, what do you mean by an eternity?"

"But what does it matter to us?" laughed Ivan, "we've time enough for our talk, for what brought us here. Why do you look so surprised? Answer: why have we met here? To talk of my love for Katerina Ivanovna, of the old man and Dmitri? of foreign travel? of the fatal position of Russia? Of the Emperor Napoleon? Is that it?"

"No."

"Then you know what for. It's different for other people; but we in our green youth have to settle the eternal questions first of all. That's what we care about. Young Russia is talking about nothing but the eternal questions now. Just when the old folks are all taken up with practical questions. Why have you been looking at me in expectation for the last three months? To ask me, 'What do you believe, or don't you believe at all'? That's what your eyes have been meaning for these three months, haven't they?"

"Perhaps so," smiled Alyosha. "You are not laughing at me now, Ivan?"

"Me laughing! I don't want to wound my little brother who has been watching me with such expectation for three months. Alyosha, look straight at me! Of course I am just such a little boy as you are, only not a novice. And what have Russian boys been doing up till now, some of them, I mean? In this stinking tavern, for instance, here, they meet and sit down in a corner. They've never met in their lives before and, when they go out of the tavern, they won't meet again for forty years. And what do they talk about in that momentary halt in the tavern? Of the eternal questions, of the existence of God and immortality. And those who do not believe in God talk of socialism or anarchism, of the transformation of all humanity on a new pattern, so that it all comes to the same, they're the same questions turned inside out. And masses, masses of the most original Russian boys do nothing but talk of the eternal questions! Isn't it so?"

"Yes, for real Russians the questions of God's existence and of immortality, or, as you say, the same questions turned inside out, come first and foremost, of course, and so they should," said Alyosha, still watching his brother with the same gentle and inquiring smile.

"Well, Alyosha, it's sometimes very unwise to be a Russian at all, but anything stupider than the way Russian boys spend their time one can hardly imagine. But there's one Russian boy called Alyosha I am awfully fond of."

"How nicely you put that in!" Alyosha laughed suddenly.

"Well, tell me where to begin, give your orders. The existence of God, eh?"

"Begin where you like. You declared yesterday at father's that there was no God." Alyosha looked searchingly at his brother.

"I said that yesterday at dinner on purpose to tease you and I saw your eyes glow. But now I've no objection to discussing with you, and I say so very seriously. I want to be friends with you, Alyosha, for I have no friends and want to try it. Well, only fancy, perhaps I too accept God," laughed Ivan, "that's a surprise for you, isn't it?"

"Yes, of course, if you are not joking now."

"Joking? I was told at the elder's yesterday that I was joking. You know, dear boy, there was an old sinner in the eighteenth century who declared that, if there were no God, he would have to be invented. *S'il n'existait pas Dieu, il faudrait l'inventer.* And man has actually invented God. And what's strange, what would be marvellous, is not that God should really exist; the marvel is that such an idea, the idea of the necessity of God, could enter the head of such a savage, vicious beast as man. So holy it is, so touching, so wise and so great a credit it does to man. As for me, I've long resolved not to think whether man created God or God man. And I won't go through all the axioms laid down by Russian boys on that subject, all derived from European hypotheses; for what's a hypothesis there is an axiom with the Russian boy, and not only with the boys but with their teachers too, for our Russian professors are often just the same boys themselves. And so I omit all the hypotheses. For what are we aiming at now? I am trying to explain as quickly as possible my essential nature, that is what manner of man I am, what I believe in, and for what I hope, that's it, isn't it? And therefore I tell you that I accept God simply. But you must note this: if God exists and if He really did create the world, then, as we all know, He created it according to the geometry of Euclid and the human mind with the conception of only three dimensions in space. Yet there have been and still are geometricians and philosophers, and even some of the most distinguished, who doubt whether the whole universe, or to speak more widely the whole of being, was only created in Euclid's geometry; they even dare to dream that two parallel lines, which according to Euclid can never meet on earth, may meet somewhere in infinity. I have come to the conclusion that since I can't understand even that, I can't expect to understand about God. I acknowledge humbly that I have no faculty for settling such questions, I have a Euclidian earthly mind, and how could I solve problems that are not of this world? And I advise you never to think about it either, my dear Alyosha, especially about God, whether He exists or not. All such questions are utterly inappropriate for a mind created with an idea of only three dimensions. And so I accept God and am glad to, and what's more I accept His wisdom, His purpose—which are utterly beyond our ken; I believe in the underlying order and the meaning of life; I believe in the eternal harmony in which they say we shall one day be blended. I believe in the Word to Which the universe is striving, and Which Itself was 'with God', and Which Itself is God and so on, and so on, to infinity. There are all sorts of phrases for it. I seem to be on the right path, don't I? Yet would you believe it, in the final result I don't accept this world of God's, and, although I know it exists, I don't accept it at all. It's not that I don't accept God, you must understand, it's the world created by Him I don't and cannot accept. Let me make it plain. I believe like a child that suffering will be healed and made up for, that all the humiliating absurdity of human contradictions will vanish like a pitiful mirage, like the despicable fabrication of the impotent and infinitely small Euclidian mind of man, that in the world's finale, at the moment of eternal harmony, something so precious will come to pass that it will suffice for all hearts, for the comforting of all resentments, for the atonement of all the crimes of humanity, of all the blood they've shed; that it will make it not only possible to forgive but to justify all that has happened with men—but though all that may come to pass, I don't accept it. I won't accept it. Even if parallel lines do meet and I see it myself, I shall see it and say that they've met, but still I won't accept it. That's what's at the root of me, Alyosha; that's my creed. I am in earnest in what I say. I began our talk as stupidly as I could on purpose, but I've led up to my confession, for that's all you want. You didn't want to hear about God, but only to know what the brother you love lives by. And so I've told you."

Ivan concluded his long tirade with marked and unexpected feeling.

"And why did you begin 'as stupidly as you could'?" asked Alyosha, looking dreamily at him.

"To begin with, for the sake of being Russian. Russian conversations on such subjects are always carried on inconceivably stupidly. And secondly, the stupider one is, the closer one is to reality. The stupider one is, the clearer one is. Stupidity is brief and artless, while intelligence wriggles and hides itself. Intelligence is a knave, but stupidity is honest and straightforward. I've led the conversation to my despair, and the more stupidly I have presented it, the better for me."

"You will explain why you don't accept the world?" said Alyosha.

"To be sure I will, it's not a secret, that's what I've been leading up to. Dear little brother, I don't want to corrupt you or to turn you from your stronghold, perhaps I want to be healed by you." Ivan smiled suddenly quite like a little gentle child. Alyosha had never seen such a smile on his face before.

CHAPTER IV

REBELLION

"I MUST make you one confession," Ivan began. "I could never understand how one can love one's neighbour. It's just one's neighbours, to my mind, that one can't love, though one might love those at a distance. I once read somewhere of John the Merciful, a saint, that when a hungry, frozen beggar came to him, he took him into his bed, held him in his arms, and began breathing into his mouth, which was putrid and loathsome from some awful disease. I am convinced that he did that from 'self-laceration', from the self-laceration of falsity for the sake of the charity imposed by duty, as a penance laid on him. For anyone to love a man, he must be hidden, for as soon as he shows his face love is gone."

"Father Zossima has talked of that more than once," observed Alyosha. "He, too, said that the face of a man often hinders many people not practised in love from loving him. But yet there's a great deal of love in mankind, and almost Christlike love. I know that myself, Ivan."

"Well, I know nothing of it so far, and can't understand it, and the innumerable mass of mankind are with me there. The question is, whether that's due to men's bad qualities or whether it's inherent in their nature. To my thinking, Christlike love for men is a miracle impossible on earth. He was God. But we are not gods. Suppose I, for instance, suffer intensely. Another can never know how much I suffer, because he is another and not I. And what's more, a man is rarely ready to admit another's suffering (as though it were a distinction). Why won't he admit it, do you think? Because I smell unpleasant, because I have a stupid face, because I once trod on his foot. Besides, there is suffering *and* suffering; degrading, humiliating suffering such as humbles me—hunger, for instance—my benefactor will perhaps allow me; but when you come to higher suffering—for an idea, for instance—he will

242

very rarely admit that, perhaps because my face strikes him as not at all what he fancies a man should have who suffers for an idea. And so he deprives me instantly of his favour, and not at all from badness of heart. Beggars, especially genteel beggars, ought never to show themselves, but to ask for charity through the newspapers. One can love one's neighbours in the abstract, or even at a distance, but at close quarters it's almost impossible. If it were as on the stage, in the ballet, where if beggars come in they wear silken rags and tattered lace and beg for alms dancing gracefully, then one might like looking at them. But even then we should not love them. But enough of that. I simply wanted to show you my point of view. I meant to speak of the suffering of mankind generally, but we had better confine ourselves to the sufferings of the children. That reduces the scope of my argument to a tenth of what it would be. Still we'd better keep to the children, though it does weaken my case. But, in the first place, children can be loved even at close quarters, even when they are dirty, even when they are ugly (I fancy, though, children never are ugly). The second reason why I won't speak of grown-up people is that, besides being disgusting and unworthy of love, they have a compensation—they've eaten the apple and know good and evil, and they have become 'like gods'. They go on eating it still. But the children haven't eaten anything, and are so far innocent. Are you fond of children, Alyosha? I know you are, and you will understand why I prefer to speak of them. If they, too, suffer horribly on earth, they must suffer for their fathers' sins, they must be punished for their fathers, who have eaten the apple; but that reasoning is of the other world and is incomprehensible for the heart of man here on earth. The innocent must not suffer for another's sins, and especially such innocents! You may be surprised at me, Alyosha, but I am awfully fond of children, too. And observe, cruel people, the violent, the rapacious, the Karamazovs are sometimes very fond of children. Children while they are quite little—up to seven, for instance—are so remote from grown-up people; they are different creatures, as it were, of a different species. I knew a criminal in prison who had, in the course of his career as a burglar, murdered whole families, including several children. But when he was in prison, he had a strange affection for them. He spent all his time at his window, watching the children playing in the prison yard. He trained one little boy to come up to his window and made great friends with him. . . . You don't know why I am telling you all this, Alyosha? My head aches and I am sad."

"You speak with a strange air," observed Alyosha uneasily, "as though you were not quite yourself."

"By the way, a Bulgarian I met lately in Moscow," Ivan went on, seeming not to hear his brother's words, "told me about the crimes committed by Turks and Circassians in all parts of Bulgaria through fear of a general rising of the Slavs. They burn villages, murder, outrage women and children, they nail their prisoners by the ears to the fences, leave them so till morning, and in the morning they hang them—all sorts of things you can't imagine. People talk sometimes of bestial cruelty, but that's a great injustice and insult to the beasts; a beast can never be so cruel as a man, so artistically cruel. The tiger only tears and gnaws, that's all he can do. He would never think of nailing people by the ears, even if he were able to do it. These Turks took a pleasure in torturing children, too; cutting the unborn child from the mother's womb, and tossing babies up in the air and catching them on the points of their bayonets before their mothers' eyes. Doing it before the mothers' eyes was what gave zest to the amusement. Here is another scene that I thought very interesting. Imagine a trembling mother with her baby in her arms, a circle of invading Turks around her. They've planned a diversion: they pet the baby, laugh to make it laugh. They succeed, the baby laughs. At that moment a Turk points a pistol four inches from the baby's face. The baby laughs with glee, holds out its little hands to the pistol, and he pulls the trigger in the baby's face and blows out its brains. Artistic, wasn't it? By the way, Turks are particularly fond of sweet things, they say."

"Brother, what are you driving at?" asked Alyosha.

"I think if the devil doesn't exist, but man has created him, he has created him in his own image and likeness."

"Just as he did God, then?" observed Alyosha.

" 'It's wonderful how you can turn words,' as Polonius says in *Hamlet*," laughed Ivan. "You turn my words against me. Well, I am glad. Yours must be a fine God, if man created Him in His image and likeness. You asked just now what I was driving at. You, see, I am fond of collecting certain facts, and, would you believe, I even copy anecdotes of a certain sort from newspapers and books, and I've already got a fine collection. The Turks, of course, have gone into it, but they are foreigners. I have speciments from home that are even better than the Turks. You know we prefer beating—rods and scourges—that's our national institution. Nailing ears is unthinkable for us, for we are, after all, Europeans. But the rod and the scourge we have always with us and they cannot be taken from us. Abroad now they scarcely do any beating. Manners are more humane, or laws have been passed, so that they don't dare to flog men now. But they make up for it in another way just as national as ours. And so national that it would be practically impossible among us, though I believe we are being inoculated with it, since the religious movement began in our aristocracy. I have a charming pamphlet, translated from the French, describing how, quite recently, five years ago, a murderer, Richard, was executed—a young man, I believe, of three-and-twenty, who repented and was converted to the Christian faith at the very scaffold. This Richard was an illegitimate child who was given as a child of six by his parents to some shepherds on the Swiss mountains. They brought him up to work for them. He grew up like a little wild beast among them. The shepherds taught him nothing, and scarcely fed or clothed him, but sent him at seven to herd the flock in cold and wet, and no one hesitated or scrupled to treat him so. Quite the contrary, they thought they had every right, for Richard had been given to them as a chattel, and they did not even see the necessity of feeding him. Richard himself describes how in those years, like the Prodigal Son in the Gospel, he longed to eat of the mash given to the pigs, which were fattened for sale. But they wouldn't even give him that, and beat him when he stole from the pigs. And that was how he spent all his childhood and his youth, till he grew up and was strong enough to go away and be a thief. The savage began to earn his living as a day labourer in Geneva. He drank what he earned, he lived like a brute, and finished by killing and robbing an old man. He was caught, tried, and condemned to death. They are not sentimentalists there. And in prison he was immediately surrounded by pastors, members of Christian brotherhoods, philanthropic ladies, and the like. They taught him to read and write in prison, and expounded the Gospel to him. They exhorted him, worked upon him, drummed at him incessantly, till at last he solemnly confessed his crime. He was converted. He wrote to the court himself that he was a monster, but that in the end God had vouchsafed him light and shown grace. All Geneva was in excitement about him—all philanthropic and religious Geneva. All the aristocratic and well-bred society of the town rushed to the prison, kissed Richard and embraced him: 'You are our brother, you have found grace.' And Richard does nothing but weep with emotion: 'Yes, I've found grace! All my youth and childhood I was glad of pigs' food, but now even I have found grace. I am dying in the Lord.' 'Yes, Richard, die in the Lord; you have shed blood and must die. Though it's not your fault that you knew not the Lord, when you coveted the pigs' food and were beaten for stealing it (which was very wrong of you, for stealing is forbidden); but you've shed blood and you must die.' And on the last day, Richard, perfectly limp, did nothing but cry and repeat every minute: 'This is my happiest day. I am going to the Lord.' 'Yes,' cry the pastors and the judges and philanthropic ladies. 'This is the happiest day of your life, for you are going to the Lord!' They all walk or drive to the scaffold in procession behind the prison van. At the scaffold they call to Richard: 'Die, brother, die in the Lord, for even thou hast found grace!' And so, covered with his brothers' kisses, Richard is dragged on to the scaffold, and led to the guillotine. And they chopped off his head in brotherly fashion, because he had found grace. Yes, that's characteristic. That pamphlet is translated into Russian by some Russian philanthropists of aristocratic rank and evangelical aspirations, and has been distributed gratis for the enlightenment of the people. The case of Richard is interesting because it's national. Though to us it's absurd to cut off a man's head, because he has become our brother and has found grace, yet we have our own speciality, which is all but worse. Our historical pastime is the direct satisfaction of inflicting pain. There are lines in Nekrassov describing how a peasant lashes a horse on the eyes, 'on its meek eyes,' everyone must have seen it. It's peculiarly Russian. He describes how a feeble little nag has foundered under too heavy a load and cannot move. The peasant beats it, beats it savagely, beats it at last not knowing what he is doing in the intoxication of cruelty, thrashes it mercilessly over and over again. 'However weak you are, you must pull, if you die for it.' The nag strains, and then he begins lashing the poor defenceless creature on its weeping, on its 'meek eyes'. The frantic beast tugs and draws the load, trembling all over, gasping for breath, moving sideways, with a sort of unnatural, spasmodic action—it's awful in Nekrassov. But that's only a horse, and God has given horses to be beaten. So the Tatars have taught us, and they left out the knout as a remembrance of it. But men, too, can be beaten. A well-educated, cultured gentleman and his wife beat their own child with a birch-rod, a girl of seven. I have an exact account of it. The papa was glad that the birch was covered with twigs. 'It stings more,' said he, and so he began stinging his daughter. I know for a fact there are people who at every blow are worked up to sensuality, to literal sensuality, which increases progressively at every blow they inflict. They beat for a minute, for five minutes, for ten minutes, more often and more savagely. The child screams. At last the child cannot scream, it gasps: 'Daddy! daddy!' By some diabolical unseemly chance the case was brought into court. A counsel is engaged. The Russian people have long called a barrister 'a conscience for hire'. The counsel protests in his client's defence. 'It's such a simple thing,' he says, 'an everyday domestic event. A father corrects his child. To our shame be it said, it is brought into court.' The jury, convinced by him, give a favourable verdict. The public roars with delight that the torturer is acquitted. Ah, pity I wasn't there! I would have proposed to raise a subscription in his honour! . . . Charming pictures.

"But I've still better things about children. I've collected a great, great deal about Russian children, Alyosha. There was a little girl of five who was hated by her father and mother, 'most worthy and respectable people, of good education and breeding'. You see, I must repeat again, it is a peculiar characteristic of many people, this love of torturing children, and children only. To all other types of humanity these torturers behave mildly and benevolently, like cultivated and humane Europeans; but they are very fond of tormenting children, even fond of children themselves in that sense. It's just their defencelessness that tempts the tormentor, just the angelic confidence of the child who has no refuge and no appeal, that sets his vile blood on fire. In every man, of course, a demon lies hidden—the demon of rage, the demon of lustful heat at the screams of the tortured victim, the demon of lawlessness let off the chain, the demon of diseases that follow on vice, gout, kidney disease, and so on.

"This poor child of five was subjected to every possible torture by those cultivated parents. They beat her, thrashed her, kicked her for no reason till her body was one bruise. Then they went to greater refinements of cruelty—shut her up all night in the cold and frost in a privy, and because she

247

didn't ask to be taken up at night (as though a child of five sleeping its angelic, sound sleep could be trained to wake and ask), they smeared her face and filled her mouth with excrement, and it was her mother, her mother, did this! And that mother could sleep, hearing the poor child's groans! Can you understand why a little creature, who can't even understand what's done to her, should beat her little aching heart with her tiny fist in the dark and the cold, and weep her meek unresentful tears to dear, kind God to protect her? Do you understand that, friend and brother, you pious and humble novice? Do you understand why this infamy must be and is permitted? Without it, I am told, man could not have existed on earth, for he could not have known good and evil. Why should he know that diabolical good and evil when it costs so much? Why, the whole world of knowledge is not worth that child's prayer to 'dear, kind God'! I say nothing of the sufferings of grown-up people, they have eaten the apple, damn them, and the devil take them all! But these little ones! I am making you suffer, Alyosha, you are not yourself. I'll leave off if you like.''

"Never mind. I want to suffer too," muttered Alyosha.

"One picture, even one more, because it's so curious, so characteristic, and I have only just read it in some collection of Russian antiquities. I've forgotten the name. I must look it up. It was in the darkest days of serfdom at the beginning of the century, and long live the Liberator of the People! There was in those days a general of aristocratic connections, the owner of great estates, one of those men—somewhat exceptional, I believe, even then—who, retiring from the service into a life of leisure, are convinced that they've earned absolute power over the lives of their subjects. There were such men then. So our general, settled on his property of two thousand souls, lives in pomp, and domineers over his poor neighbours as though they were dependants and buffoons. He has kennels of hundreds of hounds and nearly a hundred dog-boys—all mounted, and in uniform. One day a serf boy, a little child of eight, threw a stone in play and hurt the paw of the general's favourite hound. 'Why is my favourite dog lame?' He is told that the boy threw a stone that hurt the dog's paw. 'So you did it.' The general looked the child up and down. 'Take him.' He was taken—taken from his mother and kept shut up all night. Early that morning the general comes out on horseback, with the hounds, his dependants, dog-boys, and huntsmen, all mounted around him in full hunting parade. The servants are summoned for their edification, and in front of them all stands the mother of the child. The child is brought from the lock-up. It's a gloomy, cold, foggy autumn day, a capital day for hunting. The general orders the child to be undressed; the child is stripped naked. He shivers, numb with terror, not daring to cry. . . . 'Make him run,' commands the general. 'Run! run!' shout the dog-boys. The boy runs. . . . 'At him!' yells the general, and he sets the whole pack of hounds on the child. The hounds catch him, and tear him to pieces before his mother's eyes! . . . I believe the general was afterwards declared incapable of administering his estates. Well—what did he deserve? To be shot? To be shot for the satisfaction of our moral feelings? Speak, Alyosha!"

"To be shot," murmured Alyosha, lifting his eyes to Ivan with a pale, twisted smile.

"Bravo!" cried Ivan delighted. "If even you say so . . . You're a pretty monk! So there is a little devil sitting in your heart, Alyosha Karamazov!"

"What I said was absurd, but——"

"That's just the point, that 'but'!" cried Ivan. "Let me tell you, novice, that the absurd is only too necessary on earth. The world stands on absurdities, and perhaps nothing would have come to pass in it without them. We know what we know!"

"What do you know?"

"I understand nothing," Ivan went on, as though in delirium. "I don't want to understand anything now. I want to stick to the fact. I made up my mind long ago not to understand. If I try to understand anything, I shall be false to the fact and I have determined to stick to the fact."

"Why are you trying me?" Alyosha cried, with sudden distress. "Will you say what you mean at last?"

"Of course I will; that's what I've been leading up to. You are dear to me, I don't want to let you go, and I won't give you up to your Zossima."

Ivan for a minute was silent, his face became all at once very sad.

"Listen! I took the case of children only to make my case clearer. Of the other tears of humanity with which the earth is soaked from its crust to its centre, I will say nothing. I have narrowed my subject on purpose. I am a bug, and I recognise in all humility that I cannot understand why the world

249

is arranged as it is. Men are themselves to blame, I suppose; they were given paradise, they wanted freedom, and stole fire from heaven, though they knew they would become unhappy, so there is no need to pity them. With my pitiful, earthly, Euclidian understanding, all I know is that there is suffering and that there are none guilty; that cause follows effect, simply and directly; that everything flows and finds its level—but that's only Euclidian nonsense. I know that, and I can't consent to live by it! What comfort is it to me that there are none guilty and that cause follows effect simply and directly, and that I know it? I must have justice, or I will destroy myself. And not justice in some remote infinite time and space, but here on earth, and that I could see myself. I have believed in it. I want to see it, and if I am dead by then, let me rise again, for if it all happens without me, it will be too unfair. Surely I haven't suffered simply that I, my crimes and my sufferings may manure the soil of the future harmony for somebody else. I want to see with my own eyes the hind lie down with the lion and the victim rise up and embrace his murderer. I want to be there when everyone suddenly understands what it has all been for. All the religions of the world are built on this longing, and I am a believer. But then there are the children, and what am I to do about them? That's a question I can't answer. For the hundredth time, I repeat, there are numbers of questions, but I've only taken the children, because in their case what I mean is so unanswerably clear. Listen! If all must suffer to pay for the eternal harmony, what have children to do with it? Tell me, please? It's beyond all comprehension why they should suffer, and why they should pay for the harmony. Why should they, too, furnish material to enrich the soil for the harmony of the future? I understand solidarity in sin among men. I understand solidarity in retribution, too; but there can be no such solidarity with children. And if it is really true that they must share responsibility for all their fathers' crimes, such a truth is not of this world and is beyond my comprehension. Some jester will say, perhaps, that the child would have grown up and have sinned, but you see he didn't grow up, he was torn to pieces by the dogs at eight years old. Oh, Alyosha, I am not blaspheming! I understand, of course, what an upheaval of the universe it will be, when everything in heaven and earth blends in one hymn of praise and everything that lives and has lived cries aloud: 'Thou art just, O Lord, for Thy ways are revealed.'

When the mother embraces the fiend who threw her child to the dogs, and all three cry aloud with tears: 'Thou art just, O Lord!' then, of course, the crown of knowledge will be reached and all will be made clear. But what pulls me up here is that I can't accept that harmony. And while I am on earth I make haste to take my own measures. You see, Alyosha, perhaps it really may happen that if I live to that moment, or rise again to see it, I, too, perhaps, may cry aloud with the rest, looking at the mother embracing the child's torturer: 'Thou art just, O Lord!' but I don't want to cry aloud then. While there is still time I hasten to protect myself and so I renounce the higher harmony altogether. It's not worth the tears of that one tortured child who beat itself on the breast with its little fist and prayed in its stinking outhouse, with its unexpiated tears to 'dear, kind God'! It's not worth it, because those tears are unatoned for. They must be atoned for, or there can be no harmony. But how? How are you going to atone for them? Is it possible? By their being avenged? But what do I care for avenging them? What do I care for a hell for oppressors? What good can hell do, since those children have already been tortured? And what becomes of harmony, if there is hell? I want to forgive. I want to embrace. I don't want more suffering. And if the sufferings of children go to swell the sum of sufferings which was necessary to pay for truth, then I protest that the truth is not worth such a price. I don't want the mother to embrace the oppressor who threw her son to the dogs! She dare not forgive him! Let her forgive him for herself, if she will, let her forgive the torturer for the immeasurable suffering of her mother's heart. But the sufferings of her tortured child she has no right to forgive; she dare not forgive the torturer, even if the child were to forgive him! And if that is so, if they dare not forgive, what becomes of harmony? Is there in the whole world a being who would have the right to forgive and could forgive? I don't want harmony. From love for humanity I don't want it. I would rather be left with the unavenged suffering. I would rather remain with my unavenged suffering and unsatisfied indignation, even *if I were wrong*. Besides, too high a price is asked for harmony; it's beyond our means to pay so much to enter on it. And so I hasten to give back my entrance ticket, and if I am an honest man I am bound to give it back as soon as possible. And that I am doing. It's not God that I don't accept, Alyosha, only I most respectfully return Him the ticket.''

"That's rebellion," murmured Alyosha, looking down.

"Rebellion? I am sorry you call it that," said Ivan earnestly. "One can hardly live in rebellion, and I want to live. Tell me yourself, I challenge you—answer. Imagine that you are creating a fabric of human destiny with the object of making men happy in the end, giving them peace and rest at last, but that it was essential and inevitable to torture to death only one tiny creature—that baby beating its breast with its fist, for instance—and to found that edifice on its unavenged tears, would you consent to be the architect on those conditions? Tell me, and tell the truth."

"No, I wouldn't consent," said Alyosha softly.

"And can you admit the idea that men for whom you are building it would agree to accept their happiness on the foundation of the unexpiated blood of a little victim? And accepting it would remain happy for ever?"

"No, I can't admit it. Brother," said Alyosha suddenly, with flashing eyes, "you said just now, is there a being in the whole world who would have the right to forgive and could forgive? But there is a Being and He can forgive everything, all and for all, because He gave His innocent blood for all and everything. You have forgotten Him, and on Him is built the edifice, and it is to Him they cry aloud: 'Thou art just, O Lord, for Thy ways are revealed!'"

"Ah! the One without sin and His blood! No, I have not forgotten Him; on the contrary I've been wondering all the time how it was you did not bring Him in before, for usually all arguments on your side put Him in the foreground. Do you know, Alyosha—don't laugh! I made a poem about a year ago. If you can waste another ten minutes on me, I'll tell it to you."

"You wrote a poem?"

"Oh, no, I didn't write it," laughed Ivan, "and I've never written two lines of poetry in my life. But I made up this poem in prose and I remembered it. I was carried away when I made it up. You will be my first reader—that is, listener. Why should an author forgo even one listener?" smiled Ivan. "Shall I tell it to you?"

"I am all attention," said Alyosha.

"My poem is called 'The Grand Inquisitor'; it's a ridiculous thing, but I want to tell it to you."

CHAPTER V

"EVEN this must have a preface—that is, a literary preface," laughed Ivan, "and I am a poor hand at making one. You see, my action takes place in the sixteenth century, and at that time, as you probably learnt at school, it was customary in poetry to bring down heavenly powers on earth. Not to speak of Dante, in France, clerks, as well as the monks in the monasteries, used to give regular performances in which the Madonna, the saints, the angels, Christ, and God Himself were brought on the stage. In those days it was done in all simplicity. In Victor Hugo's 'Notre Dame de Paris' an edifying and gratuitous spectacle was provided for the people in the Hôtel de Ville of Paris in the reign of Louis XI in honour of the birth of the dauphin. It was called *Le bon jugement de la très sainte et gracieuse Vierge Marie,* and she appears herself on the stage and pronounces her *bon jugement.* Similar plays, chiefly from the Old Testament, were occasionally performed in Moscow too, up to the times of Peter the Great. But besides plays there were all sorts of legends and ballads scattered about the world, in which the saints and angels and all the powers of Heaven took part when required. In our monasteries the monks busied themselves in translating, copying, and even composing such poems—and even under the Tatars. There is, for instance, one such poem (of course, from the Greek), 'The Wanderings of Our Lady through Hell', with descriptions as bold as Dante's. Our Lady visits Hell, and the Archangel Michael leads her through the torments. She sees the sinners and their punishments. There she sees among others one noteworthy set of sinners in a burning lake; some of them sink to the bottom of the lake so that they can't swim out, and 'these God forgets'—an expression of extraordinary depth and force. And so Our Lady, shocked and weeping, falls before the throne of God and begs for mercy for all in Hell—for all she has seen there, indiscriminately. Her conversation with God is immensely interesting. She beseeches Him, she will not desist, and when God points to the hands and feet of her Son, nailed to the Cross, and asks: 'How can I forgive His tormentors?' she bids all the saints, all the martyrs, all the angels and archangels to fall down with her and pray for mercy on all without distinction. It ends by her winning from God a respite

253

of suffering every year from Good Friday till Trinity day, and the sinners at once raise a cry of thankfulness from Hell, chanting: 'Thou art just, O Lord, in this judgment.' Well, my poem would have been of that kind if it had appeared at that time. He comes on the scene in my poem, but He says nothing, only appears and passes on. Fifteen centuries have passed since He promised to come in His glory, fifteen centuries since His prophet wrote, 'Behold, I come quickly'; 'Of that day and that hour knoweth no man, neither the Son, but the Father,' as He Himself predicted on earth. But humanity awaits him with the same faith and with the same love. Oh, with greater faith, for it is fifteen centuries since man has ceased to see signs from Heaven.

> *No signs from Heaven come to-day*
> *To add to what the heart doth say.*

There was nothing left but faith in what the heart doth say. It is true there were many miracles in those days. There were saints who performed miraculous cures; some holy people, according to their biographies, were visited by the Queen of Heaven herself. But the devil did not slumber, and doubts were already arising among men of the truth of these miracles. And just then there appeared in the north of Germany a terrible new heresy. 'A huge star like to a torch' (that is, to a church) 'fell on the sources of the waters and they became bitter.' These heretics began blasphemously denying miracles. But those who remained faithful were all the more ardent in their faith. The tears of humanity rose up to Him as before, awaited His coming, loved Him, hoped for Him, yearned to suffer and die for Him as before. And so many ages mankind had prayed with faith and fervour: 'O Lord our God, hasten Thy coming,' so many ages called upon Him, that in His infinite mercy He deigned to come down to His servants. Before that day He had come down, He had visited some holy men, martyrs and hermits, as is written in their 'Lives'. Among us, Tyutchev, with absolute faith in the truth of his words, bore witness that:

> *Bearing the Cross, in slavish dress*
> *Weary and worn, the Heavenly King*
> *Our mother, Russia, came to bless,*
> *And through our land went wandering.*

And that certainly was so, I assure you.

"And behold, He deigned to appear for a moment to the people, to the tortured, suffering people, sunk in iniquity but loving Him like children. My story is laid in Spain, in Seville, in the most terrible time of the Inquisition, when fires were lighted every day to the glory of God, and 'in the splendid *auto da fé* the wicked heretics were burnt'. Oh, of course, this was not the coming in which He will appear according to His promise at the end of time in all His heavenly glory, and which will be sudden 'as lightning flashing from east to west'. No, He visited His children only for a moment, and there where the flames were crackling round the heretics. In His infinite mercy He came once more among men in that human shape in which He walked among men for three years fifteen centuries ago. He came down to the 'hot pavements' of the southern town in which on the day before almost a hundred heretics had, *ad majorem gloriam Dei*, been burnt by the cardinal, the Grand Inquisitor, in a magnificent *auto da fé*, in the presence of the king, the court, the knights, the cardinals, the most charming ladies of the court, and the whole population of Seville.

"He came softly, unobserved, and yet, strange to say, every-one recognised Him. That might be one of the best passages in the poem. I mean, why they recognised Him. The people are irresistibly drawn to Him, they surround Him, they flock about Him, follow Him. He moves silently in their midst with a gentle smile of infinite compassion. The sun of love burns in His heart, light and power shine from His eyes, and their radiance, shed on the people, stirs their hearts with responsive love. He holds out His hands to them, blesses them, and a healing virtue comes from contact with Him, even with His garments. An old man in the crowd, blind from childhood, cries out, 'O Lord, heal me and I shall see Thee!' and, as it were, scales fall from his eyes and the blind man sees Him. The crowd weeps and kisses the earth under His feet. Children throw flowers before Him, sing, and cry hosannah. 'It is He— it is He!' all repeat. 'It must be He, it can be no one but Him!' He stops at the steps of the Seville cathedral at the moment when the weeping mourners are bringing in a little open white coffin. In it lies a child of seven, the only daughter of a prominent citizen. The dead child lies hidden in flowers. 'He will raise your child,' the crowd shouts to the weeping mother. The priest, coming to meet the coffin,, looks perplexed, and frowns, but the mother of the dead child throws herself at His feet with a wail. 'If it is Thou, raise my child!' she cries holding

255

out her hands to Him. The procession halts, the coffin is laid on the steps at His feet. He looks with compassion, and His lips once more softly pronounce, 'Maiden, arise!' and the maiden arises. The little girl sits up in the coffin and looks round, smiling with wide-open wondering eyes, holding a bunch of white roses they had put in her hand.

"There are cries, sobs, confusion among the people, and at that moment the cardinal himself, the Grand Inquisitor, passes by the cathedral. He is an old man, almost ninety, tall and erect, with a withered face and sunken eyes, in which there is still a gleam of light. He is not dressed in his gorgeous cardinal's robes, as he was the day before, when he was burning the enemies of the Roman Church—at that moment he was wearing his coarse, old, monk's cassock. At a distance behind him come his gloomy assistants and slaves and the 'holy guard'. He stops at the sight of the crowd and watches it from a distance. He sees everything; he sees them set the coffin down at His feet, sees the child rise up, and his face darkens. He knits his thick grey brows and his eyes gleam with a sinister fire. He holds out his finger and bids the guards take Him. And such is his power, so completely are the people cowed into submission and trembling obedience to him, that the crowd immediately make way for the guards, and in the midst of deathlike silence they lay hands on Him and lead Him away. The crowd instantly bows down to the earth, like one man, before the old inquisitor. He blesses the people in silence and passes on. The guards lead their prisoner to the close, gloomy vaulted prison in the ancient palace of the Holy Inquisition and shut Him in it. The day passes and is followed by the dark, burning 'breathless' night of Seville. The air is 'fragrant with laurel and lemon'. In the pitch darkness the iron door of the prison is suddenly opened and the Guard Inquisitor himself comes in with a light in his hand. He is alone; the door is closed at once behind him. He stands in the doorway and for a minute or two gazes into His face. At last he goes up slowly, sets the light on the table and speaks.

" 'Is it Thou? Thou?' but receiving no answer, he adds at once: 'Don't answer, be silent. What canst Thou say, indeed? I know too well what Thou wouldst say. And Thou hast no right to add anything to what Thou hadst said of old. Why, then, art Thou come to hinder us? For Thou hast come to hinder us, and Thou knowest that. But dost Thou know what will be to-morrow? I know not who Thou art and care not to know whether it is Thou or only a semblance of Him, but to-morrow I shall condemn Thee and burn Thee at the stake as the worst of heretics. And the very people who have to-day kissed Thy feet, to-morrow at the faintest sign from me will rush to heap up the embers of Thy fire. Knowest Thou that? Yes, maybe Thou knowest it,' he added with thoughtful penetration, never for a moment taking his eyes off the Prisoner."

"I don't quite understand, Ivan. What does it mean?" Alyosha, who had been listening in silence, said with a smile. "Is it simply a wild fantasy, or a mistake on the part of the old man—some impossible *quid pro quo?*"

"Take it as the last," said Ivan, laughing, "if you are so corrupted by modern realism and can't stand anything fantastic. If you like it to be a case of mistaken identity, let it be so. It is true," he went on, laughing, "the old man was ninety, and he might well be crazy over his set idea. He might have been struck by the appearance of the Prisoner. It might, in fact, be simply his ravings, the delusion of an old man of ninety, over-excited by the *auto da fé* of a hundred heretics the day before. But does it matter to us, after all, whether it was a mistake of identity or a wild fantasy? All that matters is that the old man should speak out, should speak openly of what he has thought in silence for ninety years."

"And the Prisoner too is silent? Does He look at him and not say a word?"

"That's inevitable in any case," Ivan laughed again. "The old man has told Him He hasn't the right to add anything to what He has said of old. One may say it is the most fundamental feature of Roman Catholicism, in my opinion at least. 'All has been given by Thee to the Pope,' they say, 'and all, therefore, is still in the Pope's hands, and there is no need for Thee to come now at all. Thou must not meddle for the time, at least.' That's how they speak and write too—the Jesuits, at any rate. I have read it myself in the works of their theologians. 'Hast Thou the right to reveal to us one of the mysteries of that world from which Thou hast come?' my old man asks Him, and answers the question for Him. 'No, Thou hast not; that Thou mayest not add to what has been said of old, and mayest not take from men the freedom which Thou didst exalt when Thou wast on earth. Whatsoever Thou revealest anew will encroach on men's freedom of faith; for it will be manifest as a miracle, and the freedom of their faith was dearer to Thee than anything in those days fifteen hundred years ago. Didst Thou not often say then, "I will make you free"? But now Thou hast seen these "free" men,' the old man adds suddenly, with a pensive smile. 'Yes, we've paid dearly for it,' he goes on, looking sternly at Him, 'but at last we have completed that work in Thy name. For fifteen centuries we have been wrestling with Thy freedom, but now it is ended and over for good. Dost Thou not believe that it's over for good? Thou lookest meekly at me and deignest not even to be wroth with me. But let me tell Thee that now, to-day, people are more persuaded than ever that they have perfect freedom, yet they have brought their freedom to us and laid it humbly at our feet. But that has been our doing. Was this what Thou didst? Was this Thy freedom?' "

"I don't understand again," Alyosha broke in. "Is he ironical, is he jesting?"

"Not a bit of it! He claims it as a merit for himself and his Church that at last they have vanquished freedom and have done so to make men happy. 'For now' (he is speaking of the Inquisition, of course) 'for the first time it has become possible to think of the happiness of men. Man was created a rebel; and how can rebels be happy? Thou wast warned,' he says to Him. 'Thou hast had no lack of admonitions and warnings, but Thou didst not listen to those warnings; Thou didst reject the only way by which men might be made happy. But, fortunately, departing Thou didst hand on the work to us. Thou hast promised, Thou hast established by Thy word, Thou hast given to us the right to bind and to unbind, and now, of course, Thou canst not think of taking it away. Why, then, hast Thou come to hinder us?' "

"And what's the meaning of 'no lack of admonitions and warnings'?" asked Alyosha.

"Why, that's the chief part of what the old man must say."

" 'The wise and dread Spirit, the spirit of self-destruction and non-existence,' the old man goes on, 'the great spirit talked with Thee in the wilderness, and we are told in the books that he "tempted" Thee. Is that so? And could anything truer be said than what he revealed to Thee in three questions and what Thou didst reject, and what in the books is called "the temptation"? And yet if there has ever been on earth a real stupendous miracle, it took place on that day, on the day of the three temptations. The statement of those three questions was itself the miracle. If it were possible to imagine simply for the sake of argument that those three questions of the dread spirit

had perished utterly from the books, and that we had to restore them and to invent them anew, and to do so had gathered together all the wise men of the earth—rulers, chief priests, learned men, philosophers, poets—and had set them the task to invent three questions, such as would not only fit the occasion but express in three words, three human phrases, the whole future history of the world and of humanity—dost Thou believe that all the wisdom of the earth united could have invented anything in depth and force equal to the three questions which were actually put to Thee then by the wise and mighty spirit in the wilderness? From those questions alone, from the miracle of their statement, we can see that we have here to do not with the fleeting human intelligence but with the absolute and eternal. For in those three questions the whole subsequent history of mankind is, as it were, brought together into one whole, and foretold, and in them are united all the unsolved historical contradictions of human nature. At the time it could not be so clear, since the future was unknown; but now that fifteen hundred years have passed, we see that everything in those three questions was so justly divined and foretold, and has been so truly fulfilled, that nothing can be added to them or taken from them.

" 'Judge Thyself who was right—Thou or he who questioned Thee then? Remember the first question; its meaning, in other words, was this: "Thou wouldst go into the world, and art going with empty hands, with some promise of freedom which men in their simplicity and their natural unruliness cannot even understand, which they fear and dread—for nothing has ever been more insupportable for a man and a human society than freedom. But seest Thou these stones in this parched and barren wilderness? Turn them into bread, and mankind will run after Thee like a flock of sheep, grateful and obedient, though for ever trembling, lest Thou withdraw Thy hand and deny them Thy bread." But Thou wouldst not deprive man of freedom and didst reject the offer, thinking, what is that freedom worth, if obedience is bought with bread? Thou didst reply that man lives not by bread alone. But dost Thou know that for the sake of that earthly bread the spirit of the earth will rise up against Thee and will strive with Thee and overcome Thee, and all will follow him, crying, "Who can compare with this beast? He has given us fire from heaven!" Dost Thou know that the ages will pass, and humanity will proclaim by the lips of their sages that there is no crime, and therefore no sin; there is only hunger?

"Feed men, and then ask of them virtue!" that's what they'll write on the banner, which they will raise against Thee, and with which they will destroy Thy temple. Where Thy temple stood will rise a new building; the terrible tower of Babel will be built again, and though, like the one of old, it will not be finished, yet Thou mightest have prevented that new tower and have cut short the sufferings of men for a thousand years; for they will come back to us after a thousand years of agony with their tower. They will seek us again, hidden underground in the catacombs, for we shall be again persecuted and tortured. They will find us and cry to us, "Feed us, for those who have promised us fire from heaven haven't given it!" And then we shall finish building their tower, for he finishes the building who feeds them. And we alone shall feed them in Thy name, declaring falsely that it is Thy name. Oh, never, never can they feed themselves without us! No science will give them bread so long as they remain free. In the end they will lay their freedom at our feet, and say to us, "Make us your slaves, but feed us". They will understand themselves, at last, that freedom and bread enough for all are inconceivable together, for never, never will they be able to share between them! They will be convinced, too, that they can never be free, for they are weak, vicious, worthless and rebellious. Thou didst promise them the bread of Heaven, but, I repeat again, can it compare with earthly bread in the eyes of the weak, ever-sinful and ignoble race of man? And if for the sake of the bread of Heaven thousands and tens of thousands shall follow Thee, what is to become of the millions and tens of thousands of millions of creatures who will not have the strength to forgo the earthly bread for the sake of the heavenly? Or dost Thou care only for the tens of thousands of the great and strong, while the millions, numerous as the sands of the sea, who are weak but love Thee, must exist only for the sake of the great and strong? No, we care for the weak too. They are sinful and rebellious, but in the end they too will become obedient. They will marvel at us and look on us as gods, because we are ready to endure the freedom which they have found so dreadful and to rule over them—so awful it will seem to them to be free. But we shall tell them that we are Thy servants and rule them in Thy name. We shall deceive them again, for we will not let Thee come to us again. That deception will be our suffering, for we shall be forced to lie.

" 'This is the significance of the first question in the wilderness. and this is what Thou hast rejected for the sake of that freedom which Thou hast exalted above everything. Yet in this question lies hid the great secret of this world. Choosing "bread", Thou wouldst have satisfied the universal and ever-lasting craving of humanity—to find someone to worship. So long as man remains free he strives for nothing so incessantly and so painfully as to find someone to worship. But man seeks to worship what is established beyond dispute, so that all men would agree at once to worship it. For these pitiful creatures are concerned not only to find what one or the other can worship, but to find something that all would believe in and worship; what is essential is that all may be *together* in it. This craving for *community* of worship is the chief misery of every man individually and of all humanity from the beginning of time. For the sake of common worship they've slain each other with the sword. They have set up gods and challenged one another, "Put away your gods and come and worship ours, or we will kill you and your gods!" And so it will be to the end of the world, even when gods disappear from the earth; they will fall down before idols just the same. Thou didst know, Thou couldst not but have known, this fundamental secret of human nature, but Thou didst reject the one infallible banner which was offered Thee to make all men bow down to Thee alone—the banner of earthly bread; and Thou hast rejected it for the sake of freedom and the bread of Heaven. Behold what Thou didst further. And all again in the name of freedom! I tell Thee that man is tormented by no greater anxiety than to find someone quickly to whom he can hand over that gift of freedom with which the ill-fated creature is born. But only one who can appease their conscience can take over their freedom. In bread there was offered Thee an invincible banner; give bread, and man will worship thee, for nothing is more certain than bread. But if someone else gains possession of his con-science—oh! then he will cast away Thy bread and follow after him who has ensnared his conscience. In that Thou wast right. For the secret of man's being is not only to live but to have something to live for. Without a stable conception of the object of life, man would not consent to go on living, and would rather destroy himself than remain on earth, though he had bread in abundance. That is true. But what happened? Instead of taking men's freedom from them, Thou didst make it greater than ever! Didst Thou forget that man prefers peace, and even death, to freedom of choice in the knowledge of good and evil? Nothing is more seductive for man than his freedom of conscience, but nothing is a greater cause of suffering. And behold, instead of giving a firm foundation for setting the conscience of man at rest for ever, Thou didst choose all that is exceptional, vague and enigmatic; Thou didst choose what was utterly beyond the strength of men, acting as though Thou didst not love them at all—Thou who didst come to give Thy life for them! Instead of taking possession of men's freedom, Thou didst increase it, and burdened the spiritual kingdom of mankind with its sufferings for ever. Thou didst desire man's free love, that he should follow Thee freely, enticed and taken captive by Thee. In place of the rigid ancient law, man must hereafter with free heart decide for himself what is good and what is evil, having only Thy image before him as his guide. But didst Thou not know that he would at last reject even Thy image and Thy truth, if he is weighed down with the fearful burden of free choice? They will cry aloud at last that the truth is not in Thee, for they could not have been left in greater confusion and suffering than Thou hast caused, laying upon them so many cares and unanswerable problems.

" 'So that, in truth, Thou didst Thyself lay the foundation for the destruction of Thy kingdom, and no one is more to blame for it. Yet what was offered Thee? There are three powers, three powers alone, able to conquer and to hold captive for ever the conscience of these impotent rebels for their happiness —those forces are miracle, mystery and authority. Thou hast rejected all three and hast set the example for doing so. When the wise and dread spirit set Thee on the pinnacle of the temple and said to Thee, "If Thou wouldst know whether Thou art the Son of God then cast Thyself down, for it is written: the angels shall hold him up lest he fall and bruise himself, and Thou shalt know then whether Thou art the Son of God and shalt prove then how great is Thy faith in Thy Father." But Thou didst refuse and wouldst not cast Thyself down. Oh! of course, Thou didst proudly and well, like God; but the weak, unruly race of men, are they gods? Oh, Thou didst know then that in taking one step, in making one movement to cast Thyself down, Thou wouldst be tempting God and have lost all Thy faith in Him, and wouldst have been dashed to pieces against that earth which Thou didst come to save. And the wise spirit that tempted Thee would have rejoiced. But I ask again, are there many like Thee? And couldst Thou believe for one moment that men, too, could face such a temptation? Is the nature of men such, that they can reject miracle, and at the great moments of their

life, the moments of their deepest, most agonising spiritual difficulties, cling only to the free verdict of the heart? Oh, Thou
didst know that Thy deed would be recorded in books, would
be handed down to remote times and the utmost ends of the
earth, and Thou didst hope that man, following Thee, would
cling to God and not ask for a miracle. But Thou didst not
know that when man rejects miracle he rejects God too; for
man seeks not so much God as the miraculous. And as man
cannot bear to be without the miraculous, he will create new
miracles of his own for himself, and will worship deeds of
sorcery and witchcraft, though he might be a hundred times
over a rebel, heretic and infidel. Thou didst not come down
from the Cross when they shouted to Thee, mocking and
reviling Thee, "Come down from the Cross and we will believe
that Thou art He". Thou didst not come down, for again Thou
wouldst not enslave man by a miracle, and didst crave faith
given freely, not based on miracle. Thou didst crave for free
love and not the base raptures of the slave before the might
that has overawed him for ever. But Thou didst think too
highly of men therein, for they are slaves, of course, though
rebellious by nature. Look round and judge; fifteen centuries
have passed, look upon them. Whom hast Thou raised up to
Thyself? I swear, man is weaker and baser by nature than
Thou hast believed him! Can he, can he do what Thou didst?
By showing him so much respect, Thou didst, as it were, cease
to feel for him, for Thou didst ask far too much from him—Thou
who hast loved him more than Thyself! Respecting him less,
Thou wouldst have asked less of him. That would have been
more like love, for his burden would have been lighter. He is
weak and vile. What though he is everywhere now rebelling
against our power, and proud of his rebellion? It is the pride
of a child and a schoolboy. They are little children rioting and
barring out the teacher at school. But their childish delight will
end; it will cost them dear. They will cast down temples and
drench the earth with blood. But they will see at last, the
foolish children, that, though they are rebels, they are impotent
rebels, unable to keep up their own rebellion. Bathed in their
foolish tears, they will recognise at last that He who created
them rebels must have meant to mock at them. They will say
this in despair, and their utterance will be a blasphemy which
will make them more unhappy still, for man's nature cannot
bear blasphemy, and in the end always avenges it on itself.
And so unrest, confusion and unhappiness—that is the present

lot of man after Thou didst bear so much for their freedom! Thy great prophet tells, in vision and in image, that he saw all those who took part in the first resurrection and that there were of each tribe twelve thousand. But if there were so many of them, they must have been not men but gods. They had borne Thy cross, they had endured scores of years in the barren, hungry wilderness, living upon locusts and roots—and Thou mayest indeed point with pride at those children of freedom, of free love, of free and splendid sacrifice for Thy name. But remember that they were only some thousands; and what of the rest? And how are the other weak ones to blame, because they could not endure what the strong have endured? How is the weak soul to blame that it is unable to receive such terrible gifts? Canst Thou have simply come to the elect and for the elect? But if so, it is a mystery and we cannot understand it. And if it is a mystery, we too have a right to preach a mystery, and to teach them that it's not the free judgment of their hearts, not love that matters, but a mystery which they must follow blindly, even against their conscience. So we have done. We have corrected Thy work and have founded it upon *miracle, mystery* and *authority*. And men rejoiced that they were again led like sheep, and that the terrible gift that had brought them such suffering was, at last, lifted from their hearts. Were we right teaching them this? Speak! Did we not love mankind, so meekly acknowledging their feebleness, lovingly lightening their burden, and permitting their weak nature even sin with our sanction? Why hast Thou come now to hinder us? And why dost Thou look silently and searchingly at me with Thy mild eyes? Be angry. I don't want Thy love, for I love Thee not. And what use is it for me to hide anything from Thee? Don't I know to Whom I am speaking? All that I can say is known to Thee already. And is it for me to conceal from Thee our mystery? Perhaps it is Thy will to hear it from my lips. Listen, then. We are not working with Thee but with *him*—that is our mystery. It's long—eight centuries—since we have been on *his* side and not on Thine. Just eight centuries ago we took from him what Thou didst reject with scorn, that last gift he offered Thee, showing Thee all the kingdoms of the earth. We took from him Rome and the sword of Cæsar, and proclaimed ourselves sole rulers of the earth, though hitherto we have not been able to complete our work. But whose fault is that? Oh, the work is only beginning, but it has begun. It has long to await completion and the earth has yet much to suffer, but we shall triumph and shall be Cæsars, and then we shall plan the universal happiness of man. But Thou mightest have taken even then the sword of Cæsar. Why didst Thou reject that last gift? Hadst Thou accepted that last counsel of the mighty spirit, Thou wouldst have accomplished all that man seeks on earth—that is, someone to worship, someone to keep his conscience, and some means of uniting all in one unanimous and harmonious ant-heap, for the craving for universal unity is the third and last anguish of men. Mankind as a whole has always striven to organise a universal state. There have been many great nations with great histories, but the more highly they were developed the more unhappy they were, for they felt more acutely than other people the craving for world-wide union. The great conquerors, Timours and Genghis Khans, whirled like hurricanes over the face of the earth striving to subdue its people, and they too were but the unconscious expression of the same craving for universal unity. Hadst Thou taken the world and Cæsar's purple, Thou wouldst have founded the universal state and have given universal peace. For who can rule men if not he who holds their conscience and their bread in his hands? We have taken the sword of Cæsar, and in taking it, of course have rejected Thee and followed *him*. Oh, ages are yet to come of the confusion of free thought, of their science and cannibalism. For having begun to build their tower of Babel without us, they will end, of course, with cannibalism. But then the beast will crawl to us and lick our feet and spatter them with tears of blood. And we shall sit upon the beast and raise the cup, and on it will be written, "Mystery". But then, and only then, the reign of peace and happiness will come for men. Thou art proud of Thine elect, but Thou hast only the elect, while we give rest to all. And besides, how many of those elect, those mighty ones who could become elect, have grown weary waiting for Thee, and have transferred and will transfer the powers of their spirit and the warmth of their heart to the other camp, and end by raising their *free* banner against Thee! Thou didst Thyself lift up that banner. But with us all will be happy and will no more rebel nor destroy one another as under Thy freedom. Oh, we shall persuade them that they will only become free when they renounce their freedom to us and submit to us. And shall we be right or shall we be lying? They will be convinced that we are right, for they will remember the horrors of slavery and confusion to which Thy freedom brought them. Freedom, free thought and science will lead them into such straits and will bring them face to face with such marvels and insoluble mysteries, that some of them, the fierce and rebellious, will destroy themselves; others, rebellious but weak, will destroy one another, while the rest, weak and unhappy, will crawl fawning to our feet and whine to us: "Yes, you were right, you alone possess His mystery, and we come back to you, save us from ourselves!"

" 'Receiving bread from us, they will see clearly that we take the bread made by their hands from them, to give it to them, without any miracle. They will see that we do not change the stones to bread, but in truth they will be more thankful for taking it from our hands than for the bread itself! For they will remember only too well that in old days, without our help, even the bread they made turned to stones in their hands, while since they have come back to us, the very stones have turned to bread in their hands. Too, too well will they know the value of complete submission! And until men know that, they will be unhappy. Who is most to blame for their not knowing it, speak? Who scattered the flock and sent it astray on unknown paths? But the flock will come together again and will submit once more, and then it will be once for all. Then we shall give them the quiet humble happiness of weak creatures such as they are by nature. Oh, we shall persuade them at last not to be proud, for Thou didst lift them up and thereby taught them to be proud. We shall show them that they are weak, that they are only pitiful children, but that childlike happiness is the sweetest of all. They will become timid and will look to us and huddle close to us in fear, as chicks to the hen. They will marvel at us and will be awestricken before us, and will be proud at our being so powerful and clever, that we have been able to subdue such a turbulent flock of thousands of millions. They will tremble impotently before our wrath, their minds will grow fearful, they will be quick to shed tears like women and children, but they will be just as ready at a sign from us to pass to laughter and rejoicing, to happy mirth and childish song. Yes, we shall set them to work, but in their leisure hours we shall make their life like a child's game, with children's songs and innocent dance. Oh, we shall allow them even sin, they are weak and helpless, and they will love us like children because we allow them to sin. We shall tell them that every sin will be expiated, if it is done with our permission, that we allow them to sin because we love them, and the punishment for these sins we take upon our-

selves. And we shall take it upon ourselves, and they will
adore us as their saviours who have taken on themselves their
sins before God. And they will have no secrets from us. We
shall allow or forbid them to live with their wives and
mistresses, to have or not to have children—according to
whether they have been obedient or disobedient—and they will
submit to us gladly and cheerfully. The most painful secrets
of their conscience, all, all they will bring to us, and we shall
have an answer for all. And they will be glad to believe our
answer, for it will save them from the great anxiety and terrible
agony they endure at present in making a free decision for
themselves. And all will be happy, all the millions of creatures
except the hundred thousand who rule over them. For only
we, we who guard the mystery, shall be unhappy. There will
be thousands of millions of happy babes, and a hundred thousand sufferers who have taken upon themselves the curse of the
knowledge of good and evil. Peacefully they will die, peacefully they will expire in Thy name, and beyond the grave they
will find nothing but death. But we shall keep the secret, and
for their happiness we shall allure them with the reward of
heaven and eternity. Though if there were anything in the
other world, it certainly would not be for such as they. It is
prophesied that Thou wilt come again in victory, Thou wilt
come with Thy chosen, the proud and strong. but we will say
that they have only saved themselves, but we have saved all.
We are told that the harlot who sits upon the beast, and holds
in her hands the *mystery,* shall be put to shame, that the weak
will rise up again, and will rend her royal purple and will strip
naked her loathsome body. But then I will stand up and
point out to Thee the thousand millions of happy children who
have known no sin. And we who have taken their sins upon
us for their happiness will stand up before Thee and say:
"Judge us if Thou canst and darest." Know that I fear Thee
not. Know that I too have been in the wilderness, I too have
lived on roots and locusts, I too prized the freedom with which
Thou hast blessed men, and I too was striving to stand among
Thy elect, among the strong and powerful, thirsting "to make
up the number". But I awakened and would not serve madness. I turned back and joined the ranks of those *who have
corrected Thy work.* I left the proud and went back to the
humble, for the happiness of the humble. What I say to Thee
will come to pass, and our dominion will be built up. I repeat,
to-morrow Thou shalt see that obedient flock who at a sign

from me will hasten to heap up the hot cinders about the pile on which I shall burn Thee for coming to hinder us. For if anyone has ever deserved our fires, it is Thou. To-morrow I shall burn Thee. Dixi.' "

Ivan stopped. He was carried away as he talked and spoke with excitement; when he had finished, he suddenly smiled.

Alyosha had listened in silence; towards the end he was greatly moved and seemed several times on the point of interrupting, but restrained himself. Now his words came with a rush.

"But . . . that's absurd!" he cried, flushing. "Your poem is in praise of Jesus, not in blame of Him—as you meant it to be. And who will believe you about freedom? Is that the way to understand it? That's not the idea of it in the Orthodox Church . . . That's Rome, and not even the whole of Rome, it's false—those are the worst of the Catholics, the Inquisitors, the Jesuits! . . . And there could not be such a fantastic creature as your Inquisitor. What are these sins of mankind they take on themselves? Who are these keepers of the mystery who have taken some curse upon themselves for the happiness of mankind? When have they been seen? We know the Jesuits, they are spoken ill of, but surely they are not what you describe? They are not that at all, not at all. . . . They are simply the Romish army for the earthly sovereignty of the world in the future, with the Pontiff of Rome for Emperor . . . that's their ideal, but there's no sort of mystery or lofty melancholy about it. . . . It's simple lust of power, of filthy earthly gain, of domination—something like a universal serfdom with them as masters—that's all they stand for. They don't even believe in God, perhaps. Your suffering inquisitor is a mere fantasy."

"Stay, stay," laughed Ivan, "how hot you are! A fantasy, you say, let it be so! Of course it's a fantasy. But allow me to say: do you really think that the Roman Catholic movement of the last centuries is actually nothing but the lust of power, of filthy earthly gain? Is that Father Païssy's teaching?"

"No, no, on the contrary, Father Païssy did once say something rather the same as you . . . but of course it's not the same, not a bit the same," Alyosha hastily corrected himself.

"A precious admission, in spite of your 'not a bit the same'. I ask you why your Jesuits and Inquisitors have united simply for vile material gain? Why can there not be among them one martyr oppressed by great sorrow and loving humanity? You see, only suppose that there was one such man among all those who desire nothing but filthy material gain—if there's only one like my old inquisitor, who had himself eaten roots in the desert and made frenzied efforts to subdue his flesh to make himself free and perfect. But yet all his life he loved humanity, and suddenly his eyes were opened, and he saw that it is no great moral blessedness to attain perfection and freedom, if at the same time one gains the conviction that millions of God's creatures have been created as a mockery, that they will never be capable of using their freedom, that these poor rebels can never turn into giants to complete the tower, that it was not for such geese that the great idealist dreamt his dream of harmony. Seeing all that he turned back and joined—the clever people. Surely that could have happened?''

''Joined whom, what clever people?'' cried Alyosha, completely carried away. ''They have no such great cleverness and no mysteries and secrets. . . . Perhaps nothing but Atheism, that's all their secret. Your inquisitor does not believe in God, that's his secret!''

''What if it is so? At last you have guessed it. It's perfectly true, it's true that that's the whole secret, but isn't that suffering, at least for a man like that, who has wasted his whole life in the desert and yet could not shake off his incurable love of humanity? In his old age he reached the clear conviction that nothing but the advice of the great dread spirit could build up any tolerable sort of life for the feeble, unruly, 'incomplete, empirical creatures created in jest'. And so, convinced of this, he sees that he must follow the council of the wise spirit, the dread spirit of death and destruction, and therefore accept lying and deception, and lead men consciously to death and destruction, and yet deceive them all the way so that they may not notice where they are being led, that the poor blind creatures may at least, on the way, think themselves happy. And note, the deception is in the name of Him in Whose ideal the old man had so fervently believed all his life long. Is not that tragic? And if only one such stood at the head of the whole army 'filled with the lust of power only for the sake of filthy gain'—would not one such be enough to make a tragedy? More than that, one such standing at the head is enough to create the actual leading idea of the Roman Church, with all its armies and Jesuits, its highest idea. I tell you frankly that I firmly believe that there has always been such a man among those who stood at the head of the movement. Who knows, there may have been some such even among the Roman Popes. Who knows, perhaps the spirit of that accursed old man who loves mankind so obstinately in his own way, is to be found even now in a whole multitude of such old men, existing not by chance but by agreement, as a secret league formed long ago for the guarding of the mystery, to guard it from the weak and the unhappy, so as to make them happy. No doubt it is so, and so it must be indeed. I fancy that even among the Masons there's something of the same mystery at the bottom, and that that's why the Catholics so detest the Masons as their rivals breaking up the unity of the idea, while it is so essential that there should be one flock and one shepherd. . . . But from the way I defend my idea I might be an author impatient of your criticism. Enough of it."

"You are perhaps a Mason yourself!" broke suddenly from Alyosha. "You don't believe in God," he added, speaking this time very sorrowfully. He fancied besides that his brother was looking at him ironically. "How does your poem end?" he asked, suddenly looking down. "Or was it the end?"

"I meant to end it like this. When the Inquisitor ceased speaking he waited some time for his Prisoner to answer him. His silence weighed down upon him. He saw that the Prisoner had listened intently all the time, looking gently in his face and evidently not wishing to reply. The old man longed for Him to say something, however bitter and terrible. But He suddenly approached the old man in silence and softly kissed him on his bloodless aged lips. That was all his answer. The old man shuddered. His lips moved. He went to the door, opened it, and said to Him: 'Go, and come no more . . . come not at all, never, never!' And he let Him out into the dark alleys of the town. The Prisoner went away."

"And the old man?"

"The kiss glows in his heart, but the old man adheres to his idea."

"And you with him, you too?" cried Alyosha, mournfully. Ivan laughed.

"Why, it's all nonsense, Alyosha. It's only a senseless poem of a senseless student, who could never write two lines of verse. Why do you take it so seriously? Surely you don't suppose I am going straight off to the Jesuits, to join the men who are correcting His work? Good Lord, it's no business of mine. I

270

told you, all I want is to live on to thirty, and then . . . dash the cup to the ground!"

"But the little sticky leaves, and the precious tombs, and the blue sky, and the woman you love! How will you live, how will you love them?" Alyosha cried sorrowfully. "With such a hell in your heart and your head, how can you? No, that's just what you are going away for, to join them . . . if not, you will kill yourself, you can't endure it!"

"There is a strength to endure everything," Ivan said, with a cold smile.

"What strength?"

"The strength of the Karamazovs—the strength of the Karamazov baseness."

"To sink into debauchery, to stifle your soul with corruption—yes?"

"Possibly even that . . . only perhaps till I am thirty I shall escape it, and then."

"How will you escape it? By what will you escape it? That's impossible with your ideas."

"In the Karamazov way, again."

" 'Everything is lawful,' you mean? Everything is lawful, is that it?"

Ivan scowled, and all at once turned strangely pale.

"Ah, you've caught up yesterday's phrase, which so offended Miüsov—and which Dmitri pounced upon so naïvely and paraphrased!" he smiled queerly. "Yes, if you like, 'everything is lawful', since the word has been said. I won't deny it. And Mitya's version isn't bad."

Alyosha looked at him in silence.

"I thought that going away from here I have you at least," Ivan said suddenly, with unexpected feeling; "but now I see that there is no place for me even in your heart, my dear hermit. The formula, 'all is lawful', I won't renounce—will you renounce me for that—yes?"

Alyosha got up, went to him and softly kissed him on the lips.

"That's plagiarism," cried Ivan, highly delighted. "You stole that from my poem. Thank you, though. Get up, Alyosha, it's time we were going, both of us."

They went out, but stopped when they reached the entrance of the restaurant.

"Listen, Alyosha," Ivan began in a resolute voice. "If I am really able to care for the sticky little leaves I shall only love

271

them, remembering you. It's enough for me that you are some-where here, and I shan't lose my desire for life yet. Is that enough for you? Take it as a declaration of love if you like. And now you go to the right and I to the left. And it's enough, do you hear? enough. I mean even if I don't go away to-morrow (I think I certainly shall go) and we meet again, don't say a word more on these subjects. I beg that particularly. And about Dmitri too, I ask you specially never speak to me again," he added, with sudden irritation; "it's all exhausted, it has all been said over and over again, hasn't it? And I'll make you one promise in return for it. When at thirty I want to 'dash the cup to the ground', wherever I may be, I'll come to have one more talk with you, even though it were from America, you may be sure of that. I'll come on purpose. It will be very interesting to have a look at you, to see what you'll be by that time. It's rather a solemn promise, you see. And we really may be parting for seven years or ten. Come, go now to your Pater Seraphicus, he is dying. If he dies without you, you will be angry with me for having kept you. Good-bye, kiss me once more; that's right, now go."

Ivan turned suddenly and went his way without looking back. It was just as Dmitri had left Alyosha the day before, though the parting had been very different. The strange resemblance flashed like an arrow through Alyosha's mind in the distress and dejection of that moment. He waited a little, looking after his brother. He suddenly noticed that Ivan swayed as he walked and that his right shoulder looked lower than his left. He had never noticed it before. But all at once he turned too, and almost ran to the monastery. It was nearly dark, and he felt almost frightened; something new was growing up in him for which he could not account. The wind had risen again as on the previous evening, and the ancient pines murmured gloomily about him when he entered the hermitage copse. He almost ran. "Pater Seraphicus—he got that name from some-where—wherefrom?" Alyosha wondered. "Ivan, poor Ivan, and when shall I see you again? . . . Here is the hermitage. Yes, yes, that he is, Pater Seraphicus, he will save me—from him and for ever!"

Several times afterwards he wondered how he could on leav-ing Ivan so completely forget his brother Dmitri, though he had that morning, only a few hours before, so firmly resolved to find him and not to give up doing so, even should he be unable to return to the monastery that night.

CHAPTER VI

AND Ivan, on parting from Alyosha, went home to Fyodor Pavlovitch's house. But, strange to say, he was overcome by insufferable depression, which grew greater at every step he took towards the house. There was nothing strange in his being depressed; what was strange was that Ivan could not have said what was the cause of it. He had often been depressed before, and there was nothing surprising at his feeling so at such a moment, when he had broken off with everything that had brought him here, and was preparing that day to make a new start and enter upon a new, unknown future. He would again be as solitary as ever, and though he had great hopes, and great—too great—expectations from life, he could not have given any definite account of his hopes, his expectations, or even his desires.

Yet at that moment, though the apprehension of the new and unknown certainly found place in his heart, what was worrying him was something quite different. "Is it loathing for my father's house?" he wondered. "Quite likely; I am so sick of it; and though it's the last time I shall cross its hateful threshold, still I loathe it. . . . No, it's not that either. Is it the parting with Alyosha and the conversation I had with him? For so many years I've been silent with the whole world and not deigned to speak, and all of a sudden I reel off a rigmarole like that." It certainly might have been the youthful vexation of youthful inexperience and vanity—vexation at having failed to express himself, especially with such a being as Alyosha, on whom his heart had certainly been reckoning. No doubt that came in, that vexation, it must have done indeed; but yet that was not it, that was not it either. "I feel sick with depression and yet I can't tell what I want. Better not think, perhaps."

Ivan tried "not to think", but that, too, was no use. What made his depression so vexatious and irritating was that it had a kind of casual, external character—he felt that. Some person or thing seemed to be standing out somewhere, just as something will sometimes obtrude itself upon the eye, and though one may be so busy with work or conversation that for a long time one does not notice it, yet it irritates and almost torments one till at last one realises and removes the offending object, often quite a trifling and ridiculous one—some article left about

273

in the wrong place, a handkerchief on the floor, a book not re-placed on the shelf, and so on.

At last, feeling very cross and ill-humoured, Ivan arrived home, and suddenly, about fifteen paces from the garden gate, he guessed what was fretting and worrying him.

On a bench in the gateway the valet Smerdyakov was sitting, enjoying the coolness of the evening, and at the first glance at him Ivan knew that the valet Smerdyakov was on his mind, and that it was this man that this soul loathed. It all dawned upon him suddenly and became clear. Just before, when Alyosha had been telling him of his meeting with Smerdyakov, he had felt a sudden twinge of gloom and loathing, which had immediately stirred responsive anger in his heart. Afterwards, as he talked, Smerdyakov had been forgotten for the time; but still he had been in his mind, and as soon as Ivan parted from Alyosha and was walking home, the forgotten sensation began to obtrude itself again. "Is it possible that a miserable, contemptible creature like that can worry me so much?" he wondered, with insufferable irritation.

It was true that Ivan had come of late to feel an intense dis-like for the man, especially during the last few days. He had even begun to notice in himself a growing feeling that was almost of hatred for the creature. Perhaps this hatred was accentuated by the fact that when Ivan first came to the neigh-bourhood he had felt quite differently. Then he had taken a marked interest in Smerdyakov, and had even thought him very original. He had encouraged him to talk to him, although he had always wondered at a certain incoherence, or rather restlessness, in his mind, and could not understand what it was that so continually and insistently worked upon the brain of "the contemplative". They discussed philosophical questions and even how there could have been light on the first day when the sun, moon, and stars were only created on the fourth day, and how that was to be understood. But Ivan soon saw that, though the sun, moon, and stars might be an interesting sub-ject, yet that it was quite secondary to Smerdyakov, and that he was looking for something altogether different. In one way and another, he began to betray a boundless vanity, and a wounded vanity, too, and that Ivan disliked. It had first given rise to his aversion. Later on, there had been trouble in the house. Grushenka had come on the scene, and there had been the scandals with his brother Dmitri—they discussed that, too. But though Smerdyakov always talked of that with great excitement, it was impossible to discover what he desired to come of it. There was, in fact, something surprising in the illogicality and incoherence of some of his desires, accidentally betrayed and always vaguely expressed. Smerdyakov was always inquiring, putting certain indirect but obviously premeditated questions, but what his object was he did not explain, and usually at the most important moment he would break off and relapse into silence or pass to another subject. But what finally irritated Ivan most and confirmed his dislike for him was the peculiar, revolting familiarity which Smerdyakov began to show more and more markedly. Not that he forgot himself and was rude; on the contrary, he always spoke very respectfully, yet he had obviously begun to consider—goodness knows why!—that there was some sort of understanding between him and Ivan Fyodorovitch. He always spoke in a tone that suggested that those two had some kind of compact, some secret between them, that had at some time been expressed on both sides, only known to them and beyond the comprehension of those around them. But for a long while Ivan did not recognise the real cause of his growing dislike and he had only lately realised what was at the root of it.

With a feeling of disgust and irritation he tried to pass in at the gate without speaking or looking at Smerdyakov. But Smerdyakov rose from the bench, and from that action alone, Ivan knew instantly that he wanted particularly to talk to him. Ivan looked at him and stopped, and the fact that he did stop, instead of passing by, as he meant to the minute before, drove him to fury. With anger and repulsion he looked at Smerdyakov's emasculate, sickly face, with the little curls combed forward on his forehead. His left eye winked and grinned as though to say: "Where are you going? You won't pass by; you see that we two clever people have something to say to each other."

Ivan shook. "Get away, miserable idiot. What have I to do with you?" was on the tip of his tongue, but to his profound astonishment he heard himself say: "Is my father still asleep, or has he waked?"

He asked the question softly and meekly, to his own surprise, and at once, again to his own surprise, sat down on the bench. For an instant he felt almost frightened; he remembered it afterwards. Smerdyakov stood facing him, his hands behind his back, looking at him with assurance and almost severity.

"His honour is still asleep," he articulated deliberately. ("You were the first to speak, not I," he seemed to say.) "I

275

am surprised at you, sir," he added, after a pause, dropping his eyes affectedly, setting his right foot forward, and playing with the tip of his polished boot.

"Why are you surprised at me?" Ivan asked abruptly and sullenly, doing his utmost to restrain himself, and suddenly realising, with disgust, that he was feeling intense curiosity and would not, on any account, have gone away without satisfying it.

"Why don't you go to Tchermashnya, sir?" Smerdyakov suddenly raised his eyes and smiled familiarly. "Why I smile you must understand of yourself, if you are a clever man," his screwed-up left eye seemed to say.

"Why should I go to Tchermashnya?" Ivan asked in surprise.

Smerdyakov was silent again.

"Fyodor Pavlovitch himself has so begged you to," he said at last, slowly and apparently attaching no significance to his answer. "I put you off with a secondary reason," he seemed to suggest, "simply to say something."

"Damn you! Speak out what you want!" Ivan cried angrily at last, passing from meekness to violence.

Smerdyakov drew his right foot up to his left, pulled himself up, but still looked at him with the same serenity and the same little smile.

"Substantially nothing—but just by way of conversation."

Another silence followed. They did not speak for nearly a minute. Ivan knew that he ought to get up and show anger, and Smerdyakov stood before him and seemed to be waiting as though to see whether he would be angry or not. So at least it seemed to Ivan. At last he moved to get up. Smerdyakov seemed to seize the moment.

"I'm in an awful position, Ivan Fyodorovitch. I don't know how to help myself," he said resolutely and distinctly, and at his last word he sighed. Ivan Fyodorovitch sat down again.

"They are both utterly crazy, they are no better than little children," Smerdyakov went on. "I am speaking of your parent and your brother Dmitri Fyodorovitch. Here Fyodor Pavlovitch will get up directly and begin worrying me every minute, 'Has she come? Why hasn't she come?' and so on up till midnight and even after midnight. And if Agrafena Alexandrovna doesn't come (for very likely she does not mean to come at all), then he will be at me again to-morrow morning. 'Why hasn't she come? When will she come?'—as though I

276

were to blame for it. On the other side it's no better. As soon as it gets dark, or even before, your brother will appear with his gun in his hands: 'Look out, you rogue, you soup-maker. If you miss her and don't let me know she's been—I'll kill you before anyone.' When the night's over, in the morning, he, too, like Fyodor Pavlovitch, begins worrying me to death. 'Why hasn't she come? Will she come soon?' And he, too, thinks me to blame because his lady hasn't come. And every day and every hour they get angrier and angrier, so that I sometimes think I shall kill myself in a fright. I can't depend upon them, sir."

"And why have you meddled? Why did you begin to spy for Dmitri Fyodorovitch?" said Ivan irritably.

"How could I help meddling? Though, indeed, I haven't meddled at all, if you want to know the truth of the matter. I kept quiet from the very beginning, not daring to answer; but he pitched on me to be his servant. He has had only one thing to say since: 'I'll kill you, you scoundrel, if you miss her.' I feel certain, sir, that I shall have a long fit to-morrow."

"What do you mean by 'a long fit'?"

"A long fit, lasting a long time—several hours, or perhaps a day or two. Once it went on for three days. I fell from the garret that time. The struggling ceased and then began again, and for three days I couldn't come back to my senses. Fyodor Pavlovitch sent for Herzenstube, the doctor here, and he put ice on my head and tried another remedy, too. . . . I might have died."

"But they say one can't tell with epilepsy when a fit is coming. What makes you say you will have one to-morrow?" Ivan inquired, with a peculiar, irritable curiosity.

"That's just so. You can't tell beforehand."

"Besides, you fell from the garret then."

"I climb up to the garret every day. I might fall from the garret again to-morrow. And, if not, I might fall down the cellar steps. I have to go into the cellar every day, too."

Ivan took a long look at him.

"You are talking nonsense, I see, and I don't quite understand you," he said softly, but with a sort of menace. "Do you mean to pretend to be ill to-morrow for three days, eh?"

Smerdyakov, who was looking at the ground again, and playing with the toe of his right foot, set the foot down, moved the left one forward, and, grinning, articulated:

"If I were able to play such a trick, that is, pretend to have a fit—and it would not be difficult for a man accustomed to them—I should have a perfect right to use such a means to save myself from death. For even if Agrafena Alexandrovna comes to see his father while I am ill, his honour can't blame a sick man for not telling him. He'd be ashamed to."

"Hang it all!" Ivan cried, his face working with anger. "Why are you always in such a funk for your life? All my brother Dmitri's threats are only hasty words and mean nothing. He won't kill you; it's not you he'll kill!"

"He'd kill me first of all, like a fly. But even more than that, I am afraid I shall be taken for an accomplice of his when he does something crazy to his father."

"Why should you be taken for an accomplice?"

"They'll think I am an accomplice, because I let him know the signals as a great secret."

"What signals? Whom did you tell? Confound you, speak more plainly."

"I'm bound to admit the fact," Smerdyakov drawled, with pedantic composure, "that I have a secret with Fyodor Pavlovitch in this business. As you know yourself (if only you do know it) he has for several days past locked himself in as soon as night or even evening comes on. Of late you've been going upstairs to your room early every evening, and yesterday you did not come down at all, and so perhaps you don't know how carefully he has begun to lock himself in at night, and even if Grigory Vassilyevitch comes to the door he won't open to him till he hears his voice. But Grigory Vassilyevitch does not come, because I wait upon him alone in his room now. That's the arrangement he made himself ever since this to-do with Agrafena Alexandrovna began. But at night, by his orders, I go away to the lodge so that I don't get to sleep till midnight, but am on the watch, getting up and walking about the yard, waiting for Agrafena Alexandrovna to come. For the last few days he's been perfectly frantic expecting her. What he argues is, she is afraid of him, Dmitri Fyodorovitch (Mitya, as he calls him). 'And so,' says he, 'she'll come the back-way, late at night, to me. You look out for her,' says he, 'till midnight and later; and if she does come, you run up and knock at my door or at the window from the garden. Knock at first twice, rather gently, and then three times more quickly, then,' says he, 'I shall understand at once that she has come, and will open the door to you quietly.' Another signal he gave me in case anything unexpected happens. At first, two knocks, and then, afte

278

an interval, another much louder. Then he will understand that something has happened suddenly and that I must see him, and he will open to me so that I can go and speak to him. That's all in case Agrafena Alexandrovna can't come herself, but sends a message. Besides, Dmitri Fyodorovitch might come, too, so I must let him know he is near. His honour is awfully afraid of Dmitri Fyodorovitch, so that even if Agrafena Alexandrovna had come and were locked in with him, and Dmitri Fyodorovitch were to turn up anywhere near at the time, I should be bound to let him know at once, knocking three times. So that the first signal of five knocks means Agrafena Alexandrovna has come, while the second signal of three knocks means 'something important to tell you'. His honour has shown me them several times and explained them. And as in the whole universe no one knows of these signals but myself and his honour, so he'd open the door without the slightest hesitation and without calling out (he is awfully afraid of calling out aloud). Well, those signals are known to Dmitri Fyodorovitch too, now."

"How are they known? Did you tell him? How dared you tell him?"

"It was through fright I did it. How could I dare to keep it back from him? Dmitri Fyodorovitch kept persisting every day, 'You are deceiving me, you are hiding something from me! I'll break both your legs for you.' So I told him those secret signals that he might see my slavish devotion, and might be satisfied that I was not deceiving him but was telling him all I could."

"If you think that he'll make use of those signals and try to get in, don't let him in."

"But if I should be laid up with a fit, how can I prevent him coming in then, even if I dared prevent him, knowing how desperate he is?"

"Hang it! How can you be so sure you are going to have a fit, confound you? Are you laughing at me?"

"How could I dare laugh at you, and I am in no laughing humour with this fear on me? I feel I am going to have a fit. I have a presentiment. Fright alone will bring it on."

"Confound it! If you are laid up, Grigory will be on the watch. Let Grigory know beforehand; he will be sure not to let him in."

"I should never dare to tell Grigory Vassilyevitch about the signals without orders from my master. And as for Grigory

Vassilyevitch hearing him and not admitting him, he has been ill ever since yesterday, and Marfa Ignatyevna intends to give him medicine to-morrow. They've just arranged it. It's a very strange remedy of hers. Marfa Ignatyevna knows of a preparation and always keeps it. It's a strong thing made from some herb. She has the secret of it, and she always gives it to Grigory Vassilyevitch three times a year when his lumbago's so bad he is almost paralysed by it. Then she takes a towel, wets it with the stuff, and rubs his whole back for half an hour till it's quite red and swollen, and what's left in the bottle she gives him to drink with a special prayer; but not quite all, for on such occasions she leaves some for herself, and drinks it herself. And as they never take strong drink, I assure you they both drop asleep at once and sleep sound a very long time. And when Grigory Vassilyevitch wakes up he is perfectly well after it, but Marfa Ignatyevna always has a headache from it. So, if Marfa Ignatyevna carries out her intention to-morrow, they won't hear anything and hinder Dmitri Fyodorovitch. They'll be asleep."

"What a rigmarole! And it all seems to happen at once, as though it were planned. You'll have a fit and they'll both be unconscious," cried Ivan. "But aren't you trying to arrange it so?" broke from him suddenly, and he frowned threateningly.

"How could I? . . . And why should I, when it all depends on Dmitri Fyodorovitch and his plans? . . . If he means to do anything, he'll do it; but if not, I shan't be thrusting him upon his father."

"And why should he go to father, especially on the sly, if, as you say yourself, Agrafena Alexandrovna won't come at all?" Ivan went on, turning white with anger. "You say that yourself, and all the while I've been here I've felt sure it was all the old man's fancy, and the creature won't come to him. Why should Dmitri break in on him if she doesn't come? Speak, I want to know what you are thinking."

"You know yourself why he'll come. What's the use of what I think? His honour will come simply because he is in a rage or suspicious on account of my illness perhaps, and he'll dash in, as he did yesterday through impatience to search the rooms, to see whether she hasn't escaped him on the sly. He is perfectly well aware, too, that Fyodor Pavlovitch has a big envelope with three thousand roubles in it, tied up with ribbon and sealed with three seals. On it is written in his own hand, 'To my angel Grushenka, if she will come', to which he added three days later, 'For my little chicken.' There's no knowing what that might do."

"Nonsense!" cried Ivan, almost beside himself. "Dmitri won't come to steal money and kill my father to do it. He might have killed him yesterday on account of Grushenka, like the frantic, savage fool he is, but he won't steal."

"He is in very great need of money now—the greatest need, Ivan Fyodorovitch. You don't know in what need he is," Smerdyakov explained, with perfect composure and remarkable distinctness. "He looks on that three thousand as his own, too. He said so to me himself. 'My father still owes me just three thousand,' he said. And besides that, consider, Ivan Fyodorovitch, there is something else perfectly true. It's as good as certain, so to say, that Agrafena Alexandrovna will force him, if only she cares to, to marry her—the master himself, I mean Fyodor Pavlovitch—if only she cares to, and of course she may care to. All I've said is that she won't come, but maybe she's looking for more than that—I mean, to be mistress here. I know myself that Samsonov, her merchant, was laughing with her about it, telling her quite openly that it would not be at all a stupid thing to do. And she's got plenty of sense. She wouldn't marry a beggar like Dmitri Fyodorovitch. So, taking that into consideration, Ivan Fyodorovitch, reflect that then neither Dmitri Fyodorovitch nor yourself and your brother, Alexey Fyodorovitch, would have anything after the master's death, not a rouble, for Agrafena Alexandrovna would marry him simply to get hold of the whole, all the money there is. But if your father were to die now, there'd be some forty thousand for sure, even for Dmitri Fyodorovitch, whom he hates so, for he's made no will. . . . Dmitri Fyodorovitch knows all that very well."

A sort of shudder passed over Ivan's face. He suddenly flushed.

"Then why on earth," he suddenly interrupted Smerdyakov, "do you advise me to go to Tchermashnya? What did you mean by that? If I go away, you see what will happen here." Ivan drew his breath with difficulty.

"Precisely so," said Smerdyakov, softly and reasonably, watching Ivan intently, however.

"What do you mean by 'precisely so'?" Ivan questioned him, with a menacing light in his eyes, restraining himself with difficulty.

"I spoke because I felt sorry for you. If I were in your place

I should simply throw it all up . . . rather than stay on in such a position," answered Smerdyakov, with the most candid air looking at Ivan's flashing eyes. They were both silent.

"You seem to be a perfect idiot, and what's more . . . an awful scoundrel, too." Ivan rose suddenly from the bench. He was about to pass straight through the gate, but he stopped short and turned to Smerdyakov. Something strange followed. Ivan, in a sudden paroxysm, bit his lip, clenched his fists, and, in another minute, would have flung himself on Smerdyakov. The latter, anyway, noticed it at the same moment, started, and shrank back. But the moment passed without mischief to Smerdyakov, and Ivan turned in silence, as it seemed in perplexity, to the gate.

"I am going away to Moscow to-morrow, if you care to know —early to-morrow morning. That's all!" he suddenly said aloud angrily, and wondered himself afterwards what need there was to say this then to Smerdyakov.

"That's the best thing you can do," he responded, as though he had expected to hear it; "except that you can always be telegraphed for from Moscow, if anything should happen here."

Ivan stopped again, and again turned quickly to Smerdyakov. But a change had passed over him, too. All his familiarity and carelessness had completely disappeared. His face expressed attention and expectation, intent but timid and cringing.

"Haven't you something more to say—something to add?" could be read in the intent gaze he fixed on Ivan.

"And couldn't I be sent for from Tchermashnya, too—in case anything happened?" Ivan shouted suddenly, for some unknown reason raising his voice.

"From Tchermashnya, too . . . you could be sent for." Smerdyakov muttered, almost in a whisper, looking disconcerted, but gazing intently into Ivan's eyes.

"Only Moscow is further and Tchermashnya is nearer. Is it to save my spending money on the fare, or to save my going so far out of my way, that you insist on Tchermashnya?"

"Precisely so . . ." muttered Smerdyakov, with a breaking voice. He looked at Ivan with a revolting smile, and again made ready to draw back. But to his astonishment Ivan broke into a laugh, and went through the gate still laughing. Anyone who had seen his face at that moment would have known that he was not laughing from lightness of heart, and he could not have explained himself what he was feeling at that instant. He moved and walked as though in a nervous frenzy.

CHAPTER VII

AND in the same nervous frenzy, too, he spoke. Meeting Fyodor Pavlovitch in the drawing-room directly he went in, he shouted to him, waving his hands, "I am going upstairs to my room, not in to you. Good-bye!" and passed by, trying not even to look at his father. Very possibly the old man was too hateful to him at that moment; but such an unceremonious display of hostility was a surprise even to Fyodor Pavlovitch. And the old man evidently wanted to tell him something at once and had come to meet him in the drawing-room on purpose. Receiving this amiable greeting, he stood still in silence and with an ironical air watched his son going upstairs, till he passed out of sight.

"What's the matter with him?" he promptly asked Smerdyakov, who had followed Ivan.

"Angry about something. Who can tell?" the valet muttered evasively.

"Confound him! Let him be angry then. Bring in the samovar, and get along with you. Look sharp! No news?"

Then followed a series of questions such as Smerdyakov had just complained of to Ivan, all relating to his expected visitor, and these questions we will omit. Half an hour later the house was locked, and the crazy old man was wandering alone through the rooms in excited expectation of hearing every minute the five knocks agreed upon. Now and then he peered out into the darkness, seeing nothing.

It was very late, but Ivan was still awake and reflecting. He sat up late that night, till two o'clock. But we will not give an account of his thoughts, and this is not the place to look into that soul—its turn will come. And even if one tried, it would be very hard to give an account of them, for there were no thoughts in his brain, but something very vague, and, above all, intense excitement. He felt himself that he had lost his bearings. He was fretted, too, by all sorts of strange and almost surprising desires; for instance, after midnight he suddenly had an intense irresistible inclination to go down, open the door, go to the lodge and beat Smerdyakov. But if he had been asked why, he could not have given any exact reason, except perhaps that he loathed the valet as one who had insulted him more gravely than anyone in the world. On the other hand, he was

283

more than once that night overcome by a sort of inexplicable humiliating terror, which he felt positively paralysed his physical powers. His head ached and he was giddy. A feeling of hatred was rankling in his heart, as though he meant to avenge himself on someone. He even hated Alyosha, recalling the conversation he had just had with him. At moments he hated himself intensely. Of Katerina Ivanovna he almost forgot to think, and wondered greatly at this afterwards, especially as he remembered perfectly that when he had protested so valiantly to Katerina Ivanovna that he would go away next day to Moscow, something had whispered in his heart, "That's nonsense, you are not going, and it won't be so easy to tear yourself away as you are boasting now".

Remembering that night long afterwards, Ivan recalled with peculiar repulsion how he had suddenly got up from the sofa and stealthily, as though he were afraid of being watched, had opened the door, gone out on the staircase and listened to Fyodor Pavlovitch stirring down below, had listened a long while—some five minutes—with a sort of strange curiosity, holding his breath while his heart throbbed. And why he had done all this, why he was listening, he could not have said. That "action" all his life afterwards he called "infamous", and at the bottom of his heart he thought of it as the basest action of his life. For Fyodor Pavlovitch himself he felt no hatred at that moment, but was simply intensely curious to know how he was walking down there below and what he must be doing now. He wondered and imagined how he must be peeping out of the dark windows and stopping in the middle of the room, listening, listening—for someone to knock. Ivan went out on to the stairs twice to listen like this.

About two o'clock, when everything was quiet, and even Fyodor Pavlovitch had gone to bed, Ivan had got into bed, firmly resolved to fall asleep at once, as he felt fearfully exhausted. And he did fall asleep at once, and slept soundly without dreams, but waked early, at seven o'clock, when it was broad daylight. Opening his eyes, he was surprised to feel himself extraordinarily vigorous. He jumped up at once and dressed quickly; then dragged out his trunk and began packing immediately. His linen had come back from the laundress the previous morning. Ivan positively smiled at the thought that everything was helping his sudden departure. And his departure certainly was sudden. Though Ivan had said the day before (to Katerina Ivanovna, Alyosha, and Smerdyakov) that he was

284

leaving next day, yet he remembered that he had no thought of departure when he went to bed, or, at least, had not dreamed that his first act in the morning would be to pack his trunk. At last his trunk and bag were ready. It was about nine o'clock when Marfa Ignatyevna came in with her usual inquiry: "Where will your honour take your tea, in your own room or downstairs?" He looked almost cheerful, but there was about him, about his words and gestures, something hurried and scattered. Greeting his father affably, and even inquiring specially after his health, though he did not wait to hear his answer to the end, he announced that he was starting off in an hour to return to Moscow for good, and begged him to send for the horses. His father heard this announcement with no sign of surprise, and forgot in an unmannerly way to show regret at losing him. Instead of doing so, he flew into a great flutter at the recollection of some important business of his own.

"What a fellow you are! Not to tell me yesterday! Never mind; we'll manage it all the same. Do me a great service, my dear boy. Go to Tchermashnya on the way. It's only to turn to the left from the station at Volovya, only another twelve versts and you come to Tchermashnya."

"I'm sorry, I can't. It's eighty versts to the railway and the train starts for Moscow at seven o'clock to-night. I can only just catch it."

"You'll catch it to-morrow or the day after, but to-day turn off to Tchermashnya. It won't put you out much to humour your father! If I hadn't had something to keep me here, I would have run over myself long ago, for I've some business there, in a hurry. But here I . . . it's not the time for me to go now . . . You see, I've two pieces of copse land there. The Maslovs, an old merchant and his son, will give eight thousand for the timber. But last year I just missed a purchaser who would have given twelve. There's no getting anyone about here to buy it. The Maslovs have it all their own way. One has to take what they'll give, for no one here dare bid against them. The priest at Ilyinskoe wrote to me last Thursday that a merchant called Gorstkin, a man I know, had turned up. What makes him valuable is that he is not from these parts, so he is not afraid of the Maslovs. He says he will give me eleven thousand for the copse. Do you hear? But he'll only be here, the priest writes, for a week altogether, so you must go at once and make a bargain with him."

"Well, you write to the priest; he'll make the bargain."

285

"He can't do it. He has no eye for business. He is a perfect treasure, I'd give him twenty thousand to take care of for me without a receipt; but he has no eye for business, he is a perfect child, a crow could deceive him. And yet he is a learned man, would you believe it? This Gorstkin looks like a peasant, he wears a blue kaftan, but he is a regular rogue. That's the common complaint. He is a liar. Sometimes he tells such lies that you wonder why he is doing it. He told me the year before last that his wife was dead and that he had married another, and would you believe it, there was not a word of truth in it? His wife has never died at all, she is alive to this day and gives him a beating twice a week. So what you have to find out is whether he is lying or speaking the truth, when he says he wants to buy it and would give eleven thousand."

"I shall be no use in such a business. I have no eye either."

"Stay, wait a bit! You will be of use, for I will tell you the signs by which you can judge about Gorstkin. I've done business with him a long time. You see, you must watch his beard; he has a nasty, thin, red beard. If his beard shakes when he talks and he gets cross, it's all right, he is saying what he means, he wants to do business. But if he strokes his beard with his left hand and grins—he is trying to cheat you. Don't watch his eyes, you won't find out anything from his eyes, he is a deep one, a rogue—but watch his beard! I'll give you a note and you show it to him. He's called Gorstkin, though his real name is Lyagavy*, but don't call him so, he will be offended. If you come to an understanding with him, and see it's all right, write here at once. You need only write: 'He's not lying.' Stand out for eleven thousand; one thousand you can knock off, but not more. Just think! there's a difference between eight thousand and eleven thousand. It's as good as picking up three thousand; it's not so easy to find a purchaser, and I'm in desperate need of money. Only let me know it's serious, and I'll run over and fix it up. I'll snatch the time somehow. But what's the good of my galloping over if it's all a notion of the priest's? Come, will you go?"

"Oh, I can't spare the time. You must excuse me."

"Come, you might oblige your father. I shan't forget it. You've no heart, any of you—that's what it is! What's a day or two to you? Where are you going now—to Venice? Your Venice will keep another two days. I would have sent Alyosha, but what use is Alyosha in a thing like that? I send you just

* *i.e.*, setter dog.

because you are a clever fellow. Do you suppose I don't see that? You know nothing about timber, but you've got an eye. All that is wanted is to see whether the man is in earnest. I tell you, watch his beard—if his beard shakes you know he is in earnest.''

"You force me to go to that damned Tchermashnya yourself, then?'' cried Ivan, with a malignant smile.

Fyodor Pavlovitch did not catch, or would not catch, the malignancy, but he caught the smile.

"Then you'll go, you'll go? I'll scribble the note for you at once.''

"I don't know whether I shall go. I don't know. I'll decide on the way.''

"Nonsense! Decide at once. My dear fellow, decide! If you settle the matter, write me a line; give it to the priest and he'll send it on to me at once. And I won't delay you more than that. You can go to Venice. The priest will give you horses back to Volovya station.''

The old man was quite delighted. He wrote the note, and sent for the horses. A light lunch was brought in, with brandy. When Fyodor Pavlovitch was pleased he usually became expansive, but to-day he seemed to restrain himself. Of Dmitri, for instance, he did not say a word. He was quite unmoved by the parting, and seemed, in fact, at a loss for something to say. Ivan noticed this particularly. "He must be bored with me,'' he thought. Only when accompanying his son out to the steps, the old man began to fuss about. He would have kissed him, but Ivan made haste to hold out his hand, obviously avoiding the kiss. His father saw it at once, and instantly pulled himself up.

"Well, good luck to you, good luck to you!'' he repeated from the steps. "You'll come again some time or other? Mind you do come. I shall always be glad to see you. Well, Christ be with you!''

Ivan got into the carriage.

"Good-bye, Ivan! Don't be too hard on me!'' the father called for the last time.

The whole household came out to take leave—Smerdyakov, Marfa and Grigory. Ivan gave them ten roubles each. When he had seated himself in the carriage, Smerdyakov jumped up to arrange the rug.

"You see . . . I am going to Tchermashnya,'' broke suddenly from Ivan. Again, as the day before, the words seemed to drop of themselves, and he laughed, too, a peculiar, nervous laugh. He remembered it long after.

"It's a true saying then, that 'it's always worth while speaking to a clever man'," answered Smerdyakov firmly, looking significantly at Ivan.

The carriage rolled away. Nothing was clear in Ivan's soul, but he looked eagerly around him at the fields, at the hills, at the trees, at a flock of geese flying high overhead in the bright sky. And all of a sudden he felt very happy. He tried to talk to the driver, and he felt intensely interested in an answer the peasant made him; but a minute later he realised that he was not catching anything, and that he had not really even taken in the peasant's answer. He was silent, and it was pleasant even so. The air was fresh, pure and cool, the sky bright. The images of Alyosha and Katerina Ivanovna floated into his mind. But he softly smiled, blew softly on the friendly phantoms, and they flew away. "There's plenty of time for them," he thought. They reached the station quickly, changed horses, and galloped to Volovya. "Why is it worth while speaking to a clever man? What did he mean by that?" The thought seemed suddenly to clutch at his breathing. "And why did I tell him I was going to Tchermashnya?" They reached Volovya station. Ivan got out of the carriage, and the drivers stood round him bargaining over the journey of twelve versts to Tchermashnya. He told them to harness the horses. He went into the station house, looked round, glanced at the overseer's wife, and suddenly went back to the entrance.

"I won't go to Tchermashnya. Am I too late to reach the railway by seven, brothers?"

"We shall just do it. Shall we get the carriage out?"

"At once. Will any one of you be going to the town to-morrow?"

"To be sure. Mitri here will."

"Can you do me a service, Mitri? Go to my father's, to Fyodor Pavlovitch Karamazov, and tell him I haven't gone to Tchermashnya. Can you?"

"Of course I can. I've known Fyodor Pavlovitch a long time."

"And here's something for you, for I dare say he won't give you anything," said Ivan, laughing gaily.

"You may depend on it he won't." Mitri laughed too. "Thank you, sir. I'll be sure to do it."

At seven o'clock Ivan got into the train and set off for

Moscow. "Away with the past. I've done with the old world for ever, and may I have no news, no echo, from it. To a new life, new places, and no looking back!" But instead of delight his soul was filled with such gloom, and his heart ached with such anguish, as he had never known in his life before. He was thinking all the night. The train flew on, and only at daybreak, when he was approaching Moscow, he suddenly aroused himself from his meditation.

"I am a scoundrel," he whispered to himself.

Fyodor Pavlovitch remained well satisfied at having seen his son off. For two hours afterwards he felt almost happy, and sat drinking brandy. But suddenly something happened which was very annoying and unpleasant for everyone in the house, and completely upset Fyodor Pavlovitch's equanimity at once. Smerdyakov went to the cellar for something and fell down from the top of the steps. Fortunately, Marfa Ignatyevna was in the yard and heard him in time. She did not see the fall, but heard his scream—the strange, peculiar scream, long familiar to her—the scream of the epileptic falling in a fit. They could not tell whether the fit had come on him at the moment he was descending the steps, so that he must have fallen unconscious, or whether it was the fall and the shock that had caused the fit in Smerdyakov, who was known to be liable to them. They found him at the bottom of the cellar steps, writhing in convulsions and foaming at the mouth. It was thought at first that he must have broken something—an arm or a leg—and hurt himself, but "God had preserved him", as Marfa Ignatyevna expressed it—nothing of the kind had happened. But it was difficult to get him out of the cellar. They asked the neighbours to help and managed it somehow. Fyodor Pavlovitch himself was present at the whole ceremony. He helped, evidently alarmed and upset. The sick man did not regain consciousness; the convulsions ceased for a time, but then began again, and everyone concluded that the same thing would happen, as had happened a year before, when he accidentally fell from the garret. They remembered that ice had been put on his head then. There was still ice in the cellar, and Marfa Ignatyevna had some brought up. In the evening Fyodor Pavlovitch sent for Doctor Herzenstube, who arrived at once. He was a most estimable old man, and the most careful and conscientious doctor in the province. After careful examination, he concluded that the fit was a very violent one and might have serious consequences; that meanwhile he,

289

Herzenstube, did not fully undersand it, but that by to-morrow morning, if the present remedies were unavailing, he would venture to try something else. The invalid was taken to the lodge, to a room next to Grigory's and Marfa Ignatyevna's.

Then Fyodor Pavlovitch had one misfortune after another to put up with that day. Marfa Ignatyevna cooked the dinner, and the soup, compared with Smerdyakov's, was no "better than dishwater", and the fowl was so dried up that it was impossible to masticate it. To her master's bitter though deserved reproaches, Marfa Ignatyevna replied that the fowl was a very old one, to begin with, and that she had never been trained as a cook. In the evening there was another trouble in store for Fyodor Pavlovitch; he was informed that Grigory, who had not been well for the last three days, was completely laid up by his lumbago. Fyodor Pavlovitch finished his tea as early as possible and locked himself up alone in the house. He was in terrible excitement and suspense. That evening he reckoned on Grushenka's coming almost as a certainty. He had received from Smerdyakov that morning an assurance "that she had promised to come without fail". The incorrigible old man's heart throbbed with excitement; he paced up and down his empty rooms listening. He had to be on the alert. Dmitri might be on the watch for her somewhere, and when she knocked on the window (Smerdyakov had informed him two days before that he had told her where and how to knock) the door must be opened at once. She must not be a second in the passage, for fear—which God forbid!—that she should be frightened and run away. Fyodor Pavlovitch had much to think of, but never had his heart been steeped in such voluptuous hopes. This time he could say almost certainly that she would come!

BOOK VI: THE RUSSIAN MONK

CHAPTER I

FATHER ZOSSIMA AND HIS VISITORS

WHEN with an anxious and aching heart Alyosha went into his elder's cell, he stood still almost astonished. Instead of a sick man at his last gasp, perhaps unconscious, as he had feared to find him, he saw him sitting up in his chair and, though weak and exhausted, his face was bright and cheerful, he was surrounded by visitors and engaged in a quiet and joyful conversation. But he had only got up from his bed a quarter of an hour before Alyosha's arrival; his visitors had gathered together in his cell earlier, waiting for him to wake, having received a most confident assurance from Father Païssy that "the teacher would get up, and as he had himself promised in the morning, converse once more with those dear to his heart". This promise and indeed every word of the dying elder's Father Païssy put implicit trust in. If he had seen him unconscious, if he had seen him breathe his last, and yet had his promise that he would rise up and say good-bye to him, he would not have believed perhaps even in death, but would still have expected the dead man to recover and fulfil his promise. In the morning, as he lay down to sleep, Father Zossima had told him positively: "I shall not die without the delight of another conversation with you, beloved of my heart. I shall look once more on your dear faces and pour out my heart to you once again." The monks, who had gathered for this probably last conversation with Father Zossima, had all been his devoted friends for many yesars. There were four of them: Father Iosif and Father Païssy, Father Mihaïl, the warden of the hermitage, a man not very old and far from being learned. He was of humble origin, of strong will and steadfast faith, of austere appearance, but of deep tenderness, though he obviously concealed it as though he were almost ashamed of it. The fourth, Father Anfim, was a very old and humble little monk of the poorest peasant class. He was almost illiterate, and very quiet, scarcely speaking to anyone. He was the humblest of the humble, and looked as though he had been frightened by something great and awful beyond the scope of his intelligence. Father Zossima had a great affection for this timorous man, and always treated him with marked respect, though perhaps there was no one he had known to whom he had said less, in spite of the fact that he had spent years wandering about holy Russia with him. That was very long ago, forty years before, when Father Zossima first began his life as a monk in a poor and little monastery at Kostroma, and when, shortly after, he had accompanied Father Anfim on his pilgrimage to collect alms for their poor monastery.

The whole party were in the bedroom which, as we mentioned before, was very small, so that there was scarcely room for the four of them (in addition to Porfiry, the novice, who stood) to sit round Father Zossima on chairs brought from the sitting-room. It was already beginning to get dark, the room was lighted up by the lamps and the candles before the ikons.

Seeing Aloysha standing embarrassed in the doorway, Father Zossima smiled at him joyfully and held out his hand.

"Welcome, my quiet one, welcome, my dear, here you are too. I knew you would come."

Alyosha went up to him, bowed down before him to the ground and wept. Something surged up from his heart, his soul was quivering, he wanted to sob.

"Come, don't weep over me yet," Father Zossima smiled, laying his right hand on his head. "You see I am sitting up talking; maybe I shall live another twenty years yet, as that dear good woman from Vishegorye, with her little Lizaveta in her arms, wished me yesterday. God bless the mother and the little girl Lizaveta." He crossed himself. "Porfiry, did you take her offering where I told you?"

He meant the sixty copecks brought him the day before by the good-humoured woman to be given "to someone poorer than me". Such offerings, always of money gained by personal toil, are made by way of penance voluntarily undertaken. The elder had sent Porfiry the evening before to a widow, whose house had been burnt down lately, and who after the fire had gone with her children begging alms. Porfiry hastened "to reply that he had given the money, as he had been instructed, from an unknown benefactress"

"Get up, my dear boy," the elder went on to Alyosha. "Let me look at you. Have you been home and seen your brother?" It seemed strange to Alyosha that he asked so confidently and precisely about one of his brothers only—but which one? Then perhaps he had sent him out both yesterday and to-day for the sake of that brother.

"I have seen one of my brothers," answered Alyosha.

"I mean the elder one, to whom I bowed down."

"I only saw him yesterday and could not find him to-day," said Alyosha.

"Make haste to find him, go again to-morrow and make haste, leave everything and make haste. Perhaps you may still have time to prevent something terrible. I bowed down yesterday to the great' suffering in store for him."

He was suddenly silent and seemed to be pondering. The words were strange. Father Iosif, who had witnessed the scene yesterday, exchanged glances with Father Païssy. Alyosha could not resist asking:

"Father and teacher," he began with extreme emotion, "your words are too obscure. . . . What is this suffering in store for him?"

"Don't inquire. I seemed to see something terrible yesterday . . . as though his whole future were expressed in his eyes. A look came into his eyes—so that I was instantly horror-stricken at what that man is preparing for himself. Once or twice in my life I've seen such a look in a man's face . . . reflecting, as it were, his future fate, and that fate, alas, came to pass. I sent you to him, Alexey, for I thought your brotherly face would help him. But everything and all our fates are from the Lord. 'Except a corn of wheat fall into the ground and die, it abideth alone; but if it die, it bringeth forth much fruit.' Remember that. You, Alexey, I've many times silently blessed for your face, know that," added the elder with a gentle smile. "This is what I think of you, you will go forth from these walls, but will live like a monk in the world. You will have many enemies, but even your foes will love you. Life will bring you many misfortunes, but you will find your happiness in them, and will bless life and make others bless it—which is what matters most. Well, that is your character. Fathers and teachers," he addressed his friends with a tender smile, "I have never till to-day told even him why the face of this youth is so dear to me. Now I will tell you. His face has been, as it were, a remembrance and a prophecy for me. At the dawn of my life when I was a child I had an elder brother who died before my eyes at seventeen. And later on in the course of my life I gradually became convinced that that brother had been for a guidance and a sign on high for me. For had he not come into my life I should never, perhaps, so I fancy at least, have became a monk and entered on this precious path. He appeared first to me in my childhood and here, at the end of my pilgrimage, he seems to have come to me over again. It is marvellous, fathers and teachers, that Alexey, who has some, though not a great, resemblance in face, seems to me so like him spiritually, that many times I have taken him for that young man, my brother, mysteriously come back to me at the end of my pilgrimage, as a reminder and an inspiration. So that I positively wondered at so strange a dream in myself. Do you hear this, Porfiry?" he turned to the novice who waited on him. "Many times I've seen in your face, as it were, a look

293

of mortification that I love Alexey more than you. Now you know why that was so, but I love you too, know that, and many times I grieved at your mortification. I should like to tell you, dear friends, of that youth, my brother, for there has been no presence in my life more precious, more significant and touching. My heart is full of tenderness, and I look at my whole life at this moment as though living through it again.''

Here I must observe that this last conversation of Father Zossima with the friends who visited him on the last day of his life has been partly preserved in writing. Alexey Fyodorovitch Karamazov wrote it down from memory, some time after his elder's death. But whether this was only the conversation that took place then, or whether he added to it his notes or parts of former conversations with his teacher, I cannot determine. In his account, Father Zossima's talk goes on without interruption, as though he told his life to his friends in the form of a story, though there is no doubt, from other accounts of it, that the conversation that evening was general. Though the guests did not interrupt Father Zossima much, yet they too talked, perhaps even told something themselves. Besides, Father Zossima could not have carried on an uninterrupted narrative, for he was sometimes gasping for breath, his voice failed him, and he even lay down to rest on his bed, though he did not fall asleep and his visitors did not leave their seats. Once or twice the conversation was interrupted by Father Païssy's reading the Gospel. It is worthy of note, too, that not one of them supposed that he would die that night, for on that evening of his life after his deep sleep in the day he seemed suddenly to have found new strength, which kept him up through this long conversation. It was like a last effort of love which gave him marvellous energy; only for a little time, however, for his life was cut short immediately. . . . But of that later. I will only add now that I have preferred to confine myself to the account given by Alexey Fyodorovitch Karamazov. It will be shorter and not so fatiguing, though of course, as I must repeat, Alyosha took a great deal from previous conversations and added them to it.

Notes of the Life of the deceased Priest and Monk, the Elder Zossima, taken from his own words by Alexey Fyodorovitch Karamazov.

BIOGRAPHICAL NOTES

(a) *Father Zossima's Brother*

Beloved fathers and teachers, I was born in a distant province in the north, in the town of V. My father was a gentleman by birth, but of no great consequence or position. He died when I was only two years old, and I don't remember him at all. He left my mother a small house built of wood, and a fortune, not large but sufficient to keep her and her children in comfort. There were two of us, my elder brother Markel and I. He was eight years older than I was, of hasty irritable temperament, but kind-hearted and never ironical. He was remarkably silent, especially at home with me, his mother, and the servants. He did well at school, but did not get on with his school-fellows, though he never quarrelled, at least so my mother has told me. Six months before his death, when he was seventeen, he made friends with a political exile who had been banished from Moscow to our town for freethinking, and led a solitary exist-ence there. He was a good scholar who had gained distinction in philosophy in the university. Something made him take a fancy to Markel, and he used to ask him to see him. The young man would spend whole evenings with him during that winter, till the exile was summoned to Petersburg to take up his post again at his own request, as he had powerful friends.

It was the beginning of Lent, and Markel would not fast, he was rude and laughed at it. "That's all sillly twaddle and there is no God," he said, horrifying my mother, the servants, and me too. For though I was only nine, I too was aghast at hear-ing such words. We had four servants, all serfs. I remember my mother selling one of the four, the cook Afimya, who was lame and elderly, for sixty paper roubles, and hiring a free servant to take her place.

In the sixth week in Lent, my brother, who was never strong and had a tendency to consumption, was taken ill. He was tall but thin and delicate-looking, and of very pleasing counten-ance. I suppose he caught cold, anyway the doctor, who came, soon whispered to my mother that it was galloping consump-tion, that he would not live through the spring. My mother began weeping, and careful not to alarm my brother she entreated him to go to church, to confess and take the sacra-ment, as he was still able to move about. This made him angry, and he said something profane about the church. He grew thoughtful, however; he guessed at once that he was seriously ill, and that that was why his mother was begging him to confess and take the sacrament. He had been aware, indeed, for a long time past, that he was far from well, and had a year before coolly observed at dinner to our mother and me: "My life won't be long among you, I may not live another year," which seemed now like a prophecy.

Three days passed and Holy Week had come. And on Tuesday morning my brother began going to church. "I am doing this simply for your sake, mother, to please and comfort you," he said. My mother wept with joy and grief, "his end must be near," she thought, "if there's such a change in him". But he was not able to go to church long, he took to his bed, so he had to confess and take the sacrament at home.

It was a late Easter, and the days were bright, fine, and full of fragrance. I remember he used to cough all night and sleep badly, but in the morning he dressed and tried to sit up in an arm-chair. That's how I remember him sitting, sweet and gentle, smiling, his face bright and joyous, in spite of his illness. A marvellous change passed over him, his spirit seemed transformed. The old nurse would come in and say: "Let me light the lamp before the holy image, my dear." And once he would not have allowed it and would have blown it out.

"Light it, light it, dear. I was a wretch to have prevented you doing it. You are praying when you light the lamp, and I am praying when I rejoice seeing you. So we are praying to the same God."

Those words seemed strange to us, and mother would go to her room and weep, but when she went in to him she wiped her eyes and looked cheerful. "Mother, don't weep, darling," he would say, "I've long to live yet, long to rejoice with you, and life is glad and joyful."

"Ah, dear boy, how can you talk of joy when you lie feverish at night, coughing as though you would tear yourself to pieces."

"Don't cry, mother," he would answer, "life is paradise, and we are all in paradise, but we won't see it, if we would, we should have heaven on earth the next day."

Everyone wondered at his words, he spoke so strangely and positively; we were all touched and wept. Friends came to see us. "Dear ones," he would say to them, "what have I done that you should love me so? How can you love anyone like me, and how was it I did not know? I did not appreciate it before."

When the servants came in to him he would say continually: "Dear, kind people, why are you doing so much for me, do I deserve to be waited on? If it were God's will for me to live, I would wait on you, for all men should wait on one another." Mother shook her head as she listened. "My darling, it's your illness makes you talk like that."

"Mother darling," he would say, "there must be servants and masters, but if so I will be the servant of my servants, the same as they are to me. And another thing, mother, every one of us has sinned against all men, and I more than any."

Mother positively smiled at that, smiled through her tears. "Why, how could you have sinned against all men, more than all? Robbers and murderers have done that, but what sin have you committed yet, that you hold yourself more guilty than all?"

"Mother, little heart of mine," he said (he had begun using such strange caressing words at that time), "little heart of mine, my joy, believe me, everyone is really responsible to all men for all men and for everything. I don't know how to explain it to you, but I feel it is so, painfully even. And how is it we went on then living, getting angry and not knowing?"

So he would get up every day, more and more sweet and joyous and full of love. When the doctor, an old German called Eisenschmidt, came:

"Well, doctor, have I another day in this world?" he would ask, jokingly.

"You'll live many days yet," the doctor would answer, "and months and years too."

"Months and years!" he would exclaim. "Why reckon the days? One day is enough for a man to know all happiness. My dear ones, why do we quarrel, try to outshine each other and keep grudges against each other? Let's go straight into the garden, walk and play there, love, appreciate, and kiss each other, and glorify life."

"Your son cannot last long," the doctor told my mother, as she accompanied him to the door. "The disease is affecting his brain."

The windows of his room looked out into the garden, and our garden was a shady one, with old trees in it which were coming into bud. The first birds of spring were flitting in the branches, chirruping and singing at the windows. And looking at them and admiring them, he began suddenly begging their forgiveness too: "Birds of heaven, happy birds, forgive me,

297

for I have sinned against you too." None of us could understand that at the time, but he shed tears of joy. "Yes," he
said, "there was such a glory of God all about me; birds, trees,
meadows, sky, only I lived in shame and dishonoured it all
and did not notice the beauty and glory."

"You take too many sins on yourself," mother used to say,
weeping.

"Mother darling, it's for joy, not for grief I am crying.
Though I can't explain it to you, I like to humble myself
before them, for I don't know how to love them enough. If I
have sinned against everyone, yet all forgive me, too, and
that's heaven. Am I not in heaven now?"

And there was a great deal more I don't remember. I remember I went once into his room when there was no one else
there. It was a bright evening, the sun was setting, and the
whole room was lighted up. He beckoned me, and I went up
to him. He put his hands on my shoulders and looked into my
face tenderly, lovingly; he said nothing for a minute, only
looked at me like that.

"Well," he said, "run and play now, enjoy life for me
too."

I went out then and ran to play. And many times in my life
afterwards I remembered even with tears how he told me to
enjoy life for him too. There were many other marvellous and
beautiful sayings of his, though we did not understand them at
the time. He died the third week after Easter. He was fully
conscious, though he could not talk; up to his last hour he did
not change. He looked happy, his eyes beamed and sought us,
he smiled at us, beckoned us. There was a great deal of talk
even in the town about his death. I was impressed by all this
at the time, but not too much so, though I cried a great deal
at his funeral. I was young then, a child, but a lasting impression, a hidden feeling of it all, remained in my heart, ready
to rise up and respond when the time came. So indeed it
happened.

(b) Of the Holy Scriptures in the life of Father Zossima

I was left alone with my mother. Her friends began advising
her to send me to Petersburg as other parents did. "You have
only one son now," they said, "and have a fair income, and
you will be depriving him perhaps of a brilliant career if you
keep him here." They suggested I should be sent to Petersburg
to the Cadet Corps, that I might afterwards enter the Imperial

Guard. My mother hesitated for a long time, it was awful to part with her only child, but she made up her mind to it at last, though not without many tears, believing she was acting for my happiness. She brought me to Petersburg and put me into the Cadet Corps, and I never saw her again. For she too died three years afterwards. She spent those three years mourning and grieving for both of us.

From the house of my childhood I have brought nothing but precious memories, for there are no memories more precious than those of early childhood in one's first home. And that is almost always so if there is any love and harmony in the family at all. Indeed, precious memories may remain even of a bad home, if only the heart knows how to find what is precious. With my memories of home I count, too, my memories of the Bible, which, child as I was, I was very eager to read at home. I had a book of Scripture history then with excellent pictures, called "A Hundred and Four Stories from the Old and New Testament", and I learned to read from it. I have it lying on my shelf now, I keep it as a precious relic of the past. But even before I learned to read, I remember first being moved to devotional feeling at eight years old. My mother took me alone to mass (I don't remember where my brother was at the time) on the Monday before Easter. It was a fine day, and I remember to-day, as though I saw it now, how the incense rose from the censer and softly floated upwards and, overhead in the cupola, mingled in rising waves with the sunlight that streamed in at the little window. I was stirred by the sight, and for the first time in my life I consciously received the seed of God's word in my heart. A youth came out into the middle of the church carrying a big book, so large that at the time I fancied he could scarcely carry it. He laid it on the reading desk, opened it, and began reading, and suddenly for the first time I understood something read in the church of God. In the land of Uz there lived a man, righteous and God-fearing, and he had great wealth, so many camels, so many sheep and asses, and his children feasted, and he loved them very much and prayed for them. "It may be that my sons have sinned in their feasting." Now the devil came before the Lord together with the sons of God, and said to the Lord that he had gone up and down the earth and under the earth. "And hast thou considered my servant Job?" God asked of him. And God boasted to the devil, pointing to his great and holy servant. And the devil laughed at God's words. "Give him over to me and Thou wilt see that Thy servant will murmur against Thee and curse Thy name." And God gave up the just man He loved so, to the devil. And the devil smote his children and his cattle and scattered his wealth, all of a sudden like a thunderbolt from heaven. And Job rent his mantle and fell down upon the ground and cried aloud: "Naked came I out of my mother's womb, and naked shall I return into the earth; the Lord gave and the Lord has taken away. Blessed be the name of the Lord for ever and ever."

Fathers and teachers, forgive my tears now, for all my childhood rises up again before me, and I breathe now as I breathed then, with the breast of a little child of eight, and I feel as I did then, awe and wonder and gladness. The camels at that time caught my imagination, and Satan, who talked like that with God, and God who gave His servant up to destruction, and His servant crying out: "Blessed be Thy name although Thou dost punish me," and then the soft and sweet singing in the church: "Let my prayer rise up before Thee," and again incense from the priest's censer and the kneeling and the prayer. Ever since then—only yesterday I took it up— I've never been able to read that sacred tale without tears. And how much that is great, mysterious and unfathomable there is in it! Afterwards I heard the words of mockery and blame, proud words: "How could God give up the most loved of His saints for the diversion of the devil, take from him his children, smite him with sore boils so that he cleansed the corruption from his sores with a potsherd—and for no object except to boast to the devil! 'See what My saint can suffer for My sake.'" But the greatness of it lies just in the fact that it is a mystery—that the passing earthly show and the eternal verity are brought together in it. In the face of the earthly truth, the eternal truth is accomplished. The Creator, just as on the first days of creation He ended each day with praise: "that is good that I have created," looks upon Job and again praises His creation. And Job, praising the Lord, serves not only Him but all His creation for generations and generations, and for ever and ever, since for that he was ordained. Good heavens, what a book it is, and what lessons there are in it! What a book the Bible is, what a miracle, what strength is given with it to man. It is like a mould cast of the world and man and human nature, everything is there, and a law for everything for all the ages. And what mysteries are solved and revealed; God raises Job again, gives him wealth again. Many years pass by, and he has other children and loves them. But how could he love those new ones when those first children are no more, when he has lost them? Remembering them, how could he be fully happy with those new ones, however dear the new ones might be? But he could, he could. It's the great mystery of human life that old grief passes gradually into quiet tender joy. The mild serenity of age takes the place of the riotous blood of youth. I bless the rising sun each day, and, as before, my heart sings to meet it, but now I love even more its setting, its long slanting rays and the soft tender gentle memories that come with them, the dear images from the whole of my long happy life—and over all the Divine Truth, softening, reconciling, forgiving! My life is ending, I knew that well, but every day that is left me I feel how my earthly life is in touch with a new infinite, unknown, but approaching life, the nearness of which sets my soul quivering with rapture, my mind glowing and my heart weeping with joy.

Friends and teachers, I have heard more than once, and of late one may hear it more often, that the priests, and above all the village priests, are complaining on all sides of their miserable income and their humiliating lot. They plainly state, even in print—I've read it myself—that they are unable to teach the Scriptures to the people because of the smallness of their means, and if Lutherans and heretics come and lead the flock astray, they let them lead them astray because they have so little to live upon. May the Lord increase the sustenance that is so precious to them, for their complaint is just, too. But of a truth I say, if anyone is to blame in the matter, half the fault is ours. For he may be short of time, he may say truly that he is overwhelmed all the while with work and services, but still it's not all the time, even he has an hour a week to remember God. And he does not work the whole year round. Let him gather round him once a week, some hour in the evening, if only the children at first—the fathers will hear of it and they too will begin to come. There's no need to build halls for this, let him take them into his own cottage. They won't spoil his cottage, they would only be there one hour. Let him open that book and begin reading it without grand words or superciliousness, without condescension to them, but gently and kindly, being glad that he is reading to them and that they are listening with attention, loving the words himself, only stop-

301

ping from time to time to explain words that are not understood by the peasants. Don't be anxious, they will understand
everything, the orthodox heart will understand all! Let him
read them about Abraham and Sarah, about Isaac and Rebecca,
of how Jacob went to Laban and wrestled with the Lord
in his dream and said: "This place is holy"—and he will
impress the devout mind of the peasant. Let him read,
especially to the children, how the brothers sold Joseph, the
tender boy, the dreamer and prophet, into bondage, and told
their father that a wild beast had devoured him, and showed
him his blood-stained clothes. Let him read them how the
brothers afterwards journeyed into Egypt for corn, and Joseph,
already a great ruler, unrecognised by them, tormented them,
accused them, kept his brother Benjamin, and all through love:
"I love you, and loving you I torment you." For he remembered all his life how they had sold him to the merchants in
the burning desert by the well, and how, wringing his hands, he
had wept and besought his brothers not to sell him as a slave
in a strange land. And how, seeing them again after many
years, he loved them beyond measure, but he harassed and tormented them in love. He left them at last not able to bear the
suffering of his heart, flung himself on his bed and wept. Then,
wiping his tears away, he went out to them joyful and told
them: "Brothers, I am your brother Joseph!" Let him read
them further how happy old Jacob was on learning that his
darling boy was still alive, and how he went to Egypt, leaving
his own country, and died in a foreign land, bequeathing his
great prophecy that had lain mysteriously hidden in his meek
and timid heart all his life, that from his offspring, from Judah,
will come the great hope of the world, the Messiah and Saviour.

Fathers and teachers, forgive me and don't be angry, that
like a little child I've been babbling of what you know long
ago, and can teach me a hundred times more skilfully. I only
speak from rapture, and forgive my tears, for I love the Bible.
Let him too weep, the priest of God, and be sure that the
hearts of his listeners will throb in response. Only a little tiny
seed is needed—drop it into the heart of the peasant and it
don't die, it will live in his soul all his life, it will be hidden
in the midst of his darkness and sin, like a bright spot, like a
great reminder. And there's no need of much teaching or
explanation, he will understand it all simply. Do you suppose
that the peasants don't understand? Try reading them the
touching story of the fair Esther and the haughty Vashti; or

the miraculous story of Jonah in the whale. Don't forget either the parables of Our Lord, choose especially from the Gospel of St. Luke (that is what I did) and then from the Acts of the Apostles the conversion of St. Paul (that you mustn't leave out on any account), and from the Lives of the Saints, for instance, the life of Alexey, the man of God and, greatest of all, the happy martyr and the seer of God, Mary of Egypt—and you will penetrate their hearts with these simple tales. Give one hour a week to it in spite of your poverty, only one little hour. And you will see for yourself that our people is gracious and grateful, and will repay you a hundredfold. Mindful of the kindness of their priest and the moving words they have heard from him, they will of their own accord help him in his fields and in his house, and will treat him with more respect than before—so that it will even increase his worldly well-being too. The thing is so simple that sometimes one is even afraid to put it into words, for fear of being laughed at, and yet how true it is! One who does not believe in God will not believe in God's people. He who believes in God's people will see His Holiness too, even though he had not believed in it till then. Only the people and their future spiritual power will convert our atheists, who have torn themselves away from their native soil.

And what is the use of Christ's words, unless we set an example? The people is lost without the Word of God, for its soul is athirst for the Word and for all that is good.

In my youth, long ago, nearly forty years ago, I travelled all over Russia with Father Anfim, collecting funds for our monastery, and we stayed one night on the bank of a great navigable river with some fishermen. A good-looking peasant lad, about eighteen, joined us; he had to hurry back next morning to pull a merchant's barge along the bank. I noticed him looking straight before him with clear and tender eyes. It was a bright, warm, still July night, a cool mist rose from the broad river, we could hear the plash of a fish, the birds were still, all was hushed and beautiful, everything praying to God. Only we two were not sleeping, the lad and I, and we talked of the beauty of this world of God's and of the great mystery of it. Every blade of grass, every insect, ant, and golden bee, all so marvellously know their path, though they have not intelligence, they bear witness to the mystery of God and continually accomplish it themselves. I saw the dear lad's heart was moved. He told me that he loved the forest and the forest birds. He was a bird-catcher, knew the note of each of them, could call

303

each bird. "I know nothing better than to be in the forest,"
said he, "though all things are good."

"Truly," I answered him, "all things are good and fair,
because all is truth. Look," said I, "at the horse, that great
beast that is so near to man; or the lowly, pensive ox, which
feeds him and works for him; look at their faces, what meekness, what devotion to man, who often beats them mercilessly. What gentleness, what confidence and what beauty!
It's touching to know that there's no sin in them, for all,
all except man, is sinless, and Christ has been with them
before us."

"Why," asked the boy, "is Christ with them too?"

"It cannot but be so," said I, "since the Word is for all. All
creation and all creatures, every leaf is striving to the Word,
singing glory to God, weeping to Christ, unconsciously accom-
plishing this by the mystery of their sinless life. Yonder," said
I, "in the forest wanders the dreadful bear, fierce and menacing,
and yet innocent in it." And I told him how once a bear came
to a great saint who had taken refuge in a tiny cell in the wood.
And the great saint pitied him, went up to him without fear
and gave him a piece of bread. "Go along," said he, "Christ
be with you," and the savage beast walked away meekly and
obediently, doing no harm. And the lad was delighted that the
bear had walked away without hurting the saint, and that
Christ was with him too. "Ah," said he, "how good that is,
how good and beautiful is all God's work!" He sat musing
softly and sweetly. I saw he understood. And he slept beside
me a light and sinless sleep. May God bless youth! And I
prayed for him as I went to sleep. Lord, send peace and light
to Thy people!

CHAPTER II

(c) Recollections of Father Zossima's youth before he became a monk. The duel

I SPENT a long time, almost eight years, in the military
cadet school at Petersburg, and in the novelty of my surroundings there, many of my childish impressions grew dimmer,
though I forgot nothing. I picked up so many new habits and
opinions that I was transformed into a cruel, absurd, almost
savage creature. A surface polish of courtesy and society

manners I did acquire together with the French language.

But we all, myself included, looked upon the soldiers in our service as cattle. I was perhaps worse than the rest in that respect, for I was so much more impressionable than my companions. By the time we left the school as officers, we were ready to lay down our lives for the honour of the regiment, but no one of us had any knowledge of the real meaning of honour, and if anyone had known it, he would have been the first to ridicule it. Drunkenness, debauchery and devilry were what we almost prided ourselves on. I don't say that we were bad by nature, all these young men were good fellows, but they behaved badly, and I worst of all. What made it worse for me was that I had come into my own money, and so I flung myself into a life of pleasure, and plunged headlong into all the recklessness of youth.

I was fond of reading, yet, strange to say, the Bible was the one book I never opened at that time, though I always carried it about with me, and I was never separated from it; in very truth I was keeping that book "for the day and the hour, for the month and the year", though I knew it not.

After four years of this life, I chanced to be in the town of K. where our regiment was stationed at the time. We found the people of the town hospitable, rich and fond of entertainments. I met with a cordial reception everywhere, as I was of a lively temperament and was known to be well off, which always goes a long way in the world. And then a circumstance happened which was the beginning of it all.

I formed an attachment to a beautiful and intelligent young girl of noble and lofty character, the daughter of people much respected. They were well-to-do people of influence and position. They always gave me a cordial and friendly reception. I fancied that the young lady looked on me with favour and my heart was aflame at such an idea. Later on I saw and fully realised that I perhaps was not so passionately in love with her at all, but only recognised the elevation of her mind and character, which I could not indeed have helped doing. I was prevented, however, from making her an offer at the time by my selfishness, I was loth to part with the allurements of my free and licentious bachelor life in the heyday of my youth, and with my pockets full of money. I did drop some hint as to my feelings, however, though I put off taking any decisive step for a time. Then, all of a sudden, we were ordered off for two months to another district.

On my return two months later, I found the young lady already married to a rich neighbouring landowner, a very amiable man, still young though older than I was, connected with the best Petersburg society, which I was not, and of excellent education, which I also was not. I was so overwhelmed at this unexpected circumstance that my mind was positively clouded. The worst of it all was that, as I learned then, the young landowner had been a long while betrothed to her, and I had met him indeed many times in her house, but blinded by my conceit I had noticed nothing. And this particularly mortified me; almost everybody had known all about it, while I knew nothing. I was filled with sudden irrepressible fury. With flushed face I began recalling how often I had been on the point of declaring my love to her, and as she had not attempted to stop me or to warn me, she must, I concluded, have been laughing at me all the time. Later on, of course, I reflected and remembered that she had been very far from laughing at me; on the contrary, she used to turn off any love-making on my part with a jest and begin talking of other subjects; but at that moment I was incapable of reflecting and was all eagerness for revenge. I am surprised to remember that my wrath and revengeful feelings were extremely repugnant to my own nature, for being of an easy temper, I found it difficult to be angry with anyone for long, and so I had to work myself up artificially and became at last revolting and absurd.

I waited for an opportunity and succeeded in insulting my "rival" in the presence of a large company. I insulted him on a perfectly extraneous pretext, jeering at his opinion upon an important public event—it was in the year 1826*—and my jeer was, so people said, clever and effective. Then I forced him to ask for an explanation, and behaved so rudely that he accepted my challenge in spite of the vast inequality between us, as I was younger, a person of no consequence, and of inferior rank. I learned afterwards for a fact that it was from a jealous feeling on his side also that my challenge was accepted; he had been rather jealous of me on his wife's account before their marriage; he fancied now that if he submitted to be insulted by me and refused to accept my challenge, and if she heard of it, she might begin to despise him and waver in her love for him. I soon found a second in a comrade, an ensign of our regiment. In

* Probably the public event was the Decabrist plot against the Tsar, of December 1825, in which the most distinguished men in Russia were concerned.—TRANSLATOR'S NOTE.

those days, though duels were severely punished, yet duelling was a kind of fashion among the officers—so strong and deeply rooted will a brutal prejudice sometimes be.

It was the end of June, and our meeting was to take place at seven o'clock the next day on the outskirts of the town—and then something happened that in very truth was the turning-point of my life. In the evening, returning home in a savage and brutal humour, I flew into a rage with my orderly Afanasy, and gave him two blows in the face with all my might, so that it was covered with blood. He had not long been in my service and I had struck him before, but never with such ferocious cruelty. And, believe me, though it's forty years ago, I recall it now with shame and pain. I went to bed and slept for about three hours; when I waked up the day was breaking. I got up— I did not want to sleep any more—I went to the window— opened it, it looked out upon the garden; I saw the sun rising; it was warm and beautiful, the birds were singing.

What's the meaning of it, I thought, I feel in my heart as it were something vile and shameful? Is it because I am going to shed blood? No, I thought, I feel it's not that. Can it be that I am afraid of death, afraid of being killed? No, that's not it, that's not it at all. . . . And all at once I knew what it was: it was because I had beaten Afanasy the evening before! It all rose before my mind, it all was as it were repeated over again; he stood before me and I was beating him straight on the face and he was holding his arms stiffly down, his head erect, his eyes fixed upon me as though on parade. He staggered at every blow and did not even dare to raise his hands to protect himself. That is what a man has been brought to, and that was a man beating a fellow creature! What a crime! It was as though a sharp dagger had pierced me right through. I stood as if I were struck dumb, while the sun was shining, the leaves were rejoicing and the birds were trilling the praise of God. . . . I hid my face in my hands, fell on my bed and broke into a storm of tears. And then I remembered my brother Markel and what he said on his deathbed to his servants: "My dear ones, why do you wait on me, why do you love me, am I worth your waiting on me?"

Yes, am I worth it? flashed through my mind. After all, what am I worth, that another man, a fellow creature, made in the likeness and image of God, should serve me? For the first time in my life this question forced itself upon me. He had said: "Mother, my little heart, in truth we are each responsible to all for all, it's only that men don't know this. If they knew it, the world would be a paradise at once."

"God, can that too be false?" I thought as I wept, "in truth, perhaps, I am more than all others responsible for all, a greater sinner than all men in the world. And all at once the whole truth in its full light appeared to me: what was I going to do? I was going to kill a good, clever, noble man, who had done me no wrong, and by depriving his wife of happiness for the rest of her life I should be torturing and killing her too. I lay thus in my bed with my face in the pillow, heedless how the time was passing. Suddenly my second, the ensign, came in with the pistols to fetch me.

"Ah," said he, "it's a good thing you are up already, it's time we were off, come along!"

I did not know what to do and hurried to and fro undecided; we went out to the carriage, however.

"Wait here a minute," I said to him. "I'll be back directly, I have forgotten my purse."

And I ran back alone, straight to Afanasy's little room.

"Afanasy," I said, "I gave you two blows on the face yesterday, forgive me," I said.

He started as though he were frightened, and looked at me; and I saw that it was not enough, and on the spot, in my full officer's uniform, I dropped at his feet and bowed my head to the ground.

"Forgive me," I said.

Then he was completely aghast.

"Your honour . . . sir, what are you doing? Am I worth it?"

And he burst out crying as I had done before, hid his face in his hands, turned to the window and shook all over with his sobs. I flew out to my comrade and jumped into the carriage.

"Ready," I cried. "Have you ever seen a conqueror?" I asked him. "Here is one before you."

I was in ecstasy, laughing and talking all the way, I don't remember what about.

He looked at me. "Well, brother, you are a plucky fellow, you'll keep up the honour of the uniform, I can see."

So we reached the place and found them there, awaiting us. We were placed twelve paces apart; he had the first shot. I stood gaily, looking him full in the face; I did not twitch an eyelash, I looked lovingly at him, for I knew what I would do. His shot just grazed my cheek and ear.

"Thank God," I cried, "no man has been killed," and I

seized my pistol, turned back and flung it far away into the wood. "That's the place for you," I cried.

I turned to my adversary.

"Forgive me, young fool that I am, sir," I said, "for my unprovoked insult to you and for forcing you to fire at me. I am ten times worse than you and more, maybe. Tell that to the person whom you hold dearest in the world."

I had no sooner said this than they all three shouted at me.

"Upon my word," cried my adversary, annoyed, "if you did not want to fight, why did not you let me alone?"

"Yesterday I was a fool, to-day I know better," I answered him gaily.

"As to yesterday, I believe you, but as for to-day, it is difficult to agree with your opinion," said he.

"Bravo," I cried, clapping my hands. "I agree with you there too, I have deserved it!"

"Will you shoot, sir, or not?"

"No, I won't," I said. "If you like, fire at me again, but it would be better for you not to fire."

The seconds, especially mine, were shouting too: "Can you disgrace the regiment like this, facing your antagonist and begging his forgiveness? If I'd only known this!"

I stood facing them all, not laughing now.

"Gentlemen," I said, "is it really so wonderful in these days to find a man who can repent of his stupidity and publicly confess his wrong-doing?"

"But not in a duel," cried my second again.

"That's what's so strange," I said. "For I ought to have owned my fault as soon as I got here, before he had fired a shot, before leading him into a great and deadly sin; but we have made our life so grotesque that to act in that way would have been almost impossible, for only after I have faced his shot at the distance of twelve paces could my words have any significance for him, and if I had spoken before, he would have said, 'He is a coward, the sight of the pistols have frightened him, no use to listen to him'. Gentlemen," I cried suddenly, speaking straight from my heart, "look around you at the gifts of God: the clear sky, the pure air, the tender grass, the birds; nature is beautiful and sinless, and we, only we, are sinful and foolish, and we don't understand that life is heaven, for we have only to understand that and it will at once be fulfilled in all its beauty, we shall embrace each other and weep."

I would have said more but I could not; my voice broke

with the sweetness and youthful gladness of it, and there was such bliss in my heart as I had never known before in my life.

"All this is rational and edifying," said my antagonist, "and in any case you are an original person."

"You may laugh," I said to him, laughing too, "but after-wards you will approve of me."

"Oh, I am ready to approve of you now," said he; "will you shake hands, for I believe you are genuinely sincere."

"No," I said, "not now, later on when I have grown worthier and deserve your esteem, then shake hands and you will do well."

We went home, my second upbraiding me all the way, while I kissed him. All my comrades heard of the affair at once and gathered together to pass judgment on me the same day.

"He has disgraced the uniform," they said; "let him resign his commission."

Some stood up for me: "He faced the shot," they said.

"Yes, but he was afraid of his other shot and begged for forgiveness."

"If he had been afraid of being shot he would have shot his own pistol first before asking forgiveness, while he flung it loaded into the forest. No, there's something else in this, something original."

I enjoyed listening and looking at them. "My dear friends and comrades," said I, "don't worry about my resigning my commission, for I have done so already. I have sent in my papers this morning and as soon as I get my discharge I shall go into a monastery—it's with that object I am leaving the regiment."

When I had said this everyone of them burst out laughing.

"You should have told us of that first, that explains everything, we can't judge a monk."

They laughed and could not stop themselves, and not scornfully, but kindly and merrily. They all felt friendly to me at once, even those who had been sternest in their censure, and all the following month, before my discharge came, they could not make enough of me. "Ah, you monk," they would say. And everyone said something kind to me, they began trying to dissuade me, even to pity me: "What are you doing to yourself?"

"No," they would say, "he is a brave fellow, he faced fire and could have fired his own pistol too, but he had a dream

310

the night before that he should become a monk, that's why he did it."

It was the same thing with the society of the town. Till then I had been kindly received, but had not been the object of special attention, and now all came to know me at once and invited me; they laughed at me, but they loved me. I may mention that although everybody talked openly of our duel, the authorities took no notice of it, because my antagonist was a near relation of our general, and as there had been no bloodshed and no serious consequences, and as I resigned my commission, they took it as a joke. And I began then to speak aloud and fearlessly, regardless of their laughter, for it was always kindly and not spiteful laughter. These conversations mostly took place in the evenings, in the company of ladies; women particularly liked listening to me then and they made the men listen.

"But how can I possibly be responsible for all?" everyone would laugh in my face. "Can I, for instance, be responsible for you?"

"You may well not know it," I would answer, "since the whole world has long been going on a different line, since we consider the veriest lies as truth and demand the same lies from others. Here I have for once in my life acted sincerely and, well, you all look upon me as a madman. Though you are friendly to me, yet, you see, you all laugh at me."

"But how can we help being friendly to you?" said my hostess, laughing. The room was full of people. All of a sudden the young lady rose, on whose account the duel had been fought and whom only lately I had intended to be my future wife. I had not noticed her coming into the room. She got up, came to me and held out her hand.

"Let me tell you," she said, "that I am the first not to laugh at you, but on the contrary I thank you with tears and express my respect for you for your action then."

Her husband too came up and then they all approached me and almost kissed me. My heart was filled with joy, but my attention was especially caught by a middle-aged man who came up to me with the others. I knew him by name already, but had never made his acquaintance nor exchanged a word with him till that evening.

(d) *The mysterious visitor*

He had long been an official in the town; he was in a prominent position, respected by all, rich and had a reputation for benevolence. He subscribed considerable sums to the almshouse and the orphan asylum; he was very charitable, too, in secret, a fact which only became known after his death. He was a man of about fifty, almost stern in appearance and not much given to conversation. He had been married about ten years and his wife, who was still young, had borne him three children. Well, I was sitting alone in my room the following evening, when my door suddenly opened and this gentleman walked in.

I must mention, by the way, that I was no longer living in my former quarters. As soon as I resigned my commission, I took rooms with an old lady, the widow of a government clerk. My landlady's servant waited upon me, for I had moved into her rooms simply because on my return from the duel I had sent Afanasy back to the regiment, as I felt ashamed to look him in the face after my last interview with him. So prone is the man of the world to be ashamed of any righteous action.

"I have," said my visitor, "with great interest listened to you speaking in different houses the last few days and I wanted at last to make your personal acquaintance, so as to talk to you more intimately. Can you, dear sir, grant me this favour?"

"I can, with the greatest pleasure and I shall look upon it as an honour." I said this, though I felt almost dismayed, so greatly was I impressed from the first moment by the appearance of this man. For though other people had listened to me with interest and attention, no one had come to me before with such a serious, stern and concentrated expression. And now he had come to see me in my own rooms. He sat down.

"You are, I see, a man of great strength of character," he said; "as you have dared to serve the truth, even when by doing so you risked incurring the contempt of all."

"Your praise is, perhaps, excessive," I replied.

"No, it's not excessive," he answered; "believe me, such a course of action is far more difficult than you think. It is that which has impressed me, and it is only on that account that I have come to you," he continued. "Tell me, please, that is if you are not annoyed by my perhaps unseemly curiosity, what were your exact sensations, if you can recall them, at the moment when you made up your mind to ask forgiveness at the duel. Do not think my question frivolous; on the contrary, I have in asking the question a secret motive of my own, which I will perhaps explain to you later on, if it is God's will that we should become more intimately acquainted."

All the while he was speaking I was looking at him straight into the face and I felt all at once a complete trust in him and great curiosity on my side also, for I felt that there was some strange secret in his soul.

"You ask what were my exact sensations at the moment when I asked my opponent's forgiveness," I answered; "but I had better tell you from the beginning what I have not yet told anyone else." And I described all that had passed between Afanasy and me, and how I had bowed down to the ground at his feet. "From that you can see for yourself," I concluded, "that at the time of the duel it was easier for me, for I had made a beginning already at home, and when once I had started on that road, to go further along it was far from being difficult, but became a source of joy and happiness."

I liked the way he looked at me as he listened. "All that," he said, "is exceedingly interesting, I will come to see you again and again."

And from that time forth he came to see me nearly every evening. And we should have become greater friends if only he had ever talked of himself. But about himself he scarcely ever said a word, yet continually asked me about myself. In spite of that I became very fond of him and spoke with perfect frankness to him about all my feelings; for, thought I, what need have I to know his secrets, since I can see without that that he is a good man? Moreover, though he is such a serious man and my senior, he comes to see a youngster like me and treats me as his equal. And I learned a great deal that was profitable from him, for he was a man of lofty mind.

"That life is heaven," he said to me suddenly, "that I have long been thinking about;" and all at once he added: "I think of nothing else indeed." He looked at me and smiled. "I am more convinced of it than you are, I will tell you later why."

I listened to him and thought that he evidently wanted to tell me something.

"Heaven," he went on, "lies hidden within all of us—here it lies hidden in me now, and if I will it, it will be revealed to me to-morrow and for all time."

I looked at him; he was speaking with great emotion and gazing mysteriously at me, as if he were questioning me.

"And that we are all responsible to all for all, apart from our own sins, you were quite right in thinking that, and it is wonderful how you could comprehend it in all its significance at once. And in very truth, so soon as men understand that, the Kingdom of Heaven will be for them not a dream but a living reality."

"And when," I cried out to him bitterly, "when will that come to pass? and will it ever come to pass? Is not it simply a dream of ours?"

"What, then, you don't believe it," he said. "You preach it and don't believe it yourself. Believe me, this dream, as you call it, will come to pass without doubt; it will come, but not now, for every process has its law. It's a spiritual, psychological process. To transform the world, to re-create it afresh, men must turn into another path psychologically. Until you have become really, in actual fact, a brother to everyone, brotherhood will not come to pass. No sort of scientific teaching, no kind of common interest, will ever teach men to share property and privileges with equal consideration for all. Everyone will think his share too small and they will be always envying, complaining and attacking one another. You ask when it will come to pass; it will come to pass, but first we have to go through the period of isolation."

"What do you mean by isolation?" I asked him.

"Why, the isolation that prevails everywhere, above all in our age—it has not fully developed, it has not reached its limit yet. For everyone strives to keep his individuality as apart as possible, wishes to secure the greatest possible fullness of life for himself; but meantime all his efforts result not in attaining fullness of life but self-destruction, for instead of self-realisation he ends by arriving at complete solitude. All mankind in our age have split up into units, they all keep apart, each in his own groove; each one holds aloof, hides himself and hides what he has, from the rest, and he ends by being repelled by others and repelling them. He heaps up riches by himself and thinks, 'how strong I am now and how secure', and in his madness he does not understand that the more he heaps up, the more he sinks into self-destructive impotence. For he is accustomed to rely upon himself alone and to cut himself off from the whole; he has trained himself not to believe in the help of others, in men and in humanity, and only trembles for fear he should lose his money and the privileges that he has won for himself. Everywhere in these days men have, in their mockery, ceased to understand that the true security is to be found in social solidarity rather than in isolated individual effort. But his terrible individualism must inevitably have an end, and all will suddenly understand how unnaturally they are separated from one another. It will be the spirit of the time, and people will marvel that they have sat so long in darkness without seeing the light. And then the sign of the Son of Man will be seen in the heavens. . . . But, until then, we must keep the banner flying. Sometimes even if he has to do it alone, and his conduct seems to be crazy, a man must set an example, and so draw men's souls out of their solitude, and spur them to scme act of brotherly love, that the great idea may not die."

Our evenings, one after another, were spent in such stirring and fervent talk. I gave up society and visited my neighbours much less frequently. Besides, my vogue was somewhat over. I say this, not as blame, for they still loved me and treated me good-humouredly, but there's no denying that fashion is a great power in society. I began to regard my mysterious visitor with admiration, for besides enjoying his intelligence, I began to perceive that he was brooding over some plan in his heart, and was preparing himself perhaps for a great deed. Perhaps he liked my not showing curiosity about his secret, not seeking to discover it by direct question nor by insinuation. But I noticed, at last, that he seemed to show signs of wanting to tell me something. This had become quite evident, indeed, about a month after he first began to visit me.

"Do you know," he said to me once, "that people are very inquisitive about us in the town and wonder why I come to see you so often. But let them wonder, for *soon all will be explained.*"

Sometimes an extraordinary agitation would come over him, and almost always on such occasions he would get up and go away. Sometimes he would fix a long piercing look upon me, and I thought, "He will say something directly now". But he would suddenly begin talking of something ordinary and familiar. He often complained of headache too.

One day, quite unexpectedly indeed, after he had been talking with great fervour a long time, I saw him suddenly turn pale, and his face worked convulsively, while he stared persistently at me.

"What's the matter?" I said; "do you feel ill?"—he had just been complaining of headache.

"I . . . do you know . . . I murdered someone."

He said this and smiled with a face as white as chalk. "Why is it he is smiling?" The thought flashed through my mind before I realised anything else. I too turned pale.

"What are you saying?" I cried.

"You see," he said, with a pale smile, "how much it has cost me to say the first word. Now I have said it I feel I've taken the first step and shall go on."

For a long while I could not believe him, and I did not believe him at that time, but only after he had been to see me three days running and told me all about it. I thought he was mad, but ended by being convinced, to my great grief and amazement. His crime was a great and terrible one.

Fourteen years before, he had murdered the widow of a landowner, a wealthy and handsome young woman who had a house in our town. He fell passionately in love with her, declared his feeling and tried to persuade her to marry him. But she had already given her heart to another man, an officer of noble birth and high rank in the service, who was at that time away at the front, though she was expecting him soon to return. She refused his offer and begged him not to come and see her. After he had ceased to visit her, he took advantage of his knowledge of the house to enter at night through the garden by the roof, at great risk of discovery. But as often happens, a crime committed with extraordinary audacity is more successful than others.

Entering the garret through the skylight, he went down the ladder, knowing that the door at the bottom of it was sometimes, through the negligence of the servants, left unlocked. He hoped to find it so, and so it was. He made his way in the dark to her bedroom, where a light was burning. As though on purpose, both her maids had gone off to a birthday-party in the same street, without asking leave. The other servants slept in the servants' quarters or in the kitchen on the ground-floor. His passion flamed up at the sight of her asleep, and then vindictive, jealous anger took possession of his heart, and like a drunken man, beside himself, he thrust a knife into her heart, so that she did not even cry out. Then with devilish and criminal cunning he contrived that suspicion should fall on the servants. He was so base as to take her purse, to open her chest with keys from under her pillow, and to take some things

316

from it, doing it all as it might have been done by an ignorant servant, leaving valuable papers and taking only money. He took some of the larger gold things, but left smaller articles that were ten times as valuable. He took with him, too, some things for himself as remembrances, but of that later. Having done this awful deed, he returned by the way he had come.

Neither the next day, when the alarm was raised, nor at any time after in his life, did anyone dream of suspecting that he was the criminal. No one indeed knew of his love for her, for he was always reserved and silent and had no friend to whom he would have opened his heart. He was looked upon simply as an acquaintance, and not a very intimate one, of the murdered woman, as for the previous fortnight he had not even visited her. A serf of hers called Pyotr was at once suspected, and every circumstance confirmed the suspicion. The man knew—indeed his mistress did not conceal the fact—that having to send one of her serfs as a recruit she had decided to send him, as he had no relations and his conduct was unsatisfactory. People had heard him angrily threatening to murder her when he was drunk in a tavern. Two days before her death, he had run away, staying no one knew where in the town. The day after the murder, he was found on the road leading out of the town, dead drunk, with a knife in his pocket and his right hand happened to be stained with blood. He declared that his nose had been bleeding, but no one believed him. The maids confessed that they had gone to a party and that the street door had been left open till they returned. And a number of similar details came to light, throwing suspicion on the innocent servant.

They arrested him, and he was tried for the murder; but a week after the arrest the prisoner fell sick of a fever and died unconscious in the hospital. There the matter ended and the judges and the authorities and everyone in the town remained convinced that the crime had been committed by no one but the servant who had died in hospital. And after that the punishment began.

My mysterious visitor, now my friend, told me that at first he was not in the least troubled by pangs of conscience. He was miserable a long time, but not for that reason; only from regret that he had killed the woman he loved, that she was no more, that in killing her he had killed his love, while the fire of passion was still in his veins. But of the innocent blood he had shed, of the murder of a fellow creature, he scarcely thought.

317

The thought that his victim might have become the wife of another man was insupportable to him, and so, for a long time, he was convinced in his conscience that he could not have acted otherwise.

At first he was worried at the arrest of the servant, but his illness and death soon set his mind at rest, for the man's death was apparently (so he reflected at the time) not owing to his arrest or his fright, but a chill he had taken on the day he ran away, when he had lain all night dead drunk on the damp ground. The theft of the money and other things troubled him little, for he argued that the theft had not been committed for gain but to avert suspicion. The sum stolen was small, and he shortly afterwards subscribed the whole of it, and much more, toward the funds for maintaining an almshouse in the town. He did this on purpose to set his conscience at rest about the theft, and it's a remarkable fact that for a long time he really was at peace—he told me this himself. He entered then upon a career of great activity in the service, volunteered for a difficult and laborious duty, which occupied him two years, and being a man of strong will almost forgot the past. Whenever he recalled it, he tried not to think of it at all. He became active in philanthropy too, founded and helped to maintain many institutions in the town, did a good deal in the two capitals, and in both Moscow and Petersburg was elected a member of philanthropic societies.

At last, however, he began brooding over the past, and the strain of it was too much for him. Then he was attracted by a fine and intelligent girl and soon after married her, hoping that marriage would dispel his lonely depression, and that by entering on a new life and scrupulously doing his duty to his wife and children, he would escape from old memories altogether. But the very opposite of what he expected happened. He began, even in the first month of his marriage, to be continually fretted by the thought, "My wife loves me—but what if she knew?" When she first told him that she would soon bear him a child, he was troubled. "I am giving life, but I have taken life." Children came. "How dare I love them, teach and educate them, how can I talk to them of virtue? I have shed blood." They were splendid children, he longed to caress them; "and I can't look at their innocent candid faces, I am unworthy."

At last he began to be bitterly and ominously haunted by the blood of his murdered victim, by the young life he had destroyed, by the blood that cried out for vengeance. He had begun to have awful dreams. But, being a man of fortitude, he bore his suffering a long time, thinking: "I shall expiate everything by this secret agony." But that hope, too, was vain; the longer it went on, the more intense was his suffering.

He was respected in society for his active benevolence, though everyone was overawed by his stern and gloomy character. But the more he was respected, the more intolerable it was for him. He confessed to me that he had thoughts of killing himself. But he began to be haunted by another idea—an idea which he had at first regarded as impossible and unthinkable, though at last it got such a hold on his heart that he could not shake it off. He dreamed of rising up, going out and confessing in the face of all men that he had committed murder. For three years this dream had pursued him, haunting him in different forms. At last he believed with his whole heart that if he confessed his crime he would heal his soul and would be at peace for ever. But this belief filled his heart with terror, for how could he carry it out? And then came what happened at my duel.

"Looking at you, I have made up my mind."

I looked at him.

"Is it possible," I cried, clasping my hands, "that such a trivial incident could give rise to such a resolution in you?"

"My resolution has been growing for the last three years," he answered, "and your story only gave the last touch to it. Looking at you, I reproached myself and envied you," he said this to me almost sullenly.

"But you won't be believed," I observed; "it's fourteen years ago."

"I have proofs, great proofs. I shall show them."

Then I cried and kissed him.

"Tell me one thing, one thing," he said (as though it all depended upon me), "my wife, my children! My wife may die of grief, and though my children won't lose their rank and property, they'll be a convict's children and for ever! And what a memory, what a memory of me I shall leave in their hearts!"

I said nothing.

"And to part from them, to leave them for ever? It's for ever, you know, for ever!"

I sat still and repeated a silent prayer. I got up at last, I felt afraid.

319

"Well?" He looked at me.

"Go!" said I, "confess. Everything passes, only the truth remains. Your children will understand, when they grow up, the nobility of your resolution."

He left me that time as though he had made up his mind. Yet for more than a fortnight afterwards, he came to me every evening, still preparing himself, still unable to bring himself to the point. He made my heart ache. One day he would come determined and say fervently:

"I know it will be heaven for me, heaven, the moment I confess. Fourteen years I've been in hell. I want to suffer. I will take my punishment and begin to live. You can pass through the world doing wrong, but there's no turning back. Now I dare not love my neighbour nor even my own children. Good God, my children will understand, perhaps, what my punishment has cost me and will not condemn me! God is not in strength but in truth."

"All will understand your sacrifice," I said to him, "if not at once, they will understand later; for you have served truth, the higher truth, not of the earth."

And he would go away seeming comforted, but next day he would come again, bitter, pale, sarcastic.

"Every time I come to you, you look at me so inquisitively as though to say, 'He has still not confessed!' Wait a bit, don't despise me too much. It's not such an easy thing to do as you would think. Perhaps I shall not do it at all. You won't go and inform against me then, will you?"

And far from looking at him with indiscreet curiosity, I was afraid to look at him at all. I was quite ill from anxiety, and my heart was full of tears. I could not sleep at night.

"I have just come from my wife," he went on. "Do you understand what the word 'wife' means? When I went out, the children called to me, 'Good-bye, father, make haste back to read "The Children's Magazine" with us'. No, you don't understand that! No one is wise in another man's woe."

His eyes were glittering, his lips were twitching. Suddenly he struck the table with his fist so that everything on it danced —it was the first time he had done such a thing, he was such a mild man.

"But need I?" he exclaimed, "must I? No one has been condemned, no one has been sent to Siberia in my place, the man died of fever. And I've been punished by my sufferings for the blood I shed. And I shan't be believed, they won't believe my proofs. Need I confess, need I? I am ready to go on suffering all my life for the blood I have shed, if only my wife and children may be spared. Will it be just to ruin them with me? Aren't we making a mistake? What is right in this case? And will people recognise it, will they appreciate it, will they respect it?"

"Good Lord!" I thought to myself, "he is thinking of other people's respect at such a moment!" And I felt so sorry for him then that I believe I would have shared his fate if it could have comforted him. I saw he was beside himself. I was aghast, realising with my heart as well as my mind what such a resolution meant.

"Decide my fate!" he exclaimed again.

"Go and confess," I whispered to him. My voice failed me, but I whispered it firmly. I took up the New Testament from the table, the Russian translation, and showed him the Gospel of St. John, ch. xii. verse 24:

"Verily, verily, I say unto you, except a corn of wheat fall into the ground and die, it abideth alone: but if it die, it bringeth forth much fruit."

I had just been reading that verse when he came in. He read it.

"That's true," he said, but he smiled bitterly. "It's terrible the things you find in those books," he said, after a pause. It's easy enough to thrust them upon one. And who wrote them? Can they have been written by men?"

"The Holy Spirit wrote them," said I.

"It's easy for you to prate," he smiled again, this time almost with hatred.

I took the book again, opened it in another place and showed him the Epistle to the Hebrews, ch. x. verse 31. He read:

"It is a fearful thing to fall into the hands of the living God."

He read it and simply flung down the book. He was trembling all over.

"An awful text," he said. "There's no denying you've picked out fitting ones." He rose from the chair. "Well!" he said, "good-bye, perhaps I shan't come again. . . . we shall meet in heaven. So I have been for fourteen years 'in the hands of the living God', that's how one must think of those fourteen years. To-morrow I will beseech those hands to let me go."

I wanted to take him in my arms and kiss him, but I did not dare—his face was contorted and sombre. He went away.

"Good God," I thought, "what has he gone to face!" I fell on my knees before the ikon and wept for him before the Holy Mother of God, our swift defender and helper. I was half an hour praying in tears, and it was late, about midnight. Suddenly I saw the door open and he came in again. I was surprised.

"Where have you been?" I asked him.

"I think," he said, "I've forgotten something . . . my handkerchief, I think. . . . Well, even if I've not forgotten anything, let me stay a little."

He sat down. I stood over him.

"You sit down, too," said he.

I sat down. We sat still for two minutes; he looked intently at me and suddenly smiled—I remembered that—then he got up, embraced me warmly and kissed me.

"Remember," he said, "how I came to you a second time. Do you hear, remember it!"

And he went out.

"To-morrow," I thought.

And so it was. I did not know that evening that the next day was his birthday. I had not been out for the last few days, so I had no chance of hearing it from anyone. On that day he always had a great gathering, everyone in the town went to it. It was the same this time. After dinner he walked into the middle of the room, with a paper in his hand—a formal declaration to the chief of his department who was present. This declaration he read aloud to the whole assembly. It contained a full account of the crime, in every detail.

"I cut myself off from men as a monster. God has visited me," he said in conclusion. "I want to suffer for my sin!"

Then he brought out and laid on the table all the things he had been keeping for fourteen years that he thought would prove his crime: the jewels belonging to the murdered woman which he had stolen to divert suspicion, a cross and a locket taken from her neck with a portrait of her betrothed in the locket, her notebook and two letters—one from her betrothed, telling her that he would soon be with her, and her unfinished answer left on the table to be sent off next day. He carried off these two letters—what for? Why had he kept them for fourteen years afterwards instead of destroying them as evidence against him?

And this is what happened: everyone was amazed and horrified, everyone refused to believe it and thought that he was deranged, though all listened with intense curiosity. A few days later it was fully decided and agreed in every house that the unhappy man was mad. The legal authorities could not refuse to take the case up, but they, too, dropped it. Though the trinkets and letters made them ponder, they decided that even if they did turn out to be authentic, no charge could be based on those alone. Besides, she might have given him those things as a friend, or asked him to take care of them for her. I heard afterwards, however, that the genuineness of the things was proved by the friends and relations of the murdered woman, and that there was no doubt about them. Yet nothing was destined to come of it, after all.

Five days later, all had heard that he was ill and that his life was in danger. The nature of his illness I can't explain, they said it was an affection of the heart. But it became known that the doctors had been induced by his wife to investigate his mental condition also, and had come to the conclusion that it was a case of insanity. I betrayed nothing, though people ran to question me. But when I wanted to visit him, I was for a long while forbidden to do so, above all by his wife.

"It's you who have caused his illness," she said to me; "he was always gloomy, but for the last year people noticed that he was peculiarly excited and did strange things, and now you have been the ruin of him. Your preaching has brought him to this; for the last month he was always with you."

Indeed, not only his wife but the whole town were down upon me and blamed me. "It's all your doing," they said. I was silent and indeed rejoiced at heart, for I saw plainly God's mercy to the man who had turned against himself and punished himself. I could not believe in his insanity.

They let me see him at last, he insisted upon saying good-bye to me. I went in to him and saw at once that not only his days but his hours were numbered. He was weak, yellow, his hands trembled, he gasped for breath, but his face was full of tender and happy feeling.

"It is done!" he said. "I've long been yearning to see you, why didn't you come?"

I did not tell him that they would not let me see him.

"God has had pity on me and is calling me to Himself. I know I am dying, but I feel joy and peace for the first time after so many years. There was heaven and peace in my heart from the moment I had done what I had to do. Now I dare to love my children and to kiss them. Neither my wife nor the judges, nor anyone has believed it. My children will never believe it either. I see in that God's mercy to them. I shall die, and my name will be without a stain for them. And now I feel God near, my heart rejoices as in Heaven . . . I have done my duty."

He could not speak, he gasped for breath, he pressed my hand warmly, looking fervently at me. We did not talk for long, his wife kept peeping in at us. But he had time to whisper to me:

"Do you remember how I came back to you that second time, at midnight? I told you to remember it. You know what I came back for? I came to kill you!"

I started.

"I went out from you then into the darkness, I wandered about the streets, struggling with myself. And suddenly I hated you so that I could hardly bear it. Now, I thought, he is all that binds me, and he is my judge. I can't refuse to face my punishment to-morrow, for he knows all. It was not that I was afraid you would betray me (I never even thought of that) but I thought: 'How can I look him in the face if I don't confess?' And if you had been at the other end of the earth, but alive, it would have been all the same, the thought was unendurable that you were alive knowing everything and condemning me. I hated you as though you were the cause, as though you were to blame for everything. I came back to you then, remembering that you had a dagger lying on your table. I sat down and asked you to sit down, and for a whole minute I pondered. If I had killed you I should have been ruined by that murder even if I had not confessed the other. But I didn't think about that at all, and I didn't want to think of it at that moment. I only hated you and longed to avenge myself on you for everything. The Lord vanquished the devil in my heart. But let me tell you, you were never nearer death."

A week later he died. The whole town followed him to the grave. The chief priest made a speech full of feeling. All lamented the terrible illness that had cut short his days. But all the town was up in arms against me after the funeral, and people even refused to see me. Some, at first a few and afterwards more, began indeed to believe in the truth of his story, and they visited me and questioned me with great interest and eagerness, for man loves to see the downfall and disgrace of the righteous. But I held my tongue, and very shortly after, I left the town, and five months later by God's grace I entered upon the safe and blessed path, praising the unseen finger which had guided me so clearly to it. But I remember in my prayer to this day, the servant of God, Mihail, who suffered so greatly.

CHAPTER III

CONVERSATIONS AND EXHORTATIONS OF FATHER ZOSSIMA

(e) The Russian monk and his possible significance

FATHERS and teachers, what is the monk? In the cultivated world the Word is nowadays pronounced by some people with a jeer, and by others it is used as a term of abuse, and this contempt for the monk is growing. It is true, alas, it is true, that there are many sluggards, gluttons, profligates and insolent beggars among monks. Educated people point to these: "You are idlers, useless members of society, you live on the labour of others, you are shameless beggars." And yet how many meek and humble monks there are, yearning for solitude and fervent prayer in peace. These are less noticed, or passed over in silence. And how surprised men would be if I were to say that from these meek monks, who yearn for solitary prayer, the salvation of Russia will come perhaps once more. For they are in truth made ready in peace and quiet "for the day and the hour, the month and the year". Meanwhile, in their solitude, they keep the image of Christ fair and undefiled, in the purity of God's truth, from the times of the Fathers of old, the Apostles and the martyrs. And when the time comes they will show it to the tottering creeds of the world. That is a great thought. That star will rise out of the East.

That is my view of the monk, and is it false? Is it too proud? Look at the worldly and all who set themselves up above the people of God, has not God's image and His truth been distorted in them? They have science; but in science there is nothing but what is the object of sense. The spiritual world, the higher part of man's being, is rejected altogether, dismissed with a sort of triumph, even with hatred. The world has proclaimed the reign of freedom, especially of late, but what do we see in this freedom of theirs? Nothing but slavery and self-destruction! For the world says:

"You have desires and so satisfy them, for you have the same rights as the most rich and powerful. Don't be afraid of satisfying them and even multiply your desires." That is the modern doctrine of the world. In that they see freedom. And what follows from this right of multiplication of desires? In the rich, isolation and spiritual suicide; in the poor, envy and murder; for they have been given rights, but have not been shown the means of satisfying their wants. They maintain that the world is getting more and more united, more and more bound together in brotherly community, as it overcomes distance and sets thought flying through the air.

Alas, put no faith in such a bond of union. Interpreting freedom as the multiplication and rapid satisfaction of desires, men distort their own nature, for many senseless and foolish desires and habits and ridiculous fancies are fostered in them. They live only for mutual envy, for luxury and ostentation. To have dinners, visits, carriages, rank and slaves to wait on one is looked upon as a necessity, for which life, honour and human feeling are sacrificed, and men even commit suicide if they are unable to satisfy it. We see the same thing among those who are not rich, while the poor drown their unsatisfied need and their envy in drunkenness. But soon they will drink blood instead of wine, they are being led on to it. I ask you, is such a man free? I knew one "champion of freedom" who told me himself that, when he was deprived of tobacco in prison he was so wretched at the privation that he almost went and betrayed his cause for the sake of getting tobacco again! And such a man says: "I am fighting for the cause of humanity".

How can such a one fight? What is he fit for? He is capable perhaps of some action quickly over, but he cannot hold out long. And it's no wonder that instead of gaining freedom they have sunk into slavery, and instead of serving the cause of brotherly love and the union of humanity have fallen, on the contrary, into dissension and isolation, as my mysterious visitor and teacher said to me in my youth. And therefore the idea of the service of humanity, of brotherly love and the solidarity of mankind, is more and more dying out in the world, and indeed this idea is sometimes treated with derision. For how can a man shake off his habits? What can become of him if he is in such bondage to the habit of satisfying the innumerable desires he has created for himself? He is isolated, and what concern has he with the rest of humanity? They have succeeded in accumulating a greater mass of objects, but the joy in the world has grown less.

The monastic way is very different. Obedience, fasting and prayer are laughed at, yet only through them lies the way to real, true freedom. I cut off my superfluous and unnecessary desires, I subdue my proud and wanton will and chastise it with obedience, and with God's help I attain freedom of spirit and with it spiritual joy. Which is most capable of conceiving a great idea and serving it—the rich man in his isolation or the man who has freed himself from the tyranny of material things and habits? The monk is reproached for his solitude: "You have secluded yourself within the walls of the monastery for your own salvation, and have forgotten the brotherly service of humanity!" But we shall see which will be most zealous in the cause of brotherly love. For it is not we, but they, who are in isolation, though they don't see that. Of old, leaders of the people came from among us, and why should they not again? The same meek and humble ascetics will rise up and go out to work for the great cause. The salvation of Russia comes from the people. And the Russian monk has always been on the side of the people. We are isolated only if the people are isolated. The people believe as we do, and an unbelieving reformer will never do anything in Russia, even if he is sincere in heart and a genius. Remember that! The people will meet the atheist and overcome him, and Russia will be one and unorthodox. Take care of the peasant and guard his heart. Go on educating him quietly. That's your duty as monks, for the peasant has God in his heart.

(f) Of masters and servants, and of whether it is possible for them to be brothers in the spirit

Of course, I don't deny that there is sin in the peasants too. And the fire of corruption is spreading visibly, hourly, working from above downwards. The spirit of isolation is coming upon the people too. Money-lenders and devourers of the commune are rising up. Already the merchant grows more and more eager for rank, and strives to show himself cultured though he has not a trace of culture, and to this end meanly despises his old traditions, and is even ashamed of the faith of his fathers. He visits princes, though he is only a peasant corrupted. The peasants are rotting in drunkenness and cannot shake off the habit. And what cruelty to their wives, to their children even! All from drunkenness! I've seen in the factories children nine years old, frail, rickety, bent and

327

already depraved. The stuffy workshop, the din of machinery, work all day long, the vile language and the drink, the drink—is that what a little child's heart needs? He needs sunshine, childish play, good examples all about him, and at least a little love. There must be no more of this, monks, no more torturing of children, rise up and preach that, make haste, make haste!

But God will save Russia, for though the peasants are corrupted and cannot renounce their filthy sin, yet they know it is cursed by God and that they do wrong in sinning. So that our people still believe in righteousness, have faith in God and weep tears of devotion.

It is different with the upper classes. They, following science, want to base justice on reason alone, but not with Christ, as before, and they have already proclaimed that there is no crime, that there is no sin. And that's consistent, for if you have no God what is the meaning of crime? In Europe the people are already rising up against the rich with violence, and the leaders of the people are everywhere leading them to bloodshed, and teaching them that their wrath is righteous. But their "wrath is accursed, for it is cruel". But God will save Russia as He has saved her many times. Salvation will come from the people, from their faith and their meekness.

Fathers and teachers, watch over the people's faith and this will not be a dream. I've been struck all my life in our great people by their dignity, their true and seemly dignity. I've seen it myself, I can testify to it. I've seen it and marvelled at it. I've seen it in spite of the degraded sins and poverty-stricken appearance of our peasantry. They are not servile, and even after two centuries of serfdom they are free in manner and bearing, yet without insolence, and not revengeful and not envious. "You are rich and noble, you are clever and talented, well be so, God bless you. I respect you, but I know that I too am a man. By the very fact that I respect you without envy I prove my dignity as a man."

In truth if they don't say this (for they don't know how to say this yet) that is how they act. I have seen it myself, I have known it myself, and, would you believe it, the poorer our Russian peasant is, the more noticeable is that serene goodness, for the rich among them are for the most part corrupted already, and much of that is due to our carelessness and indifference. But God will save His people, for Russia is great in her humility. I dream of seeing, and seem to see clearly already, our future. It will come to pass, that even the most corrupt of our rich will end by being ashamed of his riches before the poor, and the poor, seeing his humility, will understand and give way before him, will respond joyfully and kindly to his honourable shame. Believe me that it will end in that; things are moving to that. Equality is to be found only in the spiritual dignity of man, and that will only be understood among us. If we were brothers, there would be fraternity, but before that, they will never agree about the division of wealth. We preserve the image of Christ, and it will shine forth like a precious diamond to the whole world. So may it be, so may it be!

Fathers and teachers, a touching incident befell me once. In my wanderings I met in the town of K. my old orderly, Afanasy. It was eight years since I had parted from him. He chanced to see me in the market-place, recognised me, ran up to me, and how delighted he was, he simply pounced on me: "Master dear, is it you? is it really you I see?" He took me home with him.

He was no longer in the army, he was married and already had two little children. He and his wife earned their living as costermongers in the market-place. His room was poor but bright and clean. He made me sit down, set the samovar, sent for his wife, as though my appearance were a festival for them. He brought me his children: "Bless them, father."

"Is it for me to bless them? I am only a humble monk. I will pray for them. And for you, Afanasy Pavlovitch, I have prayed every day since that day, for it all came from you," said I. And I explained that to him as well as I could. And what do you think? The man kept gazing at me and could not believe that I, his former master, an officer, was now before him in such a guise and position; it made him shed tears.

"Why are you weeping?" said I. "Better rejoice over me, dear friend, whom I can never forget, for my path is a glad and joyful one."

He did not say much, but kept sighing and shaking his head over me tenderly.

"What has become of your fortune?" he asked.

"I gave it to the monastery," I answered; "we live in common."

After tea I began saying good-bye, and suddenly he brought out half a rouble as an offering to the monastery, and another half-rouble I saw him thrusting hurriedly into my hand: "That's for you in your wanderings, it may be of use to you, father."

I took his half-rouble, bowed to him and his wife, and went out rejoicing. And on my way I thought: "Here we are both now, he at home and I on the road, sighing and shaking our heads, no doubt, and yet smiling joyfully in the gladness of our hearts, remembering how God brought about our meeting."

I have never seen him again since then. I had been his master and he my servant, but now when we exchanged a loving kiss with softened hearts, there was a great human bond between us. I have thought a great deal about that, and now what I think is this: is it so inconceivable that that grand and simple-hearted unity might in due time become universal among the Russian people? I believe that it will come to pass and that the time is at hand.

And of servants I will add this: in old days when I was young I was often angry with servants; "the cook had served something too hot, the orderly had not brushed my clothes." But what taught me better then was a thought of my dear brother's, which I had heard from him in childhood: "Am I worth it, that another should serve me and be ordered about by me in his poverty and ignorance?" And I wondered at the time that such simple and self-evident ideas should be so slow to occur to our minds.

It is impossible that there should be no servants in the world, but act so that your servant may be freer in spirit than if he were not a servant. And why cannot I be a servant to my servant and even let him see it, and that without any pride on my part or any mistrust on his? Why should not my servant be like my own kindred, so that I may take him into my family and rejoice in doing so? Even now this can be done, but it will lead to the grand unity of men in the future, when a man will not seek servants for himself, or desire to turn his fellow creatures into servants as he does now, but, on the contrary, will long with his whole heart to be the servant of all, as the Gospel teaches.

And can it be a dream, that in the end man will find his joy only in deeds of light and mercy, and not in cruel pleasures as now, in gluttony, fornication, ostentation, boasting and envious rivalry of one with the other? I firmly believe that it is not and that the time is at hand. People laugh and ask: "When will that time come and does it look like coming?" I believe that with Christ's help we shall accomplish this great thing. And how many ideas there have been on earth in the history of man which were unthinkable ten years before they appeared?

Yet when their destined hour had come, they came forth and spread over the whole earth. So it will be with us, and our people will shine forth in the world, and all men will say: "The stone which the builders rejected has become the corner-stone of the building."

And we may ask the scornful themselves: if our hope is a dream, when will you build up your edifice and order things justly by your intellect alone, without Christ? If they declare that it is they who are advancing towards unity, only the most simple-hearted among them believe it, so that one may positively marvel at such simplicity. Of a truth, they have more fantastic dreams than we. They aim at justice, but, denying Christ, they will end by flooding the earth with blood, for blood cries out for blood, and he that taketh up the sword shall perish by the sword. And if it were not for Christ's covenant, they would slaughter one another down to the last two men on earth. And those last two men would not be able to restrain each other in their pride, and the one would slay the other and then himself. And that would come to pass, were it not for the promise of Christ that for the sake of the humble and meek the days shall be shortened.

While I was still wearing an officer's uniform after my duel, I talked about servants in general society, and I remember everyone was amazed at me. "What!" they asked, "are we to make our servants sit down on the sofa and offer them tea?" And I answered them: "Why not?—sometimes at least." Everyone laughed. Their question was frivolous and my answer was not clear; but the thought in it was to some extent right.

(g) *Of prayer, of love, and of contact with other worlds*

Young man, be not forgetful of prayer. Every time you pray, if your prayer is sincere there will be new feeling and new meaning in it, which will give you fresh courage, and you will understand that prayer is an education. Remember too, every day, and whenever you can, repeat to yourself: "Lord, have mercy on all who appear before Thee to-day." For every hour and every moment thousands of men leave life on this earth, and their souls appear before God. And how many of them depart in solitude, unknown, sad, dejected, that no one mourns for them or even knows whether they have lived or not. And behold, from the other end of the earth perhaps, your prayer for their rest will rise up to God though you knew them not nor they you. How touching it must be to a soul standing in dread before the Lord to feel at that instant that, for him too, there is one to pray, that there is a fellow creature left on earth to love him too. And God will look on you both more graciously, for if you have had so much pity on him, how much more will He have pity Who is infinitely more loving and merciful than you. And He will forgive him for your sake.

Brothers, have no fear of men's sin. Love a man even in his sin, for that is the semblance of Divine Love and is the highest love on earth. Love all God's creation, the whole and every grain of sand in it. Love every leaf, every ray of God's light. Love the animals, love the plants, love everything. If you love everything, you will perceive the divine mystery in things. Once you perceive it, you will begin to comprehend it better every day. And you will come at last to love the whole world with an all-embracing love. Love the animals: God has given them the rudiments of thought and joy untroubled. Do not trouble it, don't harass them, don't deprive them of their happiness, don't work against God's intent. Man, do not pride yourself on superiority to the animals; they are without sin, and you, with your greatness, defile the earth by your appearance on it, and leave the traces of your foulness after you— alas, it is true of almost every one of us! Love children especially, for they too are sinless like the angels; they live to soften and purify our hearts and, as it were, to guide us. Woe to him who offends a child! Father Anfim taught me to love children. The kind, silent man used often on our wanderings to spend the farthings given us on sweets and cakes for the children. He could not pass by a child without emotion, that's the nature of the man.

At some thoughts one stands perplexed, especially at the sight of men's sin, and wonders whether one should use force or humble love. Always decide to use humble love. If you resolve on that once for all, you may subdue the whole world. Loving humility is marvellously strong, the strongest of all things and there is nothing else like it.

Every day and every hour, every minute, walk round yourself and watch yourself, and see that your image is a seemly one. You pass by a little child, you pass by, spiteful, with ugly words, with wrathful heart; you may not have noticed the child, but he has seen you, and your image, unseemly and ignoble, may remain in his defenceless heart. You don't know it, but you may have sown an evil seed in him and it may grow, and all because you were not careful before the child, because you did not foster in yourself a careful, actively benevolent love. Brothers, love is a teacher; but one must know how to acquire it, for it is hard to acquire, it is dearly bought, it is won slowly by long labour. For we must love not only occasionally, for a moment, but for ever. Everyone can love occasionally, even the wicked can.

My brother asked the birds to forgive him; that sounds senseless, but it is right; for all is like an ocean, all is flowing and blending; a touch in one place sets up movement at the other end of the earth. It may be senseless to beg forgiveness of the birds, but birds would be happier at your side—a little happier, anyway—and children and all animals, if you yourself were nobler than you are now. It's all like an ocean, I tell you. Then you would pray to the birds too, consumed by an all-embracing love, in a sort of transport, and pray that they too will forgive you your sin. Treasure this ecstasy, however senseless it may seem to men.

My friends, pray to God for gladness. Be glad as children, as the birds of heaven. And let not the sin of men confound you in your doings. Fear not that it will wear away your work and hinder its being accomplished. Do not say: "Sin is mighty, wickedness is mighty, evil environment is mighty, and we are lonely and helpless and evil environment is wearing us away and hindering our good work from being done." Fly from that dejection, children! There is only one means of salvation, then take yourself and make yourself responsible for all men's sins, that is the truth, you know, friends, for as soon as you sincerely make yourself responsible for everything and for all men, you will see at once that it is really so, and that you are to blame for everyone and for all things. But throwing your own indolence and impotence on others you will end by sharing the pride of Satan and murmuring against God.

Of the pride of Satan what I think is this: it is hard for us on earth to comprehend it, and therefore it is so easy to fall into error and to share it, even imagining that we are doing something grand and fine. Indeed many of the strongest feelings and movements of our nature we cannot comprehend on earth. Let not that be a stumbling-block, and think not that it may serve as a justification to you for anything. For the Eternal Judge asks of you what you can comprehend and not what you cannot. You will know that yourself hereafter, for you will behold all things truly then and will not dispute them. On earth, indeed, we are, as it were, astray, and if it were not for the precious image of Christ before us, we should be undone and altogether lost, as was the human race before the Flood. Much on earth is hidden from us, but to make up for that we have been given a precious mystic sense of our living bond with the other world, with the higher heavenly world, and the roots of our thoughts and feelings are not here but in other worlds. That is why the philosophers say that we cannot apprehend the reality of things on earth.

God took seeds from different worlds and sowed them on this earth, and His garden grew up and everything came up that could come up, but what grows lives and is alive only through the feeling of its contact with other mysterious worlds. If that feeling grows weak or is destroyed in you, the heavenly growth will die away in you. Then you will be indifferent to life and even grow to hate it. That's what I think.

(h) *Can a man judge his fellow creatures? Faith to the end*

Remember particularly that you cannot be a judge of anyone. For no one can judge a criminal until he recognises that he is just such a criminal as the man standing before him, and that he perhaps is, more than all men, to blame for that crime. When he understands that, he will be able to be a judge. Though that sounds absurd, it is true. If I had been righteous myself, perhaps there would have been no criminal standing before me. If you can take upon yourself the crime of the criminal your heart is judging, take it at once, suffer for him yourself, and let him go without reproach. And even if the law itself makes you his judge, act in the same spirit so far as possible, for he will go away and condemn himself more bitterly than you have done. If, after your kiss, he goes away untouched, mocking at you, do not let that be a stumbling-block to you. It shows his time has not yet come, but it will come in due course. And if it come not, no matter; if not he, then another in his place will understand and suffer, and judge and condemn himself, and the truth will be fulfilled. Believe that, believe it without doubt; for in that lies all the hope and faith of the saints.

Work without ceasing. If you remember in the night as you go to sleep: "I have not done what I ought to have done," rise up at once and do it. If the people around you are spiteful and callous and will not hear you, fall down before them and beg their forgiveness; for in truth you are to blame for their not wanting to hear you. And if you cannot speak to them in their bitterness, serve them in silence and in humility, never losing hope. If all men abandon you and even drive you away by force, then when you are left alone fall on the earth and kiss it, water it with your tears and it will bring forth fruit even though no one has seen or heard you in your solitude. Believe to the end, even if all men went astray and you were left the only one faithful; bring your offering even then and praise God in your loneliness. And if two of you are gathered together—then there is a whole world, a world of living love. Embrace each other tenderly and praise God, if only in you two His truth has been fulfilled.

If you sin yourself and grieve even unto death for your sins or for your sudden sin, then rejoice for others, rejoice for the righteous man, rejoice that if you have sinned he is righteous and has not sinned.

If the evil doing of men moves you to indignation and over-whelming distress, even to a desire for vengeance on the evil-doers, shun above all things that feeling. Go at once and seek suffering for yourself, as though you were yourself guilty of that wrong. Accept that suffering and bear it and your heart will find comfort, and you will understand that you too are guilty, for you might have been a light to the evil-doers, even as the one man sinless, and you were not a light to them. If you had been a light, you would have lightened the path for others too, and the evil-doer might perhaps have been saved by your light from his sin. And even though your light was shining, yet you see men were not saved by it, hold firm and doubt not the power of the heavenly light. Believe that if they were not saved, they will be saved hereafter. And if they are not saved hereafter, then their sons will be saved, for your light will not die even when you are dead. The righteous man departs, but his light remains. Men are always saved after the death of the deliverer. Men reject their prophets and slay them, but they love their martyrs and honour those whom they have slain. You are working for the whole, you are acting for the future. Seek no reward, for great is your reward on this earth: the spiritual joy which is only vouchsafed to the righteous man. Fear not the great nor the mighty, but be wise and ever serene. Know the measure, know the times, study that. When you are left alone, pray. Love to throw yourself on the earth and kiss it. Kiss the earth and love it with an unceasing, consuming love. Love all men, love everything. Seek that rapture and ecstasy. Water the earth with the tears of your joy and love those tears. Don't be ashamed of that ecstasy, prize it, for it is a gift of God and a great one; it is not given to many but only to the elect.

(i) *Of hell and hell fire, a mystic reflection*

Fathers and teachers, I ponder "What is hell?" I maintain that it is the suffering of being unable to love. Once in infinite existence, immeasurable in time and space, a spiritual creature was given, on his coming to earth, the power of saying: "I am and I love." Once, only once, there was given him a moment of active *living* love and for that was earthly life given him, and with it times and seasons. And that happy creature rejected the priceless gift, prized it and loved it not, scorned it and remained callous. Such a one, having left the earth, sees Abraham's bosom and talks with Abraham as we are told in the parable of the rich man and Lazarus, and beholds heaven and can go up to the Lord. But that is just his torment, to rise up to the Lord without ever having loved, to be brought close to those who have loved when he has despised their love. For he sees clearly and says to himself: "Now I have understanding and though I now thirst to love, there will be nothing great, no sacrifice in my love, for my earthly life is over, and Abraham will not come even with a drop of living water (that is the gift of earthly, active life) to cool the fiery thirst of spiritual love which burns in me now, though I despised it on earth; there is no more life for me and will be no more time! Even though I would gladly give my life for others, it can never be, for that life is passed which can be sacrificed for love, and now there is a gulf fixed between that life and this existence."

They talk of hell fire in the material sense. I don't go into that mystery and I shun it. But I think if there were fire in material sense, they would be glad of it, for I imagine that in material agony their still greater spiritual agony would be forgotten for a moment. Moreover, that spiritual agony cannot be taken from them, for that suffering is not external but within them. And if it could be taken from them, I think it would be bitterer still for the unhappy creatures. For even if the righteous in Paradise forgave them, beholding their torments, and called them up to heaven in their infinite love, they would

336

only multiply their torments, for they would arouse in them still more keenly a flaming thirst for responsive, active and grateful love which is now impossible. In the timidity of my heart I imagine, however, that the very recognition of this impossibility would serve at last to console them. For accepting the love of the righteous together with the impossibility of repaying it, by this submissiveness and the effect of this humility, they will attain at last, as it were, to a certain semblance of that active love which they scorned in life, to something like its outward expression . . . . I am sorry, friends and brothers, that I cannot express this clearly. But woe to those who have slain themselves on earth, woe to the suicides! I believe that there can be none more miserable than they. They tell us that it is a sin to pray for them and outwardly the Church, as it were, renounces them, but in my secret heart I believe that we may pray even for them. Love can never be an offence to Christ. For such as those I have prayed inwardly all my life, I confess it, fathers and teachers, and even now I pray for them every day.

Oh, there are some who remain proud and fierce even in hell, in spite of their certain knowledge and contemplation of the absolute truth; there are some fearful ones who have given themselves over to Satan and his proud spirit entirely. For such, hell is voluntary and ever-consuming; they are tortured by their own choice. For they have cursed themselves, cursing God and life. They live upon their vindictive pride like a starving man in the desert sucking blood out of his own body. But they are never satisfied, and they refuse forgiveness, they curse God Who calls them. They cannot behold the living God without hatred, and they cry out that the God of life should be annihilated, that God should destroy Himself and His own creation. And they will burn in the fire of their own wrath for ever and yearn for death and annihilation. But they will not attain to death. . . .

Here Alexey Fyodorovitch Karamazov's manuscript ends. I repeat, it is incomplete and fragmentary. Biological details, for instance, cover only Father Zossima's earliest youth. Of his teaching and opinions we find brought together sayings evidently uttered on very different occasions. His utterances during the last few hours have not been kept separate from the rest, but their general character can be gathered from what we have in Alexey Fyodorovitch's manuscript.

The elder's death came in the end quite unexpectedly. For although those who were gathered about him that last evening realised that his death was approaching, yet it was difficult to imagine that it would come so suddenly. On the contrary, his friends, as I observed already, seeing him that night apparently so cheerful and talkative, were convinced that there was at least a temporary change for the better in his condition. Even five minutes before his death, they said afterwards wonderingly, it was impossible to foresee it. He seemed suddenly to feel an acute pain in his chest, he turned pale and pressed his hands to his heart. All rose from their seats and hastened to him. But though suffering, he still looked at them with a smile, sank slowly from his chair on to his knees, then bowed his face to the ground, stretched out his arms as though in joyful ecstasy, praying and kissing the ground, quietly and joyfully gave up his soul to God.

The news of his death spread at once through the hermitage and reached the monastery. The nearest friends of the deceased and those whose duty it was from their position began to lay out the corpse according to the ancient ritual, and all the monks gathered together in the church. And before dawn the news of the death reached the town. By the morning all the town was talking of the event, and crowds were flocking from the town to the monastery. But this subject will be treated in the next book; I will only add here that before a day had passed something happened so unexpected, so strange, upsetting, and bewildering in its effects on the monks and the townspeople, that after all these years, that day of general suspense is still vividly remembered in the town.

This book, designed by
William B. Taylor
is a production of
Edito-Service S.A., Geneva

Printed in Switzerland

THE
GREATEST MASTERPIECES
OF
RUSSIAN LITERATURE